**Panic threatened to overcome him when the mountain opened its mouth and belched a tremendous river of star-filled black water north and south.**

Soldiers cried out in fear. The city trembled. Grass withered gray. A third wave rolled toward the western gate of the city, but it forked at the last moment, sparing them. It seemed every guard along the wall sighed with relief. The mountain settled down, its legs sinking into the soft earth.

*What does this mean?* he asked Vaesalaum. *The mountain's arrival . . . my summoning fire . . . you? Is the world ending?*

The little creature bobbed up and down, and he saw the faintest hint of a smile on its youthful face.

*No, not ending,* its cold voice spoke within his mind. He sensed within it a powerful promise, and an overwhelming sense of excitement.

*Awakening.*

# *Praise for*
# David Dalglish

"A fast-paced, page-turning ride with a great, likeable main character in Devin Eveson. It's the definition of entertaining."

—John Gwynne, author of *Malice*, on *Soulkeeper*

"A dark and lush epic fantasy brimming with magical creatures and terrifying evil....Dalglish's worldbuilding is subtle and fluid, and he weaves the history, magical workings, and governance of his world within the conversations and camaraderie of his characters. Readers of George R. R. Martin and Patrick Rothfuss will find much to enjoy here." —*Booklist* on *Soulkeeper*

"A soaring tale that nails the high notes. *Skyborn* had me gazing heavenward, imagining what could be."

—Jay Posey, author of *Three*

"Dalglish raises the stakes and magnitude, demonstrating his knack for no-holds-barred, wildly imaginative storytelling and world-building." —*Publishers Weekly* on *Shadowborn*

"Dalglish concocts a heady cocktail of energy, breakneck pace, and excitement."

—Sam Sykes, author of *Seven Blades in Black*, on *A Dance of Cloaks*

"Fast, furious, and fabulous."

—Michael J. Sullivan, author of *Theft of Swords*, on *A Dance of Cloaks*

# RAVEN
# CALLER

# By David Dalglish

## THE KEEPERS

*Soulkeeper*

*Ravencaller*

## SERAPHIM

*Skyborn*

*Fireborn*

*Shadowborn*

## SHADOWDANCE

*A Dance of Cloaks*

*A Dance of Blades*

*A Dance of Mirrors*

*A Dance of Shadows*

*A Dance of Ghosts*

*A Dance of Chaos*

*Cloak and Spider* (novella)

# RAVEN CALLER

## THE KEEPERS: BOOK TWO

# DAVID DALGLISH

www.orbitbooks.net

Copyright © 2020 by David Dalglish
Excerpt from *Voidbreaker* copyright © 2020 by David Dalglish
Excerpt from *The Ranger of Marzanna* copyright © 2020 by Jon Skovron

Cover design by Lauren Panepinto
Cover illustration by Paul Scott Canavan
Cover copyright © 2020 by Hachette Book Group, Inc.
Map by Tim Paul
Author photograph by Myrtle Beach Photography

Orbit
Hachette Book Group
1290 Avenue of the Americas
New York, NY 10104
orbitbooks.net

First Edition: March 2020
Simultaneously published in Great Britain by Orbit

Orbit is an imprint of Hachette Book Group.
The Orbit name and logo are trademarks of Little, Brown Book Group Limited.

The publisher is not responsible for websites (or their content) that are not owned by the publisher.

The Hachette Speakers Bureau provides a wide range of authors for speaking events. To find out more, go to www.hachettespeakersbureau.com or call (866) 376-6591.

Library of Congress Cataloging-in-Publication Data
Names: Dalglish, David, author.
Title: Ravencaller / David Dalglish.
Description: First Edition. | New York, NY : Orbit, 2020. | Series: The keepers; book 2
Identifiers: LCCN 2019029889 | ISBN 9780316416696 (trade paperback) |
    ISBN 9780316416689 (e-book)
Subjects: GSAFD: Fantasy fiction.
Classification: LCC PS3604.A376 R38 2020 | DDC 813/.6—dc23
LC record available at https://lccn.loc.gov/2019029889

ISBNs: 978-0-316-41669-6 (trade paperback), 978-0-316-41667-2 (ebook)

Printed in the United States of America

LSC-C

10 9 8 7 6 5 4 3 2 1

*To my twin wolves of anxiety, Fluffy and Bobo, and
to Jeannette Ng, who helped me name them.*

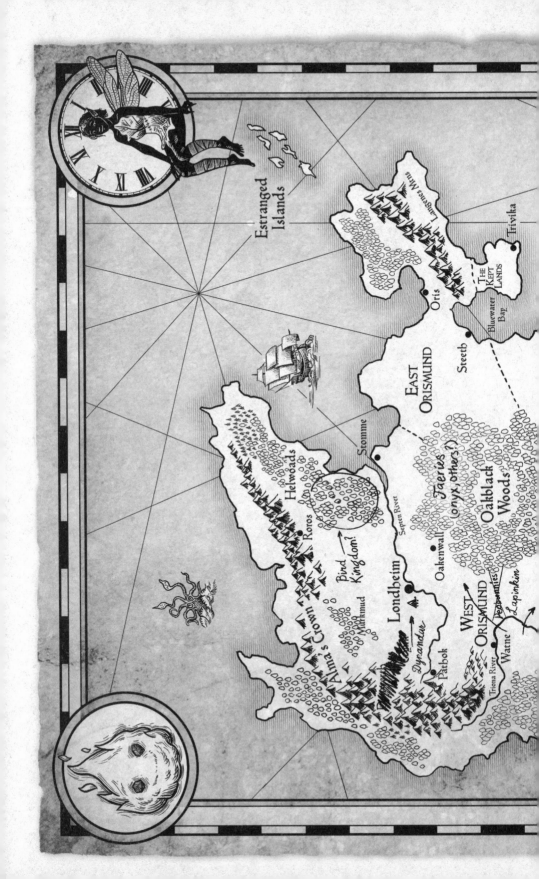

THE GENTLE OCEAN

Nelme

SOUTH
ORISMUND

Nicus

Viridi

Wardbus

Mermaids?

The Gulf
of Ianor

Por Emden

Vibrant
Isle

Devin, this is as best as
I remember it from what
Cannac showed me.
—Tommy

THE CRADLE

Copyright © 2020 by Tim Paul

# RAVEN CALLER

# PROLOGUE

## The Day of Viciss's Arrival

Dierk knelt on the cold floor of his family's cellar, the Book of Ravens in one hand and a dagger in the other, and stared at the man he'd killed. There wasn't much to him, just bruised skin, stained slacks, and a faded shirt with multiple holes. The blood trickling from his punctured neck seemed clean compared to the rest of him. The ropes binding his wrists and ankles likely cost more than anything the ragged man once possessed.

"Oh shit."

Dierk turned to the side and vomited up his breakfast. It left the muscles of his scrawny abdomen tight and his throat burning raw. All his well-crafted plans collapsed into disordered panic. He'd layered towels underneath the body but there was already so much blood. The smell of it mixed with feces. Sisters be damned, the man had defecated himself upon dying. Was that normal? Or had he done it to spite Dierk just before the dagger pierced his throat?

"This was a mistake," he whispered. "I shouldn't, I shouldn't have, oh damn it all to the void, what have I done?"

When he was ten, he'd trapped a cat in the cellar and come back a week later armed with a knife he'd stolen from the kitchen. He'd spent hours cutting into that dead tabby, flaying off the fur, untwining muscles, and sliding guts out in long, thin loops. It wasn't quite pleasure he'd felt, but something to the right of it. A satisfaction he'd unknowingly craved, each new cut or tear like a scratch upon an itch in his brain.

Then his father found out, and Dierk had learned to be much more careful over the following six years. Dogs, cats, squirrels, and rats, all easily disposed of in some gutter alley of Londheim's many disgusting districts. He'd bled, cut, and skinned all manner of creatures, but never a human. Never before today.

The ground shook, and a bottle of wine rolled off one of the racks and shattered upon the floor. Dierk screamed in surprise. That was the third quake this morning, as if the world itself were angry with his arrogance. Or maybe he overlooked the obvious. For years he'd dabbled in practices considered heretical to the tyrannical Sisters. Perhaps they had turned their eye upon him, and they were not pleased.

Dierk glared at his copy of the Book of Ravens as if it were responsible for his current predicament. One of his father's guards, Three-Fingers, had given it to him as a secret present on his fourteenth birthday.

"I know about your more ugly habits," the scarred man had whispered, his breath heavy with the scent of alcohol. "This'll give them purpose. Make it mean something."

It was the greatest gift Dierk had ever received, and it awakened a part of his mind he'd never realized was closed. What had been random cuts became runes and symbols. What had been sweaty silence became whispered prayers to the void. He'd cupped the severed head of a dog and pressed his lips to its forehead to breathe in its essence during the reaping hour. Each time he felt the tantalizing call of something greater. Fleeting ephemeral lives of animals could not compare to the eternal memories of the soul.

He was licking dew off leaves when, just outside his reach, there awaited a river.

Three-Fingers had brought him the homeless man that now lay before him. He'd given him the knife. He'd looked upon him with respect and admiration Dierk had never experienced from his father.

"When you kill him doesn't matter," Three-Fingers had said. "The reaping hour is when the magic comes. That's when you'll finally be a true Ravencaller."

*A true Ravencaller.* The sound of it had tickled his senses. He cherished the idea of his needs and impulses, always strange and discordant with society, leading him to something meaningful. A purpose to remove the aching loneliness he felt when watching others his age grow their wild interlocking relationships of love, loyalty, and respect.

But right now he felt ready to lose his mind. Someone would find out, a servant most likely. This wasn't something he could hide like a dead cat. Would he be banished from his home? All of Londheim? Or might he even be hung from the city gates and denied the dignity of a pyre?

"Stop it, Dierk, stop it, stop it, stop it," he cried, accompanying each request with a vicious punch to his leg. He had to get himself under control. Tears were rolling down his cheeks. Such a disgrace. Who ever heard of a Ravencaller bawling over some dead homeless man? Dierk curled his knees to his chest and rocked back and forth in the dark. The body was still bleeding.

Maybe it wasn't too late. He could come clean to his father. If he blamed the whole thing on Three-Fingers, he may have a chance. He could show him the Book of Ravens and claim it was thrust into his hands unwillingly. If—if he removed the ropes, maybe he could say the homeless man attacked him. Self-defense, you could kill in self-defense and no one would blame you, right?

Again the ground shook. The Cradle was laughing at him.

*Cradle never laughs. Cradle is angry. Cradle meant to be a garden, not a prison.*

Every single muscle in Dierk's body locked up. That voice, it wasn't his, yet it slid through his mind as familiar as his own skin. It was as peaceful as a winter morning, and just as cold.

"Who's there?" he asked the dark cellar.

Suddenly the cellar was dark no more. A light manifested in the air before him, taking the slender shape of a long-bodied reptile with tiny catlike paws. Instead of scales, its pale blue body rippled with soft fur akin to a rabbit's. Though its face resembled that of a child, it bore only smooth divots where its eyes should be. From nose to tail, it was barely longer than his hand.

*Human is crying*, spoke this hovering being of cold light with a voice that echoed inside his skull. *Human is afraid. I come. I choose. Human gives doubt to choice. I choose wrong?*

"What?" Dierk asked. He quickly wiped at his face, trying to clear away the snot and tears. "No, I'm not afraid."

*Human is a liar.*

Its mouth didn't move but Dierk knew it spoke. It bore no eyes but he felt certain it watched him closely.

"And who are you to call me a liar?" he asked, trying to salvage some semblance of pride.

*I am nisse.*

"Nisse?" Dierk said. "What—what are you, Nisse?"

*I am nisse as Dierk is human. I am many names. I, Vaesalaum.*

Nisse? Vaesalaum? Dierk had never heard anything of the sort. A wriggling fear in the back of his mind insisted he'd gone insane. This little creature did not hover and bob in the air in front of him. The murder had broken him. Surely this was his brain's feeble attempt to re-create order.

"How do you know my name?" he asked.

*Human mind is a book. I read pages.*

The creature, Vaesalaum, floated to the cooling corpse, traversing through the air in an S-like motion with its snakelike body. Dierk's curiosity pulled him out of his shock.

"Why are you here, Vaesalaum?" he asked. The name clunked awkwardly off his tongue.

*I seek an answer. I seek a promise. I seek a disciple. I offer much for all three.*

"A disciple?" he wondered aloud. "And you're to be my teacher?"

The nisse sank lower to the ground. Its bluish light shone across the corpse, granting an unwelcome clarity to the stiffening limbs, lifeless eyes, and drying blood. The otherworldly being turned its body into a circle and settled atop the dead man's forehead.

*Teacher. Partner. Master.*

"And why would I accept?" he asked, trying to hide the fear growing in his chest. What if this wasn't some cracked creation of his mind, but an actual being that existed? It shouldn't. Monsters, faeries, and dragons weren't real. They were stories, fables, and entertaining myths. Humanity had wisely disregarded them and moved on, except for the Sisters, which they still clung to in their naïveté. But who was he to challenge his senses? How could he deny the voice whispering in his head?

*Dierk desires what Vaesalaum offers. Dierk desired it since childhood.*

A glowing symbol appeared upon the man's forehead, carved from the touch of an invisible knife. Dierk recognized it at once. It was the inverse of the symbol of the Sisters, that of a circle enclosed around a small, upward-turned triangle. Even wearing it as a charm or necklace could earn you a week of hard labor, for that was the symbol of the Ravencallers, and the Keeping Church had done everything in its power to banish them into oblivion.

*Come closer,* Vaesalaum ordered. *Do not fear.*

Light shimmered across the symbol. Dierk's breath caught in his throat. No, it couldn't be. It was only midday, and far from the reaping hour. That was not the light of the man's soul shimmering into the air. That wasn't his eternal memories and emotions licking the dark cellar air in thin, weblike threads.

*Power in purpose*, that cold voice spoke. *Life amid death. Come breathe.*

Dierk's feet moved of their own accord. The symbol of the Ravencallers blazed upon the corpse's forehead. Silvery threads waved an inch above the charred flesh, and they were growing longer. Dierk dropped to his knees. His eyes watered. The Book of Ravens had talked much of this moment, of the sacredness of the reaping hour and the separation of the body from mortal flesh. The Soulkeepers carefully guarded humanity from that power. They buried it in rituals and masks and forced separation and distance from the weeping and the mourned.

Dierk lowered his face to the circle formed by the nisse's body, put his lips to the blasphemous symbol, and obeyed. Lips parting, tongue trembling, he breathed.

The cellar turned black. The body vanished, the nisse with it. He heard no sound, and he felt no sensations, not the cool stone against his knees, not the chill, musty air. Dierk knew he should be afraid of such sudden emptiness, just as he knew it was dangerous to put his hand to a fire, but he was not. The void encapsulating him brought sudden relief from an unknown pressure banding around his head. It was the removal of a dozen nails secretly lodged into his hands and feet. Dierk felt he belonged, this void a more welcoming presence than his pale, skinny physical body.

The darkness parted before a sudden light. It hovered in the air, at first nothing more than a faint blue spark, but it steadily grew like a well-oiled fire. Human features distinguished themselves amid the burning haze, though they never lost the cold blue shade. At last a grown man stood before Dierk, and it took him a moment to realize who it was: the homeless man he'd murdered. Except now his clothes were neat and prim, and his skin and hair immaculately clean.

"Where am I?" the ghostly man asked.

Dierk swallowed down a sharp stone in his throat. The void's comforting presence threatened to leave him. He didn't want to talk to this man. He only sought the power of his soul. And whoever he was, how would he react if he realized who Dierk was, and remembered?

"I don't know," Dierk said. "It is new to me as well."

The ghostly image didn't seem too upset with the answer. He looked around, mildly curious as to his apparent lack of surroundings. Before Dierk could say more, Vaesalaum shimmered into existence, the strange creature circling above the homeless man's head like a crown.

*Behold human, now an open book. Vaesalaum controls the pages. Dierk reads the words.*

A shudder ran through the man, and then he split in two, his front half cleaved off like a split log. The man shrieked even as his mouth elongated into an inhuman shape. Flesh peeled like smoke, and he screamed, still alive, still sentient, every piece of his essence swirling toward Dierk, and Dierk was screaming, too, just as loud, just as horrified.

A bright forest replaced the void. Dierk leaned against a tree, his arms crossed over his chest and a smile upon his face. Except his name wasn't Dierk any longer; his name was Erik. He inhabited the memory, his identity superimposed over Erik's. His movements mimicked history, his emotions echoed those of the previous time. A young woman swayed in a plain brown dress before him, shaking and tapping a tambourine as she sang. The sunlight seemed to touch her blond hair in such a perfect way that it shone like spun threads of gold. Dierk felt happiness eager to burst from his chest. He thought he knew what it meant to be happy, but this showed him how wrong he was. At best he understood contentedness. This was better. So much better.

The forest shimmered, and now he made love to that same woman. His hands massaged her breasts as he kissed the woman's pale neck, purposefully marking it with a bruise to playfully point out later. Dierk had never seen a woman naked before that wasn't drawn in a book or painting, and the idea of having himself inside another person seemed weird in a way he could never verbalize… but while inhabiting Erik it felt so *good*, Dierk wanted to push harder with his hips, he wanted to send his hands wandering everywhere, but he was not in charge of this existence, Erik was, and Erik kept his movements slow and steady as his cock stiffened, harder and harder until it felt ready to burst. And then it did, and the waves of pleasure left Dierk exhausted and overwhelmed.

As Erik rolled onto his back and put his arm across his forehead, Dierk saw Vaesalaum hovering near the rooftop of the cabin, and then the world changed again. Erik was older now, his wife (Lisa, her name was Lisa) rocking in a chair beside the fire. Her breasts were exposed, and a young infant suckled one of them. Erik stood in the doorway of the cabin, his feet frozen in place by the beautiful sight. He didn't move. He didn't want to move, only smile and laugh at her when Lisa glanced his way and asked if something was the matter.

Though Erik was smiling, Dierk wished to burst into tears. By the void, this was water on a tongue that had known only thirst. The companionship, the love, it was so simple and easy, it hurt him, hurt him in a deep, confusing way that inspired sadness as much as it did happiness.

*Does Dierk not desire joy?* It was Vaesalaum's voice piercing the suddenly frozen memory. *There are other experiences.*

Before Dierk could answer, the memory shifted, becoming another moment, another reenacted moment in time. Erik was running. His love and happiness had been replaced with stark terror. His cabin was on fire. Strange men surrounded it, and they wielded weapons. Lisa was crying. So was their child, but Lisa's hands were empty. The wail grew. The fire spread.

*No more*, Dierk screamed, but Erik's mouth would not cooperate. *Stop this, pull me out, pull me out!*

The void returned. The nisse shimmered into view. Though it lacked eyes, he felt the creature's stare boring into him.

*Dierk not like violence?*

"Not like…not like that," he said. "I never want to feel that again."

Vaesalaum bobbed up and down. Dierk swore its body had grown several inches since when it had first appeared.

*Human has more pages. I know what Dierk seeks.*

A dirty street of Londheim replaced the void. Erik huddled at the entrance of an alley. The sky was bright with stars. All he had were the clothes on his back and the leather shoes on his feet, and they were a pitiful protection against the cold wind blowing in from the west.

"Ye' awake?" a gruff voice asked. Erik looked up to see a mirrored reflection of himself. The other man was just as destitute, just as broken. There were only two differences between their haggard selves. One was that this new man was barefoot. The other was that he held a knife.

"Get lost," Erik said, refusing to reveal any fear.

"Yer shoes. Give 'em."

Erik glared him in the eye, too cold and tired to give a shit about some short, rusted blade.

"Get. Lost."

The man jabbed the knife at the air between them. The movement was quick, unsteady. His other hand reached for Erik's left foot, and when his fingers closed about the heel, he pulled.

Erik felt everything inside him break down, and what was left was decidedly not human. He leapt on the man like a savage animal. He was just another dirty, broken soul of Londheim forced to live in squalor, but to Erik's eyes, he was a piece of meat to be ripped apart. His fists rained down on him, breaking his jaw and knocking loose teeth. They wrestled, the knife fell to the street unbloodied. Erik's hands wrapped about the man's neck, and feral strength flooded his fingers. The man gasped and gargled as his face turned to blue.

And in that moment, that wild, vicious space of time strangling the life out of an enemy, Dierk felt *alive*. His every sense burned at heightened levels. Struggle. Fight. Crush. Watch the life leave the eyes of another. Dierk felt tightness in his groin and a pounding in his neck.

The moment ended. The emptiness around him returned, but only for a moment before it, too, broke. Dierk's eyes crossed, and suddenly he was back in his cellar, in his own body, feeling his own emotions. Erik lay before him, the symbol of the Ravencallers having faded away. Vaesalaum hovered a few feet above the dead man's body. Dierk pushed himself to his feet, and he realized with detached awkwardness his pants were wet with semen.

"His—his memories," Dierk stammered. "You gave them to me?"

*Not gift. Taken. Lost upon reaping hour. Dierk accept?*

Accept? How could he refuse such a tantalizing promise? What other wonders might this strange little creature teach him? The feeling of the convulsing man's throat crushed between his hands lingered in his mind like a pleasant warmth.

"Of course I accept," he said. "But what could I possibly offer you?"

The nisse hovered closer. Earnestness tinged its cold voice.

*Bring Vaesalaum bodies. Together we share. Together we grow strong.*

Dierk quivered. He was not strong like Erik had been prior to being sucked dry by years of homelessness and abandonment. Perhaps Three-Fingers could bring him another, but how would he dispose of the bodies, or keep them from being discovered?

"I don't think I can," he said. "I'm not strong, and I'm no good with weapons."

Vaesalaum floated over to his copy of the Book of Ravens, which lay discarded on the floor.

*Read*, the nisse said. *Book is key.*

Dierk tried to tamp down his excitement. The Book of Ravens was notorious for many reasons, but one was the complete anonymity of its author. The Keeping Church had launched multiple investigations, but the book appeared as old as the church itself, and its mysteries unassailable. This bizarre creature...might it be the author? Was it connected to that forgotten age when magic was real and sacrifices of blood and flesh might harness power of the void?

"Are you a raven?" Dierk asked. "A true raven, like what we aspire to be?"

*Not raven*, Vaesalaum said. *Friend of raven. True ravens are the avenria. Dierk holds avenria words. Words give power. Dierk will harness that power.*

What was an avenria? And what power did the nisse intend him to possess? He joined the floating creature at the book. Pages flipped untouched until it settled on a page Vaesalaum intended him to read. It was the ninth chapter, and one he'd read many times before. On one side it detailed the hypocrisy of the Soul-keepers and their elaborate rituals and pyres. On the other, it listed the chant that Soulkeepers once used to dispose of bodies. The words seemed to glow before him, and before he realized, he'd begun repeating them aloud.

*"Anwyn of the Moon, hear me! The soul has departed. This body before me, once sacred, is sacred no more. Make this empty vessel return to the land as ash. Give me the fire. Send me the flame. Create in me your pyre so I might burn."*

Fire burst about Dierk's hands, an all-consuming blaze of yellow light. He stared at it in awe, for only a shred of its heat bathed his skin, and his hands felt only a pleasant kiss of its fury. He did not ask the nisse what to do with it, for the desire was clear enough by the chant. He plunged both hands into the chest of the corpse. It immediately erupted in flames. They burned with terrifying swiftness, and neither flesh nor bone could resist its sudden rage. The body withered to ash. Even the blood cracked and peeled into tiny gray flecks. Dierk's eyes watered but he refused to look away.

This power. This fire. It came from within *him*. He wasn't helpless. He wasn't weak. With Vaesalaum's guidance, he could be more powerful than he ever dreamed.

Quick as it appeared, the fire faded, leaving only a small circle of ash upon the warm stone. A heavy knock on the cellar door banished the silence. Light from upstairs flooded down the stairway. Dierk squinted against it as he scrambled to his feet. He expected a servant, but instead down came the square-jawed opposite of everything Dierk was. His hair was black, his eyes gray, and his suit immaculately pressed.

"Dierk?" asked his father, Soren Becher, the Mayor of Londheim. "I sent a servant to fetch you twenty minutes ago. What are you doing down here?"

Dierk shrugged, incapable of providing a good answer. Vaesalaum floated above Dierk's shoulder, yet somehow his father gave no sign of worry or care. Instead he cast his bespectacled eyes about the cellar, no doubt searching for signs of a skinned animal. He found none. What he did notice was the stain on Dierk's trousers. His stern features hardened.

"Go clean yourself up," he said. "You're disgusting."

The heat in Dierk's neck felt unbearable. He retreated up the stairs and down the hall to his room.

"Can no one see you?" he whispered quietly while buttoning into a new pair of pants.

*Nisse seen when wanted seen*, Vaesalaum answered.

"I'm jealous," he muttered.

Dierk exited his room and slowly wandered back to the main foyer. The anxious looks on everyone's faces as they rushed about kindled his curiosity. Had something happened? It seemed every day Londheim dealt with some new emergency, but this was different. He thought he saw poorly hidden fear in the eyes of their servants.

Dierk did not address his father upon entering the foyer, only waited to be noticed.

"At least you're presentable," Soren said after a cursory examination. "Come. We're expected at the wall."

The wall? Not some family meeting or dire, droning funeral presided over by a Pyrehand?

"Why?" he dared ask. "Are we under attack?"

"I don't know," Soren said. "We'll soon find out."

A servant stepped in and bowed.

"Royal Overseer Downing has arrived," he said once Soren had acknowledged him. "He waits with his soldiers by the front steps."

"Impatient as always," Soren said, adjusting his tie so its sapphire pin was perfectly centered above the knot. "Come, Dierk. Keep quiet, and if you are afraid, keep it to yourself. We must project strength before the unknown."

Dierk did everything he could to avoid glancing at Vaesalaum floating over his shoulder. He'd look like a maniac if he spoke to the creature in the presence of others, but he desperately wished to ask the nisse if it knew what his father referenced. Strength before the unknown? What could he mean?

*He means the approach of the demigod of change,* said Vaesalaum, startling Dierk.

*You can read my thoughts?*

*Humans are books,* the nisse said, sounding exhausted. *I read pages. Dierk is slow?*

His neck flushed with anger and embarrassment, but he did not answer, not verbally nor inside his mind.

Dierk followed his father out the front door. Four armed soldiers stood stiff and passive around a well-dressed man in a tan suit. His hair was cut close to the scalp, and his smile was as bright as his skin was dark. A pendant hung from his neck, that of a scepter held in a closed fist. His name was Albert Downing, and he was the Royal Overseer elected by the landowners of West Orismund to rule in the Queen's stead. He approached the end of his second ten-year term, and all expected him to be serving a third. Dierk wasn't surprised. Albert was handsome and intelligent, and he greeted everyone as if they were a childhood friend. As politicians went, he was honest and fair. Among all of his father's stuffy, self-important asshole friends, Dierk found Albert to be a uniquely likable presence.

"Greetings, Overseer," Soren said while dipping his head in respect. "My apologies for keeping you waiting."

"Save your apologies for actual transgressions," Albert said. "Instead walk with me. I do not want to be gone long from the wall."

The seven of them exited the estate grounds and marched through the streets of Windswept District. The two older men conversed easily. Given their respective duties, they often consulted one another, each heavily influencing the other when it came to policy and law.

"When did you first see it?" Soren asked as they walked.

"My advisors tell me they spotted it this morning," Albert said. "At first we thought it a trick of the light, or perhaps a strange cloud of smoke."

"And you no longer think that to be the case?" Soren asked.

"I no longer know what to think," Albert said. "You'll understand when you see it for yourself."

Most people on the road gave way and then bowed upon their passage, but Dierk was shocked that once they were out of Windswept District, many began shouting questions as they passed. Such rudeness unnerved him. Their questions made no sense. Refugees? Black water? A mountain? Not helping was the distant sensation of the ground rumbling beneath his feet. What had Vaesalaum said earlier, something about how the Cradle was angry? Dierk was starting to believe it.

With Dierk keeping a respectable distance behind the two politicians, he could not hear them over the noise of the crowds and the rattle of the city guards' armor. More guards greeted them upon reaching the western wall at a station near the entrance. The group passed through a portcullis to reach the stone stairs upward. Dierk followed, eager for a look at whatever was causing this much commotion.

Whatever he'd expected, it was a pale comparison to the sight of the crawling mountain. Even Soren and Albert looked shaken. Six enormous legs slammed into the earth and dragged craters open with their claws. Its belly cut a groove with its approach. The sound of its passage was like thunder.

"It's so much closer," Albert said. "I was not even gone an hour."

"Will it stop when it reaches the city?" Soren asked. He'd taken off his spectacles and begun cleaning them with his shirt, a tic Dierk knew to mean his father was nervous and trying to hide it.

"I don't know."

"Should I order an evacuation?"

Again Albert shrugged.

"I've spoken to a few of the refugees coming in from the west. If that thing bears ill intent, we are already beyond hope of evacuating in time."

"So we sit here and watch?" Soren asked. "Is that all we have to offer?"

"It's that or we launch an attack against a mountain," Albert said. "You're good with numbers. Pray tell me, what do you consider the odds of that succeeding to be?"

Dierk's father had no good response, so they waited, and they watched. Minutes passed with agonizing slowness. Dierk shifted his weight from foot to foot as the mountain crawled closer. The demigod of change, Vaesalaum had called it.

*Will it destroy us?* he asked the nisse.

*Time will tell.*

Panic threatened to overcome him when the mountain opened its mouth and belched a tremendous river of star-filled black water north and south. Soldiers cried out in fear. The city trembled. Grass withered gray. A third wave rolled toward the western gate of the city, but it forked at the last moment, sparing them. It seemed every guard along the wall sighed with relief. The mountain settled down, its legs sinking into the soft earth.

Dierk gazed upon the magnificent, awe-inspiring presence that Vaesalaum had called the demi-god of change. His father and the Royal Overseer asked questions of one another, and they fielded more from a seemingly endless stream of wealthy elites scrambling to join them upon the wall. Dierk ignored them all.

*What does this mean?* he asked Vaesalaum. *The mountain's arrival . . . my summoning fire . . . you? Is the world ending?*

The little creature bobbed up and down, and he saw the faintest hint of a smile on its youthful face.

*No, not ending,* its cold voice spoke within his mind. He sensed within it a powerful promise, and an overwhelming sense of excitement.

*Awakening.*

# CHAPTER 1

Vikar Forrest leaned into his chair and stated the facts as if Devin had requested the Keeping Church to remove the moon from the sky.

"You're asking me to authorize a raid on the biggest donor to the church in Londheim," Forrest said. "And all this based on an anonymous testimony?"

"And the assassination attempt Gerag made on my life with one of his bodyguards."

"Whose body you are no longer in possession of. I'm still going on your word."

Devin fought to keep calm. This had to go through cleanly. Under no circumstances would he allow the fat bastard to escape the imprisonment he deserved. He'd marched into his Vikar's office confident in his claims, but that confidence was starting to wither under Forrest's constant questioning.

"Then put my word on the line. If I'm wrong, I'll resign from the division while Gerag watches. But if I'm right..."

His Vikar sighed.

"If you're right, we close down arguably the biggest soulless sex ring in all of West Orismund. Fine. You got your permission. I'll write a note to the Mayor tomorrow."

"Not tomorrow," Devin said. "Tonight. I fear Gerag might

know I'm on to him. The more time he has, the more likely he hides his crimes."

Forrest's frown was fouler than rancid butter.

"Fine," he said. "But I'm warning you, if you bullshit me on this, I won't be stopping at your resignation. I'll run you out of Londheim as a goddess-damned beggar."

Even though the city guard were under the direct authority of Londheim's Mayor, Vikars could command them so long as their orders did not contradict the local Mayor's. This concession was part of the agreement reached at the second council of Nicus three centuries prior. After an hour of impatient waiting, twelve city guards led by a sergeant arrived at the Cathedral of the Sacred Mother. Three of the men bore chain tattoos across their throats signifying them as soulless, and Devin tried not to be disturbed by their presence. Ever since Jacaranda's awakening, he was heavily torn on how to treat them.

"Forrest wouldn't tell me what we're here for," said the sergeant, a burly man named Bovalt sporting an overly long mustache. "I hope you know."

"I'll explain on the way. I don't want a weasel escaping the hen-house because the guard dog was too busy licking its own balls."

"Didn't know Soulkeepers had a penchant for artsy words."

"I'm giving it a try," Devin said, already liking the sergeant.

"Well, you're not good at it."

Devin explained the orders to arrest Gerag Ellington on the way to his mansion, as well as detailed where the secret tunnel beneath the district wall led to a secondary home. To Bovalt's credit, he took it all in stride.

"Quiet District, eh?" he said. "This'll be a first for me. Those rich types tend to hire personal guards. Will you help out if they get mouthy?"

"My sword and pistol are yours, Sergeant."

Bovalt grinned.

"That's what I like to hear."

They marched through the streets, taking a direct path southeast. The sooner they arrived, the less likely Gerag would have any warning. As they closed the distance, and saw smoke rising above the rooftops, Devin feared they may already be too late. A bucket brigade had formed by the time they arrived. Quiet District paid handsomely for a fire guild's protection, and they worked rapidly and efficiently. The fire seemed localized on the mansion's first floor, and guildsmen with rags tied over their mouths steadily progressed farther through the front door and into the halls. Meanwhile men with shovels dug a trench line about the house to prevent further spreading to the nearby mansions.

"I'm guessing that there's our destination?" the sergeant asked as they stopped before the blaze.

"You'd guess right," Devin said. "Have your men set up a second bucket line. We need to salvage what we can."

"You think whoever we're arresting is alive in there?"

"I pray so."

The sergeant started barking out orders. The man in charge of the fire guildsmen noticed their arrival and hurried over, offering suggestions of where else they could help. Devin stood by and watched, feeling frustrated and helpless. The fire was far too convenient in timing to be accidental. Had someone tipped Gerag off to their approach? There'd be no answers until the fire dwindled, so he joined a bucket line and helped with the rest.

An hour later the bulk of the fire guild had called it quits and returned home. A few lingered behind, keeping an eye on the smoldering remains to ensure bad luck didn't spark it back up again.

"Guild leader says it's safe enough to go in," Bovalt said after conversing with the older man in charge. "It looks like they got here in time. Didn't do much more than gut the first floor. Might be risky traveling any higher up, though. If the foundation's weakened..."

"Then I'll take the risk alone," Devin said. "Keep your men in the yard and make sure no one sneaks out from one of the windows."

"If that's what you want. It's your hide, after all."

Devin tied a rag over his nose and mouth to help against the smoke. Unsteady foundation or not, he'd risked his status and reputation convincing Forrest to allow this raid. He had no plans to go home empty-handed. He passed through the front door and peered about with watery eyes. The walls were blackened halfway toward the ceiling, and he had to carefully watch each step he took. The fire appeared to have been worst in that center hallway, and not near as widespread as Devin first assumed by the amount of smoke that'd been billowing into the air.

He found the first body near a window on the bottom floor. A servant, Devin guessed. Her body was mostly untouched by the flame. Killed by smoke then, he surmised. He glanced at the now-broken window and shook his head. So close to safety before succumbing. The poor woman. He found a second servant collapsed on the stairs, much of his skin horribly burned. Devin carefully stepped over him and onto the second floor.

Another body lay at the top of the stairs, face-first into the carpet. His feet dangled over the step, one slipper missing. His bed robe was shriveled and blackened. Burns covered his face and chest, strong enough to peel it down to the bone. The stink of charred hair made Devin turn away. Anger and frustration bubbled together as bile in his throat.

"Shit," he muttered. "At least the bastard got what he deserved."

He exited the mansion and returned to the sergeant.

"There's a hidden door leading to an underground basement," Devin told him. "You'll find it in the lone bedroom left of the entrance, back behind the closet. Have your men collect anything they find."

Bovalt saluted halfheartedly.

"Will do."

Devin watched them enter the smoky house from the entryway of the property fence. Part of him felt relief. If Gerag was dead, he couldn't challenge the accusations of the soulless slave trade. But there was someone who would definitely not approve of such an easy death.

"Is he inside?" Jacaranda asked. Devin kept his surprise down to a small flinch. He'd not heard her approach. He turned to see her standing behind him, much of her body and head covered by a long hooded coat. A white scarf wrapped about her neck, hiding the chain tattoos there. Her fingers drummed the hilts of the short swords strapped to each of her thighs.

"I thought I asked you to stay home?"

She leaned over and kissed his cheek.

"And since when do I do as you ask?"

Devin tried to smile, but his mood was too dour. That, and he was unsure of how Jacaranda would react to the news.

"Jac," he said, deciding it best to come right out and say it. "Gerag died in the fire."

Her eyes narrowed. It might have been shadows from the hood, but he swore he saw her face darken.

"Where is the body?" she asked.

"I'm not sure you should—"

"Where. Is. It?"

Devin glanced about. Most of the curious onlookers and neighbors had returned to their homes when the fire was extinguished. The city guards were in the underground cells. If he hurried, they could be in and out before anyone noticed.

"Come on," he said. "We can't let anyone see us."

She wordlessly followed him into the mansion.

"At the top of the stairs," Devin said, for she knew the mansion better than he did. Together they crossed through the blackened walls, bypassed the servant's body upon the stairs, and reached the second floor.

Devin crossed his arms and waited. How would Jacaranda react? Relieved at the monster's passing? Angry that he'd died without being prosecuted and publicly shamed for his deeds? He didn't know. He just wanted to be there for her.

Jacaranda circled the body once, her eyes locked on to the corpse with frightening intensity.

"The build's correct," she muttered. "Same as the hair."

"What are you doing?" Devin asked as she drew a small dagger buckled to her thigh. A single stab punctured the cloth of his trousers, and she viciously yanked on it to tear the fabric along the inside seam. Devin crossed his arms and accepted her silence. She sheathed the dagger and then pulled the fabric away to expose the burned man's legs and crotch. Jacaranda grabbed his testicles and pushed them to the side. It took less than a second for her to reach a conclusion.

"It's not him," she said.

"What?"

Jacaranda pointed to a bare patch of skin.

"There should be a birthmark right here." She shifted his cock the other direction. "And a small scar right here."

"Are you sure?"

Her pained look made him realize how foolish his question had been. Of course she was sure. How many years had she served as Gerag's pleasure toy?

She released the dead man's genitals and stood. The anger on her face grew.

"He's escaped," she said. "Faked his death and escaped. That fucker. I knew I should have come and killed him the moment Adria woke me."

That was how Jacaranda referred to Adria resurrecting her from the dead with the powers granted to her by the bizarre machinery buried beneath the city. Woke, as if pulled from a dream. Woke, as if a bullet had not torn through her heart and left her to die in his arms.

"If he's fled, then someone might know where," he said. "The cages beneath the mansion should be enough to convince the Mayor to issue an arrest warrant for Gerag...that is, if I can convince him this body is a fake."

"Why would he not believe you?"

Devin frowned at her.

"Are you willing to testify before Mayor Becher?"

Of course not. Even if they could convince the Mayor she were an awakened soulless, the church would find out about her existence. From there, it'd be investigations, interviews, perhaps even a judgment from the three Vikars. A judgment he had no control over.

"So be it," she said. "Let everyone else think he's dead. I'll find him. I know his tricks. I know all his little nests throughout the city." She sighed at the corpse. "Poor man. Killed because he shared a resemblance to Gerag. What a shitty fate."

Devin stared at the body, a thought squirming in his head.

"If he's faked his death, then he knows you're still alive," he said. "And he might not be done trying to bury evidence of his crimes."

Jacaranda spun from the corpse, her hands drifting subconsciously to the hilts of her short swords.

"Gerag should have done a damn better job setting this fire," she said. "Because it doesn't matter if I have to tear down every single home in Londheim brick by brick. I will find him, and when I do, he will suffer for every sick act he made me endure."

# CHAPTER 2

The floor beneath Adria hummed as it lifted her to the top of the Sisters' Tower. She stood resolute in the center, arms stiff at her sides. A desire for solitude carved away at the edges of her consciousness, and so she fled to high above the homes of Londheim. Part of her feared what might happen to her sanity if she could not attain some sense of peace for her weary mind. Part of her wondered if she had already lived through exactly that.

The statues of the three Sisters awaited her at the pinnacle. The deep sky rumbled a warning of thunder. Adria wrapped her arms around the grieving Lyra and pressed forehead to forehead with the statue. The cold porcelain of her mask dug into her skin. She'd not taken it off in the two days since escaping the prison Janus had locked her within. She wondered if she ever would.

"You never wanted this burden, did you?" Adria asked the weeping Sister. "You only wished for beings to love, and to be loved in return. How great is your burden, watching us hate and suffer? How great is the weight of every soul you must deliver to and from our world?"

Adria closed her eyes and imagined the stone arms coming to life and wrapping about her shivering body. She imagined hearing the words of her Goddess promising her a future of safety, peace, and certainty. If only she could reject this gift. If only.

When she opened her eyes, she saw thousands of little diamonds of light scattered across the sleeping city, each one the soul of a man, woman, or child. It didn't matter if stone or wood blocked the way, for the light would shine through. Adria sensed each one like the tiniest needle prick on the back of her neck, the souls of the entire population of Londheim. It was a great burden she wanted no part of, but none of that compared to the silver scar that rent the sky in twain.

"It is most appropriate that I find you here," a man spoke from behind her. "Give it a few decades and you'll have your own statue alongside them, Chainbreaker."

Adria's spine locked tight. Bile panicked into her throat. Only her pride kept her outwardly calm as she turned about to face the madman who had set this curse upon her.

"Spare me your heresy," she told Janus. "I am in no mood to hear it."

Janus crossed his arms and leaned against the statue of Alma struggling to lift a feather. His long coat fluttered in the cold breeze. How he'd joined her atop the tower, she had not a clue.

"Only the cowardly consider the truth a form of heresy," he said. "And you are no coward."

Though his skin was as pale as milk, his form seemed to shimmer darkly to Adria's eyes. No soul, she realized. There was no sparkling diamond of light deep within the confines of his skull. Instead a fog of shadow swam through his being like smoke.

"Are you here to capture me again?" she asked. Her hands clenched into fists. Her power was extraordinary, but could it compete against the shape-changing monstrosity at such close range? She didn't know, and she feared to find out.

"Come now," Janus said. He smirked at her as if her question were ridiculous. "If I wanted to capture you, I'd have done so without saying a word. I'm here to talk, that's all. I promise."

The last time he'd come to talk to her, she'd been imprisoned in a vast cavern of flesh and steel. He'd also looked dangerously unhinged, a stark contrast to his smooth, smiling visage now. What had changed?

"Fine then," she said. "I'm listening. Perhaps you can start with telling me what in the Goddesses' names you did to me?"

Janus laughed.

"Nothing in *their* name, I assure you. Is it not obvious, Adria? I'd have thought a woman with your intelligence would have pieced it together almost immediately."

Adria had her theories, of course, as did her brother-in-law, Tommy, but they were just that, theories. Here was a chance to learn the truth from the mouth of the monster himself. "You've given me mastery over souls," she said. "I can see them, manipulate them, even use their power as my own."

"That is the very short of it, yes."

"Then why?"

"Why you?" Janus shrugged. "The people loved you, you proved to be a powerful soul already with your healing prayers, and most of all, you don't appear to have the same fanatical blind loyalty to the Sisters like most of your kind. That, and it just happened to be the steps of your church where I spent my days in disguise. Sometimes the fate of nations hinges on coincidence, after all."

While Janus had spent his nights in Londheim finding and killing members of the Keeping Church, during the day he'd disguise himself as a beggar woman on the footsteps of her church. Learning of Janus's constant close proximity only heightened her fear of him. He could be anyone, anything, and she'd never know.

Adria felt little sparks of electricity travel down her arms. There was no soul to harness nearby but her own. Would that power be enough? And was it worth the risk to her own life? The world would be a better place without him and his sick "art." Laborers were still trying to find a way to disassemble the macabre crystal dome he'd built in the center of the market district from the blood and bones of those he'd murdered.

"That's not what I meant," she said. "Why give me this power? What do you hope to gain?"

Janus showed no sign of noticing the swelling power in her fingertips. If anything, he looked disappointed.

"Viciss gives you a gift, and you seek ulterior motives," he said. "Maybe you should worry less on why you have this power and more on what to *do* with it."

"I have an idea."

Adria sprang toward him, her right hand extended. Her fingers brushed his bare chest. Light swelled at the point of their contact, and Adria felt a heavy pull within her chest sap her breath. Drawing power from her own soul was a heavy burden, but if she could push through, if she could...

Janus smacked her wrist aside, pivoted, and struck her in the abdomen with his other fist. An uppercut met her chin as she doubled over. Adria fell dazed to the floor. Her mask clattered beside her upon the stone. She sucked in air as she recovered, blood dripping across her tongue and teeth from where his fist had split her lower lip. Damn it! If only she had her brother's speed and reflexes. She thought she'd surprised him, thought she'd been fast enough, yet when he reacted, his entire form had been a blur.

"So stubborn," Janus said. He paced the small space before her, his voice growing frighteningly angry. "So foolish. So *human.*"

He kicked her in the abdomen, resetting what meager improvement she'd made in recovering her breath.

"If it was my decision, I'd have the whole lot of you wiped off the face of the Cradle. The only thing that gives me comfort is knowing your existence is a giant wad of spit in the eye of your clueless Goddesses."

Adria pushed up to her knees, and she rapidly whispered through clenched teeth.

"Blessed Sisters, I seek your protection. Bind the darkness so it may not touch my flesh. Show mercy so I may stand in the light."

He tried to kick her again but his foot collided with a wall of light that shimmered into existence, then vanished the moment he pulled away. Janus's eyes narrowed, and he lashed out with a hand that turned the color of steel. Adria felt a momentary twinge within her mind, but the wall held. She rose to her feet, her glare matching Janus's strange mixture of amusement and annoyance. Her long dark hair cascaded forward from her hunched form to cover her face, not a mask, but close enough to one that she felt her confidence returning.

"You will not touch me again," she said.

She thought he'd be angry, but instead he lifted his hands in surrender.

"No, I will not," he said. "You have your role to play, Chain-breaker, whether I like it or not. I thought I'd give you the courtesy of explaining this since your friends so rudely took you from my care once the conversion process was finished."

"Then say it and be gone."

Janus's right hand sharpened into a singular spike, his skin shifting from pale flesh to brilliant jade. He slowly pressed it into the shield of light, gently at first, then steadily harder. All the while his eyes never left hers.

"I do not take orders from you," he said. "Have I not yet made that clear?"

The twinge of strain on her mind grew to a pounding headache. Sweat trickled down her neck and forehead. Her jaw shook with each word.

"Say it . . . and be gone."

She would not break before him. She would not cower. This thing, this monster that bore the name *Janus* would not lord his superiority over her for one more second. She watched him sink his heels into the floor, his shoes literally merging with the stone to give him greater stability. All his weight leaned into the thrust. The shield of light shimmered and rippled with cracks, but Adria found it easier, not harder, to keep it intact. The necessary power was within her. She just needed to believe.

"Impressive," Janus said. He withdrew the jade spear and separated his feet from the floor. "Maybe one day you'll be worth Viciss's gift. As for your purpose, it's simple, really. You are to replace the Sisters. Your power isn't quite there yet, but one day you'll render their caring and delivery of souls obsolete, and take up that task yourself. Look upon the people of Londheim and realize that you are everything they need. That alone will be a good first step."

"Replace the Sisters?" Adria asked. "Are you mad? That isn't a purpose, and it certainly isn't a need of our people. Winter comes and we have little harvest. They need food, and shelter from the cold."

"Of which your Sisters deliver neither." Janus walked to the edge of the tower and balanced upon the thin wall. "Perhaps you should start pondering why the Goddesses are as helpless as you are in the face of tribulation."

With that, he walked off the side and vanished. Adria grabbed her mask and pulled it back over her face. Only then did she feel a semblance of calm settle upon her shoulders. Damn that shapeshifting monster. It was as if his every word were meant to squirm inside her brain and set it on fire.

Adria returned her hands to the activating stones and discovered a trio of novices awaited her at the bottom of the tower. Their eyes bulged at the sight of the moving platform, but they kept their wits about them and pretended to have seen nothing.

"Yes?" Adria asked when none of the youngsters appeared ready to break the silence first.

"Vikar Thaddeus requests your presence," said the oldest of them, a pretty redheaded girl maybe a year or two away from obtaining the rank of Mindkeeper herself.

"I'll be on my way to the cathedral then."

"No, not the cathedral. Vikar Thaddeus said to meet him 'where only we might go.'"

Adria withheld a shudder.

"Very well," she said. "Thank you."

The novices bowed and left. Adria cast one last look to the Sisters' Tower, half-expecting to see Janus lurking atop it, his sick smile mocking her from afar.

There was only one place Thaddeus could mean by his deliberate wording. Adria descended the innocuous steps upon the side of the Sisters' Remembrance, passed through the dark tunnel, and traveled to the locked door barring her way into the forgotten prison of the Keeping Church. The guard checked her over from his little window before opening it. Thaddeus waited in the dim torch light, his arms crossed over his chest and a grim smile painted upon his elderly face.

"Thank you for coming so quickly," he said. "I do not know how much time we have left."

"What happened?" she asked.

"Deakon Sevold has taken a turn for the worse." The Vikar led her past the dank, empty cells. "I fear we are rapidly running out of time."

Adria remembered the horrific state Sevold had been in when she last visited. How could his health possibly get worse? Again she passed the cell with the imprisoned Mindkeeper Tamerlane, and it seemed his pale gold eyes twinkled at the sight of them. His mouth was securely covered, but there was no doubt in her mind he smiled.

To her surprise, the next cell was not empty like before. A man lay on a cot, his body twisted and contorted in a horribly familiar way. His hair had fallen from his scabbed head, and his ribs formed an unnatural wave upon his gaunt frame. His tongue hung out from a jaw stretched much too far to one side. Adria shuddered. She could see his soul, and from it wept a constant agony and torment. The temptation to free it from his broken mortal shell nearly overwhelmed her.

"Who is he?" she asked after halting before the cell.

"A man who earned the wrath of a Ravencaller," Thaddeus said. "Their numbers are growing throughout Londheim at a frightening rate. If we don't halt the spread soon, we might have more cursed citizens than we do cells to safeguard them in. We brought him down here in hopes that, should we discover a cure for Sevold, we can use it upon him as well."

"I pray we discover it soon," she said. The idea that others might suffer a similar fate as her Deakon terrified her, as did knowing there were more out there who wielded dark, blasphemous power.

"I pray you discover it now," Thaddeus said. "We have no choice."

The stench of death was overwhelming in the final cell. Adria had wondered how a man in his state could worsen, but she discovered how easily that was possible. Sevold's skin was covered with bruises, his entire right arm was a sickly yellow, and when he breathed in, it gurgled like water blown through a straw. If the Deakon was awake, he lacked the strength to open his eyes. His mouth hung limply open, and multiple teeth were missing. Those that remained were solid black.

"Goddesses have mercy," Adria whispered. "Only the cruelest of men could place such a fate upon another."

"The world is full of cruel men," Thaddeus said. "Please, I know it was difficult, but I would like you to try to cure him a second time. I fear he will die within days if he is not healed."

Adria felt her sight shifting. The Deakon's soul hovered within his skull, just as tormented as the other man's. She focused on it, dimming the outer world as her vision attuned to the spiritual. Its light was weaker than expected, due to thin black lines that wrapped about it like spiderwebs. Adria tried to fall into the soul's memories but found her path blocked. The curse, she realized. It denied her any attachment to the man's soul.

"I have something I would like to try," she said. "Please, remain still, Thaddeus, and trust in me no matter what happens."

She had told no one of the changes she'd undergone in Janus's machinery beneath the city. She feared the increased scrutiny, and she wanted nothing to do with whatever fate Janus seemed to think he'd forced upon her. What she did want was to help people, and if that meant revealing herself to her Vikar, then so be it. Her right hand settled upon Thaddeus's jaw. The other stretched toward Sevold's.

"You will feel a strain," she said. "Endure it."

Thaddeus's face was a perfect stone, revealing nothing of his thoughts and emotions. His soul, however, revealed all as she touched it with her mind. He was frightened and confused, but as the threads of his soul floated out to touch her palm, she sensed his growing curiosity. Power flowed into her, and she channeled it straight through her body and to the broken Deakon.

To her mind's eye, it was like watching opposing spiderwebs intertwine. The vibrant silver she cast from her hand twisted and broke about the black lines imprisoning the Deakon's soul. She lashed at them, tugging and pulling, but they would not break. The more she tried, the more they drew power from Sevold's own soul to lash back in return. Again she felt the similar hatred and anger as when she'd first tried to heal him, but this time she could actually see the vicious, stabbing little threads as they bit into her skin.

Adria relented to their power when the pain grew too much for her to bear. So far as she could tell, she had made not a dent upon the curse. Thaddeus gasped in a long breath upon her releasing his soul. Sweat poured down his skin, and he had to brace himself against the bars of the cell to remain on his feet.

"What did you do?" he asked.

"I...used the power of your soul to see if I could free the Deakon from his curse. Clearly I was not successful."

He looked up at her, his eyes sparkling with curiosity so strong it bordered on obsession.

"How?"

Adria almost told him, but that intellectual need broke her confidence. Janus was proclaiming her a replacement for the Goddesses. What might her Vikar do with that knowledge? Discussing how she'd gained her new powers also meant potentially revealing her rescuers, perhaps putting Puffy and Jacaranda in danger by doing so.

"I'm not ready to talk about that yet," she said. "Will you allow me my privacy for a few days longer?"

Debate raged within her Vikar, but in the end he kept to his trust in her.

"Very well," he said. He released his grip on the bar and tested his balance. His legs wobbled a bit, but he seemed to have mostly recovered from the strain of her using his soul. "Have you anything else you might try?"

"Yes, I do," she said. "Allow me to speak with Tamerlane."

"Absolutely not. We already suffer without our Deakon. I will not lose you as well to his curse."

"That curse is fueled by divine power. I can do nothing to it, for it seems the Sisters themselves want it locked upon Sevold. If you want it removed, then allow me to question him. He may be the only way we banish this curse."

"We've interrogated him relentlessly," Thaddeus insisted. "His resolve is nigh unbreakable."

"Even so, I believe I can make him talk to me."

Thaddeus crossed his arms.

"Is this linked to whatever you just did to me?"

"Yes. It is. Now will you allow it?"

Another inner debate, this one far quicker than the last.

"Very well. I pray you do nothing to make me regret this."

They returned to Tamerlane's cell. The tanned man sat on his knees, and he watched them intently. His Mindkeeper robes had broken down considerably during his stay, and his brown hair was matted from dirt and sweat. His eyes, though, were alive with thought. Thaddeus was right. They'd not broken his spirit in the slightest.

The guard opened his cell with a loud clank of metal. Adria stepped inside, her hands crossed behind her back.

"How does he eat and drink?" she asked as she studied the leather across his mouth.

"At knifepoint," the guard answered. He knelt beside Tamerlane and inserted a second key into the lock, undoing the contraption, and then pulled the saliva-coated leather away. Tamerlane wretched twice, then gathered his bearings. Despite her newfound power, Adria still felt a twinge of fear at what might happen if he decided to curse her. The guard clearly feared the same possibility, and he drew his sword and placed the edge at the man's throat.

"Hello, Tamerlane," she said. "My name is Adria Eveson. I wish to speak with you. Is that all right?"

Tamerlane worked his jaw up and down, which audibly popped twice. That done, he settled a cocky smile her way, as if they were friends meeting up at a tavern instead of in a bleak, forgotten cell tied to the church's darkest times.

"Not a word while he's around," Tamerlane said, pointing at Thaddeus. "And not with a blade at my throat, either. If I talk, it is to you alone."

Adria glanced over her shoulder, her request obvious. Thaddeus glared at the imprisoned Mindkeeper with open contempt.

"Please, be careful, Adria," he said. He motioned to the nearby guards to follow, and then he disappeared toward the exit. Tamerlane settled against the cell wall. His amusement was plain as day.

"Twice now I've seen you come here trying to undo what I've done," he said. "Both times Thaddeus held himself differently than when he'd brought scholars and doctors to investigate the Deakon. My mouth may be blocked, but my ears hear well. You prayed over Sevold the first time, to no avail. This time, you pray not a word, yet I swear it seemed our beloved Vikar was greatly moved by your actions. Tell me, Adria, what is so special about you?" His smirk grew. "Is it because your prayers for healing actually work?"

Adria kept her body stiff and relied on her mask to hide her reaction.

"What makes you believe such an outlandish claim?" she asked.

"Is it really so outlandish? The Sisters granted me strength to curse the Deakon. It only follows that others would receive strength to heal and bless, does it not?"

Goddesses above, she wanted to slap that smirk off his face so much it hurt.

"You think the Sisters granted you power to curse their own Deakon? A curse you read in the blasphemous Book of Ravens, which denounces the Sisters and denies their authority over the Cradle?"

"Have you read the Book of Ravens?" he asked.

"I have."

Immediately his attention perked up.

"Have you now?" he said. "Then you should know the book does not denounce the Sisters, but instead asks the reader to view them in a different light. Those curses are the proof. By accomplishing these supposed 'blasphemous' results, they show that the calm, pure, forgiving Goddesses we envision are capable of a far wider spectrum of concepts and emotions."

Adria thought of the horrendous shape Sevold had been cursed into and shook her head. If that ugliness were a part of the Goddesses, they could not possibly be worthy of her prayers. She could not accept that it was the Goddesses' doing.

"You purposefully lead the conversation astray," she said. "Tell me how to remove the curse. If you don't, the church will have you executed."

"If I cure the Deakon, the church will have no need of me, and then I will be executed for what I know and what I have done. I'm sorry, Adria, but try offering something more valuable than a hastening toward my own death."

"Then what is it you do want?"

Tamerlane gestured to the walls about him.

"What does every prisoner want? Freedom."

"You know I can't promise that. I'll relay the request to Vikar Thaddeus, of course. If you undo the damage you have done, then perhaps a merciful fate for your transgressions can be reached."

"You again offer me nothing," he said, and slumped back against his cell wall with a roll of his eyes. "I bore of this. Let us discuss far more interesting matters. Yourself, to be specific. You can hide behind that mask all you like, but I can sense that this line of questioning is not your desired inquiry. Sevold was the reason you were brought down here, but if we were friends in the cathedral's library, calmly conversing with cups of tea beside a fireplace, you would ask different questions, wouldn't you, Adria?"

Those pale gold eyes bored into her, and though she could see his very soul, she felt far more naked before him than he before her.

"How did you lose your faith?" she asked. "What is it you discovered that broke down your belief in the Sisters and allowed you to become such a monster?"

She worried that her question would anger him, but instead he sounded disappointed.

"You think my casting of that curse means I lost my faith in the Sisters? Far from it, Adria. I hold them close in my heart, and I assure you, they still love me as well."

An unwelcome memory flashed through Adria's mind; Janus crumbling before her, his body twisting and breaking as she wielded the words of the mutilation curse like a sledgehammer. Yes, there was one question she wanted an answer for, one that had weighed on her since that weak, frightened moment she'd committed blasphemy in a failed attempt to spare her life.

"How could that be possible?" she asked. "How can one wield such a horrific curse and still be beloved by the Goddesses?"

Tamerlane's eyes met hers, and she could almost see the mind behind those eyes at work, brilliant and fascinating. It took him but a moment to reach his conclusion, and she had no doubt it would be the correct one.

"You cursed someone, didn't you, Adria?"

She swallowed down a jagged stone that spontaneously formed in her throat.

"You didn't answer my question."

Another long stare.

"The world we live in is not simple," he said. "It is not black and white and confined to a flat page scrawled upon by the scholars. You ask about an act committed in a singular moment in time. The context of that moment must be taken into account. Can the Sisters love a person who wields their power into a curse? Absolutely. Might they also hate or condemn a person for the same act? Without question."

For the first time he stood. Adria hastily retreated two steps toward the door. For some reason she was more frightened of him than she'd been of Janus atop the Sisters' Tower.

"You committed the same act as I," he said. "Yet I am within a cage, and you are the Deakon's supposed savior. It's almost as if the act itself is irrelevant. All that matters is the framework, the victim, the purpose, and the ripples it spreads throughout the many affected lives. You know nothing of me, nor why I spoke that curse. I know nothing of you, or why you spoke a similar curse, but I do know this: The Sisters have abandoned neither of us, which means their love remains. Does that soothe your soul? Or would you rather a simpler answer, one mushed into gruel more appropriate for consumption by the children?"

Adria clenched her hands into fists. She could turn Tamerlane's physical body to ash. A mere thought, and she could spare herself the confusion...but did she truly want that? The Keeping Church struggled mightily to understand the rules and philosophical implications of this new, chaotic world. Tamerlane, though, seemed unbound by rigid dogma and tradition. One conversation with him, and she already felt she glimpsed a better understanding.

"Then let us start again with what I know," she said. "What I know is that two cells down a man I believe to be wise and just is suffering immensely by your words, and I want to end that suffering. Am I truly so terrible for wishing that so?"

Tamerlane smiled. Not a mocking, arrogant smirk. A real smile, one that made her wish she had known this man long before the world turned itself inside out. No doubt he had been handsome once. Even covered in sweat and dirt, he carried a sort of confident charisma.

"I will make you a promise, Adria, but only if you make me one in return. If you guarantee my freedom, then I will remove the curse upon Deakon Sevold's soul. I want *your* guarantee, mind you, not anyone else's. I want you to swear your very life to protect mine should anyone try to kill me or return me to this dark cell."

"Why would you undo the curse now, and why for my promise?" she asked. "I am but a simple Mindkeeper. A similar promise from my Vikar surely means much more."

"Because you're clearly precious to Thaddeus. He won't hesitate to chop off my head, but if it meant possibly losing you? Well..."

The man shrugged. "Perhaps that might cause him to think twice. And besides, I already offered such a deal to Thaddeus. He refused it."

Adria's mouth dropped open, the reaction thankfully hidden behind her mask.

"What? You lie. Thaddeus would certainly have granted your freedom to spare Sevold's life."

Tamerlane laughed and shook his head.

"You vex me, Adria. Sometimes I find myself liking you, and other times, you are insufferably naïve. If the Deakon of Londheim perishes, who replaces him?"

"A vote among all keepers decides that."

"I imagine Thaddeus has his sights on a promotion," Tamerlane said. "But maybe that's why you won't take my offer as well. If he is made Deakon, the position of Vikar of the Day suddenly opens up. My, my, I wonder who he might choose as his successor? Might it be the humble Mindkeeper who tried her damnedest to heal the previous Deakon and who wields the power of the Sisters in ways even our current Vikar does not?"

Adria wanted to shout at him how wrong he was. She wanted to crush him with her newfound power and rip his soul to the heavens. His claims...they couldn't be true. Lies, manipulative lies of a man who had turned against the Goddesses.

"You disappoint me," she said. "But I guess I should have expected no less. Farewell, Tamerlane."

"One last parting bit of wisdom," he said. "Perhaps I am insane, and your prayers are but empty words that land upon deaf ears. But if your prayers are heard, and the Sisters grant you power like they did for me, then perhaps you should worry about helping all of Londheim instead of just one suffering old man. The 19th Devotion might be a good start. Give it a try, Adria, and if it works, think on why it took so long for you, or anyone within your church, to consider it. Go on then. I look forward to hearing the results."

Adria exited the cell and gestured to the guard waiting at the far end of the tunnel. He returned carrying the leather gag, and Tamerlane made no effort to resist.

"Did you learn a cure?" Thaddeus asked. The cell door clanged shut behind them.

"No," she said. "His words twist more than a snake."

"I warned you, he is a cunning man lost to the lies of the Raven-callers. If we are to save our Deakon, it won't be through his aid, I fear."

Adria wanted to ask about the deal Tamerlane claimed the Vikar had turned down: a life for a life. Wasn't their Deakon worth it? And if Thaddeus had refused...was it for the reasons he offered? Did he seek the Deakonship? And if he was considering her as his replacement, did that mean he believed she would help him con-solidate his power?

"I am sorry I could not be of more help," Adria said. "I will pray on the matter, and if I discover any other ideas to try, I swear I will return."

Thaddeus offered her a weary smile.

"Thank you, Mindkeeper. You've already done more than I could ever ask."

Adria left the Sisters' Remembrance hurrying faster and faster until she was practically running. Once she was out of Church District, she found herself an isolated corner by the district wall and slumped against the stone. Sweat dripped down her face. Her breath clung hot to the interior of her mask. Her heart pounded. The thousands upon thousands of souls throughout Londheim sur-rounded her like a second set of stars, and no matter her attempts, she could not remove the feel of them watching her every action.

"Lyra of the Beloved Sun, hear my prayer," she whispered. "Our stomachs groan with hunger. Our hands shake with want. Deliver us that which we need, and may we rejoice in your kindness."

Adria was well familiar with the 19th Devotion, for she had prayed it often with the poor and destitute of her district, Low Dock. The meaning had always seemed obvious: Acknowledge your needs to the Sisters and trust that they will care for you and ensure your daily necessities were met, whatever they might be. It didn't actually mean you hoped the Sisters would appear and deliver bread to appease your hunger. It was symbolic, it was humbling. It wasn't literal.

Adria looked down at the small loaf of bread cradled between her palms, warm to the touch and smelling as if freshly pulled from an oven, and knew not whether to laugh or cry.

# CHAPTER 3

Sweat dripped down Dierk's neck as he hurried along the winding Low Dock street. He walked with his shoulders hunched and his eyes planted firmly toward his feet. His hands were buried into the pockets of his pale brown coat. He'd bought the cheap thing at the market thinking it an appropriate disguise, but mere minutes inside the destitute district he realized that his definition of "poor" was wildly off.

*You're too clean,* he thought as he veered away from a tired worker carrying a bucket of something on his shoulder. The bearded man glared at him as they passed, or maybe Dierk imagined it. *No holes in your clothes, no calluses or scars on your hands. Your coat may be cheap, but it's still new.*

It didn't help that he felt incredibly young compared to those who lingered in the streets or made their way to the docks. Young, spoiled, and trespassing into a world where he did not belong.

*Dierk is afraid,* Vaesalaum whispered into his mind. *Dierk is a coward. Whole city belongs to humans. Do not cower.*

"Easier said than done," Dierk muttered. The nisse floated just above his left shoulder. It had grown considerably since he'd first found it weeks ago in his family's cellar, its serpentine body now the length of his forearm. Its soft fur rippled as it flew despite the lack of wind. The air in Low Dock felt stiff and sick. Perhaps it was the proximity to the river and the many shops there. He wouldn't know. He hadn't come this far south in Londheim in years...if ever.

*Power breeds confidence*, Vaesalaum said. *Remember your power.*

"You're wrong. Confidence breeds power. My father is friends with many powerful people who are completely spineless when challenged."

*Spineless like your father's only son?*

Dierk winced at the insult. Damn it, here he was arguing aloud with an invisible creature while walking in a district he knew nothing of. People would likely think him crazy. Then again, being crazy wasn't as big a deal in a place like Low Dock as it would be in, say, Quiet District. Despite knowing it'd be smarter to answer the nisse in his mind, he whispered and muttered his responses. Mentally talking with the nisse unnerved him, for it made it feel like he had to guard his every thought lest it be seen as a dialogue. It might be an illusion of privacy, but it was an illusion he desperately needed.

"Are we close?" he asked.

*We are close. Turn left. Follow Vaesalaum.*

Dierk did as he was told. The street was lined with makeshift tents, compressing the already crowded space between houses on either side. The cries of young children grated across his spine. He wished he were in Windswept District, where his family's mansion was located. One of its many patrolling city guards would have ordered their parents to shush their children or take them elsewhere.

"Won't there be a crowd?" Dierk asked, hurriedly glancing away from a tan-skinned man in a hood who smiled at him with teeth whiter and sharper than what seemed natural.

*Vaesalaum cares not for crowds. Seen only when desired. Dierk will be calm. Dierk will remain silent. No human shall be the wiser.*

Dierk could already hear the growing commotion. Tugging on his collar (why did it have to be so damn hot, wasn't it already autumn?), he hurried after the strange, luminescent being with the paws of a cat and the face of a child. Ever since that first clumsy kill, the nisse had guided him at night to bodies of men and women who'd recently died, be it from hunger, disease, or the hands of another. Each time, their bodies had been left hidden and undisturbed so he could drink of their memories in private.

This time, though, he did not seek a body to drink of memories. This time, Vaesalaum brought him to witness a body sacrificed at the hands of a Ravencaller.

The dead man hung above the street, his head tilted backward and his mouth open as if letting out a silent cry to the heavens. Two lengths of rope had been tied to the rooftops and then bound to his wrists to keep him suspended. His clothes had been removed and his head shaved. A single spike pierced through one ankle and out the other to keep the legs together. Across his chest and cutting down to his navel was a giant, gaping triangle exposing ribs, guts, and tissue. Intestines hung like bloody streamers to decorate the street for a particularly macabre holiday.

Dierk stood at the back of the small crowd, admiring the amount of attention to detail necessary to suspend the body in such a way. The slack on the ropes was just right so the body hung perpendicular to the ground instead of slanted one way or another. The spike pinned the legs together so they did not dangle about. Even the hanging intestines, while seemingly random, were carefully positioned and stitched in place with black thread.

"Why hang the body in such a way?" he wondered aloud.

*Burial for bodies with a soul. That is Sisters' decree. Pyre for bodies without. That is Soulkeeper decree. But pyre is not opposite of burial. Give body to the air. That is avenria decree.*

"Who are the avenria?" he asked, careful to keep his words

at a barely perceptible whisper. The nisse hadn't mentioned them since his first appearance, but to refer to this as an "avenria decree" jostled his curiosity.

*Shadow walkers. The first Ravencallers. Avenria guard souls of the dead from abuse. From corruption.*

"From things like you, then?"

*Not nisse. Nisse are gifts. Nisse let grieving humans say good-bye.*

That hardly described what Dierk and Vaesalaum had been doing with the bodies they found. With the nisse's help he'd plunged through their memories, "reading their pages" as his new friend would call it. Nothing compared to its rush. Dierk felt like he was being told a story, sometimes mundane, sometimes exciting, but he experienced every sensation, felt every emotion as he peered through a dead man or woman's entire life. He was even starting to learn how to control it himself instead of relying on Vaesalaum to guide him to specific memories.

"That's it, back up, all of you," a gruff man shouted. The small crowd parted as two city guards pushed through to the space below the hanging body. One let out a loud curse, then ordered the other to enter the home on the right.

"Why did you want me to see this?" Dierk asked as he slumped against a building, shrinking into himself to make his body as small as possible.

*There are more like you, Dierk. More seeking truth. Find them. Become one with them. Ravencallers will guide humans to their new place in the awakened world.*

The other guard emerged from the waist up at a window on the upper floor. A few hacks with his sword cut the rope holding the body aloft. It immediately swung low, its momentum carrying it to the wall of the home on the other side. It struck with a wet splatter, internal organs dumping out across the dirt. The first guard swore up a storm and again shouted for the crowd to disperse.

Dierk wandered away with the rest. He tugged on the hood of his coat, wishing it would stretch even lower over his face.

"And what is our new place?" he asked the nisse.

*Not yet. You must learn. Keep learning. Wisdom comes with time.*

Dierk had plenty of experience with evasive non-answers, given his father's occupation in politics, and he easily detected another from the nisse. He decided to let the matter drop. There would be no forcing answers out of Vaesalaum. The nisse held all the cards in their relationship.

There were two exits out of Low Dock, and though the nearest led away from his mansion, Dierk hurried to it anyway. He wanted out of the crowded, somber district as fast as possible, even if it meant a longer walk back home. His "disguise" made him feel more noticeable, not less, at least here in the poorest parts of Londheim. He kept his head down, his arms crossed, and hurried through the streets. He slowed only when he heard the sounds of a crowd, but unlike before, these noises were loud and jovial.

"What leads that way?" he asked Vaesalaum at a junction. Down the other road he could hear people shouting, laughing, some even singing. It had the air of a festival in a district normally bathed in quiet struggle.

*Somewhere Dierk should not go.*

The refusal to answer, as well as the insistence not to go, was enough to convince Dierk to take a brief detour. He could sense the nisse's disapproval like a bad smell lingering around his head. Dierk relished it. Too often the strange creature commanded every aspect of his life. It was refreshing to do something against its wishes, no matter how simple and petty.

At least eighty people, maybe more, crowded around the small church. It took him a moment, but he realized they formed a haphazard line leading to the church's stairs. A dark-skinned Faithkeeper with a shaved head stood at the top, two younger novices at her side holding baskets. Distributing food, from what he could tell.

That explained the commotion. The price of bread had doubled since the black water's arrival, and from what discussions he'd overheard at his house, it was expected to double again by the time winter was in full swing. Who wouldn't be excited by a free meal?

*Foolish human,* Vaesalaum whispered, an uncomfortable reminder that it permanently haunted his mind. *Look closer.*

Dierk wasn't sure what he was supposed to be seeing, but he watched as directed. After a minute the Faithkeeper stopped helping the little ones distribute loaves of bread and instead closed her eyes and rested a hand above each basket. She was praying, he decided, based on the movement of her lips. He knew that Faithkeepers often prayed a blessing over meals, particularly during large gatherings, but what was the point of praying over empty baskets?

He blinked, and the baskets weren't empty anymore. Steam rose off loaves of bread piled so high they were in danger of spilling out across the steps of the church. A hush went through the crowd, followed by gasps and cheers. Some were even crying.

"Miracles," Dierk whispered. "The—the servants of the Goddesses perform miracles."

*As they have for weeks. Are Dierk's eyes still so closed to the world?*

He'd heard some stories of healing, yes, but all of Londheim was awash with the most ridiculous of rumors. It took just one loon insisting they saw, say, talking birds or man-eating mushrooms and the rumor would sweep through the city for a day or two before being replaced by the next asinine claim. Dierk had assumed the rumors of the church keepers healing the wounded just one more false claim, perhaps meant to inspire trust in the organization during these troubling times.

"But—but the Book of Ravens, it insists the Sisters are foolish, conceited, even liars. They don't care for us. For truth, I didn't...I didn't really think the Sisters even existed."

*Does the book ever deny their power? Does the book ever claim them to not exist? We slumbered. Sisters slumbered. The jailer and prisoner manacled in the same cell. We awaken. Sisters awaken. Dierk must learn to accept the miraculous as commonplace, or Dierk will never reach true power.*

It was the harshest Vaesalaum had talked to him since first appearing. Dierk winced at the words. They made him feel small and stupid, nothing but a dumb child needing to learn his place. It reminded him of cowering before his father, and he instinctively crossed his arms and looked to the ground.

"Sorry," he mumbled.

*Human apologizes. Vaesalaum does not want apology. Vaesalaum wants its pupil to learn. Return home. Nothing for Dierk here.*

But Dierk's curiosity was much too aflame to leave now. He wanted to see the miracle again, and he started worming his way through the crowd toward the front. Men, women, and children ate all around him, commenting and making comparisons. Apparently no one could quite agree on how the bread tasted. As he closed the distance, he heard sudden, loud sobs unbefitting the overall jovial atmosphere. Dierk turned their direction, and it was then he saw the celestial being.

Her long dark hair spilled down either side of her porcelain mask and curled about her shoulders. Her skin was as pale and perfect as the white half of her mask. Her brown eyes were the color of the stained wood that made up every piece of furniture in Dierk's family mansion. With the rest of her face hidden by her Faithkeeper mask, and the flow of her body buried beneath thick gray robes, she was an unseen mystery, but for Dierk, that didn't matter in the slightest.

He didn't need to see her physical body. He could see her soul.

It shined like a diamond behind her mask, swirling with white fire within the prison of her skull. Dierk had seen souls before, but none like this, and none while the host was alive. It pulsed with life. It cast a shadow across all else in his vision, making colors seem drab and the skin of people's bodies vaguely translucent. A separate line spread out before her, filled with dozens of sick and wounded people of Londheim. This miracle woman knelt over a young girl at the front of the line. Her skin was pale, her body weak with consumption. The Faithkeeper's hands pressed against either side of this girl's face, as if preparing for a kiss. The light of her soul flared, so beautiful, so terrible, that Dierk lifted an arm and squinted as if that would do anything. It swirled like a storm, little tendrils shooting through her bones to exit out her fingertips.

The girl's body jolted with life. A single, rapturous cry erupted from her dry throat. The family with her sobbed and worshipped in equal measure. Dierk felt tears run down his face. Was it the beauty he witnessed, or the light stinging his eyes? He didn't know. He didn't care. His awe was overwhelming. Who was this woman who possessed a soul unlike any other in all the Cradle, and who healed flesh with a kiss and a prayer?

Dierk grabbed the arm of the nearest man and pointed.

"Who is that?" he asked.

"Mindkeeper Adria," was his reply. "Some say she's the Sacred Mother reborn, others say Lyra made flesh."

Dierk released his grip, and he did not bother to thank him for the answer. In his world there was himself, Vaesalaum, and Adria. All else were bothersome statues clogging up his way toward her.

"How can I see it?" he asked Vaesalaum. "Her soul. It's—it's blinding."

*Dierk's eyes change with contact with nisse. Improve. Evolve. She is the Chainbreaker. The dragons chose her to lead humans to a new way. A way free of the Sisters. You see gifted power.*

Another family approached Adria for healing, and Dierk pushed and shoved his way forward, ignoring the angry remarks he elicited from the gathered throng. He had to see. He had to bear witness to her next wonder. Adria bent toward a sick child, from what Dierk could see, maybe six or seven years old. His skin was pale as milk, his gaze listless, and his body shivering from fever. Adria put her hands upon his face, and this time Dierk watched with utter fascination as little tendrils of the woman's soul wound through her body to her fingertips. They pulsed with life. They burned with light.

"Her power," Dierk whispered in awe. "It's like mine. She—she's like *me*."

*Not alike*, Vaesalaum spoke. *Ravencallers harvest souls of the dead. Swindle their power. Chainbreaker wields souls. Commands them. She is queen, and souls her subjects. You are a peasant compared to her.*

It didn't matter. Their difference in power might be vast, but it was the *same* power. He and Adria, they were connected, two practitioners of magics long thought impossible. His feet moved of their own accord. The urge to speak with her overwhelmed his stomach's nervous protests. Before he even knew it, he stood at the head of the line, mere feet away from this crystalline beauty. Adria's eyes fell upon him. Her head tilted slightly to one side.

"Yes?" she asked.

Dierk froze. His jaw locked tight. A hundred possible responses rattled around in his skull, not a one managing the journey to his tongue. Heat flushed up his neck to his ears just from her gaze sweeping over him. His pants tightened as blood pounded into his crotch.

*Say something*, he inwardly screamed. *Anything!*

Rough hands pushed him aside. A husband and wife, coming with an older man struggling to walk. There was no time to abide his foolishness when miracles awaited. Adria turned her attention to the new couple, breaking the spell she held over him.

"Sorry," Dierk said, far too quietly for her to hear. He slunk away, only now noticing that Vaesalaum had abandoned him. Well, why wouldn't it? Perhaps the nisse couldn't stand to watch him make a fool out of himself before the enormous crowd. Dierk broke out into a run. Who gave a shit if anyone noticed him?

They'd all seen him. They'd all laughed at him, hadn't they? He ran, ran until he found a small dark corner all alone and shoved himself into it.

"Stupid," he muttered, slamming the bottom of his fist against the wall separating Low Dock from Tradeway. The pain reverberated up his arm, and while it didn't feel good, it felt *deserved*, so he did it again and again, pounding the immovable stone with his scrawny hands. "Stupid—stupid—stupid—fucking—idiot!"

Bone cracked. A sob escaped his lips. Dierk slid to the ground, clutching his injured hand to his chest. His pinkie extended at an odd angle, and he feared what he'd done to the knuckle. Tears rolled down his face. He rolled his knees to his chest and stared into nowhere.

"What is wrong with you?" he asked himself. "Why do you have to be so...so..."

He didn't know how to answer. Or maybe he was scared to voice everything he knew. His weird habits. His need to cut and skin. How being around strangers crippled him with nerves, resulting in him pushing away those his father brought over in hopes of making "friends." And now he'd stood before the most beautiful, mesmerizing person in the entire Cradle and just...stared at her while slack-jawed and drooling.

*What did Dierk hope to accomplish?*

The intrusion of Vaesalaum's cold voice sank Dierk's head deeper into the space between his knees. To have anyone, or anything, witness his awful thoughts humiliated him further.

"I don't know," he whispered. "I wanted...I wanted to tell her that I'm like her. That I can see souls like her, that I can touch them, manipulate them like she can. That—that maybe we could talk. I could learn more about her, learn why she is what she is. Is that so fucking awful, Vaesalaum?"

He'd meant that final sentence to come across as spiteful and angry, but instead it sounded like a simpering plea in his mind.

*Not awful. Dierk is not like other humans. Vaesalaum would not have come otherwise. Do not lament for what you are not. Embrace what you have. Power. Wisdom. The eyes of a nisse.*

Dierk sniffled and rubbed at his eyes. A new emotion burned in his stomach. He'd cut animals out of a need he could not resist. He'd obeyed his father's commands out of fear. This was different. This was something he wanted, wanted so badly it frightened him.

"I will see her again," he told Vaesalaum. "I'll let her know how special I am. I don't care how hard or awkward it is, I have to become better. Adria and I—I think we're meant to be."

*Meant to be? By whom, human? Goddesses? Dragons? Uncaring fate?*

"I don't know," he said, pushing himself back up to his feet. He cradled his injured hand against his stomach as if it were his child. "And I don't care. We're meant to be, Vaesalaum. Whatever it takes, I'll do it."

Those words. Hearing them. Saying them. They lit a fire that burned in a cold, dark chamber he never knew existed within him.

*We're meant to be.*

# CHAPTER 4

Tommy couldn't understand the soldiers' lack of eagerness, nor the worry painted across the face of Jarel Downing. The gaunt man was in charge of the expedition that had taken them from Londheim to a farming village tucked against the southern bend of the Septen River some sixty miles west.

"Do you think the lapinkin would mind answering some questions after we're done discussing the boring political matters?" Tommy asked him.

"I can't imagine why they would," Jarel replied. He was a cousin to the Royal Overseer, and that family connection had landed him oversight of the thirty soldiers currently marching between the tall grass of West Orismund toward a large farming community fifty miles southwest of Londheim. Jarel had the forgettable temperament of a man destined to be a wall ornament hanging in various mansions and halls. His hair and nails were meticulously cleaned and cut, and his clothes too thin and frail for the road. Day or night, it seemed his dark face was permanently locked in a visage of mild annoyance.

"I expect us to be nuisances to them," he added. "And threats at the worst."

"There's no reason we can't get along," Tommy said, drawing from his well of eternal optimism to counter the dour man's constant pessimism. Over their past two days of travel, Tommy had learned that if something *could* go wrong, Jarel was convinced it *would* go wrong. He blamed it on fate conspiring against him to make him miserable, an odd complaint in Tommy's mind. If fate wanted to make him miserable, it'd have had him born to a destitute family in Low Dock instead of the wealthy Downing family in Quiet District.

"I can think of plenty," Jarel said. "They refuse to give up the land they stole. They don't trust us to keep our word. Void's sake, maybe they'll decide they'd rather eat us than discuss diplomacy."

"Eat us?" Tommy said. "That's ridiculous. Rabbits are herbivores."

The look Jarel gave him was certainly an interesting one.

"They're not rabbits."

"Well, they're mostly like rabbits," Tommy insisted. "Just... really big ones."

That ended their conversation, akin to how most conversations with Jarel ended: with abrupt, confused silence. Tommy was pretty sure Jarel didn't like him. It seemed the likeliest explanation for the awkward pauses and constant sighs. The silence grated on Tommy's nerves, for he was a bundle of energy with no outlet.

*Lapinkin!* How could he be so lucky? Tommy had grown up reading stories of rabbit-like humanoids called peobunnies, whose descriptions had matched perfectly to what the messenger from Coyote Crossing had described upon arriving in Londheim. The peobunnies were fuzzy and friendly beings eager to help their neighbors. In hindsight the books were thinly veiled morality stories, but still, the creatures had been dear to his heart. When orders had come to the Wise tower requesting Malik's accompaniment to the farming community of Coyote Crossing to settle a dispute with a newly arrived lapinkin family, Tommy had begged to go in Malik's stead.

"But what help could we possibly be?" Malik had asked.

"Well, I've read all the folklore about peobunnies," Tommy had argued back. "Uh, I mean, lapinkin. Surely there is some truth to the stories, given what we know about the vanishing and return of the old world? Right? Please say I'm right."

The pleading might have been a bit much, but damn it, he was going to meet real, honest-to-Goddess peobunnies! Tommy was practically bouncing off his pony's saddle. His hope was that once the dispute was settled (something about the lapinkin wanting land claimed by the farmers, he hadn't paid that much attention), he could ask them questions about their community life, their culture, and their history. Maybe he could even write books about them, just like the ones he'd read when growing up! His mind was aflame with the possibilities. Jarel and the other soldiers might not wish to discuss such matters, but at least he had one person with him who did.

"Are we there yet?" Tesmarie whispered up at him from a deep chest pocket of his robe. Tommy glanced at Jarel, who was studiously ignoring him. A little jostle of the reins had Tommy's pony fall behind several feet.

"Soon," he whispered back. "Give us twenty minutes."

The faery wiped sleep from her eyes and then stretched with a stifled yawn. "That's fine. It's nice and cozy in here."

Tesmarie had offered to accompany him on his visit, for which he was terribly grateful. Unlike him, she had actual experience interacting with lapinkin, and had been the first to correct him on the proper term. *I don't know what a peobunny is*, she'd said, *but I think you might get hit if you call a lapinkin that*. Should things get complicated, Tommy hoped Tes could guide him through. The only troublesome part was keeping her a secret from the rest of his traveling companions. He didn't know how they'd react to Tesmarie's presence, and Tesmarie herself had seemed pretty reluctant to show herself, only saying she "wasn't ready" when he asked about it. Given what she went through at the marketplace when Janus attacked, Tommy couldn't blame her.

Twenty minutes turned into half an hour, but at last the squat cottages and sprawling fields of Coyote Crossing spread out before them. Jarel marched the soldiers directly into the village's center, where a small crowd rushed to greet them.

"Have you come to drive the beasts away?" one man shouted above the others.

"We come to talk," Jarel insisted, earning himself several unhappy groans.

"Talking will do no good," an older man insisted. Others in the crowd gave him space, and Tommy guessed him to be the man who owned the land they farmed. "That's why we asked for soldiers, not diplomats."

"Well, lucky for you we came with both," Jarel said as he climbed down from his pony. "Goddesses above, how I hate riding. All right, where are these so-called lapinkin? I'd rather get this over with before it gets dark."

The old man led them westward. Tommy dismounted and quickly followed at the head of the pack. He couldn't wait to see their furnished burrows, supposedly as spacious and comfortable as any human home. Once beyond the cottages of Coyote Crossing, and with the flatlands plainly visible for miles, it was easy to spot the newly built lapinkin home, but it was no burrow.

A mansion of earth proudly faced the east. Grass grew from its rooftops. Vines stretched like spiderwebs over its walls. For doors and windows it bore spacious openings revealing short, cleanly cut grass forming a natural carpet on the floor. Flowers bloomed in tight formations between the windows, with colors carefully chosen to replicate images of forests, flowing rivers, and proud lapinkin standing atop pure white clouds. Tommy's eyes bulged at the sight, and it took all his self-control not to sprint ahead.

"That...eyesore appeared overnight," the old man explained. "Not sure how they magicked that, either. Was nothing but an empty hill, but then the hill's gone, and the mansion's there in its place. Then the first of the beasts came and told us to abandon our fields. If we try to tend them, they chase us off with spears, and they're getting aggressive. Just last week they broke my grandson's arm, all for the crime of picking green beans to eat."

"Have they made any demands?" Jarel asked.

"They want us to leave and never come back. That's it. I suspect you'll try talking with them, but good luck. They're more stubborn than mules, and just as smart, I'd bet."

Tommy saw many of the lapinkin working the fields behind the mansion, much too far away to make out their features. It was only when a trio exited the mansion's front opening that he could finally lay eyes upon the fabled beings.

Their faces were long and rounded, with flat noses befitting their namesake. Their matching marbled eyes watched the approaching soldiers carefully. Soft gray, black, or white fur covered their muscular frames, that which was visible underneath their intricately stitched leather armor. Their long ears lay flat behind their heads, the tips overlapping and linked together with thick iron piercings so that the ears seemed more like hair that hung to their waists. Two of the lapinkin wielded long spears with a particularly strange attachment, as if beneath the sharp head was an additional metal wedge like a miniature plow.

"I see the inevitable has come," said the unarmed lapinkin with a stunningly deep voice. His fur was a brown so dark it bordered on black except for his arms, which lightened into a golden color. Seven rings connected his ears together, two more than the lapinkin beside him. "Human soldiers, come to take what belongs to others. The centuries have not diminished your avarice, only fed it."

Jarel sputtered for a moment, clearly not expecting such an eloquent response.

"My name is Jarel Downing," he said at last. "I come with the authority of the Royal Overseer to discuss matters troubling our citizens here in Coyote Crossing." He hesitated, but the lapinkin did not offer up his own name. "With whom do I speak?"

"I am Warrenchief Naiser," the lapinkin said. "And we have nothing to discuss. These lands are ours. We gave the humans here time to pack their belongings and leave, but instead they argued and stalled, and now we see the reason why. They hope force of steel will save them. It will not, Jarel Downing. Leave, and take these people with you. Do not force my windleapers to spill blood upon this green earth."

Jarel looked beyond flustered. Given the man's birth and connections, Tommy couldn't imagine *anyone* talking to him in such a way. When it was clear the man's tongue was too tied to be useful, Tommy stepped forward, hoping he might salvage the situation.

"I, um, my name is Tommy," he said. He waved. "Hello."

Naiser and Jarel stared at him with a shared sense of mild confusion.

"Yes?" the lapinkin asked.

"I just wanted to say that, uh, that the soldiers here were just for our safety since we didn't really know anything about...you. You lapinkin. It is lapinkin, right?"

"It is," Naiser said, his annoyance growing.

"Great, great. But as I was saying, we're not here to fight, right, Jarel? We just want to talk, and get all this figured out. Most of the people here have farmed this land since they were born, and they know of no other home. It'd be most cruel to force them out, wouldn't you agree? I think that, if we sit down and talk, we can come up with a solution that makes everyone happy."

He smiled, relieved he finally got all that out. Naiser took that relief and stomped on it with one of his long, bare feet.

"Force *them* out?" he said. "Our castle warren was built long before this village sprung up in its shadow. We have woken from your Goddesses' imprisonment to find *our* lands taken, and so we have taken them back. We have already begun planting our crops. In time, we will rebuild our homes. We will plant the roots of our communities deep down into the stone itself. Heed my warnings, humans. Any who would attempt to move us will die."

"But these lands are ours," Jarel said. Splotches on his neck were turning red from anger. "We won't give them up just like that!"

"Your lands?" Naiser took a step forward. Armor rattled throughout the accompanying soldiers. "How great your greed. How swollen your arrogance. We *had* an agreement in ages past. Londheim was the farthest west humanity would settle, and we *shared* that magnificent city."

The lapinkin stepped so close, his and Jarel's noses were inches apart. He showed no fear at the swords the human soldiers drew. His marbled eyes bore into Jarel's with the viciousness of an angered wasp.

"From the very first breath drawn by the very first human created by the Sisters, humanity has warred against us. There will be no happy solution to this, nor will there ever be." He cast his gaze to the entirety of the gathered humans. "Leave. Now. Our patience is at its end."

And with that, Naiser spun about and marched back into the mansion. The two spear wielders took positions at either side of the entrance, and they glared with undisguised anger. Jarel stood and blubbered angrily for a bit.

"Back to the village," he said at last. The soldiers put their backs to the earthen mansion and marched. Tommy lingered, a frown plastered to his face. It felt like his heart had been broken to pieces like so much cheap glass.

"Is something the matter?" Jarel asked upon realizing Tommy wasn't following.

Tommy sighed long and deep, exhaling broken pieces of his childhood.

"That wasn't very fuzzy and friendly of them *at all*."

The villagers offered their homes to the soldiers, and while most gladly accepted a bed over another night sleeping on the hard ground, Tommy turned them down and staked his tent on the village's outskirts. A snap of his fingers set his small bundle of twigs to burning, and he slumped before it with his head in his hands. The stars winked into existence one by one as the sun dipped below the horizon.

"Try not to let it get you down," Tesmarie said. She floated above the fire, appreciating the warmth and glad to stretch her wings after such a long journey stuffed in Tommy's robe pocket. "Most everyone is cranky after waking up from a long nap. No doubt they're the same."

"I'm not sure what happened is all that comparable to a nap," Tommy said.

"Fine. But it doesn't change how cranky they are. I bet with just a little bit of time, they'll warm up to you."

Tommy smiled at the onyx faery.

"I hope so, but the lapinkin being rude isn't what really bothers me."

"And what is that?"

He chewed on his lip as he tried to put his thoughts into proper order.

"It's that...well, I don't have any way to argue with them. Why does the claim of those living here now outrank the claims of those who lived here centuries ago? Especially when it sounds like their disappearance was the fault of the Sisters? You know, *our* Goddesses? At best we could appeal to their sense of decency by showing how difficult and traumatic it'd be to uproot an entire community. But then again, why is that worse than *their* trauma at being put into some strange sleep and awakening to the entire world having moved on, their homes destroyed and their lands taken? It's not worse. So I find myself sitting here thinking, if I wasn't a human, and hadn't come here with representatives of West Orismund...I think I'd be arguing on behalf of the lapinkin."

Tesmarie zipped over and sat down on his shoulder. He felt the soft hint of her hair upon his skin as she leaned against him.

"You're a good person, Tommy. I'd take a world full of people like you over anyone else, human or dragon-sired. Try not to beat yourself up thinking of a solution. Some problems don't have one."

"Every problem has a solution," Tommy said. "Just sometimes they're not ones we like."

Tommy stared at the fire. A thousand ideas bounced around inside his skull as he tried to find an outcome to their current predicament that didn't end with bloodshed.

"Do you think it'd help if you go talk to the lapinkin instead?" he asked Tesmarie.

"I thought it would when I agreed to come with you," she said. "Now, though? They seemed awfully angry. I don't think they'd be more open to talking with me on your behalf. I think they'd view me as..."

Her voice drifted away.

"As what?" Tommy prodded.

Tesmarie's wings hummed to life, and she lifted a few inches off his shoulder.

"As a traitor," she said softly.

The remark left Tommy feeling sick and stupid. Of course they'd view her as a traitor. Why didn't he see that before? The whole trip he'd hoped she could show the lapinkin that they were perfectly fine people. Goddesses above, why did he have to be so naïve?

"I'm sorry," he told the faery. "I should have thought of that before inviting you to come with me."

"Don't make yourself feel worse than you do. I *did* think of it. I just hoped it'd be . . . better." Tesmarie let out a dramatic sigh. "No wonder the dragons and Goddesses struggled so much to fill our world with life and love. Everything gets so *complicated*."

She suddenly startled, and before he could ask about what, she dove back into his robe pocket.

"There you are," Jarel said, his voice disturbing the peaceful quiet. "We've reached a decision, and you weren't there for it."

Tommy spun in his seat to face the highborn dullard.

"What decision is that?" he asked.

"You're supposed to be our lapinkin expert," Jarel said, completely ignoring his question. "Well, you've met them now. Does anything match up? Do they have any abilities my soldiers should worry about?"

"Their overall physique resembles the stories," Tommy said, frowning. "Though they're a bit leaner and more muscular than usually described. As for powers . . . they're giant rabbits. I guess they might jump really high? That might pose a threat to your men."

Jarel's eyes narrowed.

"You're not mocking me, are you, Tomas?"

"No, no, of course not. I really do mean that, every story insists they are incredible leapers. I'm not a soldier, so I can't imagine how that might affect a battle, but it seemed prudent to mention it nonetheless."

"What about their eyesight? Can they see well in the dark?"

Tommy didn't like where this line of questioning was leading.

"I can only make guesses," he said. "Rabbits see best in dim light, dawn and dusk, mostly. They'll see better than human eyes at night, but not significantly. Why do you ask?"

Jarel motioned for Tommy to rise from his seat and follow.

"Because we're mobilizing tonight," he said. "And the only surprise I want is our attack on their castle."

# CHAPTER 5

Y ou've got to stop this," Tesmarie whispered into Tommy's ear as they marched toward the lapinkins' castle. "It feels so *wrong.*"

Tommy hardly disagreed, but what could he do to stop thirty soldiers hurrying across the flatlands beside him?

"I can't," he said, careful to keep his voice down so the clatter of armor and footsteps drowned it out. Jarel walked beside him, and the last thing he wanted was the man in charge to think he had taken up a habit of chatting with himself.

"You have your magic," the faery insisted.

"Magic they don't know about. What do you think will happen if I attack the Royal Overseer's men with spells?"

Honestly he didn't know the answer, either, but it was a good question, and a major reason he grumpily marched along. He and Malik had kept their magical abilities a secret, and often discussed the best way to introduce their abilities to the world. Generally they agreed it would be in a lengthy, detailed demonstration with fellow members of the Wise in the organization's First Tower all the way east in Steeth. Revealing them with a potentially treasonous demonstration in the middle of nowhere was not exactly part of the plan.

"If you don't stop them, then I think I might," Tesmarie huffed.

"Please don't," Tommy said, struggling to keep the panic out of his voice.

"What's that?" Jarel asked.

The faery zipped into Tommy's pocket so fast, his eyes could not follow.

"Nothing, nothing," he said. "Just…thinking to myself, hoping the lapinkin don't fight back."

Jarel grunted.

"Let them. Like it will matter. We outnumber them, we're better trained and better equipped. Lyra's tits, they don't even have doors on their mansion. This will be a breeze."

They were almost to the mansion. The villagers insisted the lapinkin slept inside, and come night, it would be completely dark and silent. From what they could see in the starlight, there were no patrols or guards posted, either. Jarel clearly thought it meant incompetence or foolishness on their part. Tommy's nervous stomach insisted otherwise.

"There's still time to barter," he said, only for Jarel to ignore him. The arrogant oaf drew the slender sword from his waist. Jarel would not participate in the fighting, instead command from the back, but he seemed to like wielding it anyway. Perhaps it let him pretend to participate as others risked their lives.

"Kill them where they sleep," he shouted to the rest. The mansion was barely two hundred feet away. The likelihood of them crossing such a close distance stealthily in their armor was nil. Jarel pushed for shock and speed instead. "Go, go, let us go hunting rabbits!"

Tommy felt tiny feet kick his chest.

"Let me kill him," Tesmarie huffed. "Please let me kill him."

He patted his pocket, hoping that might keep her calm, and watched the soldiers race toward the mansion. They rushed the wide front door…and then slammed to a halt as a torrent of wind blasted against them, as if the door were the mouth of an exhaling giant. The soldiers raised their arms and pushed, but they could gain no headway. After a long few seconds, the wind halted, and out stepped Naiser, accompanied by four of his windleapers armed with spears.

"Such is the honor of humans," Naiser shouted. "I expected better. We always do. And as always, you disappoint."

"I don't give a shit about his blustering," Jarel yelled to his men. "Kill him and be done with it."

The lapinkin tensed their legs and curled their backs.

"Come try," said Naiser.

The soldiers charged. Air gathered at the lapinkins' feet, flattening the grass, and then they *leapt*. A sound like thunder marked their launch. Their bodies soared into the air, above the soldiers, above the mansion, seemingly to the sky itself. The humans collectively stared up at them with dumbfounded looks. They raised their shields and prepared for the inevitable fall, only the lapinkin did not fall.

The windleapers hovered, small clouds swirling underneath their feet.

"We told you to leave," Naiser shouted, and his deep voice rumbled like the angry voice of a storm. "This death is on your own heads."

Another thunderous boom. The lapinkin streaked downward like comets, their spears leading the way. This was no fall. This was a charge. They slammed into the heart of the soldiers' formation, their spears puncturing armor like cloth to continue into the earth itself. Tommy's eyes widened as he realized the reason for the strange plow-shaped hook on their spears. It dug into the ground as the lapinkin dragged their victims, carving shallow grooves into the earth to halt the momentum of their dive.

For one long moment the soldiers stared at their foes in shocked horror, and then they charged, fueled with rage for the dead and fear for their own lives. The lapinkin waved their hands, gusts of wind shoving the soldiers back like leaves in a breeze. Space regained, the five leapt back into the air. Tommy's ears ached from the concussive noise.

"Sisters help us, we have to flee," he shouted to Jarel. "We can't fight them, can't you see that?"

The spoiled brat of a noble offered no words, only watched as the lapinkin crossed from the sky to the ground in a flash, their spears like plows carving a home for seeds, and the soldiers' blood like water that would nurture them. In only moments a third of the soldiers were dead, and they were yet to swing a sword. Soldiers rushed them again, fighting against new surges of wind. This time the windleapers ripped their spears free and twirled them above their heads. Perhaps they didn't have the strength to leap again. Perhaps they felt like fighting fair. Tommy didn't know. He only knew the human soldiers had no chance.

Precise, controlled movements batted aside their swords. The bloodied points of spears found openings in their armor, sliding past shields into armpits and stomachs. A whirlwind swirled through them, as if the wind were their ally guarding their flanks. Soldiers died, and at last their courage broke. Only fifteen soldiers remained, and they fled back toward Jarel, who had finally regained his senses.

"Flee!" he screamed, his order thoroughly unnecessary. "Flee these horrid monsters!"

The lapinkin, however, did not appear willing to let them escape. They blasted into the air, hovered momentarily as they adjusted the aim of their spears, and then crashed down with an eruption of earth and steel. Tommy watched with his mouth hanging open as Naiser landed atop a soldier, his spear piercing right through his chest and out the other side in an explosion of gore. The spear hit ground and then dragged the both of them for over thirty feet, coming to a halt not far from where Tommy stood frozen in place. Despite his own plea to flee, he could not seem to make his legs work.

A sharp tugging on his ear snapped him from his paralysis. It was Tesmarie pulling with both hands.

"Go, go, go, go-go-go-go," she cried.

Tommy looked to the soldiers, and to the windleapers soaring skyward for another attack. There was no chance they'd escape, not without his help. He had to do something, but to kill the lap-inkin? Could he? Should he?

*It's that or die*, he told himself, and even then he wanted to argue. His hands spread wide to either side of him, and his mind raced through the many spells he'd memorized. One chance. The lap-inkin were about to descend.

*"Aethos glaeis surmu."*

Frost spread like a fog from his fingertips, settling in a long line enveloping all the soldiers as well as himself in its center. A wall of ice rose from the frost's circle, its top curling inward to form a dome. It had barely completed when the five windleapers struck. Ice cracked, but it did not break. Windleapers slid across the top, spears carving a spiderweb of cracks along every side.

"To-To-Tomas?" Jarel stammered, his eyes so wide, they looked ready to fall out. Tommy ignored him. There wasn't any time to explain how he did what he did.

"Can you get us out of here?" he asked Tesmarie.

"I could help speed up your run," the faery said. "I'm not sure what else I could do. Will they break through your ice?"

Storm winds rocked the sides of the ice dome in answer. Three windleapers stood with their hands extended, guiding the air into vicious, focused gusts. The cracks in the ice thickened.

"I've got to dismiss the ice, or it'll collapse on top of us," he said. "Can you convince them to spare us?"

Tesmarie clutched her arms to her chest.

"I don't know," she said. "I don't think they'll care."

"Very well. We'll go with my plan. Hide in my pocket. I don't want the lapinkin to know you're here."

She reluctantly obeyed. Tommy closed his eyes, and with but a thought he banished the ice into nothingness. Wind ripped through their huddled formation from all directions, then halted. The three windleapers closed in, murder in their eyes and blood on their spears.

"*Aethos creare fulgur,*" Tommy said, but he did not release the power. Fire swirled around his fingers, and a great stream of smoke rose from his palms, which he kept aimed firmly at the ground. He had to keep it at the ready. He needed the lapinkin to understand he could fulfill his promised threat. Hopefully that was soon, because it felt like trying to hold back the charge of a bull.

The windleapers readied for a jump, and though they were outnumbered five to one, not a soul in that field thought the humans had a chance.

"Mercy!" Tommy screamed. "Mercy, or I burn this whole damn field to the ground, and all of us with it!"

The remaining three windleapers hesitated. Naiser aimed the tip of his spear directly at Tommy's head.

"One throw, and I remove your head from your shoulders," he said. "Do you think you can finish your spell before I do?"

Sweat rolled down Tommy's neck in rivers.

"You don't get it," he said. "The spell's already cast. All that matters now is the direction it goes."

Naiser glared, and for a moment Tommy expected the last thing he'd ever see was to be that furry man's angry frown. Instead he lowered his spear and gestured for the other two windleapers to do the same.

"I accept your surrender," Naiser said. "Throw down your weapons."

The soldiers quickly obeyed, even Jarel. Tommy raised his hands above his head, and at last he released the spell. Fire roared into the sky, shapeless and wild. It continued for a long three seconds, then ceased. Tommy breathed out a sigh of relief. While casting the spell took a toll on his body, at least the incredible strain was gone.

"Whew," he said. "I feel so much better now."

"I am happy for you," said Naiser, mere moments before the butt of his spear struck Tommy square in the forehead, knocking him bewilderedly into unconsciousness.

Tommy woke with his hands bound behind his back, a gag tied across his mouth, and a pounding headache focused in the center of his forehead. He grunted and sat up as best he could. His vision was blurry, and his surroundings dark, so it took a moment for him to gain his bearings. He checked his pocket, immediately worried for Tesmarie, but found her missing.

"So you finally come around," Jarel said. "About time."

The two of them were tied shoulder to shoulder to a thick wooden stake in the center of a field. Campfires burned across the fields, and Tommy struggled to focus his vision on them. Why so many campfires when the lapinkin lived in their earthen mansion? He tried to see who surrounded them in the starlight. A lot of shadowed figures, hundreds at the least. What in Anwyn's name was going on?

"Where are we?" Tommy asked, but from behind his gag, it came out a muffled garble of nonsense.

"I can't make out a word you're saying," Jarel said. His face sported a few new bruises, but other than that, he appeared unharmed.

"What. Happened?" Tommy tried again, speaking slowly and using extra emphasis on each syllable.

"What happened?" Jarel laughed. "What happened is somehow

you can summon ice from your fingertips and you didn't bother to tell me this before we attacked those fucking rabbits. *That's* what happened."

Tommy blinked at him and said nothing. Jarel wasn't wrong, technically, but that hardly answered his question.

"Fine," Jarel said. "A whole *army* of those lapinkin arrived from the west. They disarmed my soldiers and marched them into Coyote Crossing. The town's been taken hostage. They've rounded everyone up like cattle and stuck them in some weird dirt cage. Other than you and me, obviously. I'm not sure if that's a good or bad thing. The last thing I want right now from those monsters is special treatment."

Well, that was interesting. Tommy wondered how the lapinkin might execute someone they strongly disliked. Impaled with their spears? Or perhaps something more ritualistic involving wind. Could you kill someone with just wind? He didn't know. What he did know was that tonight was not the night to discover the answer to that question.

"Can you get us out?" Jarel asked. "You know, with your spells, or whatever you did?"

He shook his head. With his hands bound and his mouth gagged, he couldn't speak the necessary words. There were a few spells he could summon with just mental command, but they were raw and simplistic. Given the way his hands were bound, closed with his palms facing one another, the magic would just wash over his own arms. Not an appealing scenario.

"Wonderful," Jarel said. He slumped against the stake. "Damn it all, I knew I should have said no when Albert asked me to come here. '*I need someone I can trust.*' Fuck him. He can come talk with whatever bizarre creature decides it wants our land next." Tommy realized the man had begun to cry. "Assuming there is a next time. Damn it. Goddess fucking damn it."

He fell silent, his rage impotent and his tears more important.

Tommy did his best to remain calm. Whatever the reason he and Jarel were separated from the others, he had to hold hope it was for something other than execution. Besides, if execution was on the menu, it didn't really matter if he was calm for it or not. He'd still end up dead.

After an interminable amount of time a windleaper approached from one of the many distant campfires. His fur was black as coal but for the puddles of white splashed across his face and ears. His spear hung across his back, and he held a slender knife.

"I know about your magic," he said to Tommy. "Make the slightest noise and I cut out your throat."

Tommy nodded as fervently as possible.

The windleaper cut the rope tying each of them to the stake, starting with Jarel. Once both were free, he tugged them to their feet and gave them a shove in the direction from which he'd come. They crossed the field, their destination a particularly large bonfire. A log lay atop the grass some space away, and after a gesture, the two took a seat.

Warrenchief Naiser waited beside the fire, his arms crossed over his chest and a dour frown on his face. Tommy could not help but notice his fingers drumming the long hilt of his spear. Impatient. Eager.

"Remove their bindings," Naiser said. "I need them to talk."

Their escort used a knife to cut the ropes and gags. Tommy gladly spat out the rough cloth and stretched his sore jaw.

"Thank you," he said, though it didn't look like the lapinkin wanted to hear it. Jarel looked disgusted but thankfully kept his mouth shut. Tommy did not trust the dour man to handle any meeting gracefully unless the other party was busy kissing his ass. Once they were freed, the lapinkin bowed and left. Naiser glared at them, clearly displeased about something.

"You both are to receive an honor clearly undeserving of you," he said. "It is rare for a human to meet with the King of the dyrandar. Be respectful, or I will have him explode your mind into jelly."

Jarel scoffed while Tommy's mind had to go over the previous sentence twice before he might respond.

"He might *what?*"

Naiser gave no answer. A figure approached from the darkness, and the Warrenchief dipped his head low in respect.

At nearly eight feet tall, the humanoid deer towered over Naiser, and that didn't count the additional three feet of antlers growing from the sides of his skull. Those antlers curled inward to form a complete circle, their sharpened tips halting inches away from their opposite. Strips of cloth hung like ribbons from the dark bone, matching his loose robe, whose stripes were the colors of autumn. His upper half was very much like a muscular human's, albeit giant and layered with chestnut-colored fur. The legs of his lower half were reversed at the knee like a deer's, and they ended with giant hooves instead of feet.

"Welcome to our grasslands, King Cannac," Naiser said. "I trust your journey here was uneventful?"

"Not uneventful, but it was peaceful," Cannac said. His voice was deeper than the night was dark. He turned to Tommy, and it seemed his ashen, unblinking eyes stared right through him. "Come forth, onyx one. You need not hide from us."

*Onyx one?*

Tommy glanced about, confused, until Tesmarie flew out from behind the log he sat atop. He hadn't known she was there, she was so swift and quiet, but somehow Cannac had known. The faery hovered before the two dragon-sired with her arms behind her back and her head respectfully bowed.

"I'm sorry," she said. "Tommy is my friend. Please don't hurt him, that's all I ask."

"Friend?" Naiser said, the word never before spoken with such ugliness and contempt in all the world.

"Friendship among our kind was never rare before our

imprisonment," Cannac said, and he dipped his head to the faery. "And I pray it stays so now. Stay with us, little one. In this gathering of royalty, you may represent your fae."

Tommy's jaw dropped open. Tesmarie...royalty?

"It's—it's true," she said, looking embarrassed. "I'm the matriarch's daughter."

"A pointless connection," Naiser said, unimpressed. "Will the fae listen to her? Will they help us fight for our lands?"

"She stays," Cannac said again. Just like that, the matter was settled. Tommy felt in awe of the respect the giant deer-man commanded. Tesmarie's wings buzzed. She zipped over to Tommy's knee and sat. Cannac sat as well, his elbows on his knees and his palms facing the night sky.

"Well then, let's get this over with," Naiser said. He pointed at Jarel, who had remained pale-faced and perfectly still the whole time. "You said you speak for the human's ruler. That's good enough for us. We need you to listen to our demands, and then if you value your life, agree to them."

Jarel was clearly unhappy being forced to participate. Whatever bluster he'd shown earlier was long gone.

"I—I don't think you understand how things work in Orismund," he said. "The Royal Overseer isn't the ruler of all humans, just those here in West Orismund."

"And you are of his blood," Naiser said. "Which makes you royalty. You may still speak for him."

"But the Royal Overseer isn't royalty," Jarel insisted. "He's elected by our land owners to serve as official proxy for the Queen in Oris. I have no authority, none, I just...I just, I'm close to my uncle. He listens to me. He'll accept what I say."

"Oris is hundreds of miles to the east, if it is the same Oris that existed in our time," Cannac said. "We cannot wait for word from there. Too many will die. The Royal Overseer rules in the Queen's stead?"

"Y-yes," Jarel stammered. "It might seem a little complicated, but it's because of the Three-Year Secession. Originally the King or Queen would choose their Overseer, but then—"

"Enough," Naiser interrupted. "Your uncle rules West Orismund. That's all that matters at this point. You can convey our message, and you can make him listen."

"Sure, of course," Jarel said. "Tell it, and I'll bring it to Albert, I promise."

Cannac brought his hands together so his fingertips touched, but not his thumbs, which he kept pointed skyward.

"It will not be told," he said. "It will be shown."

Tommy's eyes darted about, curious as to what the dyrandar meant. His bones vibrated from the deep hum emanating from Cannac's throat. The space between his hands shimmered as if the dyrandar held a captive rainbow. The circle of space in the heart of his antlers swelled with light. What began as smaller than a star bloomed to a full sun burning above the dyrandar's head. Tommy stared in wonder, for despite its brightness, it did not hurt his eyes.

"Thanks be to Gloam," Cannac said. "Let our thoughts be one."

Light rolled from the sun in five distinct rivers, each one traveling to a person seated about the bonfire. It flowed like water but looked like a white wave of fire. When it struck Tommy in the chest, he felt light-headed and dizzy, and he clutched his seat to steady himself. New colors rolled back out of him, as if Tommy were a mixture of paints spilling into this clean, pure river. He need not ask, for somehow he knew what they represented. A pale white for his fear. Cerulean for his curiosity. Olive for his confusion. Pink for his love. His entire being retold in color that swirled and blended without ever losing an individual shade.

Similar rivers of color rolled from the others. He saw Naiser's pride in deep violet. He saw Jarel's fear in a sickly green. Tesmarie's hopeful optimism swirled with cerulean and sunlight yellow. For Cannac, every shade was overwhelmed with the brilliant, calm white of peace. These rivers flowed to the bonfire, where they collected in a great, chaotic sphere.

Cannac spoke without moving his lips, his voice emanating from the sun burning between his antlers.

*Naiser, reveal your strength.*

The sphere unfolded. Tommy felt his mind pulled toward the lapinkin, as if it had left his body and traveled elsewhere. The colors of the sphere re-formed into shimmering valleys dotted with farms and villages. Instinctively Tommy knew he gazed upon the grasslands southwest of Londheim, viewing them as if from the eye of a soaring hawk. The vision shifted westward, to the Triona River. Thousands of lapinkin leapt over its surface with ease. Those who'd come to Coyote Crossing were merely the far-reaching scouts, Tommy realized, not their true power. The pull toward Naiser weakened, and the sphere folded back in on itself.

*Queen Viera of the Viridi, do you hear my voice?*

A woman of grass appeared to hover in the heart of the sphere. Every inch of her body rippled in the cool night air, the grass blades overlaid much like the scales of a reptile. Instead of eyes, she had pure black crevices that repelled even the light of the stars. The way she moved and shifted, it was as if there were no bones or muscles in her body, just flowing grass growing from some unseen center deep within.

"I hear you," Viera said. There was a playfulness to her voice, like a deeper-toned version of Tesmarie. Cannac bowed his antlers.

*Then reveal your strength.*

The sphere unfolded. The flatlands even farther south greeted him, hundreds of miles of rocky soil and fading grass occupying the space between the Triona River and the Oakblack Woods. Cities of viridi rose among them, building spires of twig, vine, and grass that rivaled the tallest buildings of Londheim. Walls of thorns thirty feet high surrounded these cities, adorned with roses that bloomed in streams like blood. Viera's dominance of the vision sphere weakened, and it folded back in on itself. As quickly as she had appeared, the Queen was gone.

*Arondel, Queen of the Winged, do you hear me?*

A white-feathered owl appeared in the heart of the sphere. Tommy held back a gasp. It was the same snow-white owl that had accosted him and Devin on his lone attempt accompanying the Soulkeeper on his nightly patrols.

"I hear you, dyrandar," the owl said.

*Then reveal your strength.*

The sphere unfolded. Countless birds of all sizes flew the skies over the Helwoads to the northwest. Tommy sensed but did not see their nests in the tall branches. Lord over these flocks were the mighty owls. They soared down from Alma's Crown, commanding the others with deep shrieks and hoots. Deer, coyotes, and even cattle fell to the iron grip of their claws. Anger mixed with fear inside Tommy's stomach as he watched a force of thirty such owls slam their way into a village along the Helwoads' border, ripping off rooftops and knocking over walls as they chased its inhabitants out.

The owl vanished from the sphere, and another took her place. A parade of various creatures, bearing names and titles Tommy struggled to remember. Creatures made of stone and silver, with arms like a mantis, faces like carved masks, or skin like flowing clouds. One by one they revealed their people awakening throughout the western reaches of West Orismund, reestablishing their homes, warrens, nests, and crypts. Last was the dyrandar king, and it seemed the sphere struggled to contain his presence.

*I am Cannac, and I reveal my strength.*

The sphere unfolded. Dozens of dyrandar men, women, and children marched with their belongings tied into heavy sacks on their backs. They traversed the southern tip of Alma's Crown, passing through areas forever scarred by the flow of the black water. Their caravan halted near where Tommy believed was Pathok, one of the mountainous villages built near the start of the Septen River. Pathok looked empty, the black water no doubt to blame, and the dyrandar began tearing down buildings. Time slipped by as easily as water, the dyrandar building new homes with their carried supplies of wood and fur, replacing squat, square structures with tall tents and huts. Tommy's vision pulled outward, and he saw a similar story playing out again and again in abandoned towns all across the mountain's southern curl.

Cannac's calm, peaceful white washed away everything. Tommy felt his nerves cease. His mind was calm as a pool of water on a clear day, and he never wanted it to end.

"Thanks be to Gloam, and the power granted," Cannac said. He clapped his hands together. "This meld is at its end."

The sun blinked out of existence. The connecting rivers and colors of emotions faded away like the morning dew beneath a warm summer sun. Lingering effects of Cannac's peace settled on Tommy's mind, and he stared at the dyrandar with unabashed admiration.

"Do you understand now?" Cannac said, this time with a voice born from his physical form. "These lands were ours upon our forced slumber, and they are ours again. We are united in our vision, and if we must, we shall march as one army, I as its general, and Naiser as my left hand. Please, listen to our words. Respect our ways. Honor our claims. If you do so, then you may spare us from bloodshed. In its absence, we may grow as neighbors and not as rivals."

Jarel nodded, his eyes glazed over as if he were still inside a dream.

"So you want me to tell Albert all...that," Jarel said.

"Is it really that complicated?" Naiser answered. "Tell him of our claims, or simpler yet, that everything west of Londheim belongs to us. Other than that, tell him of what you saw, our armies, our numbers. Tell him how easily we could crush you if you tried to challenge us."

"I—I can try. This is, this vision, it's..." Jarel shrugged. "I don't know if I could ever have the words to convey what I just saw."

"So you're saying your uncle won't believe you?" Cannac asked.

The answer Jarel gave looked like it physically hurt him to speak.

"No," he said. "I fear he won't."

Naiser let out a derogatory sigh.

"I warned you this was pointless, Cannac," he said. "Humans spread like roaches. History proves war inevitable."

"Nothing is inevitable," Cannac insisted. He rose to his full height. "I will go with these two to Londheim. I will share my wisdom with their ruler. I will give him two visions so he may choose. Let him see a world of peace and prosperity, with the dragon-sired trading and building a life as their neighbors. Let him see a land bathed in fire and his people slain by the thousands by our combined might. Only a fool would choose the death and suffering over happiness and equality."

Naiser frowned and shook his head. The rings in his ears rattled against one another.

"We're repeating all our old mistakes," he told Cannac. "We should treat their presence like a full-scale invasion. Meet strength with strength. My lapinkin are eager to shed blood in the name of our freedom."

"We did that once," the dyrandar said. "And we paid dearly for it."

The lapinkin had no retort. He glared at the two humans still remaining.

"I'll leave you to deal with them," he said. A single leap, an accompanying blast of air, and he was gone. Cannac watched him go with an unreadable gaze. After a long moment he turned his attention back to the other three.

"I must inform my people of my plans," he said. "Follow me to my camp. It will be safer for you there than with the lapinkin, I fear."

Both Tommy and Jarel quickly nodded. Tesmarie fluttered to the giant's side, and he dipped his head the slightest amount.

"Yes, Tesmarie?" he asked. "I sense a question in you. Have no fear. Speak it."

The faery rubbed her elbows, her face etched with worry.

"Is Naiser correct?" she asked. "Will the dragon-sired wage war on humans?"

The wise dyrandar offered the faery his gentlest smile.

"We fear only what history taught us time and time again. It is not we who war against humanity, onyx one. Humanity wars against us, and our very existence."

He lifted an arm as thick as a tree branch, his hand clenched into a fist. Tommy envisioned it carrying a sword or axe and shivered with unease.

"This time," Cannac said, "in this age that we have newly awakened, we will sacrifice everything to ensure we are not the ones who lose."

# CHAPTER 6

**Y**ou still with me there, old man?" Lyssa asked, stirring Devin from his thoughts. The two walked a night patrol through the streets of Low Dock, and his mind had wandered off while staring at the sky. Focusing on anything other than Gerag's disappearance had proven difficult.

"Old man?" he asked. "Do you see any gray hairs? I think not."

She stood on her tiptoes and pushed his tricorn hat to one side to check.

"None yet. Give it time. You have a habit of worrying yourself to death even in the best of circumstances."

Devin fixed his hat and jostled hers off in return.

"You're only a year younger than I. Does that make you an old woman?"

"I like to think of age in terms of life lived. Given what we've all gone through since the black water came, I think we're both older than dirt."

She bent at the waist to scoop up her fallen hat. He noticed she avoided using her arm injured a week prior.

"Are you sure you'll be fine for tonight?" he asked. "No lingering effects?"

"None that I'm aware of," Lyssa said. She pulled the hat low over her face and straightened its five crow feathers. "Though if magical healing has a catch, I'm sure I'll be the unlucky sod to discover it."

"When did Adria heal your arm?" This was Lyssa's first patrol since breaking it in a battle against two gargoyles. He'd only found out she'd be accompanying him minutes before his patrol started. She'd announced her health by using that previously injured arm to punch him square in the chest and then laugh.

"It wasn't your sister, actually," she said. She squinted, something in the sky not seeming right to her, but after a moment it passed and she looked back. "Faithkeeper Gruneir did. He's actually the seventh keeper I know of that's started praying over the sick and injured at the Cathedral of the Sacred Mother. Have you not been by recently? People line up in droves at Alma's Greeting each morning waiting for the doors to open. Novices let people in at sunup, and they'll go until the entire courtyard is overflowing. It's a madhouse, really." Lyssa seemed to realize something and grunted. "That's funny. I think your sister is the only one *not* healing the sick at the cathedral."

Not exactly a surprise to Devin. The whole ordeal with Janus, as well as whatever change had come over her from the otherworldly machinery buried beneath Londheim, had taken its toll. When she did heal others, she made sure she did so from her church in Low Dock.

"Adria's always been one to shy away from attention," he said. "So long as she's helping people, I think she'll be happy."

The pair paused at a corner and carefully examined each direction. Gargoyles had long vanished from the rooftops, but they could always be hiding. They scanned the stars for the shadowy outlines of owls, and they searched the ground for a suspicious character that might be Janus in disguise. It was exhausting being so careful all the time. Devin longed for the peace and quiet of a campfire far from civilization. It wasn't until his travels had ceased that he realized just how much he missed the days and nights journeying the wildlands of the west.

"So have I missed anything since I was knocked out of commission?" Lyssa asked.

"Things have gotten…strange over the last few days," Devin said. His fingers brushed the small pouch tied to his belt, and the three unique flamestones within. Knowing they were there eased his nerves. "I can't explain it, but it seems the day-to-day stress of living under these conditions is wearing people down. Been finding more and more people wandering about at night despite the curfew. Their behavior is erratic, on edge. Wish I could describe it better, but I know I don't like it."

"It was bound to happen," Lyssa said. "Having a giant mountain crawl to your city's doorstep will lead to a few mental breakdowns."

Devin hoped it was that simple. Truth be told, he was glad to have Lyssa with him. The previous night had been the worst so far, with over twenty people ignoring the curfew and resisting when he tried forcing them back inside.

An hour passed in relative peace. Only once did they spot a giant owl. Thankfully it circled twice and then continued on. Devin prayed for Lyra to show mercy to whoever the creature might pick as its eventual target. Owl attacks had grown rarer as patrols had grown in strength and number, but in a city so large as Londheim, there were always people foolish enough to brave the night.

"Hear that?" Lyssa asked halfway through the second hour. Devin shook his head. "Follow me, then."

They cut through an alleyway shielded from the sky by sheets and tarps, and stepped out the other side. A woman knelt in the middle of the street, her back hunched and her head bowed low. A sound like a low sob pulsed from her throat. Devin approached, looking to comfort her, but his insides twisted in fear. Some instinct inside him screamed warning, and he paused to reassess. It took only a second to discover why. Blood. It darkened the hem of her plain dress, and little rivulets of it trickled to the street on either side of her.

Devin drew his sword from its sheath.

"Miss?" he said. "Are you all right?"

Her head twisted. The sob, he realized. It wasn't a sob at all. It was a guttural moan of pleasure. Blood caked her face and neck. Her long dark hair hung in thick wet clumps. Her bloodshot eyes widened at the sight of him. She smiled, flashing teeth dripping with gore.

"Not fine," the woman said. Her voice was rapid, and clipped. "Still hungry. Always hungry."

Her body twitched, and she was on her feet. Devin never saw the upward motion. It was as if she rematerialized in that new position. Her bloodied hands held what had once been a cat, before its body had been ripped open and its fur peeled away. Devin watched with paralyzing horror as she brought the body to her lips. She crunched pieces of bone between her teeth, shivering with joy at every crack.

"Anwyn spare us," Lyssa said. She raised her pistols. "What new monster is this?"

"Monster?" the woman asked. She took a step, slow and unsteady, but her next was so fast her body was a blur to Devin's highly trained eyes. The cat corpse slipped from her fingers and landed upon the stone with a wet *plop*. "Where? Protect me, Soulkeepers. Protect me from the monsters!"

She was laughing, laughing even as tears fell from her eyes.

"I'm so tired," she said. "So tired, and so...damn...*hungry!*"

The woman lunged at Devin with the speed of a panther on the hunt. A sound like thunder boomed through the street, echoed by another less than a second later. The woman froze in front of

Devin, one hand grabbing the front of his coat, the other clasping at his trachea. He hadn't seen her cross those final few feet. One moment she had been before him, the next, she reappeared with her hands upon him. Her entire body shuddered. A giant hole in her forehead gushed blood and fluid, and a matching one in her chest did likewise.

She crumpled at his feet, her eyes locked open in surprise. The feel of her wet fingers sliding free of his throat would haunt his nightmares for weeks to come.

"What was that?" Lyssa asked, smoke rising from the barrels of her pistols. Her entire form was as still as a statue. "What—the *fuck*—was that?"

Devin pulled a handkerchief from his shirt pocket and wiped away the warm blood on his neck. His mind reeled, and he felt his hands shaking. Had to regain his composure. Had to remain calm. After sheathing his sword, he knelt at the body and examined it with as much indifference as he could muster.

"I don't know," he said. "But I think she was human."

Her blood was dark and red, not blue like several magical creatures they'd fought and killed. A rudimentary scan of her body showed no abnormalities. It could still be a creature disguised as a human, he supposed, but so far as he could tell, there was no evidence of that beyond paranoia.

"That's bullshit," Lyssa said. "No human acts like that. No human moves like that. She wasn't just running, Devin. She was...flickering."

A distant scream pulled him back to his feet. Lyssa reloaded her pistols and gestured the direction it came from.

"Another?" she asked, voicing Devin's mirrored fear.

"Pray not," he said. He loaded flamestone and lead into his pistol. "I'll lead. Save your shots for whatever I can't handle with my sword."

Together they sprinted down the narrow street, urged on by

a second scream that choked to a sudden halt. At the turn of the corner he paused, and he was glad he did. A group of five ravenous beings clustered around the body of an elderly woman, ripping and gulping down pieces as fast as their dull human fingers allowed. The door to the nearby home was broken open, and a trail of blood led from it to the center of the street, where the poor woman had been dragged out to her death. That the cannibals were working together only heightened Devin's already growing horror.

Devin flashed a hand signal to Lyssa, ordering her to fall back and remain silent. It was time to try something new. His hand slipped inside the secondary bag of flamestones. These were the magically altered stones Tommy had given him prior to his patrol. Spellstones, Tommy called them. He pulled the hammerlock back, slid the spellstone into the chamber, and cocked it all the way. There was no need to insert a lead shot. The spellstone was all he needed.

"Hope you knew what you were doing," Devin whispered. He stepped around the corner, aimed straight into the heart of the five, and pulled the trigger.

The pistol rocked backward in his hand with abnormal recoil. A glowing red dot crossed the distance so rapidly, it seemed a singular line, and then it connected with the shredded corpse. The spell detonated in a roaring explosion of flame that swirled upward like a spontaneously formed tornado. The five cannibals shrieked before the fire stole the breath from their lungs and charred their flesh down to the bone.

"Damn," Devin said, in awe of the damage. "You went all out on that one, Tommy."

He turned to find Lyssa staring at him with her mouth hanging open.

"How in blazes did you do that?" she asked.

"Magic," he said.

Her head tilted to one side, the gears within catching and grinding as she tried to process what she'd seen and heard.

"Later," she said, snapping out of it. "When this is over, you owe me an explanation, maybe even two or three. Got it?"

Before he could answer, the heavy toll of a bell sounded from a quarter mile to the west. It was a warning to the citizens to stay indoors, as well as a call to arms for any and all city guards. Other districts soon answered. Devin tried to take comfort in knowing the patrols would keep people safe. That comfort paled with each additional bell. This curse wasn't localized in Low Dock, or even just the southern portions. Every single district had been struck by the ravenous cannibals.

"Let's keep on the move," Devin said. He began the process of loading a regular flamestone and shot into his pistol. "It sounds like the whole city is in under attack."

"Keep your ears peeled for screams, then," Lyssa said. "And pray we arrive in time."

It did not take long for another cry to pierce the night. The two Soulkeepers dashed toward it. A mere block over they found two crazed cannibals beating on the door of a bakery, and when it failed to open, one of them moved to the window and flung himself through with no regard to the shattering glass that cut into his flesh. Devin readied his sword, but before he charged, he heard the woman's scream that had pulled them this direction coming from the opposite end of the street.

"Go," Lyssa said. "I'll take these two."

"Are you sure?"

She winked at him as she lifted her pistols.

"Two targets, two shots. I'll be fine."

Devin sprinted in the opposite direction, offering no other protest. Lyssa was deadly accurate with her pistols, and could reload her pair faster than most could load a single flamestone and shot. He only feared what might happen if there were more lurking nearby. Granted, he was the one running blind, perhaps he should fear for himself…

Two more screams guided him onward to an alley, and he dashed in with pistol and sword raised. The sight within rooted his feet in place and left his jaw hanging.

The screams came not from another innocent victim, but from the ravenous cannibals themselves. A whirlwind of shadow and steel blazed through them. Blood exploded in showers from their bodies and fell upon the stone like rain. A lone woman danced around their eager hands and teeth, outnumbered five to one, yet not once did Devin feel she was in danger. One after another they fell, until the last ravenous collapsed, a long spike of steel driven through his forehead. The battle over, Devin got his first good look at the woman he thought he'd come to save.

A thick, downward-pointed beak covered much of her face, the blackish silver coloring reminding him of a raven. A thick hood hung over her face, its shadows unnaturally deep so that only the beak and her silver-blue eyes were visible underneath. She wore dark gray trousers and a gray shirt with long, buttoned sleeves. Every part of her bore some flicker of silver, either the buckles at her waist, on the tops of her tall black boots, or most striking of all, as ornaments over the fingers of her gloves, giving a distinct impression of sharpened claws.

No part of her clothing was as striking as the wings that stretched from her upper back. They were as tall as her, long and black, and though they bore distinct raven feathers near the top, by the bottom of the wings they dissolved into a shadowy smoke-like substance that hid much of her lower body. The front of the wings folded around and over her shoulders until they touched, and the flowing feathers and shadow gave a distinct impression of a heavy cloak.

The woman put her heel on the dead man's skull and held it in place so she could yank the blade of her sickle out. It slid free with a sickening slurp. She wielded two such sickles, the handles made of wood and bearing dozens of chips and scars. The blades themselves were nearly as long as the handles, and though they were clearly sharpened to a vicious edge, they bore just as many signs of wear and tear along the steel. Everything about her bore that feel, Devin realized, from her clothes to her weapons. Not old, exactly, but experienced. Weathered.

"Have you come to rescue me?" she asked. Her beak did not move to produce words, giving it a masklike presence, but he felt certain it was real. Only her throat flexed to produce the sounds, deep and calm. "I appreciate the concern, but I can quite take care of myself."

"So it seems," Devin said. "I am Devin Eveson, Soulkeeper of the three Sisters. Might I have the name of one so skilled?"

Her eyes narrowed. From a smile, he wondered, or from distrust?

"Evelyn," she said. "These men and women you see before you have lost themselves to a poison of our making. I will do my best to solve the crisis, but until then, I would recommend you humans locking your doors and boarding up your windows anytime the sun goes down. Oh, and if someone shows signs of insomnia, separate them. You can't risk a killer hiding in your own home."

Her wings spread out, tips touching from wall to wall of the alley. A single beat lifted her to the rooftop. The wings closed back around her, turning her into a deep shadow nearly invisible in the starlight.

"Your partner is in danger," she said. "I would hurry if I were you."

Evelyn spun around and vanished into the night. If not for the piled corpses, Devin might have thought the whole encounter a vivid dream. Her warning echoed in his mind. He sheathed his weapons and sprinted, praying he was not too late.

The space before the bakery was empty. A knot grew in his

throat, and he pumped his legs faster. The sounds of struggle greeted him as he closed the distance. *Still alive*, he begged to Lyra. Still alive, and not lying on the ground with her throat opened and her innards spilled out like a goddess-damned gourmet meal for the sick, ravenous humans.

Through the broken windows, Devin could see two corpses beside a table, while a third doubled over halfway out the window, a hole in its head and its stomach serrated by the broken glass that held it in place. Lyssa lay atop that table, stale bread haphazardly spilled across the floor. A ravenous cannibal pinned her, his wrists held back by her trembling grasp. Every few seconds both she and the ravenous would flicker from view and reappear, their positions changed. The tubby man Lyssa wrestled was a good hundred pounds heavier than her, and the difference was steadily exhausting her. Her face was red, and those clacking teeth kept getting closer and closer to her exposed neck.

Devin raised his pistol. No time to hesitate. Had to take the shot, no matter how closely they struggled. No matter that one more flicker might throw off his aim. He squeezed the trigger, his heart freezing in his chest as time itself seemed to hold its breath. The thunder of the exploding flamestone filled his ears. The cannibal's forehead caved inward. His spine went rigid, and he collapsed over Lyssa, who cursed loudly as she shoved the body aside.

"Good timing," she said, using her sleeve to wipe some of the gunk off her face and neck. "I swear, Londheim's just full of things eager to eat you, and not in a pleasant way."

Devin normally would have appreciated the terrible joke, but he was too busy staring at the front of the bakery. A memory from weeks earlier flashed through his mind, that of a jittery, nervous man banging on that same bakery's door. He, too, had insisted he was hungry, and that he could find no sleep. His movements had also come in rapid bursts, though not quite to the extent of the ravenous creatures they currently fought.

"Lyssa, do you remember the night the gargoyles attacked?" he asked.

"Remember it? They broke my arm. Of course I remember it."

"I'm not talking about the gargoyles, but the man they attacked. The one trying to break into this bakery."

Lyssa hesitated a moment, and then he saw the same connection click in her own mind.

"This has been building for a while," she said.

Devin surveyed the horrific mess of broken glass, stale bread, and drying blood.

"How many were affected?" he asked. "How many now prowl the streets? There could be hundreds, even thousands throughout all of Londheim."

"Doesn't matter how many," Lyssa said. She stepped through the broken window. Glass crunched underneath her boots. "One is too many. Anwyn have mercy on us all. As if the owls and gargoyles weren't enough."

A guttural moan pulled their attention down the street. A man and woman hurried toward them, by-now familiar grins on their faces and lustful hunger in their eyes. Devin braced his legs and raised his sword as he watched their forms flicker and reappear closer each time.

"Forget the number," he said. "Forget everything but the here and now. We fight to the dawn. You with me, Lyssa?"

The other Soulkeeper twirled her short swords in her hands as the ravenous closed the distance.

"I always am," she said. A tired, crazed grin crossed her face. "To death or the dawn, whichever comes first!"

# CHAPTER 7

Jacaranda crouched on the worn shingles of a modest (by the wealthy Windswept District standards) home and put her hand over the chimney's crown. No heat. No smoke, either. Good enough for her. She dropped down into the flue, and then braced herself with her knees. It was a tight fit, but that was fine with Jacaranda. It meant her slide would be easily controlled. Only at the bottom might things get complicated.

A minute later her feet touched a half-burned log in the heart of the fireplace. She crouched her knees to her chest and ducked her head, becoming a little ball of dark leather and cloth. A single roll had her out of the fireplace and into the living room of Wolter Horry, Gerag's premiere book fixer.

Not a single candle or lantern lit the place, leaving only a thin ray of starlight from one of the windows to guide her. She carefully followed the nearby wall, taking plenty of time between each step. She was in no hurry. She and Wolter would have all night to discuss Gerag's sudden disappearance. A hallway branched out near the fireplace, and she followed it to a closed door. She tested the handle and found it unlocked. Good. She slowly opened it an inch or so at a time, just in case the hinges were loose or squeaked.

Inside was a four-poster bed surrounded with heavy curtains. A dim candle burned atop the nearby dresser. Jacaranda held her breath and listened. When she heard a soft rattle of air, she knew Wolter was asleep. One last detail to take care of. She had replaced the scarf she used to cover her neck with a much thicker and wider black cloth, and she lifted it up over her nose to hide the bulk of her face as well. Combined with her hood, only her eyes would be visible. She feared even those might be enough for Wolter to recognize her. They'd interacted several times while she served as Gerag's puppet. If he realized who she was . . .

Best not to think on that prospect. She drew her short swords, crossed the gap between the door and the bed, and lifted her leg. Wolter gagged awake from the pressure of her heel pressing down upon his throat. He instinctively grabbed at her ankle, then froze when he saw the glint of her swords in the candlelight. The sleep faded from his eyes. His chest rose and fell as he sucked in what little breath she allowed.

"Do anything stupid and you die," she told him. "No one's coming to help you, and no one will hear you if you scream. If you do as I say without blustering or lying, then I will let you live. Do you understand?"

She lifted her heel a fraction of an inch.

"Yes," Wolter said.

"Good."

Jacaranda withdrew her leg and stepped back to ensure she could watch him carefully. Wolter was an older man well into his fifties, his graying hair marked by an enormous bald spot atop his head. He'd be no threat in a fight so long as he didn't surprise her. To Wolter's credit, he did not panic or scramble for a means to defend himself. Instead he calmly sat up in his bed, rubbed his sore throat, and met her careful gaze.

"I have few enemies," Wolter said. "But those I work for have many. If you're hoping to hurt them through me, you waste your time. I always plan for this eventuality. You will find nothing incriminating on my clients."

"I'm not looking for evidence to present to the Mayor," Jacaranda said. "I know well of Gerag's crimes."

Wolter was an accountant who fixed Gerag's various business records to hide the income he earned from his illegal soulless trade. Generally that meant increasing the amount of trees cut and worked by his many camps and then selling those imaginary trees to imaginary buyers in the east. If anyone might know where Gerag had gone into hiding, it'd be the man still in charge of his money.

At the mention of Gerag, he visibly paled.

"I see," he said. "Am I a loose end you've come to clean up now that Gerag's in your custody?"

"In custody?" she asked. "So you know he wasn't killed in the fire at his mansion?"

Wolter swung his legs out from underneath his thick blankets. Jacaranda lifted a sword at him in warning.

"I seek only a drink," Wolter said. He pointed to a metal pitcher atop his nightstand. "It's not poisoned, I promise. I have no desire to end my own life tonight."

She nodded to show she'd allow it. Wolter limped on a bad knee to the stand, opened its small drawer, and pulled out a tin cup. Once the cup was full of a red liquid from the pitcher, he downed it all in a long series of gulps.

"Much better," he said, shaking his head. "And of course Gerag didn't die in that fire. No one who knows him believes that. Burned to death in a fire that barely blackened one floor? Sloppy work, if you ask me. If someone wanted him dead, especially in this chaotic day and age, they'd have just slit his throat and been done with. The only reason for the fire was to disguise the identity of whatever body they used."

"But you said in custody, not in hiding," Jacaranda said. "Why?"

Wolter smiled at her with far too much pride.

"I'm his bookkeeper," he said. "He'd need my help to transfer and liquidate his investments and accounts, help that he has not requested. You and I both know Gerag would be incapable of leaving a single copper penny behind when fleeing this cesspit of a city. His greed overrides even his most basic survival instincts, the dumb bastard."

Jacaranda's heart plummeted into her stomach. She thought she'd kept her disgust with Wolter hidden, and kept her face sufficiently disguised. Apparently not.

"Why would I know of Gerag's greed?" she asked, hoping she hadn't revealed her identity somehow.

He tilted his head slightly.

"You need not keep up your ruse with me, soulless," he said. "I find this fascinating. Did Gerag train you to find him should he ever go missing? I assumed you'd have killed yourself to erase any lingering evidence."

It seemed her violet eyes had indeed given her away. She almost pretended to still be soulless, but the thought of doing so sickened her already upset stomach. Fuck that. She kicked Wolter in the chest, her heel stealing the breath from his lungs and smacking him against the wall. His head bounced off it with a loud crack. Wolter's legs went weak, and he slid down to his rump while clutching his ribs.

"Damn it, Jac, have you gone insane without your master? Do not hurt me again, do you understand? That is an order."

Jacaranda knelt before him and placed the tip of a short sword underneath his jaw.

"I don't take orders anymore," she said. "I give them. If you think someone took Gerag, then give me a name. Who's your best guess?"

For the first time since waking, Wolter looked legitimately frightened.

"I don't know," he said. "Gerag trusted me with the nature of his business but never the names of his buyers. I'd wager everything

I owned on the abductor being one of them. If Gerag ever went down, he could bring a lot of wealthy, powerful names down with him. Perhaps someone decided to be proactive about the whole situation."

*Damn it, why didn't I think of that?*

Gerag had always been a weaselly survivor, and she'd assumed he faked his death to avoid the arrest that had been on its way. But Wolter was right. Gerag knew the identity of many wealthy buyers, and with Jacaranda and Devin killing guards and breaking Marigold free before her auction, all of those potential buyers would have known Gerag was compromised.

"Who has him?" she asked, feeling her rage rising. "Who is keeping him from me?"

Gerag's death was hers to inflict. No one else had suffered at his hands like she had. No one had been used, tortured, and humiliated like she'd been. Her anger seethed and grew, a fire that shocked her with its fury. It made thinking difficult. It made her limbs tremble against her will, and it clouded her every thought with an overwhelming desire to inflict pain.

"I don't know," Wolter said. He shrank before her, his eyes widening at the sight of her rage. "What the void are you? No soulless behaves in such a way."

"I'm not soulless anymore," she said.

"How is that possible?"

"I don't know. Ask the Sisters when you see them."

He opened his mouth to respond, and she promptly shoved her short sword up to the hilt inside it. The back of his skull cracked at the force, and she felt her blade travel through the thin wallpaper and hit the outer wall. Wolter's body convulsed as he bled out. Jacaranda watched without pity as he died. How many criminal enterprises had this one man allowed to flourish? How much blood had he washed off silver and gold coins so they might be spent without fear?

The last whisper of a dying breath escaped Wolter's lips. Jac-aranda ripped her short sword free. Her rage was unquenched. Wolter's death was a wad of spit on a campfire. She needed the real thing. She needed Gerag gone from this world. She needed, she needed...

"Get a grip, Jac," she whispered to herself. Goddesses help her, she was almost afraid of how overwhelming her hatred and lust for killing had become. Gerag was a monster, of that, she held no doubt. But she did not wish to become a monster when hunting him.

Several long, deep breaths later she sheathed her short swords and walked out the front door.

While Windswept District wasn't as wealthy as Quiet District, it was still home to a slice of society's upper crust. Mainly this consisted of shop owners, guild leaders, and those with the education to work with paper and numbers instead of their bare hands. Its streetlamps were well lit despite the threat of owls and gargoyles. At least two groups of city guards patrolled the area when she'd sneaked in, as well as a duo of Soulkeepers. Hiding from them was still relatively easy for her, given the trees and bushes that dotted the tiny little rectangle of land each plot possessed. Easy, but time consuming, especially when she dared not traverse the rooftops. Doing so seemed to be tempting fate to end her life as a snack for a gargantuan bird.

This time, though, she need not hide from the patrols. She heard bells sounding in the distance. The first patrol she spotted rushed along as if the city were under siege and they moved toward a breach in its walls. Twice she heard distant screams.

"What is going on?" she whispered while peering out from behind the thick trunk of an oak tree dominating its small yard. The duo of Soulkeepers sprinted past with their swords and pistols drawn.

The sudden sound of a fist pounding of glass behind her nearly caused her feet to leave the ground. She spun, her hands already on the hilts of her short swords. Small fists were striking the pane of glass positioned near the end of the home. Jacaranda didn't hesitate. Something was wrong, horribly wrong, she knew it in her gut. She crossed the lawn and peered inside the house.

A frightened girl, maybe ten to eleven years old, stared back at her with huge saucers for eyes. Blood was on her shift, but it didn't appear to be hers.

"Let me out!" the girl screamed. "Mom is…Mom is…please, let me out!"

A low candle burned atop a dresser inside the girl's room. The door to her room was closed and locked, and it shook from heavy blows on the opposite side.

"Step back," Jacaranda ordered. "I said, step back!"

The girl finally backed away from the window and clutched her elbows, her head on a swivel to watch the rattling door. Jacaranda smashed the glass with the hilt of her sword, then knocked loose several more jagged pieces along the bottom.

"Come on," she said after sheathing her sword. The girl ran to the window and began crawling out. Jacaranda caught her by her armpits to keep her balanced as she exited. The girl was mostly through by the time the door to her room banged open, and Jacaranda saw the threat.

She'd assumed thieves or rapists had targeted the home, but to her shock, a woman in her thirties barged in. She wore a night robe that hung loosely open. Blood coated her face and bare chest. Her eyes had the wild stare of one who had consumed some of the harsher mushrooms grown in the mountains near Watne.

"Little ditty," the woman said. "Where'd you go?"

Jacaranda never saw the woman move. Instead she flickered. One moment, she was standing in the doorway. The next, she was at the window, her hand latched on to her daughter's foot. The girl shrieked and kicked. Jacaranda braced one leg against the wall and pulled. For one agonizing second it seemed the woman would not relent, but then the foot slipped free of her blood-soaked hand. Together, Jacaranda and the girl toppled to the grass.

"Don't run, ditty," the woman said. "I won't hurt you. Mother's hungry, that's all."

She began climbing through the window, showing not a care to the remaining shards of glass that cut into the skin of her back. Jacaranda rolled to her feet and drew her swords. Panic threatened to overwhelm her control. Had to fight it. Countless hours of training had formed her combat instincts, and she relied on them above all else. These emotions of fear, panic, horror...if she dwelled on them, she'd be helpless. They were too new. Too powerful.

Even prepared for the woman's charge, she still nearly failed to react in time. The bloodied woman was halfway out the window, her body flickered, and then she was on her feet a mere foot away. Jacaranda fell back to gain what little space she could and thrust her swords deep into the woman's belly. Together they fell, the crazed mother atop her, flailing wildly. But the woman could not close the space, and her teeth snapped futilely at the air.

Within moments she'd lost too much blood. Her strength left her, and she slumped in Jacaranda's arms.

"My...my..." the woman gasped, struggling to breathe. Her pupils widened. "Is my...little ditty all right?"

She died without receiving an answer.

Jacaranda pushed her body off and rose to her feet. The daughter sobbed on her knees beside the body, her little shoulders trembling with each cry.

"Is there anyone else in the house?" Jacaranda asked.

"My father," she said. "But he's—he's dead. My mom ate him." Tears streamed down the girl's face despite the surreal calm in her voice. "She ate him. She *ate* him. Oh Goddesses, I'm going to—"

She turned and vomited upon the grass. Jacaranda could hardly blame her. Everything about this was beyond insane. Was this happening all across Londheim? Oh shit, what of Devin? He was on out patrol during this mess.

"I need to get you somewhere safe," she said, doing her best to focus on the task at hand. "Come with me. I'll find you a guard who can escort you to one of their stations."

The girl wiped her mouth and then nodded. Jacaranda led the way, the girl trailing a few steps behind her. There'd be no stealth to their travel now, so Jacaranda kept her swords at the ready at all times.

"What's your name?" she asked as they hurried down the street.

"Abigail," she said.

"All right, Abigail, I want you to keep an eye on the sky. If you see anything that looks like a bird, even just a shadow, you let me know."

"I'll try."

Jacaranda could tell it frightened the girl to imagine owls attacking them, but it also gave her a task to focus her mind upon. Keeping calm was of the utmost importance. A mother going insane was a freak occurrence, but the alarm bells ringing from towers throughout Londheim filled her with dread that the incident was not isolated. If this was widespread…

There was no need to wonder at that horror, because she was living it. Smoke rose from a fire in a nearby district, and she doubted anyone would come to put it out. She spotted a man in the distance beating at a door in an attempt to break in, but he fled long before Jacaranda was near enough to make him out.

"Soon," she said, for the girl's comfort or her own, she wasn't sure. "We'll find some guards soon."

But it was another of the bizarre cannibals that found them first. A woman approached in the center of the street, everything about her movements and appearance crying warning in Jacaranda's mind.

"Stay behind me," she told Abigail. "I'll keep you safe."

The woman approached with an unsteady gait. Her movements were rapid, too rapid, but only in little bursts. She was naked from the waist up, as if she'd woken up in the middle of the night and given no thought to her appearance before exiting to roam the street. What in all the darkness of the void had happened to these people? Jacaranda hoped someone smarter figured it out, because this was beyond nightmarish. She'd thought the woman held something to her mouth to eat, but as she neared, Jacaranda realized the woman was gnawing at the skin of her own thumb.

"More?" she said when she removed her thumb, revealing it stripped to the bone from the knuckle up. "So hungry. Could you give more?"

Jacaranda braced herself for any sudden movements.

"Walk away," she warned.

Instead the woman took another uneasy step. Blood soaked the thin sleeve of her shift from her gnawed thumb. Instead of showing fear, she smiled.

"You," she said. "You'll help."

The woman's body flickered closer, but this time Jacaranda was ready. The moment it happened, she dashed closer, determined to be the one on the offensive. The woman raised her arms in defense, and Jacaranda was shocked at the speed of her reaction. Trained fighters would be envious. Jacaranda's swipes struck the bones of the woman's forearms, halted from scoring lethal damage. The woman snap-kicked with the force of a man twice her weight, and when Jacaranda doubled over in pain, she leaned in with teeth wide.

Her teeth nipped but a small cut before Jacaranda slipped away. This time she gave every bit of respect to her foe's speed. She cut once, twice, expecting them to be blocked by her gashed forearms, and then hesitated. The woman flickered again, and suddenly her arms were already wrapped around Jacaranda's waist. Her hungry mouth closed in for a bite on Jacaranda's vulnerable neck.

Jacaranda gave her the steel of her short sword to bite instead. Teeth cracked with a sound that sent shivers down her spine. Still the madwoman refused to relent. Had to act fast, she thought. Jacaranda's left arm was trapped against her side due to the woman's grasp, but her right was free. She slid the blade downward, scraping and chipping teeth on its way out. The moment the sword was free, the woman bit again. Jacaranda didn't bother defending. This time she slammed the tip of her sword straight into her trachea, enduring another bite on her shoulder that drew blood.

Two sawing motions and the woman collapsed at Jacaranda's feet, her throat gushing blood upon the street. Jacaranda stared at her dying body. Horror crept at the corners of her consciousness. This wasn't real. This was all a cruel, sadistic delusion of her mind. It had to be.

But the wind on her skin was cold, and the pain in her shoulder sharp and real. She took in a long breath and then let it out. The act returned some semblance of calm to her mind.

"It's done," she said, turning to Abigail. "Let's go."

Her heart froze. A glass-eyed man clutched Abigail's neck with both hands, his mouth open and a long strand of drool dripping down his chin.

"It's just meat," he said. "And any meat'll do."

Abigail flailed and kicked, but he ignored every blow. She couldn't make a noise. She couldn't breathe.

"Let her go!"

Jacaranda lunged across the distance, her short swords leading. She buried the first into his forehead, the second into that drooling mouth of his. He collapsed, yet still he would not let go. Jacaranda pried at his fingers, and when that did not work, she sliced several off with her sword. Finally the grip relented, and Abigail rolled free and onto her back.

"I'm sorry," Jacaranda said. "I should have paid more attention. I should have . . . Abigail?"

The girl clutched her throat. Huge welts were already growing from the man's grip. Her mouth opened and closed, simulating breathing, but Jacaranda could only hear the faintest wheeze to show for it. Her mind blanked. The girl was staring at her, begging for help with her eyes. Help she couldn't offer.

Her throat. Her tiny little throat. The man had permanently crushed it in his grasp.

"I don't know what to do," Jacaranda said. "I don't know. Abigail, I don't know!"

Her lips were turning blue. Her eyes had rolled back into her head. Jacaranda held her mouth open with shaking fingers, and she pressed down on her tongue, but it didn't matter. Her throat was crushed. Convulsions soon started.

"No," Jacaranda whispered. "Please, no. Just breathe. You can do it."

Wait. One of the Sisters' keepers! They could heal her! She slid her arms underneath the girl's back and knees to lift her. She never did. There was no life left in the body she held. No breath. No heartbeat. She held a corpse. Jacaranda slumped over her, her vision blurring with tears.

How worthless was she? One girl. She couldn't even save one girl. Jacaranda bathed Abigail's face with her tears as she beat her fists against the cold stone. Damn this night. Damn this city. In that moment, if the Goddesses would have granted her any wish, she'd have burned the entire labyrinthine city to ash. Anything to stop the hurt.

Jacaranda forced herself back to her feet and ran. She left the girl's body where she lay. The guilt she felt for doing so didn't matter. She couldn't look at her anymore. The swirling, tumultuous mixture of emotions clawing at her heart and lungs were more than she could bear.

After some time she grabbed a windowsill and used it to vault to the roof of a random home. She pressed her back to the chimney, pulled her legs to her chest, and cried. She let the horror of the night wash over her, and this time she didn't try to maintain control. Why bother? There was no one to protect. Let her tears fall. Let it all crush her under a weight she was painfully unfamiliar with. Gerag's vanishing. Abigail's death. Devin's safety. So many things beyond her control. How did people live like this? How did they deal with such constant uncertainty?

In time her tears slowed to a stop. She stared at the night sky and let its starlight soothe her. Even amid this pain, she reminded herself it was better than her previously soulless self. Others dealt with uncertainty, and so, too, would she learn.

Jacaranda waited out the night on that rooftop. She tried to sleep, but between the bells and the distant screams, there'd been no rest for her. Occasionally she'd get the impulse to sprint toward Low Dock to find Devin on patrol. The rational part of her mind choked that impulse down every time. She didn't know his location, nor could she guarantee her own safety during the journey. Devin knew what he was doing, and he'd shown a remarkable ability to adapt to any situation. He'd survive. Of course he'd survive.

She wished those rational thoughts had any effect on the constant fear twisting at her insides.

Just before dawn she climbed back down to the street. It seemed with the rise of the sun, the madness ceased, and a heavy silence settled over the blood-soaked streets. Jacaranda hurried to the Church District, refusing to entertain the bleak thoughts running round and round inside her mind.

The door to Devin's home was locked. Jacaranda leaned against the wall beside the front door, her arms crossed over her chest, and waited. The sun steadily crept over the city walls. Half an hour or so later she saw Devin come walking down the street. His shoulders drooped, and it seemed the weight of his heavy coat was more than his tired body could bear.

"Hey, Jac," Devin said as he neared. Dark circles rimmed his eyes, and dried blood spackled much of his coat, but his smile was soft and genuine.

"Hey, you."

She slid her arms underneath his coat and around his waist. Her eyes closed, and she buried her face into his chest. After a moment his arms pulled her against his body as he returned the embrace. Only then did she relax, her silent tears wetting his shirt as she grieved. They said nothing, merely held one another as the sun rose and the city of Londheim awakened to the horror that had unfolded throughout the night.

# CHAPTER 8

Faithkeeper Sena bowed low before her Vikar and kept all hints of frustration buried deep down and out of her voice.

"I understand," she told Caria of the Dawn.

*Understand that Low Dock is being abandoned.*

"This isn't a decision I make lightly," Caria said. The Vikar sat on the edge of her desk and folded her hands in her lap. The two discussed provisions for the upcoming night while inside the Vikar's office located within the Faithkeeper's Sanctuary of the Grand Cathedral. Much like Caria, the office was perfectly neat and orderly. Not a speck of dust dared show its face. The bookshelves were as immaculate as the tight curls underneath the Vikar's black church hat. Behind her desk was a grand painting of the Cradle surrounded by a protective ring of stars. Beyond that ring lurked the void, painted in the darkest blacks possible and scraped across the top to give the appearance of clawing hands and fingers.

"But it is still a decision made," Sena said. Even that was more confrontational than she'd intended. The lack of sleep was getting to her.

"The church's priorities must be upon the largest districts. We Vikars are in agreement on this."

"Then help us evacuate Low Dock completely," Sena insisted.

"Don't leave us on our own to fend off those—those things people are becoming when the moon rises."

"It won't be on your own," the Vikar said. "After all, you have the supposed reborn Sacred Mother to protect you."

Sena crossed her arms and counted to three before answering. She would not dare risk a careless word here, not about her friend. The two of them had fought for Low Dock's heart and soul over many hard years, and she would not betray her now, not even to her Vikar.

"That is a title Adria has not once embraced," she said. "The people are frightened and seeking prophets and saviors. Do not cast harsh words upon a Mindkeeper who has done nothing but aid this city with the gifts given to her by the Sisters."

Caria slid off the desk to her feet. She didn't look at Sena as she smoothed out the wrinkles in her finely tailored black suit.

"She has not condemned the praises, either," Caria said. "But she is a Mindkeeper, after all. Perhaps she does not understand the public the way you or I do. Counsel her, Sena. I would hate to see blasphemy spread throughout your corner of Londheim at a time when we most desperately need unity."

Sena wondered if the reason she was called to the Cathedral of the Sacred Mother was not about the complete lack of aid for the coming night, but instead so she might be reprimanded for her handling of Adria's newfound stardom. Neither possibility left her in a decent mood.

"The people of Low Dock are some of the most faithful and worshipful servants of the Sisters in all of Londheim," she said. "And sadly they are used to hardships. We will endure. We always do. May I be dismissed? I dare not waste a second of daylight with how much left there is to do."

Upon her dismissal, Sena kept a practiced look of contentment upon her face as she walked the halls of the Faithkeeper Sanctuary.

It was only when she exited Lyra's Door and strode the crowded city streets that she allowed a scowl to emerge.

*I expected so much better of you, Caria,* she thought. *And perhaps you don't understand the people as well as you claim. Abandoning them to Adria's protection will only encourage the devotion you fear is growing blasphemous in its intensity.*

Sena would never have believed as much about her Vikar before the black water came and changed the world. Perhaps the woman had changed. Perhaps Sena had been blind to her own Vikar while focusing on the faults of the other two Sacred Divisions. It didn't matter now. Coming up with a plan to protect innocent men, women, and children from being eaten by the flickering ravenous needed to be her focus.

"Coming through, miss!" a cart driver hollered as politely as he could from the driver's seat. Sena stepped aside while mouthing an apology. The stench that followed pulled her out of her daze. Corpses were piled into the back of the cart, and though they were covered with a heavy blanket, humanoid shapes still emerged, and errant limbs poked out the edges. Sena stared at the cart as the clop of the horse's hooves faded into the distance. Londheim's Pyre-hands would be busy tonight sending souls to the stars during the reaping hour. A stone settled into the pit of her stomach as she wondered how many carts would be needed to haul away the dead that amassed from another set of attacks in Low Dock.

Sena's stomach grumbled, reminding her she had not eaten since the night before. She adjusted her path to swing through one of the smaller nearby markets. The winding street looked like it'd been decimated by a storm. Many stalls were broken or knocked over, and many others were stripped of their wares and left unattended. Windows were smashed in and hastily replaced with nailed boards. Sena settled into the back of a line for one of the few tent stalls still open. Several ahead of her quickly gestured for her to take their place.

"Rumors say the Sisters are punishing us for our gluttony," a gruff bearded man ahead of her said. "That true, Faithkeeper?"

"The Sisters do not punish," Sena said, keenly aware of how others in the line were listening for her answer. "They are beings of love. We seek them for comfort and succor, not punishment."

"Then what is this curse?" asked another. "People eating other people. It's sick."

Sena wished she had an answer, but none were forthcoming. Was it a curse? A plague brought by magical creatures? Or were people's minds breaking completely from the strain of understanding the new?

"Together we are strong," she said, emphasizing a point she'd focused on ever since the crawling mountain arrived at their city's doorstep. "And together we will endure."

Sena bought a roll stuffed with apple jelly and devoured it as she walked. Every part of her wanted to lie down in her room and sleep the day away. Sisters knew she wasn't getting much rest between fleeing survivors coming to her church and the need to guard against the monstrous people beating on the church doors seeking blood.

"Alma give me strength," she muttered through her full mouth. "Have we no chance for peace?"

Londheim was already a city of fear and paranoia, but the new threat had worn everyone thin. It seemed every man and woman was a carpenter now, applying boards to windows and new locks for their doors. Worst was how even that might not be enough. The city guard had been forced to knock on every home during their daytime patrols, and break into those that did not answer. Stories of the carnage they discovered flowed like poison throughout Londheim's veins.

That paranoia fueled the arguments she heard as she neared the entrance to Low Dock.

"I'm telling you, Jora's one of them sick fucks," a dark-haired dockworker shouted. "I saw him pawing at my window last night, trying to get in."

A man in the other of the two groups squaring off shouted back.

"It weren't me. I was watching after my little ones. They'll swear by me."

Two families, by Sena's guess. They looked ready to come to blows.

"You mean they'll lie for you. I'm trying to help you, all of you. Don't let Jora behind your barricade tonight. It'll be the death of you."

"Just look at his eyes," a relative of Jora chimed in. "He ain't sleeping a wink."

"*No one* is sleeping a wink lately," an older man of Jora's family roared back. "You want all folk with dark circles under their lids to be executed? Piss off."

Sena had hoped to ignore the brewing problem, but that seemed no longer an option. She stepped between the groups and stood at attention. Her gaze moved from one family to the other. She said nothing, not one order or command, but both sides withered underneath her vicious glare. The shouts dwindled until she might speak without raising her voice.

"This ends," she said. "There is enough bloodshed at night to last us twenty lifetimes. We will not devour each other in the day as well. Am I understood?"

"They're putting children at risk," one of them said, but his tone was more of a plea than an argument. Sena turned to Jora, and she pitied his helpless frustration. Was he one of the ravenous? Come daylight, those afflicted succumbed to sleep, and when they awoke, they remembered nothing of their nightly horrors. Perhaps Jora was one of them, perhaps not, but if she let him be, there was a chance someone would kill him out of mere suspicion.

"Are your families gathering together for safety when night falls?" she asked.

"We are," Jora said.

"Then I ask that you yourself come to my church in Low Dock. I'll watch over you personally to ensure you are no danger to others."

"That ain't necessary," an older woman of the other family offered. "Lock him in his room. We'll know well enough if he turns violent."

"No," Jora said. "I'll—I'll go. None of you trust me. I'll stay with the Faithkeeper."

That seemed to finally settle the matter. Sena noted none of them protested that doing so put people in *her* church at risk. That, sadly, was a common part of life in Londheim. Once the problem was in someone else's hands, it was quickly forgotten.

"You'll be sleeping on a hard bench tonight," Sena told Jora. "I assume that will be sufficient."

"Better than sleeping out in the street, which is where the Dorseys wanted me."

Sena escorted him to her church, which, as usual lately, was crowded with all sorts of visitors. Some sought bread and water, others a kind word from Mindkeeper Adria. It seemed Adria herself was resting, though, for the dozen or so in waiting lingered absently near the steps.

"Good day to you," Sena told several, and she put on a pleasant face as much a lie as the mask Adria wore. Once inside, she found Adria sitting alone in a pew near the front, her hands in her lap and her thumbs twiddling.

"What is the word from the cathedral?" Adria asked as Sena partly collapsed beside her.

"Unified agreement to do nothing," she said. "At least for us in Low Dock. I was too harsh with you earlier, it seems. Even my Vikar cares not for the poor here."

"She cares," Adria said. Her voice behind the porcelain mask was painfully weak and tired. "They all care. But it's a distant caring. A dull, numbed ache for the poor and tired that spurs speeches but never actions."

"You sound like a jaded idealist," Sena said, and she wrapped an arm around Adria. "I hate it. Is my old Adria under that mask somewhere?"

"Deep, deep down," she said. "A few days of peace and quiet would probably unearth her. What are the chances of us having that, I wonder?"

"The same chances of Lyra walking into our church and offering us pudding."

"I'll keep an eye on the doors, then."

Sena squeezed Adria's shoulders and then stood up.

"I need a moment to gather myself," she said. "I'll come out here and help you with the crowds afterward."

Once alone in her room, Sena loosened the buttons of her suit and pulled out a hand mirror from one of her dresser drawers. Goddesses, she looked a mess. Thick bags drooped underneath her eyes. Red, angry veins stretched toward each side of her irises. Normally she was very consistent with shaving her head the day before every ninth-day sermon. Now she couldn't remember when she'd last done so, and guessing by the thick shadow growing from her scalp, it'd been a few weeks.

"You can get through this," she whispered as she stared into the mirror. The weight of the coming night sagged her shoulders, and she felt her pulse quicken. So much to do. Not near enough time to do it.

"Sena?" someone asked from the other side. "Are you all right?"

"Yes, of course," she said upon opening the door to find Adria standing on the other side. "Why do you ask?"

"You've been in there for over an hour."

"Was I?" She rubbed at her temples. How strange. She wasn't prone to dozing off like that. "Forgive me. I must have fallen asleep."

The day did not become easier, and however long her nap had been, it hadn't been long enough. They set up rows of blankets and pillows. Anyone who lacked a secure home came to them, which at least granted them a decent number of burly men with clubs and knives eager to volunteer as guards. Both Adria and Sena insisted it'd not be necessary. When night came, they'd shut and bar the doors. They picked four to keep watch just in case, and insisted the rest sleep with their families.

Inside the church would be safe from the horrors outside, they told all comers. Of course, there was still the risk of someone inside the church becoming one of the ravenous, but no one spoke that dreaded fear. Several soldiers stayed on guard all night against that exact possibility.

By the time night came, an eerie silence fell over Low Dock, broken by the occasional tolling of a distant watch tower bell.

"Last night may have been a singular event," Adria whispered as the two stood at the cracked doors of the church.

"And it may have only been a taste of what's to come," Sena replied. "Caution is the wisest course of action." She glanced at Jora, who sat looking miserable in a far corner. Sena had assigned a single guard to watch over him in particular, a younger man in his twenties who twirled a finely sharpened knife between his fingers. Caution would have had him locked in another room. Perhaps she wasn't so wise as she pretended.

The stars twinkled into view. Adria and Sena watched the sky together, the cool night air a blessed feeling on their sweaty skin. A bell tolled to the north, followed by another, and then a third to the west.

"It's starting," Adria said. She tugged on the chin of her mask, pulling it down slightly. The Mindkeeper hadn't removed it all day. Sena was starting to suspect she even slept with it on.

"Not a onetime curse," Sena said, and she shook her head. "May Anwyn have mercy upon our city."

They retreated to the safety of their church.

"Half-tempted to leave it open," one of the men at the doors joked. "I say it'd be better we kill those who come our way than hide and hope they wander off."

Yet they locked it nonetheless, then slid a thick block of wood over two newly installed metal hooks. Sena felt the eyes of her congregation upon her, dozens of little white orbs hovering in the dimness.

"Within these walls, huddled in the arms of the Sisters, we are safe," she told them. Her voice held firm with strength she certainly did not feel herself. "Sleep, and fear not. You will all see the dawn."

It was one thing to ask for confidence amid the calm tolling of bells. It was another when the first of the ravenous beat their arms against the solid doors and begged for entry.

"Let me in!" a woman screamed. "I'm scared, I'm so scared... let me in, I'm only a little hungry. A little, just...let me in! Let me in!"

Fists pounded on the wood.

"Let! Me! In!"

Sena pretended not to hear as she moved to her lectern. Her appearance might be calm, but her heart raced. It'd be better if the ravenous were completely mindless creatures. If they didn't speak, and only ate, then it'd be easier to ignore them. It'd be easier to cut them down.

More shouts. Sena clung to the lectern with her eyes closed and face down as if in prayer. A man's voice, indecipherable through the thick wood.

Screams.

A snapping of bone. Long, long minutes of silence.

"Not enough," a man suddenly shouted. The door rattled from his body slamming against it. "It's not enough. It's never enough! You hear me in there? *Never enough!*"

The men guarding the door readied their weapons, but their earlier bravado was long gone. No one wanted that door to give.

Sena looked about the church, certain something was amiss. Everyone was locked frozen in place, as if all time had ceased. Not for her, though. Her pulse pounded in her neck, and her every breath felt hot and rushed inside her lungs. Her temples throbbed from the worst migraine she'd suffered in years.

"Adria?" she asked as she looked for her friend. There, kneeling beside a father holding his crying child. Sena stepped toward the Mindkeeper and gestured to gain her attention. She kept still until Adria joined her and leaned in close, for she didn't want to cause a panic.

"I think...I think something is wrong."

"What do you..." Again the world stopped, only not quite. It moved at a snail's pace, as if all the world swam through freezing water. Sounds elongated in her ears, warbled and stretched beyond deciphering. A sharp pain hit her stomach, accompanied by a wave of dizziness. For a moment she thought she might collapse from weak knees.

"...mean, Sena?" Adria finished.

Sena rubbed at her eyes and then rolled them back in her sockets. Goddesses above, it was so hard to concentrate. Between the headache and her stomach, it felt like her body was completely surrendering to the stress that had overtaken her lately. And would those sick bastards at the door stop beating on the other side?

"I forgot supper," Sena said. "Stupid of me. Just an apple pastry for lunch, that's all. Have you anything? Not much, I'm just...I'm hungry." A little bit of drool slid down her lower lip. "So hungry."

A crumb of bread crust. A boiled egg. A scrap of pork baked in fat. Goddesses, she couldn't say for certain she wouldn't devour a half-eaten apple she found on the floor. What had been a headache was suddenly replaced by an airy light-headedness.

How long had it been since she asked her question? Time was

so weird now. Unsteady. Almost random. It must be because of hunger, she decided. Some people did poorly if going too long without food, after all.

"I think I do have something," Adria said. "In my room."

"You're a lifesaver," Sena said.

She followed her to the door in the far back, but twice she bumped into Adria, who seemingly froze at the most random of times. Sena felt her hands shake with impatience. If only she'd hurry up. It'd been a long day, a truly long day, damn it. She deserved at least this.

Sena stepped inside when Adria opened the door to her room, but couldn't smell any food. No stashed bread crust, no leftover plate from an earlier meal. She whirled on the Mindkeeper, her eyes wide with betrayal to see the woman with her hands raised toward her, palms open. Faint light flickered from her fingertips.

"Blessed Sisters, I seek your protection," said Adria.

Sena lunged at her, every corner of her mind flaring with rage. Adria would betray her? *Her*? After all she'd done, after sticking up for her to the Vikar? What selfishness. What wretchedness. Time warped and slowed with her approach, the words on Adria's tongue dragging out into one long, indecipherable syllable. Sena's hands wrapped about the woman's throat. How dare she pray to the Sisters against her? She'd choke those words. She'd slap that mask aside and teach her respect.

Her mouth watered.

Sena's fingers closed around Adria's throat right as time crashed back to normal. Adria's prayer halted, and a shocked gasp came from behind her porcelain mask. She grabbed at Sena's wrists, but her ineffectual pawing didn't loosen a single finger.

"So hungry," Sena said. Her vision had started to blur. The light-headedness was only growing stronger. Despite the anger she felt in her breast, she laughed as if just hearing the funniest joke. "I'm sorry, Adria, so sorry, I'm not *me* when I'm hungry."

Adria's fingernails sank deep into Sena's skin, and the pain was enough to cause her to gasp and release.

"I'm sorry, Sena," Adria said with a hoarse, croaking voice. Her hand extended, and for one brief moment it seemed a star opened up in the center of her palm.

An invisible hook sank into Sena's forehead, followed by an irresistible pull. Her body slid away, along with her sight, her hunger, her pain. She felt like a snake shedding its skin, or a butterfly emerging from its cocoon. The outer world faded into darkness as Sena's mind collapsed in on itself. In that sudden void she felt warmth, a pleasant calm, and nothing else.

# CHAPTER 9

So the city of compromise has become the city of humans,"
Cannac said as the four crossed the last stretch of road leading to
Londheim's western entrance. The morning was chill but pleasant,
as it had been for most of their travel to Londheim. "Strange how
little it appears to have changed over the centuries."

"It has changed plenty," Tesmarie said. She hovered just above
Tommy's right shoulder, his constant companion on their return
trip. The two humans rode their horses, with Cannac easily keeping up with his long, steady strides. "But only where our kind
lived. Everything unique was boarded up and painted over. It's
still a pretty city, though! And maybe when things are peaceful, it
might be made even prettier with our help."

"I wouldn't hold your breath," Jarel muttered.

"You think cooperation impossible?" Cannac asked.

"No, I think it will be years before things resemble anything
close to 'peaceful.'"

Tommy disliked the pessimism but found it hard to argue against.
Ever since the black water had washed over West Orismund, it felt
like they'd not had a single day of rest. Given that civilizations
such as the dyrandar, lapinkin, and viridi were reemerging on supposed "human" lands, brand-new conflicts loomed heavy on the
horizon. If only people could see these new magical creatures like

he saw them! Puffy, Tesmarie, even Cannac, they were honorable and funny and wonderful in a myriad of ways.

But until that happened, anything the slightest bit different would be terrifying, which led to a concern that'd pressed on his mind during their journey home.

"So what do we do about, um…" Tommy gestured at Cannac. "Minimizing panic?"

"People will panic at the sight of me?" the dyrandar asked.

"Everyone's been jumping at shadows since that damn mountain crawled to our doorstep," Jarel said. "And given how the first few creatures we met started *eating* us humans, can you really blame us?"

Displeasure crossed the dyrandar's face, a unique expression to see on a deer. Tommy assumed it was displeasure anyway. Reading any emotion on Cannac's face was always a trick.

"I warned Arondel to keep her flocks in check," he said. "Short moments of petty rage may seed years of consequences. So be it. I would not cause undue fright in the populace. Halt, please, so I may prepare."

Their ponies shook their heads in annoyance at the delay. Both could see home ahead, and they knew water and rest awaited in their stables. Tommy soothed his mount as best he could by patting it on the side.

"Not long," he whispered to it. "I promise."

Cannac pressed his fingers together and lifted his arms up to eye level. His deep chant emanated from his throat with the depth of stone. It felt like the words and voice had existed since time began, and Cannac were merely a conduit for its release. Tommy watched with unabashed awe. To think mere months ago he had lived in a world without magic or magical creatures. Despite the occasional terrors, Tommy wouldn't go back for anything.

"I am a man of the human world," Cannac said with eyes closed. "So I dream, so it becomes truth."

Clean white light swelled between Cannac's palms, lifted to the space above his antlers, and then silently burst into a thousand little stars that fell like rain upon the dyrandar's body. A haze washed through Tommy's mind, and when he blinked it away, he discovered a muscular man with dark trousers and a faded gray shirt standing where Cannac had been.

"Let us continue," the man said, his voice still the same. "I can maintain this dream only for a few hours."

Tommy desperately wanted to ask questions as to what spell the dyrandar had used, but Jarel merely rolled his eyes and ushered them both along with a smack of his reins. With Jarel's accompaniment, they easily passed through the checkpoint at the gates, with Tesmarie hiding in Tommy's pocket and Cannac earning only a curious glance due to his still intimidating size. Once they'd returned their ponies, Jarel crossed his arms and gestured northward.

"I take it you can handle him until my uncle is ready," he said to Tommy.

"Wait, what do you mean?" Tommy asked. "Aren't we going to meet the Royal Overseer?"

"I'm not bringing a shapeshifting, mind-reading deer person to my uncle's mansion without proper preparation. You've already threatened us with your growing army, Cannac. It'd be foolish of me to risk you learning more than we wish to reveal, and that's assuming your intentions are purely benign. I'm sorry, but I need to be smart about this."

This didn't seem smart at all, but Tommy's frustration was not mirrored by the dyrandar.

"I understand your caution," Cannac said. "Where shall I stay until then?"

"You'll lodge with Tommy in the Wise tower. Consider that an order from Albert himself."

Tommy stammered a moment, totally flustered. The whole

time he'd assumed the Royal Overseer would house Cannac like he would any other honored diplomat.

"I—I—I guess that'll be fine," he said.

"Very well," Cannac said. He bowed his head to Jarel and then turned. "Lead on, Tomas."

Tommy hurried down the main roads toward the Wise tower. He cast occasional glances Cannac's way, paranoid that his disguise would falter and a crowd would form. He was so nervous that it was Cannac who first noticed the city's strange quietness.

"Tell me, Tomas," he said. "Are all homes usually boarded up in such a manner?"

Tommy glanced about. Ever since the owls started attacking at night, the occasional paranoid person had boarded up their windows, but now it seemed every single building had covered its windows, and some even their doors. He turned his attention to the people milling about the streets, saw how nervous they looked, how bloodshot their eyes. Fear hung in the air like a stench.

"Something's wrong," Tesmarie said. She'd poked her head out from his pocket and was frowning at a group of four men chatting quietly by a lantern pole. "Everyone's time feels...messy. Impatient. And that man there, he's completely unstuck."

"Unstuck?" Tommy asked, bewildered. "What do you mean?"

She shook her head and slipped back out of sight.

"I don't know how to explain it. Let me think for a bit, all right?"

"Of course," he said. His throat constricted, and he felt his pulse quickening. "No problem. I'm sure it's nothing, nothing at all."

Tesmarie flew out of his pocket once they reached the Wise tower. Malik was yet to meet the onyx faery, and given Cannac's arrival, it seemed a bad time to start.

"I'll wait out here," she said. "Try to be quick. I'm really worried about these unstuck people. We need to talk to Devin and find out what he knows."

Tommy knocked five times before Malik unlocked and unbarred the heavy wood door.

"Thank the stars you're back," Malik said, flinging his arms around Tommy. "I feared you'd return after dark and be caught completely unaware."

"Unaware?" Tommy asked. "Unaware of what?"

Except his mentor and friend had already turned his attention to their seemingly unassuming guest, who had followed Tommy into the wide foyer.

"Hello?" Malik asked. "Might I ask who you are?"

Tommy had hoped to explain everything to Malik over a relaxing cup of tea, and warn him about Cannac's disguise. The dyrandar, however, held no such concerns. A press of his fingers and his body shimmered a rainbow of colors, followed by a single flash. In its wake returned Cannac's original, enormous form. He looked almost comical in a room far too small for him, and he had to bow his neck and shoulders to keep his antlers from pressing the low ceiling.

"Cannac, this is Malik," Tommy said, trying not to laugh as he made the introductions. "Malik, this is Cannac, a dyrandar."

Malik's jaw dropped open, and he grabbed the edge of a side table to steady himself.

"Shame on you, Tommy," Malik said, his voice surprisingly calm. "You should warn me when we're having guests."

"I have come to speak with your Royal Overseer as a representative of the dragon-sired," Cannac said. "Tomas was kind enough to offer me a place to stay as I wait."

"Of course he did," Malik said. He looked torn between laughing and fleeing the room screaming. "Please, have a seat. I need to speak with Tommy a moment in private."

Cannac glanced at the two human-sized chairs beside the fireplace.

"I shall stand," he said.

"Right," Malik said. "Sorry. Just a moment."

He pulled Tommy through the doorway into what served as the tower's tiny kitchen.

"The city is tearing itself apart at night and you show up with a half-deer, half-human giant and expect us to play host?" Malik asked.

"What do you mean?" Tommy asked. "What's happening at night?"

"You don't know. Of course you don't know." Malik rubbed at his temples. "Some sort of curse has hit Londheim, especially the southern portions of it. When night falls, a fraction of the people turn mad. They—they're eating people, Tommy. It's a fucking nightmare. No one knows the cause, or who'll be affected next."

Tommy stammered for a moment as his brain tried to digest the information. People were turning into crazed cannibals? Goddesses above, that couldn't possibly be right.

"There's—there's got to be a reason," Tommy said. "We can investigate it, find the cause, find a cure."

"And how do we do that with Cannac in our tower's living room?"

"This wasn't my choice. Jarel ordered him to stay here. I thought he'd be at the Overseer's mansion!"

"I will leave if my staying here is unacceptable," Cannac called from the other room. "I do not wish to be a burden."

Malik shot Tommy a bewildered look as to how the dyrandar overheard their conversation.

"He can read emotions and thoughts," Tommy explained.

"Wonderful." Malik returned to the living room, and he put on his best welcoming face, which meant it was slightly less rigid than normal. "Do not mistake surprise for disapproval. I am happy for you to stay here, but I fear our tower was not constructed with someone of your proportions in mind."

"A matter of little concern," Cannac said. "Worldly limitations often fall to otherworldly solutions."

Before Tommy could ask what that meant, the dyrandar began chanting. His strange words washed over them, and it seemed the tower itself vibrated to the sound of each ringing syllable.

"Take hold, dear Gloam," Cannac whispered upon ending the chant. "I relinquish this world to your pristine thought."

Sweat rolled down Tommy's forehead and neck despite the bite of early winter that crept through cracks in the walls. His heart pounded in his chest, and he realized a panic attack was threatening to overwhelm him. It wasn't because he was afraid. It was because the world before him had stopped resembling the firm reality he'd understood his entire life.

The room expanded, the walls billowing outward as if they were curtains and not stone. The ceiling did not lift. It simply ceased to be. An infinite expanse of darkness replaced it, formless and empty. Tommy couldn't decide if he'd grown, the furniture had resized, or Cannac had shrunk, but suddenly the chairs and couch by the hearth seemed the perfect fit for all three of them. The dyrandar carefully settled into one, a contented sigh escaping his lips as he was able to relax his neck and shoulders without a roof to constrict his antlers.

"How—how did you do this?" Tommy asked. It felt like reality had turned wobbly.

"I am a master of visions and dreams," Cannac said. "And what is this world but a dream?"

Malik looked like a child standing before a wealth of presents.

"Gloam," he said. "Your power comes from Gloam?"

The connection clicked in Tommy's mind. *Gloam* was the only school of magic that Malik could successfully manifest, and before him sat a creature with power leagues beyond what they'd encountered in scrolls and books of spells concerning the discipline.

"We dyrandar were Gloam's very first creation," Cannac said.

"As such, he bestowed us a great portion of his power. You intrigue me, Malik. What do you know of Gloam?"

Malik was suddenly tripping over himself grabbing at books scattered throughout the side tables and floor. He thrust several at Cannac's face, their pages opened to spells that he'd been studying.

"What does this one do?" he asked. "I cannot ascertain its function from context alone, and it's driven me mad."

Cannac looked pleasantly intrigued, and he detailed the spell, one for granting wishes in a mental, imaginary form. Tommy listened to them talk while standing awkwardly in the center of the room. Just like that, Tommy felt like he ceased to exist. Was that it? He'd been gone several days, his life in danger, and after a brief greeting, Malik had turned his focus to other matters?

"I need to leave," Tommy interrupted. "I need to make sure Devin and Adria are safe."

"Of course, of course," Malik said. His hand raced over the lines in one of the tomes he held. He didn't even bother to look Tommy's way when he answered. "Go on. We'll be fine here. So Cannac, the initial declaration of *Gloam* at a spell's initiation, is this necessary for all spells, or only ones with significant power requirements?"

Tommy hurried out the door, berating himself even as he hurt. Well, what had he expected from his mentor? A kiss and a welcome-back snuggle? Malik had made clear their relationship, and Tommy felt stupid for hoping for something more to emerge.

"Are you all right, Tommy?" Tesmarie asked as he closed the tower door behind him. Immediately the dreamlike feeling of the tower faded. The cold, dreary reality of Londheim greeted him with the gentleness of a brick to the face.

"Huh? Oh. Yes, I'm fine. Really." He wiped at his eyes, then smiled up at the faery. "Come on, I bet Devin's been just flabbergasted without us around to solve his problems, so let's hurry along!"

It was late afternoon by the time Tommy knocked on his brother-in-law's door, but already the city was hunkered down as if to weather a terrible storm. Several times Tesmarie pointed to a man or woman hurrying down the street, insisting something was significantly wrong with them, but Tommy saw no difference between them and any other random passerby. Still, it put a chill into his bones that could not be explained by the biting wind, and he stomped his feet impatiently as he waited. The boards nailed over the lower floor windows of the houses on either side of Devin's didn't help, either.

"Yes?" Devin said when he flung the door open. A half second later he realized who had come, and a smile spread across his tired face from ear to ear. He wrapped Tommy in a warm hug. "You're back."

"I've got about ten stories to tell when we have the time," Tommy said. "But from what I gather, you've got a few to tell yourself."

His smile flickered but a moment before returning.

"You could say that." He smiled to Tesmarie. "Did you make sure Tommy behaved while he was gone?"

"As well as one my size could," she said. A soft buzz of her wings catapulted her from Tommy's shoulder to Devin's, and she planted a kiss on his cheek. "I'm happy to be home."

They stepped inside from the cold. Jacaranda sat on the couch facing the fire, and her smile was a salve to Tommy's wriggling nerves. He approached for a hug, and when Puffy flickered from the hearth in greeting, he waved back. The pleasantries didn't last long. Tommy sat on the couch, and he brought up the bizarre curse that had besieged the city in his absence.

"Malik told me a little bit about what's going on," he said. "I was hoping you could fill me in about the rest. Something about insane cannibals attacking at night?"

"That's one way to put it," Devin said. His easy smile faded into nothing. "This is gruesome stuff, Tommy, but I'll do my best to explain."

Tommy listened in horror as Devin described the nighttime attacks. It sounded too macabre to be real. People attacking others to *eat* them? What in the world was going on?

"It happens only at night?" Tesmarie asked. She sat upon Devin's shoulder, a look of worry etched onto her onyx face.

"Seems so," Devin said. "The moment the sun rises, the attacks stop. Guards have captured men and women suffering the same deranged symptoms, and when daylight comes, they immediately collapse into a deep sleep. If they're forced awake, they remember nothing of the previous night. It's baffling."

"No," Tesmarie said. "Not baffling. I—I think I know what is happening to them."

Devin bolted upright in his chair.

"You do? How? What is going on?"

Tesmarie fluttered to the center of the room so she could address them all.

"Tommy, do you remember that mushroom I gave you so you didn't need to sleep while we looked for Adria?"

"Sure, the timeshroom," he said. It'd been the weirdest thing when he ate it. Tesmarie had told him to lie down as if to nap, and though he felt like he'd slept for a full night's rest, he'd been keenly aware that the sleep happened during a single blink of his eyelids.

"They're called chronimi mushrooms," she gently corrected. "They were meant as a gift to humans to remove their need for sleep."

"Remove it how?" Devin asked.

"By . . . um, how do I put this? By making the person momentarily unstuck in time so they could sleep for a full eight hours or so, but to everyone else, it'd appear they slept only a moment. Does that make any sense?"

"I think so," Tommy said. "When I ate the time...chronimi, it felt like hours of sleep passed in the blink of an eye."

"This is fascinating," Jacaranda said. "But Tommy didn't become a maniac and attempt to eat all of us. How does this explain what's happening to Londheim?"

"That's because he wasn't allergic," Tesmarie said. "Some people are extremely susceptible to the mushroom's effects, and it causes everything to go wrong. They still become unstuck, but they don't sleep. Hours pass for their bodies, but they get no rest. Worse, it happens continuously, and at random amounts and lengths."

"They're sleep deprived," Tommy blurted out. His excitement had him leaping off the couch, and he sheepishly sat back down before continuing. "If they're experiencing hours, and even days, in the blink of an eye without rest and without food, it must take its toll on their bodies and minds. I've read about the effects of extreme sleep deprivation. It can get quite ugly."

"But why eat people?" Jacaranda asked.

"Are they eating only people?" Tesmarie asked.

"No, they're not," Devin said. He frowned in thought. "They've broken into bakeries and stores searching for food. They're always hungry, though, and if their mind finally cracks under the strain..."

"They go for whatever food they can find," Jacaranda finished. She shivered. "These poor people. I wonder if they're even aware of what's going on around them. It sounds awful. But why does it only affect them at night? And why isn't everyone else having a normal reaction to this mushroom?"

Tesmarie shrugged.

"You must not be getting enough of the mushroom to notice. As for when, the chronimi was designed to activate upon nightfall and then disperse from the body upon morning in an attempt to prevent, well, what's happening right now. Once daylight touches their bodies, the activated spores destroy themselves, which is why those suffering can finally sleep. Only activated spores, though. Newly ingested ones will wait until nightfall. Somehow, the people of Londheim must be continuously taking in low amounts of the chronimi."

Now it was Devin's turn to rise from his chair. He hurried to the door and began strapping on his thick belt for his sword and pistol.

"Tes, I think you've changed everything," he said. "All of you, come with me. We've work to do."

Adria's room was a small fit, but everyone did their best to cram inside. The firekin hopped into the fireplace and settled in, its warmth welcome in the cold room.

"I—I didn't know what to do," Adria said. She leaned against the wall, her porcelain mask held in her hands. Her eyes were red, from tears or exhaustion, Tommy couldn't tell. "It's daytime now, so she should be safe, but…"

Her voice trailed off. Tommy grabbed her hand and squeezed it.

"I'm sure you did the right thing," he said. "Trust Tes to fix it, all right?"

"That's right," Tesmarie said, trying to sound chipper. "Everything's fine. I'll make her better, I promise!"

Faithkeeper Sena sat perfectly still upon Adria's bed. Her hands rested on her lap, and her eyes gazed into nothing. It was the calm look of a soulless, for hovering in the air beside her was the pure white shimmering star that was her own soul. Adria had removed it the night before, rendering Sena's newly soulless body unwilling to act on any of its impulses.

"It won't take but a moment," Tesmarie added as she landed atop Sena's shoulder and pressed her hands upon the dark skin of her neck. The faery's eyes closed, and she murmured something quietly. A few seconds later she buzzed back into the air and let out a long, satisfied sigh.

"Her time's properly set now, promise," she said. "You can, um, give her back her soul."

Adria beckoned the soul back into her body with a simple gesture of her hand. The gleaming orb sank through Sena's forehead, darkening the room in its absence. For a long moment it seemed all there held their breath, and then Sena gasped in air.

"Adria?" she murmured, but her eyelids were so heavy. Her body slumped to the side, sleep immediately overtaking her. Tommy smiled, thrilled to see the cure worked.

"See, I told you to trust her," he said, clasping Adria's hand in his. His sister-in-law joined Sena on the bed, and finally the long-held tears broke free. Adria wept with relief over her friend, planting several kisses on her forehead before closing her eyes and recollecting herself. The intimate moment left Tommy feeling uneasy, and he turned to give them privacy. Devin snapped his fingers to grab his attention and beckoned him to the door.

"This changes everything," Devin said, keeping his voice low. "We know the cause of this plague, which means we know how to end it. These mushrooms, where do they grow?"

"Somewhere always wet and dark," Tesmarie said, having flown back over to sit atop Tommy's shoulder. "I found the one I gave Tommy growing in a little tunnel you humans built near the river."

"An underground tunnel," Tommy said. "The timeshrooms must be growing in the water. That's how it's affecting everyone all across the city! If we figure out where is being hit the worst, then we can narrow our search down."

"Southeast Londheim," Devin said. "Low Dock in particular."

"Where does Low Dock get its water?" Tesmarie asked.

"An underground cistern. The chronimi mushrooms must be

growing down there, and their spores are entering the water. It's the only explanation that works. If we find them, and destroy them, we'll save all of Londheim."

"Destroying the mushrooms will prevent another attack from happening tomorrow," Jacaranda said. "But it won't help those suffering tonight. It's already in their blood."

"I can help the people who are reacting poorly," Tesmarie offered. "If someone can keep them still and from eating me, that is."

"Then we split in two groups," Devin said. "Jacaranda and I will check the cistern. Tommy, you and Tesmarie will patrol Low Dock for people suffering the effects of a chronimi." A burst of fire from Adria's fireplace caused Devin to quickly reassess. "Sorry, Jacaranda, *Puffy*, and I will check the cistern. Sound good?"

"Sure," Tesmarie said. She gave Tommy a worried smile. "Are you ready to keep me safe as I do my magic?"

Tommy gulped down a giant knot of worry.

"Sure," he said, his voice cracking. "Using my magic to hold crazy time-unstuck sleep-deprived ravenous cannibals at bay so you can cure them? I've never felt more confident in my entire life."

# CHAPTER 10

Before heading underground, Devin needed to address one detail that brought him to the steps of Anwyn's Gate outside the cathedral.

"Ready to kick more ass tonight?" Lyssa asked Devin as he approached. The sun had begun its descent, and it painted an orange hue across the old stone of the city.

"I actually need to talk to you about that," he said. Several other Soulkeepers lingered nearby, and he gestured for her to walk with him. Once they were at the very bottom step, he lowered his voice to just above a whisper. "I won't be accompanying you tonight, but I'd appreciate it if you didn't mention this to Vikar Forrest."

Her left eyebrow arced high up into her forehead.

"Explanation, please?"

Devin debated for the twelfth time whether or not to tell Lyssa his plan. She was a skilled shot, and had proven herself capable of thinking on her feet over the past weeks. How might she react to Puffy's existence? And what of Jacaranda? Would Lyssa keep silent if she noticed the chains tattooed across her throat? He wanted to believe her trustworthy, but he dealt with matters that allowed no margin of error.

"I think I've discovered the reason for the nightly attacks," he said. "If I'm right, tonight should be the last time we deal with this threat."

"What? Devin, that's great! Where is it? How can I help?"

This was his chance. All he had to do was ask her along…

"I can't say. I'm sorry. You'll have to trust me."

He couldn't do it. He couldn't risk Jacaranda's safety. All they were doing was clearing out some mushrooms underneath the city. There was no need for the risk.

Lyssa stepped back, and she shoved her hands into the pockets of her coat.

"Sure," she said. There was no hiding the upset in her voice. "I trust you, Devin. Good luck with…whatever it is you're doing. Don't worry about me. I'll find a squad of city guards to patrol with instead."

She trotted up the steps without another word. Devin sighed. Had he made the right choice? Only the Goddesses knew at this point, but the one thing he did know was that Lyssa was hurt by his lack of trust. Damn it all, what he'd give for Jacaranda's condition to be known and understood by the church. She was a miracle, and yet he had to keep her hidden like a criminal.

Jacaranda waited for him two blocks south of the cathedral, short sword in one hand and a blazing torch in the other for Puffy to travel upon.

"Everything good?" she asked.

"As well as can be expected," he said. "Come on. The cistern entrance is a good half mile from here, and I'd like to be down there before the sun sets."

From what information Tommy had gleaned from the Wise tower as they prepared for their excursion, the underground cistern should be a small room about the size of a house, with several cramped tunnels leading to multiple wells throughout Low Dock and the neighboring Tradeway District. So far as Tommy knew, it was the only cistern in Londheim, with the rest of the city using wells dug deep into the soil.

The moment Devin stepped off the ladder into one of those tunnels, he knew Tommy's information was woefully incorrect.

"Where are we?" Jacaranda asked as she quickly followed. "Are you sure this is it?"

The entrance had been a small shed with a broken lock that covered a hole in the ground. A metal ladder was bolted into the stone at the top, and it'd rattled from their weight. The shoddy work seemed completely opposite to the grand sight before him. The tunnel was fifteen feet across, with stone walkways on either side. Between them flowed a veritable river of water. There were no bricks, no chip marks, no signs of any working of the stone to create the arched ceiling above them and the perfectly smooth walkways below. It was as if the stone had simply formed into such a shape. Mushrooms grew in four strict, unending lines across the ceiling, their heads glowing a bright cyan so that they had no need for Puffy's light.

"Humans didn't build this," Devin said as he leaned closer to the wall. It wasn't perfectly flat as he'd first thought. Little grooves ran throughout the stone, curling and rolling like waves of the Gentle Ocean. Carved figures decorated with sapphires danced amid the waves, strikingly similar in appearance to Puffy when it ran about on two legs. Devin had expected the tunnel to be cramped and smell of mold. Instead the roof was at least five feet above his head, well lit, and if he inhaled strongly enough, he caught the scent of open fields.

"How could something like this go unnoticed for so long?" Jacaranda asked.

"Maybe it changed when the old world returned," Devin said. "Or maybe it's always been like this and our eyes could not see it."

Puffy elongated to see better and glanced in both directions, then pointed.

"Follow the firekin's lead," Devin said.

Tesmarie had described the chronimi as resembling the cabbage-shaped sheepshead mushrooms, only instead of a light brown, they were stark white. Devin kept an eye on the water as they walked alongside it. A layer of deep green moss completely covered the walls where the water flowed.

"This feels like it was built for a reason," Jacaranda whispered as they walked. Something about the tunnel and its bluish glow lent it a somber air. "And it wasn't as a cistern."

"Not at first anyway," Devin agreed.

They followed the tunnel for several minutes, traveling upstream to the river that flowed beside them. It contained few curves or turns, and Devin did his best to map their progress in his head compared to the above ground. They were steadily traveling away from the Septen River and toward Tradeway. Twice they passed ladders he was tempted to climb. Where did they exit? Were they forgotten like so much else from centuries ago was forgotten, buried beneath a sheen of illusion by the hands of the Sisters?

Splashing up ahead pulled Devin from his thoughts. He readied his sword and pistol, fearful of what monster might emerge from the water's flow. Jacaranda lowered to a crouch. Puffy shook its arms to grab their attention from atop the torch.

CALM, it spelled out in the air. NOFITE.

Devin uncocked his pistol to its neutral position, holstered it along with sheathing his sword, and then awaited the mysterious creature's arrival.

The sound of splashing echoed through the tunnel as if invisible fish were thrashing at the surface. Devin and Jacaranda watched the water, confused. Large jets of water would fly into the air, buoyed by some unknown force, and then land with a great splash. They rushed on by, the sound thunderous in the quiet tunnel, then halted. The water grew perfectly still. Puffy put its hands on its hips and tilted its head to one side, seeming almost impatient.

And then the first of the waterkin leapt out of the river and onto the edge of the stone. It was triple the size of Puffy, and composed solely of crystalline clear water akin to how Puffy was formed of perfectly controlled flame. It bore the same deep black orbs for eyes, like two floating obsidian spheres. Three more burst out of the water and landed around them upon the walkway. Water leaked out of their feet and steadily pooled back into the river flowing between the pathways so that they shrank in size to match Puffy's. For a long moment they stared at one another, and if they were communicating, Devin did not see how.

One of the waterkin poked Devin's leg. Somehow, against all logic his brain could follow, it did not make his pant leg wet. Another hopped atop his arm, becoming snakelike as it swirled up to his shoulder. Devin kept perfectly still, trusting Puffy to keep them safe. So far the firekin had not moved from its spot, which led him to believe things had not yet turned dangerous. The waterkin lifted his tricorn hat off his head, hopped again, and then with a great splash it soaked his entire head and face, the drops racing down his chin to plop down to the ground and re-form.

Beady little black eyes bobbed up and down. That reaction Devin did understand. The bratty little waterkin was laughing at him.

"Devin," Jacaranda said with the stern tone of an adult chastising a child as her hand closed around his wrist reaching for his pistol. "Behave."

"Tell them that," he muttered. Two more waterkin shot into the air like projectiles, one splashing his face, the other his rear. Puffy's shoulders sagged, as if disappointed in his fellow elementals.

"I think they're adorable," Jacaranda said as more waterkin emerged from the river. She held up her hand, and one of them hopped up, took the shape of an orb, and somehow rolled across her palm. She gently lobbed it toward the ceiling, where it splashed, re-formed, and pirouetted during its descent. Several other waterkin dove back into the river, melding halfway into the flow so they appeared to zip about the surface like skaters atop ice.

Puffy returned to Jacaranda's torch. Its body elongated and shrank to form letters so they might understand it.

U NICE. THEY NICE. C?

"I see," Devin said. "We'll keep our weapons stowed away, assuming our weapons could even do anything to a waterkin. They *are* waterkin, aren't they?"

Two circles of smoke drifted above Puffy's head in confirmation. The firekin hopped back atop Jacaranda's torch. The remaining waterkin returned to the flowing river, merrily splashing and leaping about. The sound of their play slowly faded as the trio crossed the remainder of the tunnel, which broadened widely upon their arrival to the cistern's main chamber.

"Bless the stars above," Devin whispered. "This is incredible."

Hundreds of pillars the height of five men spaced the cavernous cistern. The effervescent blue mushrooms, which had grown in straight lines above their heads while in the tunnel, painted the ceiling in long, swirling patterns that never seemed to end. The pillars themselves were decorated with five dragons chasing one another through the sky in loops. Water gently flowed down the pillars from distant pipes across the ceiling. Grooves upon the bottom of the pillars were cut so that the water's flow across it mimicked the sound of a rocky spring. Green moss carpeted the entire underwater floor, and when Devin tested it with his foot, it was soft and spongy.

"Only Low Dock and Tradeway draw water from this cistern," Jacaranda said. "But there's so much here...surely this was meant for the entire city?"

"I think you're right," Devin said. "It wouldn't surprise me if what people think are underground wells in the other districts also draw from this cistern's tunnels."

There was no walkway to use once out of the tunnel, so Devin waded into the knee-high water to examine the nearest pillar. Each dragon carved upon it bore a distinct look from the others, varying in length and size, some even the number of legs. There was no question as to the identity of one of the five, its tall, spiky back and six stubby legs a clear imitation of the crawling mountain resting outside Londheim's gates.

"We knew about you once, didn't we, Viciss?" Devin whispered as he trailed his fingers across the carving. He examined the others, wondering at their names. Which was Nihil, and which was Aethos? Was it the dragon with a body longer than a snake and a dozen arms? Or was it the one with three hills atop its back and its sides marked with caves? Only one dragon bore wings, and Devin felt a chill tickle his spine at the thought of something as gargantuan as the living mountain flying overhead.

"I don't see any of the chronimi mushrooms," Jacaranda said, interrupting his thoughts.

"It's a big cavern," Devin said. "Let's not write this place off yet."

Devin took point, and he set their path so the wall to their right always stayed in view. If need be, they'd check row by row until they found their culprit. The mushrooms were down here, he felt certain of that in his gut. It was just a matter of finding where they grew.

Water splashed to their left, too far to see in the dim light, but Devin assumed it was the playful waterkin keeping an eye on their progress. Jacaranda kept alert, and was clearly more nervous than him about their search. It almost made Devin laugh. Was he so inured to the strange and bewildering that water beings playing in a hidden cavern filled with magic mushrooms barely gave him pause?

It took nearly five minutes to walk from one side of the cistern to the other, and they passed multiple side tunnels branching out for who knew what part of Londheim.

"Surely this cannot all be rainwater," Jacaranda said.

"Maybe, maybe not," Devin said. "How many secret little funnels throughout the city carry the water down here? And Londheim rarely floods no matter how hard it rains. Perhaps now we know why."

"Whoever built this system must have been brilliant."

"I'll agree with you on that."

Devin shifted their path so they continued following an outer wall, figuring they'd loop toward the center of the room. They slowly covered ground, the sound of water a babbling brook in their ears. Devin could imagine himself coming down here just to relax in the peaceful atmosphere, away from people and the noise, and instead embraced by cool blue light and the steady flow of water.

Neither Devin nor Jacaranda first spotted the house. Puffy had to hop twice atop the torch to get their attention and then guide them along by pointing the way. The house seemed to emerge from the darkness, a tall, square structure with four pillars as its cornerstones. From wall to ceiling, it appeared less built and more grown. Its color and texture were of deep brown mushrooms, and several types of fungi, notably little button mushrooms and the larger fieldcaps, sprouted like natural decorations. The roof was one enormous flat cap that sagged over the walls. The windows were oval gaps in the sides, with only the door appearing to be made of wood. Yellow light flickered through the windows, but something about its color was odd, convincing Devin that whatever cast it, it wasn't fire.

"How long do you think this home has been here?" Devin asked. This wasn't something built, but something grown. Like with much of the changes throughout Londheim, it felt less like it had been constructed upon the black water's arrival, and more like it had been revealed to the world.

"It looks old," Jacaranda said. "Very old."

"What do you think? Do we go up and knock?"

"I don't have any better ideas," Jacaranda said.

They both looked to Puffy. The firekin huddled a moment, then rapidly spelled out six letters.

BCRFUL.

"We will," Devin promised. He kept a hand on the hilt of his sheathed sword. Jacaranda hung back a step as he waded to the enormous door, lifted his hand to knock, and then found it swinging open. A slim form towered over him, its skin wrinkled and dark like a raisin, and its head capped akin to the roof of its home. Long arms reached down to its knees, its eyes shone blue, and though it had no mouth, it somehow spoke with a voice that was a calm, soothing whisper into his ears.

"Humans?"

"Yeah, humans," Devin said. "That's us."

Normally he prided himself on being more diplomatic than that, but it was hard to think straight with the fungal humanoid leaning over him. He couldn't shake the feeling that it was looking right through his skull and picking at bits of his mind.

"Come in."

The creature moved aside and gestured for them to enter. Devin swallowed down his unease and stepped inside, Jacaranda at his heels. Despite the fact that it was all crafted from living mushrooms, the interior was surprisingly similar to a human home. There was a table with quite literal toadstools to sit upon, shelves with small wood covers, even a strange circular bed in one corner. Most important of all was the far side wall, which opened up into a sort of garden. Among the various mushrooms was a gigantic cabbage-shaped collection so white it seemed to glow.

"Would you like tea?"

"I, uh, sure," Devin said. "My name is—"

"Devin Eveson, son of Domnall and Rhonda Eveson," the giant walking mushroom interrupted. "Jacaranda, forgotten daughter, and Crksslff, firekin ember of Fifissll and Chffswy. I am Trytis, a leccin grown of Gloam himself."

Trytis pulled a bowl of wood from one of his cupboards and dipped it into the water near its feet. Devin stood awkwardly by the door while Jacaranda moved to one of the stools and sat down.

"What do you mean, 'forgotten daughter'?" she asked.

"You have forgotten their names, so I cannot know them," it explained.

"You—you can read our minds?" Devin asked.

The leccin put the bowl to its hand. A slit opened across its wrist, and a dark powder trickled out of it into the bowl. Afterward it set the bowl into the center of its palm. Steam rose almost instantly as it began to boil, though from what heat, Devin could only guess.

"I do not read minds," Trytis said. Such a soft voice for a creature so large. "Your thoughts float. I taste them. Absorb them. I learn of who you are in all your contradictions and wonders."

It retrieved two cups from another shelf, emptied the bowl into them both, and then offered Devin and Jacaranda the steaming tea. Devin took his and smelled the contents. Mushroom tea, as he expected. Should he drink? Would it be considered rude not to? He had no idea. This was far from what he'd expected when traveling into the cistern. Jacaranda held hers to her lips and gently sipped at it.

"So how does one end up with a home down here?" Devin asked. He kept an eye on Jacaranda to see if she showed any ill effects from the tea. So far, nothing.

"This grand hall was built for the waterkin," Trytis said. "And they were not always alone, but time has not been kind to us. This was my home before your Goddesses forced us into slumber, and it is my home once more."

Still Jacaranda showed no symptoms as he watched her from the corner of his eye. He lifted the tea to his lips, then checked with Puffy. The firekin remained atop Jacaranda's torch, and it seemingly had no dire warnings for him, either. Deciding to the void with it, he took a sip of his tea. He expected a much stronger flavor, but it was just a hint of mushroom mixed with a bitter but pleasant combination of herbs. Devin stifled a chuckle. If Trytis set up shop in the market selling its tea, it'd be a wealthy leccin in no time.

"We should focus on the task at hand," Jacaranda said. She was frowning at him, he noticed, but he didn't know what for. "People are dying, so we cannot afford delays. Trytis, those mushrooms growing in that garden, they are chronimi, are they not?"

"They are," the leccin said. "Though I marvel that you know their name. Did Crksslff tell you of their nature?"

A tingly warmth ballooned in Devin's stomach. He set his cup down and wiped at some sweat building on his forehead.

"An onyx faery did, actually. Those chronimi are killing us up above, Trytis. We need you to destroy them."

The giant mushroom-person crossed its arms. Its blue eyes narrowed.

"And so humans request more death to enable their continued spread across the Cradle. Is that not always the way of things?"

"Our people are going mad," Jacaranda said with a hard edge in her voice. "They're murdering and eating each other. Call us monsters if you wish, but I think a small collection of mushrooms isn't worth that much death."

The warmth traveled up from Devin's stomach into his chest. The sweat had reached his neck now. Panic forced his hands to his weapons, but he found his fingers uncooperative. They slipped off the hilt of his sword, too weak to grasp it.

"No," Trytis said. Its calm whisper changed instantly, becoming louder, stronger. It should have put fear into his heart, but Devin found himself struggling to care. "Those mushrooms aren't worth the death. That is not why I grow them. Logarius asked for them, and so I have delivered. I will not destroy them, and nor will I let you destroy them. They stay."

Devin stood on wobbly legs. Concentrating was increasingly difficult.

"What—what did you do?" he asked.

Trytis grabbed him by the front of his coat and lifted him off his feet. Jacaranda remained seated, her eyes glassed over. If she cared that he was about to die, she didn't show it.

"I bear you no malice," it said. It pulled back a giant fist. "But I cannot have others come down here looking for the chronimi."

Puffy shot off the torch like a comet, the ball of flame aimed straight for Trytis's chest. The leccin caught it with its free fist and slammed the firekin straight down into the water. Steam exploded throughout the room, coupled with an agonizing *hiss*. Devin fought his lethargy, feeling a steady bubble of rage counteracting the warmth in his gut. He'd drunk only a sip, he told himself. Just a sip. He could fight this poison. He had to!

Bubbles formed a line to a wall, and then Puffy jumped out of the water. The firekin was dramatically smaller in size, and Devin's heart ached at its weak tremble.

"I find no joy in this," Trytis said. Again it pulled back its other fist.

Jacaranda moved with speed beyond what Devin's hazy mind could follow. He saw her swords cut across both the leccin's arms, then come together to slice a massive gash into its chest. Gray fluid poured out in a resemblance of blood. The leccin dropped Devin, and he landed in the water with a splash. Jacaranda and Trytis exchanged blows, her short swords cutting thinner and thinner grooves into its massive form as she was forced to duck and weave around its powerful punches.

"Just hold on," Devin said as he drew his pistol. It took all his concentration to pull the hammer back with his thumb. His other hand reached into the special bag of spellstones and drew one out at random. It was gold and black, its interior sparkling with trapped power. Devin slid it into the chamber and pulled the hammer all the way back. He had to use both hands, but he lifted it up and pointed in the general direction of the leccin.

"Jacaranda!" he screamed. "Move!"

She turned and dove face-first into the water beside Devin. He pulled the trigger. Down came the hammer, it pierced the spellstone in half, and then a blinding light filled the interior of the home, followed by such force that it flung the pistol from his hands. Lightning ripped through Trytis like a lance of the Goddesses themselves. When it passed through the leccin's back, it hit the wall and scattered in all directions. Devin screamed as zaps of it sparked through the water. His muscles seized. He feared his heart would explode.

At last it faded. A smoking husk was all that remained of Trytis, and it crumpled to the water. Devin reached for Jacaranda but she had no need of his help. She pushed herself up and glared in his direction.

"I thought you would use fire," she said. "Lightning? While we're submerged in water?"

Under normal circumstances that death glare would have shriveled his testicles, but the lingering effects of the mushroom tea left him grinning.

"Didn't have time to choose, Jac. I just grabbed one and pulled the trigger."

Jacaranda stood, pulled her hair from her face, and then grabbed Devin by an arm to help him up. While he still felt sluggish, she appeared otherwise unaffected.

"How are you unfazed?" he asked her. "You drank it before I did."

"I only pretended to drink the tea," she said. "I didn't think you'd be so stupid as to actually drink it yourself."

"You pretended too well." Devin sagged his weight upon her. "Guess that'll teach me to trust you."

"I'm the only reason you're alive. I think you can trust me just fine."

"Got me there."

The little spot of flame that was Puffy hopped atop the chronimi mushrooms and settled in. Fire steadily spread across the mushrooms' surface, feeding the firekin with its healthy blaze. Smoke built at the ceiling as Puffy grew in size. Jacaranda guided Devin to the door, and together they stepped out into the cistern's cool air.

Two waterkin waited with their bodies halfway out of the water. They stared with their beady black eyes. Ripples shook through them. Their anger was undeniable.

"This doesn't look good," Devin muttered.

"You have a bad habit of stating the obvious," Jacaranda said.

"Sorry, I'm used to having only myself as a conversation partner."

Puffy hopped out the door and onto Jacaranda's torch. It blazed with heat that defied its size. The waterkin backed away slowly, but they were not gone. The surge of water coming from all directions proved that.

"I don't know how well I can run," Devin said. "But I think it's time we damn well try."

Arm in arm, they waded through the water as fast as their legs could manage. Puffy spun in circles atop the torch, scanning all directions. The waterkin seemed fearful of its fire so far, but Devin didn't want to risk any harm befalling the little guy.

Thin sprays of mist washed over them from afar. Testing them. Taunting them.

"Almost there," Jacaranda said. Once they reached the tunnel, they'd be able to use the walkway instead of wading through the knee-high water.

The adrenaline in his veins and the pumping of his legs steadily worked away the hazy fog Trytis's tea had latched upon his brain. Devin watched for the waterkin, but they were distant blue glows just outside the light of Puffy's torch. Would they allow them to leave? He prayed so. There didn't seem much his sword could do against a being of water.

His feet touched dry stone. Devin let out a sigh.

"Praise Anwyn," he whispered.

They managed a dozen steps into the tunnel before they heard the roar. Jacaranda twisted to look over her shoulder, her eyes wide with fear.

"What is that?"

Devin recognized that sound. Twice he'd been summoned to help with reaping rituals in the floodlands east of the Septen River. It was the sound of overwhelming amounts of water.

"Run," he cried, and so they did.

It didn't matter.

A tremendous wave flowed from the cistern into the tunnel, six waterkin on its crest. They guided it like drivers of an oxen train, and when the surge of water slammed into them, it felt like it carried the same strength and power.

Devin twisted and fought, his strength useless in the current's power. It battered him back and forth, slamming him against the stone walls before pulling him away. Air was a luxury. Direction was meaningless. Every now and then he'd catch a glimpse of Jacaranda beside him, gulping in a greedy breath before ducking back below the surface. He saw not a sign of Puffy.

At last the wave lost its power. Devin and Jacaranda rolled to a stop upon the walkway, just out of reach of a ladder and potential salvation. They coughed and gagged as they freed up their water-logged lungs. The waterkin hopped up on land to surround them, taking on the forms of canines. They steadily closed the distance. Could they tear him apart? Or would they drown him on dry ground with their own bodies? There was another fire spellstone in his pouch. If he could reach it, and maybe shoot it near enough to the waterkin...

Shadow curled around Devin and Jacaranda like a morning fog. The waterkin recoiled. Boots landed between them, coupled with the rustle of cloth and metal. Black feathers floated from wings that enveloped them in safety. Devin could not see her face, but he knew her by her voice, which was deep, tired, and dangerous.

"Be gone from here," Evelyn ordered. "My sickles reap water as well as blood."

The waterkin hesitated. The strange woman pulled her two sickles from their hooks upon her belt. Their blades flickered with shimmering blue flame. Her point delivered, the waterkin jumped into the river between the walkways and fled back toward the cistern. Evelyn watched them go for a long moment, then rehooked her sickles and offered Devin a hand.

"What brings you down here?" he asked. "I assume it wasn't just to save our miserable lives."

"I suspect I came down for the same reason you did," Evelyn said. "I am not native to Londheim, and it took me time to discover there was a cistern built below its streets. Did you destroy the chronimi?"

"We did," Jacaranda said. She warily accepted Evelyn's offered hand. "And the leccin who grew them."

Evelyn sighed from a slender gap in her long black beak.

"A shame," she said. "There are few leccin left in this world, and most hide in caves far from your civilizations. I wish it had not been pulled into this dreadful conflict."

Jacaranda stepped closer to Devin, and he noticed she still held her weapons. Her eyes had not once left the avenria.

"Who are you?" Jacaranda asked. "*What* are you? Do you two know each other?"

"I am Evelyn, an old avenria come to Londheim under the delusion she might accomplish something good." She tipped her head. "I met Devin a few nights ago. He thought I needed saving from those suffering under the effects of the chronimi. He was wrong."

"What is an avenria? Shouldn't you be called . . . I don't know, a ravenkin?"

Evelyn let out a snort from the tiny nostrils atop her beak.

"Kin are so named for they were created in the image of what came before. I cannot be ravenkin for the ravens were created in *our* image."

Devin looked up and down the tunnel, and he tried not to let his worry reveal itself in his voice.

"Speaking of kin, have you seen Puffy? A little firekin, he was with us when the waterkin attacked."

"I see only you two, but do not fear. Firekin are notoriously hard to kill." She bowed low with a strange flourish of her left hand. "I must be going. Travel further onward to the tunnel's end so you'll exit in the area you call Tradeway."

"And why not here?" Jacaranda asked, gesturing to the ladder. The avenria looked away.

"Because that ladder leads to Low Dock, and you are not ready to witness the carnage unfolding."

"What?" Devin asked. "What are you talking about?"

Evelyn put a hand and foot on the ladder's rungs. Her wings sagged from a heavy burden.

"Low Dock is no longer a place for humans," she said. "The

Forgotten Children have claimed it. Logarius will find you, I promise."

"Then we fight him, whoever he is," Devin said.

Evelyn's laughter echoed down the ladder as she departed.

"The only ones who seek out Logarius are fools with a death wish. Flee, humans. As much as it burns your pride, accept that tonight belongs to the dragon-sired."

# CHAPTER 11

Come on, come on, come on!" Tesmarie called to Tommy. "This city isn't going to save itself!"

The young human huffed and puffed as he ran after her in his thick, cumbersome robes.

"You need to slow down," he said, gulping in breaths between every other word. "Book reading isn't...isn't the most energetic... of activities."

Tesmarie swallowed down another sigh. It was maddening how quickly humans moved through time while physically traveling at such slow speeds. It was like trying to hold a conversation with a snail riding a galloping horse. For not the first time she wondered if the humans' Goddesses had accidentally or intentionally built them with such a weird discordance.

"Not far, he's not far," she called to Tommy, hoping to encourage him. He really was trying his hardest, after all. "I can see his glow just around the corner."

Despite her best efforts, impatience set her wings to a flutter, and she zipped around the corner. What had once been a window shutter lay in broken chunks on the ground. She peered inside to find an older man sitting before a cold pantry busily stuffing cheese and salted ham slices into his mouth. He ate as if each bite might be his last, hardly chewing before gagging down the next bite. When he saw Tesmarie, he flashed her a food-filled grin.

"Faery?" he asked. "You're so little. Little faery. Little, little faery."

Tesmarie fought back a shiver. There was no doubt he was suffering from an adverse reaction to the chronimi. When night fell, she had cast a simple spell upon her eyes that allowed her to view the flow of time as a multicolored river. Most of the world flowed in a steady dark blue, but the man before her flickered like a firefly between a sickly violet and a vibrant orange. Tesmarie could soothe it like one smoothed wrinkles out of a bedsheet, but to do that she needed time and the ability to touch him. With the man's meal rapidly vanishing, she doubted she could do either safely, but that was where Tommy came in.

"Just a thin layer around his legs this time," she told Tommy as her friend more stumbled than ran around the corner. "It does no good saving them from the chronimi if they die of frostbite."

"I'm doing my best here," Tommy said. His hands touched at the wrist. He gulped. The old man had risen to his feet, and a flicker of orange time carried him from the pantry to the broken window.

"Am I one of them?" the man asked. Drool dripped down his chin. "The hungry ones?"

"Hopefully not for long," Tommy answered. "*Aethos glaeis influu.*"

Ice flowed from his hands in a steady stream that sounded like cracking glass. It struck the old man at the knees and then shifted lower, locking him in a prison of ice several feet thick. He shouted and clawed at it but could not gain an inch of give.

"Great job!" Tesmarie said. She zipped above the old man's head and then dove toward his back. She needed somewhere he couldn't reach, a tricky prospect given his flexibility. Her brief stop at the small of his back ended with her flying away from swiping fingers.

"More ice," she told Tommy. "Get his arms locked down!"

"You said not to give him frostbite!"

The old man blurred with a particularly brilliant red flare. The ice at his feet cracked.

"Now, Tommy!"

"All right, all right. Uh, *glaeis influu*."

A smaller stream of ice shot from his palm. It struck the man at the shoulder and then curled low, pinning his upper arm and elbow to his side.

"Let me go!" the old man cried. He screamed with pain as he violently fought against the ice, and she feared he might break his brittle bones trying to escape. "Let me go, I'm hungry, can't you see that? Evil, evil, you're evil!"

Tesmarie flew to the trapped side, cut a hole in his shirt with her moonlight blade so she could touch his skin, and then began channeling her magic. The name of her creator, Gloam, echoed through her mind as she closed her eyes. The flow of magic brightened, and she felt it across her hands like she would a physical river.

*You poor human*, she thought. Everything about it was wrong. Squirrelly, disjointed, full of little prickles and jumps. It was like putting her hands into a current of fleas. Thankfully the dragon Gloam had gifted her people with mastery over time. It would obey her demands. Her breath turned shallow as strength flowed out of her. The spikes of orange ceased. The sickly purple lost its reddish hue, returning to a deep, satisfying blue.

The moment Tesmarie removed her hands, the old man collapsed into an awkward bend at the waist. His eyes rolled back into his head. Sleep, deeper than most ever experienced in their lives, overcame him.

"Whew," Tesmarie said. She forced a chipper tone to hide her growing exhaustion. This was the ninth person they'd saved that night, and each one felt harder than the last. "I wish they wouldn't fight so much. We're trying to help!"

Tommy climbed through the broken window, and he frowned

upon examining his work. Once he was supporting the old man's weight properly, he pointed a finger at the ice. Little jets of fire spurted from his fingertip, weakening it, but much too slowly.

"Damn it, I made it too thick," he said.

Tesmarie clenched a fist to create her moonlight blade.

"Allow me."

She swirled around the ice dozens of times, her blade carving grooves and showering the ground with white flakes. It didn't take long before the ice started falling off in chunks, and after a minute, Tommy pulled him completely free.

"Is anyone else here?" he asked as he guided the old man to the floor.

"I'll check." Tesmarie flew to each of the home's rooms and then returned faster than Tommy could blink twice. "Nope, no one, which is good. We got here before he could hurt anyone."

The ice around the man's arm was much thinner than the rest, and after a bit of fire, Tommy cracked it free.

"There we go," Tommy said. "Hopefully he'll wake up no worse for wear."

They found a blanket and placed it over him for warmth. Tesmarie locked the door after Tommy's departure, then slipped out through a crack in the window. Hopefully that would keep the sleeping man safe from any other potential ravenous who stumbled along.

"Another one up ahead," Tesmarie said as she eyed the offending aura. The orange flicker shone through walls with ease, time caring not for physical barriers. "We need to hurry, though. He's clearly on the hunt."

She led the way, Tommy doing his best to keep up.

Bells sounded, seemingly from all directions. Tesmarie fought off a momentary wave of disorientation before continuing. She was never good with extremely loud noises, and those warning bells carried an unusually strong depth to them.

"What are they ringing for?" she asked Tommy.

"Warning people about the crazy time-unstuck people, I guess?"

They cut through a gap between two homes and emerged onto one of the larger streets in Low Dock that connected both main entrances into the district. Sure enough, the flickering human was there, but so were over a dozen city guards corralling her against a wall. She tried to break through their ring, but two men grabbed her by an arm and pinned her to the ground while a third prepared for a killing blow. Tesmarie quickly darted behind Tommy's back as her friend rushed toward the soldiers.

"Wait!" Tommy shouted. "I can cure her!"

The lead guard spun on him, his expression softening upon realizing Tommy was a member of the Wise.

"You can?" he asked.

"Well, sort of." Tommy kicked his foot. "I know someone who can."

Tesmarie appreciated his caution. Tommy wouldn't reveal her to the city guards, but instead leave it as her choice. Memories of her body slamming into the glass walls of a bottle trembled through her. The faery clenched her teeth and fought them away. No, she would help people. That was what she did, what she would always do!

"That's right," she said, flying around Tommy to position herself directly before the lead guard. "I can fix what's making them act so deranged."

It took the man a long moment to carefully respond.

"And you are?"

"Tesmarie! I'm an onyx faery of the woods. If you give me a bit of time, I can return that lady back to normal. Just a little bit of time, that's all, I promise."

Tesmarie wasn't sure if he'd accept or not, but to her relief, he nodded.

"So be it," he said. "Go do what you can, faery."

"I will!" she said with her most hopeful smile.

With the woman pinned, it was much easier to find a safe spot to touch her skin. Tesmarie landed atop her arm and began smoothing out the time flow. Exhaustion tugged at her eyelids, and she had to restart twice. Dragons above and below, why was this suddenly so hard? Was it the bells? Or had she pushed herself too hard? No matter. Sheer effort carried her along, and in but a moment the woman's body went limp as she collapsed into sleep.

"Good work, faery," said the lead guard. He turned to one of the guards. "Carry her out."

Another guard lifted her into his arms and trudged west. Tesmarie let out a long sigh, glad that was over with. Her wings felt heavy, and she found herself dipping lower and lower to the ground. Tommy saw and tapped his shoulder in offering. She was more than happy to settle there to gather her strength.

"What's with the bells?" Tommy asked. "Surely everyone already knows it's not safe to be out at night."

"It's not a warning," the lead guard said. "It's an order. Low Dock is to be evacuated completely by mayoral decree. Too many lives are at risk, and this is where things are at their worst."

"Why not order that *before* nightfall?" Tommy asked, bewildered.

"Do I look like the fucking Mayor? Everyone inside Low Dock needs to go. If you want to help, then come along. Otherwise, evacuate the district yourselves."

Tommy scratched his head and looked to Tesmarie.

"Well? Do you have a preference? You look beat. It's quite all right if you need to take a break."

She floated up and kissed the tip of his nose.

"We help," she said. "Nothing's changed."

But their immediate concerns did change. Instead of hunting for more crazed chronimi victims, the guards methodically banged on the doors of one home after another, ordering the inhabitants to evacuate.

"Bring only the clothes on your backs," they'd say to those who inquired. "You'll be returning soon."

They encountered several more time unstuck, the armed and armored guards easily wrestling them down so Tesmarie could work her magic. She tried to ignore the blood that often marred their teeth and hands. At least these people would not remember their actions the following day. Could they continue on if they knew what they'd done to strangers, friends, perhaps even loved ones?

The night wore on, and the streets of Low Dock filled with people making their way to the district exits. Guards knocked on the doors and gave no care to any excuses given by the denizens within.

"I don't care if you disagree," the lead guard shouted to a half-naked man standing in the doorway to his tiny home while holding a thick wooden club. "It isn't safe in this part of the city anymore."

"It's *safe* in here," the man with the club said. "It's out on those streets that's dangerous."

"The Mayor has ordered everyone to evacuate, and that means you."

"The Mayor don't give a shit about Low Dock, and I don't give a shit about the Mayor. Fuck off."

When he tried to shut the door, one of the guards jammed his sword in the way.

"Wrong answer."

Tesmarie choked down a little cry as they smashed the door in and forcibly dragged the man into the street. He fought, and his reward was a brutal hit to the temple with a sword hilt. High-pitched cries turned her attention deeper inside, to where two little boys and their mother shrieked with worry.

"You three, come on out," said the lead guard. "I don't want to get violent with youngsters, but I will if I must."

The injured man staggered to his feet.

"You wouldn't dare," he said.

Tesmarie clung to Tommy's hair from her perch on his shoulder.

"They wouldn't dare, would they?" she asked softly.

"Orders are orders," Tommy said, but she could tell he didn't believe a word of it.

The father charged the soldiers, and in return they beat him to the ground. Two others ushered the rest of the family out, showing not a care to their crying.

"Get out of Low Dock and don't come back until the bells are done," the lead guard ordered. He spat on the father's head, then glared at the mother. "Help him walk. He tripped coming out the door and hurt himself."

Tired and bleary-eyed neighbors emerged from their own homes. Had they witnessed what happened? Would they even care? Tesmarie felt sick. She'd accompanied Tommy into the night to help people. This wasn't helping people, this was hurting them!

"Surely it won't cause any harm if some people stay behind," she offered despite knowing her opinion would be unwanted.

"I'm saving his life," the guard said. "Spare me the guilt trip over a few bruises."

The evacuation continued, though far slower than the guards preferred. Tesmarie noticed little groups of people lingering behind. They huddled in alleys and street corners, as if waiting for the guards to leave so they might return home. She couldn't shake the entirely valid point Tommy had brought up. Why wait until nightfall? This wasn't safe. This wasn't orderly. The group of twelve soldiers wasn't nearly enough to escort all the people in the district to safety, either. Why come in such low numbers? She and Tommy certainly hadn't heard or seen of any other such groups.

At one home the guards kicked and slammed their shoulders upon a door but could not get it to budge.

"It's barred shut," one explained to their leader. "Can't get in, but we know there's a good number on the other side."

"I can help with that," Tommy offered. "So long as you don't mind me using a bit of magic."

The guards exchanged glances.

"If it gets the people to evacuate, then do so."

Tesmarie lingered behind as Tommy went with the guard to the home's front door. Another round of bell ringing washed over her. She winced at the noise. Where was it coming from? It didn't sound like any normal tower the humans built. Then again, she didn't remember hearing too many bells other than the hourly chimes from the few squat clock towers in the northern half of the city.

"Do the bells bother you?" the lead guard asked her. She nodded, having no real desire to talk to someone so callous toward the people he supposedly protected. "Try to pay them no mind. I know they are powerful, but it must be done to ensure this evacuation. Otherwise we will have a massacre."

A massacre? What did he mean? She stared at the lead guard as the bells seemed to vibrate her skeleton inside her skin. Something about him was off, but she couldn't place it. Was it his hair? No, it was...it was...

She couldn't decide what color his hair was. She squinted and rubbed her eyes. She couldn't picture him in her mind. What color was his hair? What shade his skin? When she reopened them, she realized he was staring at her. Answers to her questions came to her. He was dark skinned and with brown hair. His eyes were pale yellow with rounded irises. Pale yellow...and not human.

"Tommy?" she called as the guard flashed her a smile with teeth much too white and much too sharp.

"I wondered when you'd see through us," he said. "I expected better of you, Tesmarie. We Forgotten Children have been here for weeks, and yet you have never sought us out."

"Who—who are you?" she asked.

"Gerroth Crimshield." His illusionary appearance faded completely, revealing his red fur and white tail wrapped about his waist. Even his armor changed, turning to leather instead of steel. "Son of Aerreth. Surely you remember her, don't you?"

Aerreth, the phantom death of Nicus. Everyone knew her name, especially the humans . . . at least they did, before tales of her likely turned to fables and disbelieved horror stories.

"What is going on?" she asked. "Why are you evacuating the people?"

In answer he looked to the heavens. Tesmarie followed his gaze to the starlit sky, and the dozens of black shapes flying in scattered formations.

"They're early," Gerroth said. "I should have expected as such. Arondel has always been an impatient queen once a plan is set in motion."

The owls dove amid a nightmare chorus of shrieks. The men and women who had been foolish enough to linger outside soon found themselves easy prey for the winged beasts. Nowhere was safe this time, not even the homes, for they crashed through rooftops as if they were built of twigs and kindling. Screams pierced the night air. Tesmarie clutched her arms to her chest, paralyzed with confusion and horror.

"Holy shit, they're all over the place," Tommy shouted as he rushed to join them. "We need . . . to . . ." The thought trailed off as he saw Gerroth's true form. "Hey, uh, Tes? Who's your new friend?"

A spear butt connected with the back of his head, toppling him onto his stomach.

"Please, don't!" Tesmarie screamed. She repositioned into a

hover above Tommy's body with her moonlight blade shimmering in her clenched fist. "He's kind, and he's never harmed one of us, never, I swear. Don't hurt him, please!"

The rest of the foxkin, their disguises likewise abandoned, looked to their leader for an answer.

"If he is your friend, then we shall show him mercy," Gerroth said. "Let him up."

Tommy slowly rose to his feet, his hands extended with his palms outward. She worried at the unfocused haze that seemed to have settled over his eyes.

"She's right, I don't want to hurt anyone," he said. "Tell me what you want and I'll do it, I promise."

"We want you to leave," Gerroth said. "We have claimed this territory for the dragon-sired. Low Dock no longer exists. This is Belvua now, and if the Mayor wishes to avoid further bloodshed, he will acknowledge our autonomy."

"Belvua. Autonomy. Got it." Tommy took a careful step toward the ring of foxkin. They gave way, but their reluctance was obvious in their greedy eyes and bared fangs.

"Never forget this is your true home," Gerroth said, turning on Tesmarie. "But if you come back, make sure it's alone. Belvua is a place for the dragon-sired, and the dragon-sired alone. We will not repeat the kindness we have shown tonight."

Such kindness, indeed. The rest of the foxkin yipped as they rushed through the streets, ripping open doors and barking orders to those still foolish enough to remain. Those who refused were met with quick, brutal slaughter.

"Come on, Tommy," she said, pulling on his sleeve. "Let's get you home safe."

Low Dock was dead and gone, its bones being picked clean by the great flock of owls diving from the sky with eager talons. Only Belvua remained, and together Tesmarie and Tommy fled its blood-soaked streets.

# CHAPTER 12

A moment," Adria muttered as someone hammered on the other side of her bedroom door. She sat up and wiped the sleep from her eyes. Her dreams had been strange and oddly disconcerting. Something about a thin strand of silver hovering just out of reach, and her panicking at her inability to grab a hold of it. What she'd do with it, or why she needed it in the first place, were questions for the cosmos. Adria looked to the shining soul visible through the door and immediately sensed the fear and uncertainty leaking out of it. Deciding not to bother putting on anything over her shift, she crossed the small room and stepped out to address one of the volunteers who had pledged to her church after her procession of bread.

"Is something amiss?" she asked.

The volunteer, a young woman with hair down to her waist and a nervous tic to her face, did her best to explain.

"There's a lady, she says owls destroyed her home. She wants to stay here, which I told her was fine, but then she started talking about an evacuation, and the bells..."

"Bells?" Adria asked.

The volunteer tilted her head slightly.

"You don't hear the bells?"

In fact, she did not, but she decided it best not to answer in case it upset the volunteer further. Instead she asked for a moment, ducked back into her room, and changed into her dress. Bells? Evacuation? What insanity had befallen Londheim now? She ran her fingers through her hair to untangle it into something resembling order, then reached for her mask. Only when it was safely tied over her face did she exit.

"Take me to her."

Many of the thirty people or so still bunking in the church had stirred from their slumber and gathered around the woman. Adria groaned with annoyance. Whoever this woman was, she should have been separated to prevent a panic.

"We have to run, now, before we're trapped!" her frantic plea sounded over the growing din.

"Make way, please," Adria said, her tone harsher than her words. The pale woman was dressed in a bed robe and nothing else, lacking even shoes on her feet. Upon seeing Adria, she quickly dropped to her knees.

"Sisters' mercy, it's you. You'll keep us safe, won't you?"

Safe from what? The owls? Or had something else sparked such a panic?

"Tell me your name," she asked.

"Beverly."

"Then get back on your feet, Beverly, so we may talk plainly."

The trembling woman obeyed. Adria tried to focus on her face instead of her soul. She'd found her attention on the physical realm slipping lately. The soul didn't lie, not to her eyes. Beverly was frightened, all her willpower currently spent keeping her on the sane side of panic. Publicly explaining why might make things worse. That left a much more direct approach.

"I do not need words," Adria said. "Close your eyes, and when you sense my presence, let me in. Can you do that, Beverly?"

The woman nodded. Adria put her hands on either side of her face and pressed forehead to forehead. Their souls were so close, the white fire within them almost licking the other. Like knocking on a door, Adria gently requested entrance into that burning heart of memories and emotions. She could shatter her way in, deep down she knew that, but it felt much better to be allowed. After a momentary hesitance, Beverly relaxed, and Adria dipped inside her most recent memories.

A flock of owls dove from the sky, their talons ripping chunks off rooftops, their beaks snapping up men, women, and children on the run. Fires burned in the distance. For the first time, Adria heard the bells, deep, powerful, and certainly not from any bell tower in Londheim she knew of. From Beverly's eyes, Adria watched what appeared to be a foxlike human approach with a sword drawn.

"Start running," the foxkin said. "The owls like a bit of chase for their hunts."

Beverly did. She passed by others ordered from their homes. She ducked through alleys when spotting more of the foxkin. She screamed at the top of her lungs as an owl swooped up a man into its talons mere feet away from her. All the while, her path never changed. Low Dock's church was ahead. It'd be her safety. It'd be her salvation.

Adria broke her connection, grabbed a volunteer by the wrist, and pulled her close.

"Wake Sena," she said. "And do it quickly."

She turned her attention back to Beverly, who had a dazed look in her eyes, as if just waking from a dream.

"Sit down on a bench," Adria said. "Pray to the Sisters for strength and comfort, and tell no one of what you saw."

"As you wish, blessed one."

Adria pushed through the gathering crowd. Their questions bounced off her. If she surmised correctly, she didn't have time to answer them. The Mindkeeper exited her church and stood at the top of her steps. The dark corner of her city stretched out before her, and it was a battlefield. She put a hand to her throat. Her mind focused on the blazing soul within her own body, and silently she prayed the 34th of Lyra's Devotions.

*Lyra of the Beloved Sun, hear my prayer. Give me courage to speak your words, and a heart strong enough to believe them. In your bosom may we find the strength to face our troubled times, and may we lift our voices to the heavens and shout our glorious defiance.*

The prayer finished, she licked her dry lips and spoke. Her every word echoed for miles, calm as a meadow and loud as thunder. "All in Low Dock with nowhere else to go, come to my church. Here it is safe, and by my word, and until my death, so shall it stay."

The power in her throat faded. Adria touched her mask, feeling its cool porcelain beneath her fingers for comfort. She'd given her promise. It was time to fulfill it.

A few minutes later, the first family approached the church, the husband holding their son in his arms. Adria beckoned them inside. The shadows of owls blocked the stars, and she feared they'd descend upon the three before they arrived. None did. A small mercy in a night full of slaughter.

A lone man followed, and soon another thirty or so people in various states of disarray dashed to the church in search of safety. Adria watched for dangers, but so far none approached. Sena joined her side before long, perfectly dressed in her blinding white suit.

"What madness befalls our little corner of Londheim?" she asked.

"The magical creatures," Adria said. "They've decided to take Low Dock for themselves."

Sena looked to the growing fires, the owls diving upon random rooftops, and the armed foxkin marching their way.

"I hope they leave anything to take."

There were ten foxkin in the group that approached the church, plus a handful of gargoyles crawling on all fours, and they yipped and laughed as they neared. Adria spared a glance to the stars. Three owls circled like vultures in the sky above. Just wonderful.

"It seems some of you didn't get the message," one of the foxkin called out. "This is Belvua now. No humans allowed, and no exceptions for churches."

The owls were circling lower and lower, silent killers at the ready.

"I need you to pray the 59th with me," Adria whispered. "And even if I stop, you must continue. Will you?"

"Of course," Sena said. "These people are my children. Whatever it takes to protect them, I'll do it."

Adria took Sena's hands in hers and squeezed to show the appreciation her mask would not.

"We are not leaving," she shouted to all who'd listen. "Take your threats and your blasphemy and be gone."

The leader of the foxkin flashed a toothy grin.

"Truth be told, I was hoping you'd say that. We tried to make everyone leave without a fight. You want to be stubborn? Then be stubborn. Take her out, ladies."

Owls dove from the sky, but the words were already on Adria's and Sena's tongues.

*"Blessed Sisters, I seek your protection."*

Power exploded out from their physical bodies long before the prayer completed. It was the need, Adria was learning, that focused the prayer as much as the words itself. The first time it had been only for herself, but now with Sena's help, it was the entire church that sought the Sisters' protection, and protect it, they did. Brilliant flashes of light marked two owls striking invisible barriers, their hollow-boned bodies easily breaking against that immutable wall. Their death cries were pitiful shrieks added to a night already full of screams.

A foxkin pulled a crossbow off its back and aimed their way.

Sena repeated the prayer on a loop, and with her new soul-kissed eyes, Adria could see the steady strain it took on the Faithkeeper's soul. The arrow plinked off the barrier, as did two more that followed.

"Sena keeps us safe," Adria told them. "Which means I have all the freedom I need to burn your group to ash. Continue to threaten those I have sworn to protect and meet your death."

The lead foxkin muttered something she couldn't hear to the rest, then made an exaggerated bow.

"Not bad," he said. "We'll let Logarius be the one to deal with you."

"Logarius?" Adria asked.

She received no answer. The group spread out, forming a circle around the little church with their weapons sheathed. Adria put a hand on Sena's shoulder. She'd begun to sweat, and her every muscle was locked tight.

"Enough," she said. "You've done enough."

Sena's body immediately relaxed when she ceased the prayer. The barrier around the church ceased to be.

"Goddesses help me, that was exhausting," she said. "I'm not sure I can keep that going for more than a few minutes."

"May you have no need to do so again," Adria said. "They're waiting for Logarius, whoever that is."

"Let's pray it's someone willing to listen to reason."

The night wore on, and with it grew the number of creatures surrounding their church. Adria guessed at least sixty foxkin, another twenty gargoyles, and over a dozen circling owls. No more survivors came, and even if they did, they'd have no way to break through the dragon-sired circle. Despite their numbers, Adria still believed she could hold them off with her prayers.

And then the first of the shadow wings arrived.

They landed atop nearby buildings and perched much like the gargoyles, only they were twice their size. They wore hoods sewn into their pale gray shirts, and long pants the color of smoke. Black beaks peaked out from underneath their hoods, and they gazed upon the church with blue eyes that seemed to glow in the starlight. Enormous black-feathered wings stretched from their backs and wrapped about them like cloaks. Those feathers trailed into an ethereal mist by the time it reached their knees. From within that curling flow of feathers and shadow glinted steel daggers, swords, and sickles.

"What in Alma's name are those creatures?" Sena asked.

"I don't know," Adria said. "But they terrify me."

There was something about them, something that had Adria slipping deeper and deeper into the new sight granted to her by Viciss's machine. Souls...the winged creatures had a power over souls, but they were different than hers. Her soul was a shimmering light of memories and emotions. Their souls were black voids upon a colorful canvas. She was a painter wielding a brush. They were madmen holding a torch.

An hour before dawn their numbers were fully gathered, and a lone winged monster approached. He was dressed akin to the others but for a single deviation: Sewn across his breast was an enormous silver crest, a small, upward-pointed triangle enveloped by a circle. The inversion of the Keeping Church. The symbol of the Ravencallers.

"Greetings, keepers," this wearer of blasphemy said. His beak did not move to speak. It was as if his gravelly voice were ground out from stones lodged in his throat. "I am Logarius, leader of these Forgotten Children. Tonight has been a grand night. Low Dock is no more. We have Belvua now, a place to call our own. The only hiccup is this ugly little church at the end of a dark street run by two stubborn women refusing to evacuate like they should."

"That sounds like something to be proud of," Sena said. "Might I meet these two women?"

Logarius stepped closer.

"I do not fear your prayers, little keepers. Every mark of humanity within Belvua will be erased. To let a church to the Sisters remain? Unacceptable. Order those within to leave, or they shall become ash when we burn this church to the ground."

Adria put one hand to her breast and the other to touching the forehead of her mask. She felt power swelling within her skull, the fire of her soul, and she knew she would need its raw energy to survive what was to come.

"We are not leaving," she said. "Not under threat of violence, and not so you may insult the Sisters with your destruction. Have I made myself clear?"

Logarius seemed almost pleased with the response. He drew two long daggers with blades curving like waves upon the ocean and held them in hands covered with dark, scaled skin.

"Then I will kill you myself."

The rest of the Forgotten Children tensed, eager for blood. Adria drew in a deep breath as Sena began murmuring the 59th prayer to herself, preparing another shield about the church.

"You will *not!*"

That voice. She recognized that voice, but why would he be here now?

Janus leapt from the roof of the church and landed between the two parties with a flourish of his black coat. An ugly look of anger covered his normally handsome face. Instead of addressing Adria, he marched right up to Logarius and jammed his finger against the monster's chest.

"Adria Eveson shall not be harmed," he said. "Her church is off-limits, do you understand me, avenria?"

"You're an unwanted, unloved bastard creation," Logarius retorted. "Why should we not kill you where you stand?"

"Because this isn't my order," Janus practically growled. "*Viciss* demands her survival. You couldn't kill me if you tried, you petulant child. Do you think you can also kill the dragon?"

Logarius's hands clenched tightly around the hilts of his wicked-looking daggers.

"We emerge from our prison abandoned and alone, given no comfort or answers from our makers, and yet the Dragon of Change would protect this human keeper?" He turned away. "You merely offer proof of our abandonment. Do Viciss's bidding if you must, Janus. We will look after our own."

He motioned a signal with his hand, and just like that the circle of magical creatures receded into the rest of Low Dock. *Or Belvua*, Adria corrected in her mind, at least until human soldiers stormed into the district to take it back. Janus remained where he stood, and after a long, awkward silence, Sena brushed Adria's shoulder with her fingers.

"I'll be inside calming the others."

Adria waited until the door shut behind her to speak.

"Thank you for stopping them. If you hadn't..."

Janus whirled to face her.

"I'm not here to babysit you," he snapped. "And I do not enjoy spending my time ensuring your survival. Stay on your guard. Logarius has been warned, but that doesn't mean he'll obey."

"He would ignore the order of his maker?"

"How often do humans disobey the orders of their Goddesses?" He smirked. "Your eyes have opened to wisdom beyond your fellow humans, Adria, but they are still blind to a great many things. The Forgotten Children bear no love for Viciss, and I cannot blame them. Antagonize them at your own risk, and do not think your importance will keep you safe forever. At the end of the day, you are an object of our creation, and should you fail, well..."

He leapt back to the church's rooftop. His mocking smile didn't reach his eyes.

"We can always make another."

# CHAPTER 13

It would have been better if the men and women were shouting, Dierk decided as he stood in the corner of his family's grand
library. If they were shouting, then the fear and confusion wouldn't
seem so overwhelming. Twelve people surrounded a stained oak
table in the library's center. They were the usual suspects of his
father's meetings, men and women in charge of Londheim's fate.
Seated next to his father was Royal Overseer Albert Downing,
looking cool and collected as ever in his tan suit. Next to Albert
was the world-weary and heavily scarred city guard commander,
Nikos Flynn. General Kaelyn Rose stood instead of sitting, as if
she needed her legs stiff and her arms locked behind her to remain
calm. Vikar Caria paced nearby, though despite her constant
movements, she appeared the least worried of the bunch. Scattered
among the rest of the chairs were their retainers and assistants,
doing their best to keep their heads down and their presence out
of sight.

"What you're asking for is a military-style invasion," Nikos
argued. He jammed a finger at the elaborate map of Londheim
spread across the table. "Both entrances are completely blocked
with debris, and who knows what other barricades the monsters
have erected further inside Low Dock. My guards are trained
for keeping the peace, not marching in formations into enemy

territory. If you want to use them for such, at least give me time to train them accordingly."

General Kaelyn audibly scoffed. Her hair was an apt fiery red, and she kept it combed over the left half of her face to hide the ugly scar that had taken out her eye. Her lone good eye glared contempt in Nikos's direction.

"If we had time, we wouldn't need your guards," she said. "We could wait until my soldiers arrived from Wardhus or Stomme to do the job properly."

This was a sore fact the entire council lamented daily since the living mountain had crawled its way to Londheim's gates. Though Londheim was the official seat of power for West Orismund's Royal Overseer, the vast bulk of their soldiers were stationed at the easternmost cities of Wardhus and Stomme, protecting both the ports from piracy as well as managing the borders of East and South Orismund. Stomme in particular had suffered a brutal siege during the Three-Year Secession, and had it fallen, Dierk held no doubt it'd have been transferred into the Queen's direct control in East Orismund. There remained a fear, however poorly founded, that the Queen might still send her troops to finish the job.

"That's if the troops have remained loyal," Vikar Caria said. She was a beautiful woman unsuccessfully attempting to downplay that fact with her dark hair wrapped into a bun and her rich brown skin lacking any cosmetics. "Something we cannot know for certain in this new world that has emerged. At least we've received reports from Stomme now that trade's been reestablished. We're still completely in the dark about Wardhus."

"Distant cities are not our concern," Soren said, his father's commanding voice steering the conversation with ease. The entire morning had gone as such, wild speculation led back into organized discussion by Soren's hand. The takeover of Low Dock the previous night had unnerved them all a great deal. "Londheim is what we must focus on. Until matters change, we work with what we have, not complain about what we don't have."

"And what we have is a pile of flamestones below a hammer," Albert said. "We are one good strike from everything going up in flames. Our citizens are terrified. At any moment that mountain outside our walls could come alive, and we still have no contingency plan in place. Now magical creatures have assaulted one of our districts and claimed it as their own? This is unacceptable. If the people feel we've lost control, they'll hang us from city gates and replace us with those who *will* give them safety. Tell me, Nikos, would your guards do better attacking Low Dock, or attempting to hold off riots throughout every single district in Londheim?"

The men and women present were all keenly aware of what might happen if they lost the illusion of control. It amused Dierk knowing how fearful they truly were of the populace. It stripped their aura of prestige from them in his mind.

"I'm not saying we won't do it," Nikos conceded. "I'm just worried we'll be in over our heads."

"We're all in over our heads," Caria said in a smooth voice Dierk jealously coveted. The Vikar of the Dawn could make even the most terrifying pronouncement sound inviting. "What matters is we adapt and persevere. I have reliable reports that one of my Faithkeepers is trapped in her church within Low Dock, along with many other refugees. Their safety is my current priority. Have these creatures offered any demands? Perhaps we might reason with them before we commit to further violence."

Dierk snapped to attention. The church in Low Dock? That was where the heavenly Adria resided. She was trapped there, too?

"My offices have not received any such communication," Albert said. "As best we know, their only demand is for Low Dock to be theirs, and us to allow it."

"Not Low Dock," Dierk interjected. "Belvua. They want it called Belvua now."

All eyes turned his way. Dierk had entered the library without explicit permission, relying on his relationship to his father to avoid any questioning of his presence. Now that he'd broken his silence, several there seemed eager to see him gone.

"And how do you know that?" his father asked. His tone was far from inquisitive. It sounded more like when he'd caught Dierk masturbating in the hallway when he was nine.

"I just heard it is all," Dierk said, his gaze drifting to the floor. "Don't remember where. Everyone's gossiping, even the servants."

In truth, he'd heard it from Vaesalaum, but he wasn't going to say *that* to the ruling council of Londheim. An agonizing silence followed.

"Belvua," Kaelyn said. She looked ready to spit. "Those fuckers have already renamed it? This cannot stand. Albert, we have to assert control. I have one hundred well-trained soldiers at my disposal. I assure you, they will be more than enough to retake the district. Give me the order. Show humans and monsters alike that in our lands, our *human* lands, we shall have law and order."

Albert looked to Soren. As Mayor of Londheim, Soren directly controlled the city guard, and those guards vastly outnumbered the soldiers stationed for Albert's protection. Albert could use his elected authority to co-opt them from Soren, but doing so risked losing a key ally. Cooperation between Mayor and Royal Overseer was always important in Londheim. Making an enemy of Soren meant, even if they survived the current chaos, that Albert wouldn't stand a chance of reelection when it came about two years from next spring.

"The creatures have already set up barricades," Soren said. "A few more days won't matter. Let us set up our own barricades and then study our opponents. We've a hundred conflicting reports of what these 'fox people' can do, plus there's the owls, the rumored shadow people…" He shook his head. "While we learn and prepare, Kaelyn can run drills with the city guard. When we retake

*Low Dock*"—he paused and glanced at Dierk—"it must be on the first try. We've already received one black eye. We can't afford a second."

There was unanimous agreement on that final point. The men and women disbursed without any formalities. There was too much work to do. Dierk hung back in the corner. Even from there he could feel the cold fury rolling off his father. When the library was empty, Soren shut the door, turned the lock, and then gestured for Dierk to join him by the table. Walking to it felt like he was walking to his own execution.

"Yes, Father?" he asked.

In answer, Soren backhanded him across the mouth. A heavy ring split his lip, and blood spilled across his tongue as he cried out. Dierk immediately choked the cry down. Making any noise, or showing any weakness, would only antagonize his father further. As for Soren, he crossed his arms over his chest and stared. His face was calm. His voice didn't even sound angry.

"Who told you to speak up?"

"N-no one," Dierk said. "But I had relevant information, and I thought—"

"You thought?" His father's arm moved so fast it was a blur. A single hand flung him backward. He was so much bigger, so much stronger. Dierk sucked in a breath through his teeth as pain rolled up and down his back. He'd caught the edge of a bookshelf with his spine and it hurt like the void.

"I'm sorry," Dierk said. It was practically a reflex at this point.

"If you think you know something useful, you tell *me*," his father continued. "I will decide if it is useful, if I want it shared, and if it is even true in the fucking first place. Am I understood?"

Dierk bobbed his head up and down, his eyes not leaving the floor.

"I said, am I understood?"

"Yes."

Soren stepped back and smoothed out his suit, oblivious to the nisse that now floated angrily above his head. Long claws stretched from its paws, and they were black as the night itself. Dierk mentally begged for the creature to leave them be. He just wanted this confrontation over with.

"I allow you inside these meetings so you might learn," Soren said, as if all were well between them. "That means paying attention, listening to what others say, and thinking over the arguments as they are presented. You aren't here to influence these proceedings. One day perhaps, but not yet. Now can I rely on you to do that?"

"Yes."

"Good. Now who told you these monsters wanted Low Dock renamed Belvua?"

*Tell rotten human I am near,* Vaesalaum spoke into his mind. *My claws are ready. Is Dierk ready to stand tall, too?*

"I heard it this morning at the market," Dierk blurted out. "It was a group of merchants. I don't know who they were, but they sounded convinced."

The lie seemed to have worked.

"A rumor," Soren said. "Of course. I pray your rumor is true, otherwise you have humiliated me for nothing."

Dierk wiped more blood onto the back of his hand, then sucked on his lower lip. Staining his clothes might earn him another rebuke.

His father turned, and Dierk thought he would finally leave him be, but instead he went to a bookshelf, scanned a few titles, and returned holding a book finely bound in blue leather.

"Here." He handed the book over. "Read this, cover to cover. Then you can leave."

Dierk glanced at the title. *On Maintaining Proper Public Persona.*

"I will."

Soren straightened his suit. There was blood on his knuckles. He didn't notice.

"Good. Once you have, then maybe you'll understand why your outbursts and unpleasant habits reflect poorly on everything I worked so hard to accomplish."

The door to the library shut, and with his father finally gone, Dierk dropped to his knees and clutched his arms to his chest. A trio of sobs escaped his throat, each one quieter than the last. He didn't need to release much, just enough to restore order to his mind. Once finished, he grabbed a candle off the table and carried it with him to a table tucked between two bookshelves. He'd need to finish the book his father gave him quickly to have any time for himself today. There'd be no pretending or skipping. His father had a keen mind, and sometime in the next day or two he'd make a passing reference or pointed question involving a matter discussed within those pages. Failing to answer risked far a worse punishment than what he'd endured today.

*Dierk should not suffer for speaking truth. Father is a brute. Father should be punished.*

"This is his household to do as he pleases," Dierk muttered as he opened to the first page. "I shouldn't have interfered with his work."

The nisse floated above the candle. Disgust registered on its weird, childlike face.

*Is Dierk truly so weak? Is Dierk a beaten dog? Bite your master. Remember who is stronger.*

"I *know* who is stronger," Dierk snapped. "And I'm lucky he didn't break a bone. Never should have spoken up. Stupid of me, so stupid."

Vaesalaum lowered itself so it blocked the pages.

*Dierk thinks of himself in the past. Dierk is Ravencaller now. Bite. Back.*

Dierk tried to turn a page but couldn't. His hand was shaking too much. He thought of the rituals he knew, of the power he'd begun harvesting from souls after their body's destruction. To use that power against his father? It was...it was unthinkable. It was awful. It was...it was...

"You in there, kid?"

Dierk slammed the book shut and startled out of his chair.

"Yeah, I'm here."

The door opened, and in strutted Three-Fingers. He was a gigantic man who towered a good foot taller than Dierk. His chin and neck were covered with coarse brown hair, his nose was crooked, and his smile was missing teeth. His eyes, however, sparkled with intelligence whenever he spoke to Dierk of other cities, other wild lands, and of the magic long forgotten to the Keeping Church. True to his name, he had only three fingers on his right hand.

"Such a dumb nickname, really," Three-Fingers would often say when discussing his name. "Nothing's wrong with my left hand. Shouldn't I be called Eight-Fingers?" To which he'd laugh and pound back whatever cup of alcohol he was currently favoring that month. The servants of the mansion treated Dierk gingerly, like a stray animal brought in from the cold to be nursed back to health. Soren treated him like a fungal growth with the unfortunate sharing of a last name. Only Three-Fingers treated him like a friend.

"So what's your father got you doing in here?" Three-Fingers asked.

"Reading," Dierk said.

The mercenary sauntered over and grabbed the blue book off the table. One glance at the title was enough to make him roll his eyes.

"The three divine whores have better taste than your da," he said. "Is he trying to make you learn, or to make you take a nap?"

"It doesn't matter," Dierk said, snagging the book back. "Why are you here?"

"Because there's a party tonight, and I wanted to make sure you were invited."

Vaesalaum zipped closer to the mercenary, suddenly showing great interest. Dierk did his best to ignore it.

"I'm not much for parties," he said.

"I'm not talking about your da's parties, with tailored suits and pretty dresses. A real party. A Ravencaller party." Three-Fingers pulled out a tiny scrap of paper. An address was written on one side. The symbol of the Ravencallers, a circle swallowing a small, upturned triangle, was drawn on the other side. "Take this, and go where it says. Make sure you arrive before the reaping hour. That's when the fun starts."

Dierk stuffed the scrap of paper into his pocket and tried to hide his excitement. His heart pounded in his chest as he thought of what the meeting might entail.

"Will you be going?" he asked.

"Can't. I've been roped into helping Kaelyn train the local pissheads into a pretend army, so we'll be drilling long after dark. You'll have to have fun without me."

Three-Fingers bade him farewell and exited the library. Dierk pulled the piece of paper back out and stared at the address. It wasn't too far from Windswept District. He could get there and back in under an hour.

*Dierk should go,* Vaesalaum said as it bobbed up and down over the paper. *Dierk might learn of this city. Of its many secrets.*

"A Ravencaller party," Dierk whispered. "Do you know what one is like?"

*Vaesalaum knows. The students meet the teacher. The servants meet the master.*

"Teacher? Master? What do you mean?"

The nisse looped a circle around his head. A bright smile lit its
smooth face.

*The true Ravencallers. Dierk will meet the avenria. Dierk will meet*
*Logarius.*

Three-Fingers's role as leader of the Becher Estate's guards made
it an easy task to sneak out at night. All eyes turned the other way
when Dierk slipped through the gates, a hood pulled low over his
face and the invitation shoved deeply into his pocket. He rushed
through dark streets to the written address, expecting to find some
empty warehouse or abandoned home. Instead a well-lit mansion awaited him, with two men standing guard beneath the front
door's awning.

"I'm here for the party," Dierk said, practically flinging the
invitation at them when they ordered him to halt.

One of them glanced at the paper, then nodded.

"You're cutting it close," he said. "Hurry on in."

Dierk had spent his whole life in mansions like the one he
entered. Its ceilings were tall, its walls were covered with paintings
of long-dead artists, and it seemed every other room was for eating or lounging about. Who was the wealthy man or woman that
owned this home? he wondered. Surely they'd have met at one of
his father's many gatherings. He followed the noise of people talking to a cramped dining hall. Its long table was pushed to one side
to make room for the thirty men and women within. Dierk's heart
fluttered with excitement as many eyes turned his way.

They were...normal. No masks, no dark robes, no exotic tattoos. Other than the prominently displayed circle-and-triangle
pendants, the gathered crowd wouldn't have looked out of place in
his own mansion. By the void, he even recognized a few of them!

"I see we have a new member among us," an older woman said,

her face impossibly pale due to the powder covering it. "And so young!"

"Better we start them young," said the man beside her. "It's easier to learn the real truths when the falsehoods haven't had decades to settle."

"So how did you come upon our wisdom?" a tubby man asked, joining the other two so that Dierk felt surrounded and claustrophobic.

"A—a friend," he said. "He gave me the Book of Ravens."

"Well, you picked a fine time to join," the powder-faced woman said. "Tonight is special. Very special, indeed."

"So I gather," Dierk muttered. Why did people have to greet him? He just wanted to lurk in a corner somewhere and observe.

*So fearful of attention,* Vaesalaum whispered inside his mind. The nisse floated above the dining table and its scattered half-eaten plates of tarts and cakes, seemingly intrigued by their variety. *Dierk must learn confidence, or waste his power. A proud peasant may slay a fearful Goddess.*

Thankfully a sudden burst of clapping turned everyone's attention to the far side of the room, where a mustachioed man in a finely tailored burgundy suit had stepped up onto a chair.

"Thank you for coming to my home," he said. Dierk's mind scrambled to recognize him. A trader of some sort, he vaguely remembered, some well-off man from the east who'd traveled west with business in mind. "This is an exciting time for all of us. A momentous time. Many of you have waited years for such a privilege, and so I will not drag this out further. Please, dim the lamps. Candlelight will suffice."

Those near the lamps quickly turned their little handles to seal off the oil. The room darkened considerably. Long shadows stretched across their host's form, and suddenly his face seemed far more ominous.

"Excellent," he said. The air in the room had turned thick.

Many held their breath. "Fellow Ravencallers of Londheim, please bow in respect to our teacher and master, Truthsayer Logarius."

A shadow plummeted from the ceiling, uncurling to display wings that stretched nearly wall to wall. Even in the dark those black feathers were a stark contrast to all else. Logarius landed before them and stood, and he peered at them with his glowing blue eyes. Men and women gasped. His long beak and scaled hands added to his otherworldly nature. The farthest reaches of his wings shimmered away into a pitch-black smoke, yet it flowed to the ground in a manner eerily resembling water.

"Greetings, fellow Ravencallers," Logarius said. "I am an avenria, one of many that now call Londheim home. It strengthens my heart to see that even among the Goddesses' coddled race, there are those willing to walk the hard path to truth."

Immediately every Ravencaller dropped to one knee and bowed their head. Dierk scrambled to mimic their clearly rehearsed response.

"We walk the hard path," the crowd pronounced in unison.

"And make no mistake, it will be a hard path indeed," Logarius continued. His voice was hard and rolling, and it reminded him of his father. "I wish I could say otherwise, but our centuries of absence have only added to the difficulties we face. Hard times come. Bloody times are upon us. Have you the strength to face them?"

"United in faith, we are strong," spoke the crowd.

Logarius surveyed them as if they were his own children. Chills coursed up and down Dierk's spine. He felt an intense need for approval from those blue eyes. He wanted to grab the avenria by the hem of his pants and plead for a blessing. What wisdom did such an ancient creature possess? How great was its mastery over secrets and shadows?

"By now I am sure most of you have heard of our victory in claiming Belvua as our own. It is but a small step toward a greater future. Your Goddesses whispered lies of humanity's superiority. Your time of solitude at the top of creation was never true, never just, and never destined to last. A new order rises, and you shall be at the forefront of its creation! Equality among all creations. A shedding of morality built to cage your kind and justify the killing of ours. Are you willing to bleed for this, Ravencallers? Are you willing to break bones? To lift corpses to the sky?"

Somehow Dierk knew the correct response, and he spoke with a solemn heart and an earnest tongue.

"We are willing. We are ready."

Logarius folded his wings over his shoulders, hiding all below the neck in that roiling shadow.

"Then let us partake."

A naked man tumbled out from the darkness of Logarius's wings and lay still upon the floor. His hands and feet were bound behind his back, and a thick wad of cloth was tied across his mouth. The precautions seemed unnecessary, for the man offered no sign of resistance.

"Bring the ropes."

The men and women rose to their feet, eager to witness. Two rushed to the table and returned carrying ropes already tied with loops on one end. Logarius wrapped them about each wrist and then hovered into the air with a single beat of his wings. The avenria tied both ropes about the rafters, then floated down to slide each loop around the catatonic man's wrists. Gripping both ropes in his fists, he lifted the man into the air, then passed the ropes off to be tied down.

"The Goddesses blessed you with a soul," Logarius said as he drew one of his wickedly curved daggers. "But then they demanded you wield none of that power for yourselves. Elevated and then shackled. Blessed and then cursed. This is the way of the Three Sisters. I ask of you, recite the thirteenth chapter. Give voice to the truth!"

The thirteenth chapter...Dierk recognized that one. It was one of the very few curses he was frightened to attempt even with Vaesalaum's help. Like all of the Book of Ravens' chapters, it bore a single title: "Harvest."

The gathered Ravencallers lifted their arms. Their combined chant gave Dierk the courage to join them. Only Logarius stayed silent, an omission that would have given him more pause had the words to "Harvest" not swept him up in its cadence.

"Anwyn of the Moon, hear us! Our strength wanes. Our burdens bend our backs and twist our necks. Before us lies one who has walked their final steps, and whose body crumbles, and whose soul is unfit to return to your bosom. Harvest their passing so we may carry on."

One truth Dierk had never understood was why they pleaded to Anwyn when the entire purpose of the Book of the Ravens was to denounce the Goddesses' righteousness. Did this power sparking through his veins like fire belong to the Goddess of the Dusk? Or was this cry one of mockery? He didn't know, but it seemed knowing was not a requirement. The belief, the strength of purpose, was all that mattered.

The sky opened. A swirling flower of stars, its outer ring bearing hints of blue while the center pulsed a pale yellow, replaced roof and ceiling. Dierk gazed in wonder upon its majesty. Though it encompassed only a hundred feet from side to side, and it hovered not far above Logarius's fingertips, something about the image defied those simple definitions. It was larger than all the Cradle. It was farther away than the sun. To touch it, to hold it in his hands, would elevate him to a god.

The sacrifice's body withered beneath the starscape. Color drained from his skin. His head drooped and his tongue lolled out the side of his mouth. Silver light shone through his forehead, his soul already starting to break free of its mortal shell. Something about it was different than usual. It was larger, paler. Little wisps broke from the outer edges, becoming like smoke. The tendrils wafted toward the onlookers, and Dierk eagerly drank it in.

"Breathe deep," Logarius said. "Remember who you were meant to be."

A haze settled over his mind. Images and emotions danced about him, and he shared them with his fellow Ravencallers. This wasn't like when he stole memories with Vaesalaum's help. This was a communal sharing. Energy sparked through his limbs. His back straightened, and he stood taller. His thoughts might be a fog, but his body felt ready to climb a mountain. With each passing moment, the bound man's body aged and shriveled until he appeared a living skeleton wrapped in leathery flesh. As he weakened, so did they become stronger.

A long tendril rose from the soul into the starscape, a trail of smoke from a dwindling fire. Vaesalaum hovered in a tight circle above it, growing fat off the memories. Tears ran down Dierk's face. Such beauty. Such otherworldly wonder. When Logarius's dagger split the sacrifice's chest open, not a man or woman there noticed his scream, nor cared for the life taken. Only the avenria's words finally punctured Dierk's hazy mind, embedding a thorn of panic.

"I have chosen a task to prove your loyalty," Logarius said. "Deep in Belvua, a church for the Sisters remains a thorn in our sides, and it is helmed by a blasphemy in human form bearing the name Adria Eveson. Prepare your knives and ready your curses. Come three days, your faith turns to action. Three days, and we hang the Chainbreaker from the steeple of her own church. A proper death. A *Ravencaller* death."

# CHAPTER 14

Next to the Soulkeeper's Sanctuary and cordoned off from the courtyard of cherries by a tall wooden fence was the novice training yard. It was primarily used for those hoping to become Soulkeepers, so one side was covered with firing ranges while the other two-thirds was full of sparring rings, training dummies, and lifting weights carved from wood. Devin strode through the center pathway observing the frantic pace in which the novices trained, particularly the older groups a year or two away from graduating.

*They believe they'll be conscripted early,* Devin thought. *They might even be right.*

Vikar Forrest himself monitored the firing range. His neck bulged against the constraints of his suit. His hollering was audible all the way across the yard.

"Three steps, three goddess-damned steps, is that so hard? Take a firm grip on the handle, line up the sight, and then *squeeze* the trigger. Squeeze, not tug it like it's your own cock. The world's going to the void in a handbasket, do you think we can afford wasted flamestones when three steps is too-fucking-much for your sorry asses to remember?"

The unfortunate recipient of Forrest's ire had turned beet red from neck to forehead. Devin didn't envy him. Forrest hadn't been a Vikar yet when Devin went through his years of training under the giant man's tutelage. Undertaking the responsibilities of the entire Soulkeeper organization had mellowed the man out, something his current body of students would probably disbelieve. There was a fine line between a good teacher and an asshole, and Forrest had carved a canyon across that line and pissed in it.

"Is this what you summoned me for?" Devin asked as he joined them. "To watch you lose your temper at a few senior students?"

Forrest glanced over his shoulder. His mood did not improve upon seeing Devin. A bad sign.

"I want each of you to take five shots while I'm gone," Forrest said. "When I come back, you'll show me your sixth, and if it's not improved, you'll be running laps around the entire cathedral."

The young men and women bobbed heads, each eager to prove their worth, or at the least, avoid adding several miles of jogging to their daily schedule. Forrest gestured for Devin to follow him as they walked the grounds toward an empty corner of the yard.

"It's quite a story I'm hearing about your sister," he said. "Creating food from nothing? The farmers will be pitching fits from dawn to dusk. Thank the Sisters we're in the middle of a famine, or they'd be extra pissed."

"Yes, thank the Sisters," Devin said.

"Don't get smart with me. I get enough of that with those brats over there. They think we're desperate enough to promote them all no matter how bad they are at the job. A good number have a surprise coming their way at year's end. I'd rather the whole world end than give some unprepared pimple-popper the title of Soulkeeper."

They were far from the students, yet still Forrest lowered his voice and ran a hand through his long blond hair. Devin's stomach twisted. His Vikar was nervous. Under no circumstances could that be good.

"Look, I don't want to pry like this, but some accusations have reached my ears and I need to address them."

"By all means, let me hear them," Devin said. "I've nothing to hide."

Except he did have something to hide. Thankfully there was no reason to think Forrest would...

"Supposedly you're romantically involved with a soulless. One of Gerag's soulless, to be precise."

Devin used anger to hide the sudden swelling of fear throughout his entire body.

"Magical creatures have forcibly taken Low Dock and laid siege to my sister's church, and you want to waste my time with rumors about me having sex with a soulless? What kind of priority is that?"

"My Soulkeepers are *always* my priority," Forrest snapped. A bit of his anger returned, and he towered over Devin while jamming a finger into his breastbone. "And yes, I'd be disturbed if you were taking advantage of a soulless, something that's fucking illegal, Mister High-and-Mighty. Oh, and there's the whole matter of it being *Gerag's* soulless. In case you forgot, I relied pretty heavily on your word to issue his arrest in the first place. People whom I respect have heard these rumors about you, and they've suggested the reason you discovered Gerag's sex racket was because you yourself were a buyer."

Devin met his Vikar's gaze and refused to back down. If he broke now, if he gave even the slightest hint at the truths intermixed with the falsehoods, Jacaranda's life would be in danger.

"You know me, Forrest," he said. "You've traveled at my side. We've killed bandits together and suffered through a thunderstorm convinced a tornado would sweep us both into the sky. You know damn well I would never buy a soulless, I would never use one for sex, and the only reason I was involved with Gerag in the first place was because his camp was attacked by Janus."

"And what of the woman who disappeared? Gerag filed a complaint before his death that a soulless servant of his, Jacaranda, I believe, accompanied you to Oakenwall. That soulless died, according to your own report. Now I'm worried your report wasn't entirely truthful."

*Shit, shit, shit, shit.*

"Stop insulting me," Devin said. His voice was barely above a whisper, and he fought to keep it calm and measured. "Listen to what you're saying. I faked a soulless servant's death to keep her as my own sexual pet? This is horse shit, and you know it. What proof do any of these rumors have?"

Finally a crack in Forrest's confidence.

"None," the Vikar said. "So far."

"And you won't receive any."

"So you deny it?"

This was it. His last chance. He could come clean about what happened, and explain that Jacaranda had awakened. He'd still be at fault for certain things, particularly in hiding her awakening from the church, but it'd be better than being proven a liar. Normally hiding anything from his Vikar would have never crossed his mind, but Jacaranda...

He let out a low sigh. No. If Jacaranda wanted to make her presence known to the church, it would be her own decision, not his.

"Yes, I deny it. Every word."

Forrest looked to his little squad at the firing range. It was like he was embarrassed to even make eye contact.

"Good. I hope to Anwyn that's the last I hear of this, Devin. You're a good man, and a great Soulkeeper. I can't afford to lose you to something like that. You have plenty of coin, and a lot of night women to choose from. Stick to what's legal."

Devin swallowed down his indignation.

"Is that all you needed of me?" he asked.

"Yeah. That's all."

Devin bowed with a fist to his breast.

"Then excuse me, but I have more important matters to attend to."

Devin hung his belt by the door, and he spared a glance at the fireplace. Still empty, as best he could tell. Puffy had not returned since their trip into the cistern. He prayed the little firekin was safe.

"Hey, Devin," Tesmarie said, perking up from her padded shelf. "Is something wrong? You look...upset."

"It's fine." He set his sword and pistol on their hooks, then removed his coat. "Jac in her room?"

Tesmarie zipped over to him and yammered away a few inches from his ear.

"Yup-yup. We went to market for some milk, a book, and some bread, and you wouldn't believe how much the price of every-thing has gone up. I mean, I barely understood it, but Jacaranda did! And it's a lot! Anyway, we came home not long after, and she had her book to read, and I was tired, so I napped. I assume she's still in there, yes."

"Thanks." The little faery appeared hurt he was done talking to her so quickly. Devin quickly added an addendum. "I'm sorry, Tes, but this is urgent."

"Sure," Tesmarie said. She flew back to her shelf. "Of course. Big people stuff, right?"

"The biggest."

He knocked on the door to Jacaranda's room and then waited.

"Come in."

Over the past two weeks Jacaranda had worked to make the room more into her own. The curtains were blue instead of their original gray. Her growing collection of books was arranged upon a little shelf Tommy had brought her. Even the thick comforter on her bed was new, and of course, chosen by her. Jacaranda lay atop it, reading what appeared to be one of the penny pamphlets the newer presses cranked out by the dozens.

"I've a weakness for those myself," Devin said as he closed the door. "I used to take a few with me on lengthy trips prior to the black water arriving. Which is that one?"

"A story of some woman whose lovers are killed by a jealous ghost." She glanced at him and immediately sat up. "Devin, is something wrong?"

He sighed and rubbed his temples.

"Am I that obvious?"

"Sometimes you're easier to read than this book. Have a seat, and get whatever it is off your chest."

Devin sat at the edge of the bed. He found it hard to look at her. He didn't want to see the potential hurt in her eyes.

"I had a meeting with my Vikar," he said. "According to him, he's heard rumors that I am...romantically involved with one of Gerag's soulless."

"Rumors," she said, her entire body locking in place.

"Yeah, rumors. Pretty damn accurate ones, I'd say, given the circumstances."

"What did you do?"

He shook his head and chuckled.

"Denied them, of course. I'm not going to reveal you to my superiors, Jac. It's your life, and your decision, not mine."

Jacaranda put aside her book and slid across the sheets. He noticed her feet were bare, and her toenails painted a lovely lavender. Such a random detail, but it pulled his mind from the terrible ramifications of his news.

"No one could possibly know I'm here with you," she said. "The only person who did was Tye the White, and you killed him."

"Tye saw us together, yes," Devin said. "But he might have told someone before I got to him."

Jacaranda hissed air through her teeth.

"The only person he would have reason to tell was Gerag," she said. "This confirms it. The bastard is alive out there, and he's try-ing to strike at us from wherever he hides."

"If so, he picked a clever way to go about it. If we are discovered together, it could cost me my station as a Soulkeeper, perhaps even worse. I've lied to my Vikar and denied what is technically an ille-gal act. I just want to help, but I'm terrified everything I do is only going to make things worse."

Jacaranda placed her hand over his.

"Devin?" she asked. "You don't...regret me, do you?"

"Regret you?"

She suddenly had trouble looking his way.

"Regret meeting me. Helping me. I dragged you into Gerag's mess, and nearly killed you in the process. I've put your position in jeopardy. Now you're lying to your Vikar, and..."

Her voice trailed off. Was she waiting for his answer? Or did she just not have the ability to say what else she feared? Her face was tilted to the side, half-hidden by her short red hair. He took her chin in his fingertips and gently turned her gaze toward him. Her violet eyes met his. She was so beautiful. Devin wanted to give her the world, to promise her an eternity of love and safety, but that was beyond him. All he could offer was himself, and so he did.

"Never," he said. "Not once, and I never will."

He'd not kissed her since that moment Tye temporarily stole her life away. He'd almost been afraid to do so again, as if it might resummon the trauma and pain. He leaned closer, hesitant, wait-ing. She tilted her head, and that inch of movement toward him was enough. His lips met hers with a soft, gentle kiss. Her breath was a trembling whisper as she closed her eyes. He felt her hands grasp his shirt. It felt like an eternity, but at last he pulled away.

"I'm sorry," he said, "if that was too bold a—"

Her lips banished his question. Her body pressed against his, and he closed his eyes and allowed himself to enjoy it. Her presence, her need, the hint of rose perfume he never knew she purchased and the softness of her hair running through his fingers, it was a pure joy he'd not experienced since the passing of his wife. Though he expected that kiss to be the last, she followed it up with another, and another, steadily melting his insides.

He started to position them more comfortably but she hardened herself against any such movement. When he brushed her cheek with his thumb, she gently set it back at his side. When he leaned forward to kiss her more deeply, she pushed him to a distance. Every kiss was hers, begun when she leaned in, and ended when she needed to draw a breath through her flushed lips.

*She needs to be in charge*, he realized. *She needs to feel in control.*

After all she'd endured at Gerag's hand, he could only sympathize and do his best to accommodate.

After a minute a change passed through her. Her aggression increased. Her tongue flicked across his. Her mouth drew kisses as if he were a river and she dying of thirst. She shifted from her seat atop the bed so she could face him better. One hand held him close. The other traced lines across his neck, hooked underneath his shirt to brush across his chest and stomach, and then, after a hesitation, slipped into his trousers.

Devin gasped in surprise. His breathing turned rapid as she took him into her hand and started slowly stroking up and down. Her head shifted lower, her lips latching on to the side of his neck. Her teeth nipped at his skin, only to then immediately caress it with her tongue. Devin fought to contain a steady stream of moans. It was ridiculous to try to be quiet in his own home, but Tesmarie lingered just outside the door, and he didn't want her to overhear.

"I take it you like this?" Jacaranda whispered when she pulled back a moment. She emphasized the question with a flex of her fingers around his now fully erect shaft. He grinned at her like an idiot.

"Maybe."

"Maybe?" She kissed his lips, then his cheek, then nibbled on his earlobe. "Maybe, he says?"

Her motions were growing faster, matching the pounding of his blood in his veins. Her thumb began to slide across the very tip of his cock, which grew slicker with his excitement and all the more sensitive. A shudder ran through his abdomen, and his thoughts blurred from pleasure and anticipation.

"Just like that," he whispered. "Keep going. Just like that."

The difference was stark and immediate. Her thumb pulled away. Her arm continued its up and down motion, but the energy, the fiendish joy of it, was gone. She kissed his neck, but only a few more times, as if out of obligation. Devin put his arms around her, and as she leaned closer to him, he pulled her hand from his trousers.

"It's all right," he said. "I'll be fine. You don't have to."

She was crying. Not much, and not loudly, but tears fell upon his shirt. After a moment she managed to offer an explanation.

"Gerag, he...he'd say things to me when we...and that was... that was one of them. Just like that. Just like...*fuck*."

Shudders overwhelmed her upper body, and Devin clung to her and prayed for the Goddesses to shower Jacaranda with their compassion and mercy. He held her and prayed as his own blood cooled and his breathing returned to normal.

"I need to know," she said. "I need to know he's dead. Until I know for sure, until I *know*, he'll haunt me. He won't stop haunting me. I'm so sorry, Devin. I thought I could, but I—"

"Shhh," he whispered. "You have nothing to apologize for."

She looked up at him with hair sticking to her face from her tears.

"I don't believe you."

He laughed and kissed her forehead.

"Too bad," he said. "We'll figure this out together, all right? You and me against the world if we must."

"Thank you," she said. Her head settled across his chest.

The chaotic surge of emotions seemed to have drained most of her energy. He stayed there, lying together on the sheets and offering whatever comfort his closeness could bring her until sleep came and took her away. All the while, his thoughts turned dark, and Gerag's smug, sickening face floated red in a sea of black.

*The Goddesses show you mercy if I find you*, he thought. *Because I sure as death won't.*

# CHAPTER 15

There's no way we're getting through all that," Dierk whispered to his nisse as they joined the outer ring of gawkers at the western gate to Low Dock. Tables, chairs, and crates were piled on one another to form a ten-foot barricade. Even if he could climb over it, the city guards stationed on the human side would prove troublesome. Even if he could order them to let him through (doubtful), the incident would certainly reach back to his father.

*Dierk should return home,* Vaesalaum said. Displeasure caked its every word. *Dierk should not interfere with events set in motion.*

"I can't do that." He flinched when a man nearby glanced at him curiously. Dierk wore the same clothes as his last trip to Low Dock, and he couldn't afford to let anyone know he traveled inside the newly crowned Belvua. His father's status in the city balanced on a knife point. Having a troublesome son meeting with the monsters could be all the difference between maintaining control and losing his head to riots.

*Vaesalaum reads all pages. Think the words if Dierk is fearful of unwanted ears hearing his spoken words.*

Dierk retreated away from the crowd, happy to melt into the flow of tired traffic on Tradeway. He knew he could converse with the nisse mentally, but he'd avoided doing so lately. It just felt...uncomfortable.

"Adria's in trouble," he continued once certain no one would overhear. "I have to warn her."

*This is a mistake.*

"Too bad. I'm still doing it. At least, I will once I find a way inside."

From what he'd heard, the northern entrance was similarly blocked, as well as the eastern side leading to the actual riverside docks. Belvua was completely isolated, no one going in, and no one going out.

*Logarius wants the Chainbreaker dead*, Vaesalaum interrupted. *Logarius oversteps bounds. We walk dangerous paths, Dierk. Tread carefully.*

Relief swept through him upon realizing the nisse was willing to help him.

"Thank you," he said. "So how do we get inside?"

The creature sighed.

*Walls do not mean much to our kind. I shall show one way, if Dierk insists.*

Dierk climbed the ladder out of the cistern with his wet pant legs clinging to his skin. He'd been surprised by the scope and size of its construction when Vaesalaum led him to a seemingly forgotten entrance shed. That surprise paled in comparison to the shock that overcame him upon entering Belvua, for it was as if he had stepped into another world.

"How have they changed so much in so short a time?" he asked in awe. "These buildings look like they'd have taken years to build."

*They did. This part of Londheim always belonged to dragon-sired. Human eyes were blinded. Fooled with illusions. Foxkin are tearing down illusions now they have taken over.*

Low Dock had always seemed squat and small compared to the

rest of Londheim, lacking the winding streets, towers, and inter-locking architecture of other districts. No longer. Buildings rose for multiple stories on either side of him, and their frames curled toward the road in a mockery of gravity. Some bore colorful win-dows showcasing dozens of creatures for which Dierk had no name. Others were wrapped in red and purple vines that cared not for the coming winter. Dierk walked past one three-story build-ing that more resembled an enormous tree than a house, for rough bark protected its sides.

"All this, hidden by illusions?" Dierk whispered. "That's—that's not possible."

A long stretch of buildings to his left were composed solely of sticks and grass, yet they looked no less sturdy than the surround-ing spires that were as tall as any other building in Londheim. Birds flocked around the highest spires, many of which bore open-air rooms.

*Has Dierk learned so little since my arrival? Human minds are frail. Human minds are brittle. So stiff. So unyielding. Sisters did you disservice limiting your faith and wonder.*

The mystery and wonder of Belvua threatened to overwhelm Dierk completely. So many varying styles, yet they came together beautifully. Little rivers of clear water flowed through grooves in the street no wider than his thumb, spiraling together and apart before branching off toward more vine-covered homes that grew out of the ground. One home looked built of crystal atop a walled pond, and a dozen little humanoid creatures of pure water danced and dove off its many edges. Those waterfalls eventually spilled out into more little grooves that cut through the stone and van-ished into homes. Fresh drinking water, he realized. Right inside people's homes.

*Belvua was a wonder of its time*, Vaesalaum said. *Humans built their stone homes in pale re-creations. Jealous. Petty. They could never succeed without help, which they refused.*

Despite all the changes, the roads still flowed in the same over-all directions as they had before. Dierk forced his feet to move. As much as he wanted to explore every nook and cranny, he had come for a reason. He passed homes, shops, even ornate fences surrounding staircases leading down into what he presumed were underground constructions. The only mark against their beauty was the silence and emptiness. What he would give to have walked these streets when they were filled with magical creatures, or dragon-sired as Vaesalaum called them.

"Why would the Sisters banish such wonders from us?" Dierk asked.

*There is no greater question in all the Cradle.*

The only time Dierk was stopped was at a narrow intersection. Two foxkin dressed in colorful silks stepped out from a doorway, each brandishing a long, skinny blade. Vaesalaum quickly inter-cepted their advance.

*Dierk is friend,* the nisse said. *Dierk is Ravencaller.*

Dierk tried not to gawk at the two, who turned his way, seem-ingly unconvinced by Vaesalaum's vouch.

"What are you doing here, boy?" one asked. "Your cult isn't expected yet. And why do you have a nisse accompanying you?"

*Vaesalaum is teaching Dierk,* it responded before he might answer. *Dierk is son of Mayor. Much could be gained by a leader open to our plight.*

The foxkin exchanged glances.

"Try to keep it quick," the same one said. "We'll leave you be, but I make no promises that others will feel the same way, espe-cially Logarius."

"Of course," Dierk said, hurrying on toward his destination. "Thank you, thank you both."

Compared to the wonders of its surroundings, Adria's church was plain and small. Dierk spotted a lone person watching them from a rooftop nearby, a raven-faced man that he presumed to be an avenria like Logarius. The avenria did not intervene, so Dierk pretended not to have seen him. He climbed the steps and, after a moment to gather his nerves, knocked on the door. After a minute it opened, and out stepped the woman of his dreams.

"Hurry inside," she said. "I don't know how long you'll be safe."

Instead Dierk shook his head and refused.

"I'm not some refugee seeking shelter," he said. "I...um, I've come to talk to you, actually."

He could not view her face through her mask, but he did see the way her body tensed with caution. She slowly shut the church door behind her and stood upon the top step with her arms crossed.

"All right," she said. "I'm here. Let us talk, starting with who you are."

Sweat trickled down Dierk's neck and back. An immense need to confess everything constricted his throat. He wanted to tell her how he'd dreamt of her performing miracles every night since meeting her. He wanted to tell her how her dark hair was like obsidian silk, her pale skin was as pure as the stars, and that no one else in all the Cradle felt such intense love as he did toward her.

"Can you take off your mask?" he asked instead.

"It stays on," she said. "Answer my question."

"My name, I'm, my name is Dierk. Dierk Becher. I'm the son of the Mayor."

Adria tilted her head to the side. Not much, just a slight shift, but the movement burned into his memory, just like everything else she did.

"That's...unexpected," she said. "Why are you here? For that matter, *how* are you here? Low Dock's streets are certainly not safe."

Dierk looked behind him, but just like the last time he spoke with Adria, Vaesalaum had abandoned him to his own devices. Shit. He was hoping to reveal the nisse's presence to help explain why he could see the shining light of her soul, and why he was so perfect a complement to her divine radiance.

"I had help," he said. "It doesn't matter. I've come to warn you. You're in danger."

"Look around, Dierk. Of course I'm in danger."

Fuck, shit, damn it, why was he being so stupid? It was so hard to think in her presence. Her beauty shriveled him like a grape beneath a hot summer sun. His heart pounded in his chest like a startled rabbit.

"You don't understand," he said. "There's a meeting, with Ravencallers, and the leader of the dragon-sired. They're going to attack in three days. They—they—they want to hang you from your church's steeple."

That got her attention. Her spine straightened, and he heard her suck in a harsh breath.

"Is that so? Let them try. I hold no fear of blasphemers and midnight creatures."

Of course she wasn't scared, she was a living wonder, but he had to convince her. That's why he was here!

"They're strong," he insisted. "Maybe not as strong as you, but they're so many, and they'll have help. I came here to tell you that you have to leave now, while you still can!"

"And abandon the people under my care?"

Dierk hadn't thought of that. Of course she wouldn't turn tail and run when she had others to protect.

"Bring them with you," he said lamely, realizing even as the words left his lips how ridiculous an idea it was. If the people inside could safely leave, they most certainly would have already.

"Leaving now only endangers them further," she said. "My church has been granted sanctuary, and until they revoke it, I will trust these creatures to hold to their word."

She'd been granted sanctuary? By whom? Certainly not Logarius, for he wanted her dead. Dierk didn't understand, and as he pondered, he realized she was still staring at him in silence.

"Are—are you sure you won't remove your mask?" he blurted

out. It felt a cruel fate to have his heart so smitten and yet that Mindkeeper mask deny him the sight of her cheeks, her nose, her precious lips.

"Yes, I am sure," she said. "Thank you for your warning. It was very brave of you to come here to share that. Now please forgive me, but I have faithful to attend."

Panic gave him the strength his adoration could not. He grabbed her hand in his. Her fingers were cold, her bones thinner than he'd anticipated. His mind wanted to linger on every single facet of her touch, but he could not. There was no time.

"Listen, I've told my father about the attack," he said. "Soldiers and guards will invade Belvua to protect you. Is your church truly worth this bloodshed?"

Her eyes would not leave his. They were unflinching, as powerful and vibrant as the gleaming diamond of her soul. At last he let go. The moment their fingers lost contact, he felt an immense desire fill his chest to confess.

*I can see your soul*, he'd tell her. *No one else in Londheim understands how special you are like I do. Your power, my station, our shared wisdom . . . we're perfect for one another, Adria! Can't you see that? Perfect!*

"Sorry," he said instead. "I needed you to listen."

"It's fine," she said. Still her eyes held him prisoner. "And yes, this church, and the tired and frightened people within, are absolutely worth dying for. Tell your father we await his soldiers to come escort these people safely out of Low Dock."

"Belvua," Dierk said. "Low Dock, it's called Belvua now."

"Let the monsters rename it whatever they want," Adria said. "This is Low Dock, this church is my home, and I'll turn to ash anyone who tries to tear either from my arms."

Goddesses and dragons help him, she was so proud, so strong. He felt like a blade of grass before a towering oak. No wonder Vaesalaum had fled. Dierk doubted the nisse could withstand such a stare.

"I understand," Dierk said. "Stay safe, all right? You, you're powerful. I know that, I can see that. I'm sorry I doubted you."

Dierk fled Belvua for home, his heart aflutter. Despite his awkwardness, she'd seen his bravery and thanked him for it. One memory in particular played on a permanent loop in his mind, exciting his every nerve and flooding blood down into his crotch.

When he'd taken her hand in his, their fingers intertwining, their bare skin touching bare skin, she had not pulled away.

# CHAPTER 16

Tommy focused his attention on the flamestone as the words of an ice spell echoed in his mind. It lay on the floor in the corner of the Wise tower's cellar, while he himself knelt behind an overturned table for cover. He might have made seven such flamestones successfully, but he was messing with time-delayed arcane magic. Precaution, however flimsy, felt wise.

"*Aethos glaeis,*" he whispered. "*Chyron tryga. Aethos Chyron, Chyron Aethos . . .*"

He felt the magic pour out of him, followed by a visual representation in the form of blue mist that crossed the dark cellar and swirled into the flamestone, darkening it the same color. Tommy wiped sweat off his brow and sighed with relief.

"One of these days I'm going to blow myself up doing this," he said. "I hope you appreciate these, Devin."

Footsteps alerted him to Malik's arrival. He turned to see his friend holding back a nervous frown.

"We finally received word from the Overseer," Malik said. "They're ready to meet Cannac."

"That's great," Tommy said. He pocketed his newly created spellstone, which was icy to the touch. "Why such a glum face?"

"Has it occurred to you that this meeting may go poorly?"

Tommy smacked Malik across the shoulder as he passed him up the stairs.

"You should try optimism sometime. It adds years to your life."

"Or ends it prematurely."

Cannac sat by the fireplace, slowly leafing through one of many books the two had brought the dyrandar to occupy his time. That the fireplace was twice the size it'd been a week ago should have bothered Tommy, but such things were commonplace to him now. Living with Cannac was like living inside a hazy dream.

"You need not tell me," Cannac said as he closed his book. "It is written as plain on your faces as it is on your minds. I am to meet with someone important?"

"Royal Overseer Downing, to be precise," Malik said.

"The man you say rules the western lands of Orismund?"

"Not exactly."

Tommy cinched his thick robe tighter about himself and grabbed a scarf and hat to help with the cold.

"Let's explain on the way," he said. "But first...um. Maybe we should do something about...you."

Cannac sighed with a great huff through his wide deer nose.

"You wish me to disguise myself on the journey there."

Tommy doubted any thought-reading powers were needed for that observation.

"Yeah," he said. "Exactly that. Can you?"

Cannac stood to his full height. Light flickered in the center of his horns.

"I come to establish peace and friendship," he said. "It is poor diplomacy that begins with deception and my existence hidden from the populace."

"It's for your own safety, really," Malik insisted. "After what's happened in Low Dock, I'm not sure how the general populace will react to seeing you in the streets."

"I am not afraid of the populace," the dyrandar said as his form began to shrink. "I am afraid of the rulers who guide and enable their fear."

The three exited the tower, with Cannac appearing nothing more than a tall man in a shoddy, old-fashioned suit.

"This overseer, what is he like?" Cannac asked as they walked.

"I've spoken with him a few times," Malik said. "He is a good man, a rarity for a person in power. I believe he will hear whatever you wish to say with an open mind."

"And how did a good man come to such a position of power?"

"Election," Tommy said. "The result of the bicentennial celebration of West Orismund's founding. Normally the Royal Overseer was just that, someone stationed in Londheim to oversee the west chosen by the Queen. A push for increased autonomy, coupled with a series of scandals by overseers who were, well, just terrible, led to an election every ten years. So long as you own land, you get to have your say."

"And what of those without land bearing their name?"

"Those without an ownership of land do not deserve a say in what is done with that land," Malik said. "It is a simple concept, really."

"Perhaps, if the decisions of the Royal Overseer affect only those who own land. Is that the case?"

Malik looked upset and quickly deflected. "Is it any worse than a King chosen by birth?" he argued. "At least we have a say in who holds power over us, unlike those who live in East Orismund. Yes, the Queen or King can overrule our Overseer, but given the significant distance between us, it happens rarely."

Tommy winced. Malik was criticizing the concept of royalty to an actual king.

"I wonder what your Goddesses think of this form of rule," Cannac said, thankfully showing no sign of insult. "They wished for the Keeping Church to lord over your race in both heart and law."

"Trust me," Malik said. "The church still holds plenty sway on both."

Highlighting that point, the three passed through a gate into Church District, where the overseer's mansion was also located. It was a far cry from the majestic castle in Oris, or even the sprawling estate located in Nicus for South Orismund's Royal Overseer, but that was just fine with Tommy. He personally preferred those who ruled in power to do so in the most modest of environs.

Soldiers stood guard at the tall iron fence that surrounded the mansion. A massive oval stretch of grass surrounding the building marked it as unique in a city largely built of stone towers and cobbled roads. A line of traders, farmers, bankers, guild leaders, and the like stretched over one hundred people long from the mansion's front doors, across the stone path, and out the opened gate. The three joined the tail end, much to Tommy's disapproval.

"We were explicitly invited," he grumbled as he stomped back and forth, trying to generate some acceptable measure of warmth underneath his robe. "That we should wait in line feels preposterous."

A husband and wife wrapped in thick furs ahead of them glanced over their shoulders, the woman looking amused, the man annoyed.

"You've not experienced much of Londheim politics," Malik said, lowering his voice. "Half the people ahead of us have also been invited."

"And yet I am a king," Cannac said. "Are they?"

"They don't know that."

The dyrandar shook his head, quickly fed up with the glacial progress of the line.

"Then I will show them."

His disguise fell away from his body like a discarded cloth, revealing his enormous frame, his curled antlers, and his long, flowing robes. The first to notice was the couple ahead of them, who caught sight of Cannac from the corner of their eye, turned, and screamed.

"Oh no," Tommy said, and he hunched his head and shoulders and wished to disappear. Soldiers came running by the dozens, shouting a confusing mix of orders. Cannac remained perfectly still, waiting patiently for those in line to scatter and the soldiers to fully surround them with weapons drawn. The armed men looked like children compared to his enormous frame.

"I am King Cannac of the dyrandar," he said. His voice traveled like an avalanche. "Your Royal Overseer has invited me, and I come to speak matters of peace. Will you take me to him?"

Several soldiers shared glances, and one in charge shouted repeatedly for all three to lie upon the ground. Cannac instead crossed his arms and waited. Tommy wished he could be so calm. He was half convinced he was about to die upon the blade of some frightened and confused soldier. Before the situation could escalate further, an older man came running out the front doors of the mansion, his white hair blowing in the wind and his arms flapping up and down like he were attempting to become airborne.

"Weapons down, all of you, weapons down! He is our guest!"

"Thank the Sisters," Malik muttered. "Someone with a head on their shoulders."

The man may have looked old, but he moved with the energy of a spry youth as he pushed soldiers aside to greet Cannac.

"Hello," he said, first offering his hand in greeting and then changing his mind to bow instead. "I am Scotti Tharsus, Albert's advisor."

"Albert Downing, the Royal Overseer?" Cannac asked.

"Yes, that Albert. Might you please follow me? We've been watching for your arrival, and we did not expect you'd look, uh, how you looked when you first arrived."

"It is no matter. Lead the way, Advisor. We have much to discuss."

Scotti straightened the jacket of his suit and wiped a hand through his hair, accomplishing nothing. He turned his attention momentarily to Malik and Tommy.

"And you two, please come as well," he said. "An opinion from Londheim's Wise would be much appreciated."

The mansion was divided into two wings. The left wing was where servants worked and Albert's family lived, and it housed the bedrooms, kitchens, and servant quarters. The right wing was dedicated to politics. Scotti led them through multiple lounging rooms, and when Tommy glanced through open doorways, he saw tables full of documents, fireplaces surrounded by chairs, and bookshelves stacked with yellowing paper filed away with care that made Malik look sloppy.

They also passed dozens of men and women waiting their turn to speak with the Royal Overseer. Tommy did his best not to laugh at their bug-eyed stares.

There seemed nothing special about the final lounge they entered other than that Albert Downing stood waiting by its fireplace, his hands crossed behind his back and his tan suit freshly pressed. Two soldiers stood by the door, loaded rifles in hand. Three others waited along with Albert. One was a dark-haired man with a jaw strong enough to rival Malik's, his apparent son sitting beside him on the couch. On the other couch, Tommy recognized the overseer's cousin, Jarel, looking as annoying and bothered as ever.

"Royal Overseer, Mayor," Scotti said, splitting his attention between Albert and the man on the couch, "May I present King Cannac, the ruler of the dyrandar."

"The dyrandar?" asked Mayor Soren. "Who are they? Creatures like you, or is it a kingdom we must now acknowledge?"

A look of annoyance flashed over Albert's face toward Soren, clearly unhappy that he'd been denied speaking first. Tommy quickly found a wall to support with his back, glad to be away from the conversation. The others were much too focused on Cannac to notice him.

"The dyrandar are my people," Cannac said. "Beloved firstborn of the dragon, Gloam. I would speak on important matters, if you would deign to listen."

"We have much to discuss, indeed," Albert said. "Perhaps you might start with an explanation as to what happened in the Low Dock district, or what your kind are now calling Belvua."

Cannac's ears lowered, a trait Tommy had learned meant the dyrandar was upset.

"And what might I offer that you do not already know?"

"A list of demands might be a good start," Soren said. "So far we're yet to receive any."

"Demands." Cannac crossed his arms. His entire demeanor hardened. "You think I speak for the dragon-sired who attacked your city?"

"Is that not what you're here for?" Albert asked.

The dyrandar stood to his full height. His antlers scraped the ceiling.

"I am King of my people, and I speak for a growing coalition. The dyrandar, the lapinkin, the viridi, and the winged all accept my representation. We seek the peaceful creation of nations, Overseer. I have no interest in an insignificant portion of this city. The Forgotten Children are their own beast, and they neither accept my rule nor listen to my wisdom. Do not put their sins against you upon my head."

All humans there, even Tommy, trembled at the sudden force of his voice.

"I told you, that's what he showed me," Jarel piped up for the first time when the silence dragged uncomfortably. "They're building an army. I bet Low Dock is just the beginning."

"That's not true," Tommy interjected. "Cannac, he's good, he's kind, he's—"

"Enough." The dyrandar held a hand before Tommy, silencing him. Golden light grew between his antlers. "I am tired of being interrupted, and tired of others interrupting the Royal Overseer. Let us truly speak."

The gold light washed over the entire room like a sunset. The two soldiers lifted their rifles, but they suddenly seemed confused as to how to use them. Tommy tried to speak, but his tongue felt made of lead.

Another wave of gold and the walls of the room fell away, revealing an expansive darkness stretching to infinity. Cannac and Albert stood in its focal point, and their thoughts washed over Tommy clear as day.

*Do you think there is no disagreement among our kind?* Cannac asked. *Do you think we are of one mind, and of one voice, upon waking into this changed world? You understand the complicated nature of humanity, yet think of all dragon-sired as simple as ants?*

*Please, do not misunderstand,* Albert responded. He seemed almost surprised by his own words. *I am frightened, as are our people. You raise an army outside Londheim while others like you have brought an army within. We do not know your factions, your groups, or your disagreements. We only know that we feel attacked, and I am desperately hoping you will help remove our confusion before more people die.*

Even Tommy knew such honesty during a negotiation was terrible strategy. He had a feeling that Albert's inner thoughts were spilling out regardless of whether or not he wished them to do so.

*I can only speak for whom I represent,* Cannac replied. *And our desire is for humanity to relinquish claims on all lands west of Londheim and north of the river you call the Triona. Respect our border, and we shall respect yours. Together, I hope to build a lasting peace.*

Albert's face paled.

*All lands west of... that is insane. I could never convince anyone to accept such conditions. Not even if I wanted to.*

The darkness faded. The golden light vanished. Tommy startled as if waking from a dream. Nothing appeared out of the ordinary, other than the presence of the towering dyrandar in an otherwise lavish and human surrounding. Everyone there seemed upset by such a revelation but for the Mayor's son, who seemed enthralled by the dyrandar's display.

"My terms are not negotiable," Cannac said. "All that is west of Londheim is ours. That was the agreement we reached before your Goddesses forced us into slumber, and it is the agreement we expect you to honor. Break it, and there will be blood."

"Are you threatening us?" Albert asked quietly.

"It is not a threat," the dyrandar said. "It is a statement of fact."

Another long, awkward silence.

"Very well," Albert said. He straightened his coat and gestured toward the door. "Please, return to the Wise tower. I must discuss these terms with my friends and advisors. Do not expect a decision anytime soon."

"He'll keep staying with us?" Tommy asked. "I thought he would move in here with you."

"I cannot have a King of...foreign entities staying in my home when that King is capable of reading minds," Albert said. "I mean no offense, but doing so would be unacceptably reckless."

"I understand," Cannac said, though his tone certainly implied he did not like it. "Then let us go while you discuss."

The three made for the door, but a quick command from Albert changed that.

"You two, stay."

They exchanged glances. Cannac dipped his head to the both of them.

"I shall wait for you," he said. "And if it makes you feel better, I shall wait in a form that will allow us a quiet, uneventful return to your tower."

He left the room, accompanied by the advisor, Scotti. Soren called for something stiff to drink, and servants from outside the room seemed to magically appear carrying a variety of options on a silver tray. Tommy shifted his weight awkwardly from one foot to the other as he waited for Malik to talk for the both of them.

"My cousin told me some very interesting stories when he was setting up this meeting," Albert said. He leaned against the fireplace and crossed his arms. "Stories involving you, Tomas, casting spells from your fingertips."

Tommy felt his neck and face starting to blush.

"I, um, did he now?" he said.

"Indeed. And I would like to know if he is lying through his teeth."

"He might pretend that he can't," Jarel muttered. "But I *am* telling the truth, Uncle. Why would I lie? A thought-reading mandeer just left the room, yet you wonder at spellcasting humans?"

"I know little about whatever a dyrandar is," Albert said. "But I know much about humans, and what they can and cannot do. I am eager to discover if my understanding is faulty."

Tommy glanced to Malik. They'd discussed several times how and when they'd reveal their magical abilities. Was it finally time to get on with it?

"Go on, Tommy," he said. "It'll be all right, I promise."

"All right, everyone," Tommy said. He cracked his knuckles. "Just...don't judge me too harshly if I screw something up. I'm still learning."

After having shown so many different people his abilities, Tommy had learned a bit or two on how they might react. The flashier spells worked best, so he went with his tried-and-true bolt of flame. A whip of his wrist, a quick mutter of the words *parvos fulgur*, and a ball of fire shot from his fingertips and struck the interior wall of the fireplace. The little ball detonated in a plume, its flames safely contained within the stone.

Albert's clapping broke the ensuing silence.

"Wonderful," he said. "Absolutely wonderful. Malik, are you capable of the same?"

"Sort of," Malik said. "Though my specialization falls similar to what Cannac is capable of."

The Royal Overseer looked like he was barely listening. His smile stretched ear to ear.

"Then the both of you shall join tonight's raid. Your abilities may well be the tipping point between victory and defeat."

"Raid?" Tommy asked. "What raid? I don't understand."

"The raid on Low Dock," Soren chipped in. He swirled the ice in his drink and stared at Tommy, his expression unreadable. "We're going to drive every last one of those monsters out."

The warm glow of having impressed men of such high station rapidly turned to fearful ice inside Tommy's chest.

"What? But I don't..."

Malik's hand closed about Tommy's wrist and squeezed so hard he feared it might bruise. Tommy slammed his mouth shut.

"We are happy to lend our aid wherever necessary," Malik said. "Do you mind if we leave now so we might prepare?"

"Of course," Albert said. "Scotti will inform you of the time and place. And say nothing to Cannac about this, nor give him any reason to think something is amiss. I believe him when he says he is uninvolved with matters in Low Dock, but that doesn't mean he will *stay* uninvolved if he discovers our plans."

"Completely reasonable," Malik said. "I bid you good day, Royal Overseer, Mayor."

Tommy followed his superior out the door and down the hall. The moment they were alone, he tugged on Malik's sleeve to turn him about.

"Why did you agree?" he asked. "That's—that's not what I want to do at all! Actually the opposite! I get so nervous during combat, you can ask Devin, we once faced a single giant owl and I failed so badly that I nearly—"

"Tommy, listen to me," Malik interrupted. He dropped his voice to a whisper and leaned in close. "Their minds were already made up before Cannac ever walked through the door. We don't have a choice, not if we want to keep our heads. Please, will you trust me on this?"

Tommy wanted to argue, to insist that reason could still win out, but in the end he succumbed to the wisdom of his superior.

"Yes," he said. "I'll trust you."

"Good." Malik clapped him on the shoulder. "Then steel yourself for the troubles ahead. Tonight is going to be extra ugly."

# CHAPTER 17

Evelyn halted before a dark stone tower tucked into a quiet corner of Belvua. A shudder trickled down her neck and fluttered out through her wings.

"Home," she whispered, as if the word were magic and could make it so.

She yanked the ugly wooden door open. A modification by the human inhabitants, though she knew she should count herself lucky the building still stood after their long imprisonment. Her fingers closed around the hilt of her left sickle, Whisper, and pulled it free of its belt hook. Three quick slashes broke the door's hinges and sent it toppling to the ground. Satisfied, she rehooked the sickle and entered her abandoned home.

The circular stone tower had originally been divided in half by a wall, and she saw the humans had broken a doorway through. The floors were spotted with dusty rugs, the walls were covered with painted plaster, and the windows had been built over with wood shutters. It was all...human. Evelyn spread her wings. That the first floor would be reclaimed was not a surprise, but what of the second? Stubborn hope sparked in her breast. There had been no ladder or stairs to reach it, for this was an avenria home.

A single leap catapulted her to the ceiling and beyond. Her wings touched the stone and spread like black water, her feathers dissolving into star-filled magic to grant her passage. She emerged onto the second floor like a rising phantom. Her wings became feathers once more, and she landed upon solid stone. Evelyn gazed upon the room, her breath immediately taken away.

Home. Yes, this was most definitely home. The walls were clean gray stone. The floor was a soft carpet of dark feathers plucked from the corpses of their family's ancestors. A circular straw-stuffed mattress positioned inside a wood half-sphere, the avenria equivalent of a bed, occupied the room's center. Two large dressers were stacked against one wall. An ornately carved crib was tucked into the corner, and her eyes teared up at the sight of it. There wasn't even a layer of dust upon its polished surface.

"Trapped in time along with us," she whispered. She removed a glove and slowly felt the cradle's surface with her dark, scaly fingers. Her claws clacked against the wood bars. A thousand memories crossed over her like a wave, and it took all her willpower to fight off sobbing.

There was no door to the other room, for there was no need of it. Evelyn wrapped her wings about herself and walked straight through the stone. Her vision turned to star-filled darkness for but a moment as her wings gave her passage. This was her room, the smaller bed in the center *her* bed, the dresser in the corner *her* dresser, the painting along the wall *her* painting.

It had taken her three years to finish the painting thanks to her obsession over detail. An orange sun set over the homes of Londheim. Several little avenria children played in the street with foxkin and lapinkin of similar age. Evelyn herself sat upon a stool, her hood pulled back from her head. Her feathers were dull compared to the vibrant shine of her children. Her hands, which were in mid-clap, showed little gray spots of discoloration, and its scales were rougher, the claws longer and sharper, than the silky smooth, clawless hands of her grandchildren. Even her beak looked cracked

and weathered compared to theirs, a fact her oldest son had protested against.

"You exaggerate your flaws," he'd said. "It's not true to life."

"I paint myself how I feel," she'd responded. "And right now I
feel very, very old."

Evelyn's feet rooted in place as she observed the painting. Tears
trickled down the sides of her beak as she soaked in every single
face. Her cruel mind declared their fates.

*Died in battle. Died of a diseased wound. Murdered. Taken, presumed
murdered.*

Yes, she felt old, and though her body had not changed a bit
during the Sisters' banishment, every one of the approximately
eight hundred years that had passed weighed down on her like
stone feathers strapped to her wings. She'd spilled so much blood
with her two sickles, Whisper and Song, fighting against the ravenous swarm of humanity. And now she awakened to find it had
all been for naught. Humanity had won.

Of the dozen avenria she'd painted in the picture, only two still
lived, having survived the wars against humanity prior to the Sisters banishing them into centuries of sleep beneath the dirt. She
was one, her oldest son the other.

"Come out, Logarius," she told the silence. "I know you're
here."

Shadows pooled along the floor, and from within them rose
her son. He shook out his wings and dipped his head in a mocking bow.

"I figured it was only a matter of time before you returned
here," he said.

Evelyn fought to keep a sharp edge from her voice. Logarius
had never responded well to her parental scolding.

"You've been waiting for me?" she asked.

"I told the foxkin to keep an eye out for you, yes," he said. "And

I have ever since the waterkin informed me of your arrival in Londheim. You helped put an end to the chronimi plague. Why is that?"

"No one deserved such a punishment," she said. "Not even the humans. What you did was cruel and reckless."

Logarius took a step back. When he spoke, he sounded truthfully hurt.

"Cruel? Reckless? I am yet to take a pittance of the lives that you claimed with Whisper-Song's blades. Why do you berate me so? Why do you not join us in defending Belvua?"

"Because of how you're doing it," she said. "Claiming the Book of Ravens as your own. Using it to wield angry, misguided humans as a weapon. You abuse your authority. You insult our very purpose."

"Our *purpose?*" Logarius seethed. "You'd have us go back to slavering over those pitiful creatures? We owe humanity nothing."

"We owe them our very existence."

"Yet without the humans' cruelty, you'd still be a grandmother. Perhaps a compromise then. We kill the humans down to the same numbers that we ourselves remain. Would that suffice?"

Evelyn recognized his bloodlust, his smug detestation, and his stubborn pride. It reminded her so much of herself when she was his age.

"Do whatever it is you wish," she said. "Lead these Forgotten Children, as you call them, into a war you cannot win. I am here solely to slay the men and women who have declared themselves Ravencallers."

"You know I cannot allow that. They are of use to me."

Her hands drifted to the hilts of her sickles, an act that did not go unnoticed.

"You would fight me?" Logarius asked. "Fight your own feathers and blood?"

"I have seen what my legacy has become," Evelyn said. "I will not indulge it further. The Cradle belongs to humanity. Accept that, and we might still craft a peaceful future."

Logarius drew his long, curved daggers from his belt.

"I don't want a peaceful future," he said. "I want Whisper-Song. They belong in the hands of the clan leader, a role you are not worthy to hold. Stop this posturing and pretended moral superiority and maybe we can be a family again. Give them to me, or I shall take them by force."

"Do you think you can?" Evelyn asked. She pulled her sickles free of their hooks and lowered into a combat stance. "You forget who trained you to use those blades."

"I will never forget," Logarius said. His wings closed tightly about himself. "But that proud, vicious avenria is gone. What I see before me is an old woman too tired and stubborn to defend her people in this hostile world."

It was Logarius who attacked first. Evelyn should have expected it. Between the two, she had always been the more sentimental one. His two daggers curled in from either side, aiming for her shoulders—nonlethal targets. A little chirp of laughter died in her throat as she fell backward. Perhaps she wasn't the sentimental one after all. She should have hit the wall, but her wings turned to shadow, and she passed right on through to the other bedroom.

Logarius followed soon after, but he had to wrap his wings about himself first, allowing her to steal the initiative. She spun in a tight circle, Whisper slicing upward starting at Logarius's ankle, Song echoing behind it with a cut that would carve out half of Logarius's waist. The hit would be lethal, but she both trusted her son to properly block as well as understood that fighting at a limited intensity would only guarantee her loss.

Sickles met daggers, their steel scraping against one another as each jockeyed for positioning. Logarius's elbow clipped her beak, her knee caught his side, and then they broke apart with a flash of sparks as their weapons danced. She had the better angle, which forced Logarius to leap toward the wall, kick off it, and vanish into the ceiling. Evelyn lunged after him, her wings curling above her head to grant her passage to the tower's third floor. When she emerged, her son was ready, and he struck the top of her head with the hilts of his daggers.

"Damn it," she swore as she staggered away. Logarius stalked her, his daggers twirling in his gloved hands. They stood in what had been a gathering place for eating and storytelling.

"You can't win this fight," Logarius said. "Surely you understand that."

He thrust for her rib cage. She rolled over the table, knocking red-wax candles to the floor, and stumbled back to her feet. An armoire halted her momentum. Dishes clattered and broke inside. Logarius hopped atop the table, and she was reminded of when he'd done the same as a small child. Back then he'd laughed when she yelled at him to get off for the hundredth time. He was not laughing now.

"Don't you understand?" she told him as he prepared a leaping attack. "I've made all the mistakes you're about to make. I've fought this war. I've buried the bodies. I've cried over the dead. The only thing awaiting you is misery, my son, and I want to spare you that pain."

"I will suffer any misery if it grants a home for my children," he said. "I thought you felt the same. I was wrong. Deep down, you were always just a bitter, angry coward."

He lunged. Her anger gave her strength where her old limbs could not. Would he mock her entire brutal legacy? She'd given everything for him. She'd slaughtered human men, women, and children. Hundreds of souls had returned to their Goddesses because of Whisper-Song's blades. How dare he? How *dare* he?

Evelyn stood strong against his attack, her sickles expertly parrying away his thrusts. Her son positioned his knee to strike her abdomen upon landing, but she adjusted with the tiniest movements, deflecting the force away. He landed awkwardly, his daggers pushed out of position. Evelyn rammed the long hard edge of her beak into his temple, and as he stumbled, she kicked him for separation.

Finally she had her opening, and she swung her two sickles in a high, powerful arc. Their blades flared with blue light. In an age past, firekin had blessed the weapons with their magic, granting their edges a searing heat when called upon. She could cut through stone like butter, and even the steel of her son's daggers would crumble and crack against their power. It was why Whisper-Song was given only to the clan leader of the avenria, and why Logarius sought them so desperately.

Blocking would be disastrous so Logarius took the best option available. He dashed toward her, not away, his body shifting sideways and his wings turning fully to shadow so that Whisper and Song slashed harmlessly through them. Damn it! She was getting too old, too slow! His leg swept underneath her, and she toppled to the floor with a painful jarring of her back and shoulders.

Logarius dove atop her with his daggers leading. Evelyn crossed her arms. Her wings flared outward so wide they reached wall to wall. She fell through one floor, then another. Logarius followed, the sharp points of his daggers pulled back mere inches behind his curled wings. Instead of falling through the third floor, she solidified them back into feathers. Air blasted out of her lungs from the hard landing, but she needed that sudden, awful halt to her momentum. It was the only way to catch her son by surprise.

Closing in on her much faster than he'd anticipated, he rotated briefly so that his heels would strike first. She rolled, not bothering to attack. The heel of his boot hit stone, the angle awkward and wrong. Logarius shrieked as he collapsed to his knees. Evelyn ducked her head and leapt blind through the outer wall, caught the windowsill upon exiting, and used it to shift her momentum upward. Two flaps of her wings and she landed atop her tower's point.

Logarius appeared moments later, his body exiting out a shimmery starscape along the northern wall. He clung to the side of their home with his clawed left hand, his weight braced by his good leg, but he did not attempt to chase.

"I will not rest," she told him. "Not until I have burned every copy of that damn book and scattered every last Ravencaller's ashes to the fields and mountains of the Cradle."

"Don't you understand?" her son yelled at her. "You should feel pride at your place in history. The Book of Ravens is the key! With it, humanity can understand its true place: beneath the dragon-sired."

Evelyn leapt off the rooftop, caught the wind with her wings, and glided away. Logarius did not chase, not physically. He used his words instead.

"This is our home, Mother! I will defend it to the last. Better the void take it than humanity!"

Evelyn landed on a rooftop several hundred feet away, her feet a blur. She ran, and ran, leaving her empty home behind. She ran as her guilt and sorrow chased her, ran as fast as her old legs could carry and her brittle wings propel, but it was never fast enough.

# CHAPTER 18

Devin knelt behind the corner of a shuttered tavern, a little spot of privacy amid the gathered crowd of keepers, soldiers, and city guards.

"Keep us safe, Sisters," he prayed with eyes closed and head bowed. "And please, let this night be one of peace instead of bloodshed."

It was an impossible prayer, but he prayed it nonetheless. A small army was marching into occupied territory to halt a nighttime attack on Adria's church. Bloodshed felt all but guaranteed. His prayer finished, he moved his fingers in a triangular pattern over his heart. Such acts were usually done by children first learning their faith, but given his uncertainty and confusion, Devin felt very much a child in this new world.

"Welcome back," Lyssa said when Devin joined the rest of the keepers lingering together a few dozen feet from the soldiers. She stared at him intently, and he wondered what she might be looking for.

"I think I'd rather be home," he said. "Alas, the powers that be have other ideas."

"We're helping the defenseless. This is right where you know you should be."

"Is that so?" He shook his head. "I don't know. Remember

when we traveled to places in need and offered them services? I spent most of my time tending the sick and comforting the hurting. Now I feel like we're just a military arm of the church. If we're not patrolling the streets, we're here as part of an invasion force."

"Invasion force?" Lyssa punched his shoulder. "Have you forgotten these creatures evicted hundreds from Low Dock by knifepoint? We're not invading. We're taking back what is ours."

No doubt the Forgotten Children believed the same, but Devin kept that to himself. There was no point arguing such matters well beyond the point of no return. At any moment they'd receive a signal from up front, and the whole force would march to the west gate of Low Dock. No doubt it would be barricaded, but they had a trick up their sleeves for that eventuality: Tommy and his magic.

Devin peered over Lyssa's shoulder to where his brother-in-law and his mentor, Malik, huddled together under an awning to avoid the biting wind. Tommy looked unbearably nervous, the poor guy. Battle would never be his forte. It was such a shame he couldn't have discovered his powers in a time of peace. He'd be so much happier creating silly trinkets for children and wondrous illusions for crowds than wielding fire and frost as weapons for the city. At least Tesmarie was with him, hidden in his pocket. Devin trusted the onyx faery to keep his brother-in-law safe should things turn dire.

"You still with me?" Lyssa asked.

"Yeah, sorry." Devin shook his head and forced himself to dwell on the matters at hand. "Just worried is all."

"Don't be. We got this. Anything goes wrong, I'll have your back." She grinned at him, half-cocked and matching the tilt of her feathered cap. "So, what's this I hear about you shacking up with a soulless?"

Oh Goddesses above, that rumor had made its way through the ranks?

"And where did you hear that?" he asked.

"You're avoiding the question."

He absolutely was, and it drove him nuts that Lyssa could read him so easily. It made the following lie that much harder.

"I'm not," he said. "Whatever nonsense rumor you heard is just that, nonsense."

Lyssa's fingers drummed the two hilts of her pistols, and he was surprised by the earnestness of her voice when she responded. He'd expected sarcasm or mockery, not sympathy.

"That's good to hear," she said. "Devin, you know that if you need companionship, I'm here for you, right? What we do, it isn't easy. Don't spend nights cold and alone if you feel them wearing you down. Far too many of us never learn to escape it."

Devin took Lyssa's hand and squeezed. There was a reason one rarely saw elderly Soulkeepers. It wasn't just the dangers of the occupation. After a lifetime of praying over sickly men and women who would still die, of killing those who had already murdered the innocent, and standing by helplessly as disease or famine ravaged a village, it was painfully common for a Soulkeeper to choose to take their own life during the reaping hour rather than face the memories that came at night.

"I'm good, I assure you," he said. "But thanks for caring."

The smaller woman rolled her eyes.

"Don't get used to it, you stubborn lug."

A few minutes later Vikar Forrest joined the group of Soulkeepers to give the call to march. That their Vikar was coming into combat only showed how important the church viewed the attempt to retake Low Dock. The giant man wore his old Soulkeeper outfit instead of his traditional black suit and vest. His billowing coat would have engulfed a smaller man, and Devin doubted few could heft his two-handed axe with such ease.

"It's almost time," Forrest said as he stood in a loose ring of

Soulkeepers. "We should have them vastly outnumbered, but don't get cocky. Stay loose, and stay together with your partners. Their best bet will be to get us separated, so don't fall for it. Other than that, may your swords be wet and your aim be true. If Anwyn's kind, she'll only be taking a few of us into her arms at the end of this night."

"I feel so motivated," Lyssa said to the chuckles of many.

"Speaking's never been my forte," Forrest said. He hoisted his ax above his head. "That's why I have this giant-ass thing speak for me."

Shouts from ahead ordered the troops to march. Devin inhaled deeply and breathed out his anxiety. *You're doing this for Adria,* he told himself. Reports insisted the Forgotten Children were moving in on her church tonight. At least when it came to protecting her, Devin knew they were doing the right thing.

There were three hundred total troops between the city guard and the royal soldiers. Twenty Soulkeepers trailed after them, paired up in twos. Devin glanced toward the rooftops only once as they marched, for he feared doing so more often might allow Lyssa to notice. Sure enough, Jacaranda followed at a low crouch, dressed in black. She had insisted on coming along, and even if he had refused, nothing would have stopped her.

Their formation halted at the west district gate. The interior of the gate was sealed off by an enormous pile of boards and furniture taken from the many abandoned homes within and piled up overnight after the Forgotten Children had taken over. Devin couldn't see Tommy from way in the back, but he certainly could see the enormous fireball that lit up the night. It exploded into the barricade, scattering flaming chunks all throughout the interior street. A cheer went up through the crowd. Devin grinned, imagining Tommy's reaction. Never one comfortable with attention, he was probably blushing from neck to forehead.

The soldiers marched onward, and the Soulkeepers followed up at the rear. The streets of Low Dock were dark and empty, with not a single hanging lantern lit. Devin questioned the wisdom of coming at night. Perhaps their leaders thought it poetic to retake the district in the same way the Forgotten Children had taken it from them. Perhaps they hoped to catch the magical creatures off guard during their attack on the church. Whatever the reason, it meant that many soldiers throughout the formation had to forfeit a hand to carry a torch.

Soldiers checked the first two dozen homes, finding no one. Worry built into a solid knot inside Devin's stomach. He couldn't shake the feeling that the Forgotten Children were ready for them. It seemed he wasn't the only one with that concern. At the next crossroad the entire formation halted, and a runner arrived from up front.

"General Kaelyn is worried you'll get picked off if you remain in the back," he told Forrest. "She wants you to take the middle position."

"Just this morning she wanted us guarding her flank," the Vikar grumbled. "I wish she'd make up her mind."

The Soulkeepers shuffled forward, and once repositioned, the troops began anew. Devin scanned the surroundings, always on the lookout for a peering set of eyes or a huddled shape waiting in ambush. It was by the third street that Low Dock began to appear unfamiliar. Had the buildings always been so tall? And why did some walls shimmer like pearl or alabaster instead of brick or stone?

"This is giving me the creeps," Lyssa said, and she pointed at a cylindrical building three stories tall. "No doors, no windows. How the void does anyone get in?"

Devin tried to spot Jacaranda but could not. He trusted her to keep pace with them, just camouflaged and hidden. Again the troops halted, and murmurs from up front trickled their way. General Kaelyn was lost.

"That's impossible," Devin said. "It's a straight shot until a turn at the shuttered shoemaker store. I'd have seen it if we passed it."

"Are you sure?" Lyssa asked. She eyed the homes around her distrustfully. "Things don't feel right. I'm not certain we should believe our eyes."

"Getting nervous, keepers?" asked the soldier to Devin's right. The bearded man held a torch aloft, and he winked with his lone good eye. "I'm sure the little buggers fled the moment they saw us coming. Surely they're a cowardly lot."

That certainly didn't match what Devin knew of them. Their attacks were well coordinated and daring. A panicked retreat was the exact opposite of what he expected that night.

"Devin, they're disguised!" Jacaranda's shout split the quiet night like a thunderbolt. He glanced up to see her kneeling at the side of a home, her right arm extended in a point. "Hidden with illusions! Look around you, all of you!"

Devin spun on his heels, baffled. He caught the man with the torch leering at him. Smiling. His teeth a bit too clean and sharp.

"Nosy little bitch, isn't she?" the man asked, and suddenly his skin was fur, his hands bore claws, and he had not one eye but three. Dozens of other soldiers and city guards dropped their illusions, becoming foxkin armed to the teeth with swords and daggers. There was a single, horrified second of calm as the shock and surprise rippled through the humans in a wave, and then the bloodshed began.

A roar like thunder sounded as over a dozen pistols fired simultaneously. Devin shot his own at the torch wielder, but the flash of light from the other pistols sullied his vision, as did the torch when the foxkin chucked it at his forehead. The shot went wide, and his attempt to duck came too late. The torch struck the side of his face, and the fire and wood combined for a vicious sting. He prayed it did not scar as he staggered with his sword held up in defense. The last thing his poor face needed was another permanent decoration.

Scarring might be the least of his worries, though, as the foxkin pressed the assault. He wielded a long, curved blade with both hands, and he used that power to slam Devin's sword up and nearly out of his grasp. Devin retreated backward, desperate for space, but the foxkin was faster. His sword curled downward at an arc that brought its sharp edge in for a sideways slash. Devin's pistol was empty, his sword out of position, and his fall backward too slow. The blade would open up his belly and spill his guts upon the cold, dark street.

One booming crack, followed by a second. Two shots of lead pounded into the foxkin's chest and out his back. They robbed his swing of its strength so that when Devin turned, the weapon's edge caught only the side of his long jacket. Devin spun and saluted Lyssa in thanks.

"Cover me," she said, her fingers already a blur as she simultaneously loaded both pistols. Devin put his back to her, searching for nearby foes. Despite the advantage of a surprise attack, the foxkin were outnumbered at least five to one. Already many had begun to retreat, which only added to the confusion. Some soldiers chased, while others called for a return to formation. The nearest foxkin stood over the corpse of two men, blood dripping from his twin dirks. He grinned at Devin, almost daring him to charge.

"Not a chance," Devin said, grinning right back. Lyssa's pistols would be more than enough.

A piercing cry stole his attention to the sky. His stomach dropped. His throat tightened. The rooftops were filled with a mixture of magical creatures. He saw tall, long-eared men and women wielding spears that matched Tommy's description of the lapinkin. He saw multiple avenria, their bodies shrouded by their long, shadowy wings and their faces covered with hoods. Gargoyles clung to rooftop edges, their teeth bared and hungry. Enormous owls circled amid the stars, overlooking all and waiting for their time to dive.

"You shouldn't have come," the grinning foxkin said, drawing Devin's attention back down to him. "But we're glad you did."

The earlier confusion paled in comparison to the absolute chaos unleashed by the rooftop ambush. Lapinkin blasted soldiers off their feet with torrents of wind before soaring high into the air with their spears at the ready. Several owls crashed through their ranks, grabbing soldiers with their talons and dragging them along the cobblestones. Gargoyles leapt upon the nearest men and women like attack dogs, their teeth and claws making short work of their armor to tear at the flesh beneath. The avenria were the worst. They assaulted the outer lines of soldiers, their weapons wielded with such skill they found blood with nearly every thrust and stab.

"It's on us, Soulkeepers!" Vikar Forrest bellowed over the din. His axe cleaved a gargoyle in half in mid-lunge. "Bring the bastards down!"

Devin charged the nearest foxkin. He couldn't afford to wait, not with so many skirmishes all about. The foxkin twirled his dirks, and when Devin was halfway there, he met his charge with a leap of his own. The creature had speed on him, but Devin had the far better reach. He feinted an overhead chop, which baited out a sidestep and counterthrust. The foxkin had to close the distance for his dirks, just as Devin predicted. He swept his sword sideways. The foxkin's speed was incredible, and he almost drew blood before Devin's sword chopped through his extended elbow and then crashed through his rib cage.

Pained screams formed a constant chorus punctuated with pistol fire. Devin turned in place, searching for his next opponent, when a fleeing guard collided with him shoulder-to-shoulder. He staggered for balance. Before he could even call for the man to stand his ground, a lapinkin slammed down from the sky, his spear skewering the man through the back. Both lapinkin and corpse slid several feet across the cobbles, the steel of his weapon scraping the stone.

"Anwyn have mercy," Devin whispered. He dashed after the lapinkin, who turned toward him and extended his hand. Wind soared out from his palm, and Devin felt its impact like a solid wall. His legs strained to keep himself standing. Closing the gap between them was impossible. The dragon-sired couldn't keep the wind up forever, though, and eventually Devin felt the pressure ease. He charged, but the lapinkin was faster. He leapt several dozen feet into the air and then froze in place, a faintly visible vortex of air just beneath his feet. The lapinkin took aim with his spear.

Devin picked a random direction and dove. The lapinkin dove forward, slamming into the ground, and the force of his passage sent Devin rolling. The spear caught in cobbles and wrenched from the lapinkin's grasp. Devin rolled to his knees, judging if he could reach the spear before the lapinkin did. He need not have worried. A pistol shot ripped through the dragon-sired's face and exited out the back of his skull to punch an accompanying hole through the overlapped ears behind it.

"You're a good distraction," Lyssa said, offering him a hand.

"Glad I can be useful."

An owl's cry turned his head toward the center of their formation. Forrest stood over the body of an ashen gray owl, his axe embedded in the space between its enormous eyes. The bird shrieked and flailed its wings in its death throes. Forrest yanked his axe free, hefted it above his head, and put an end to its suffering with another blow that cracked deep into its skull.

"This clusterfuck is hopeless," the Vikar shouted. Blood darkened his shirt and coat, not that he seemed to care. "Retreat, everyone retreat! Save what lives you can and then go!"

Devin couldn't argue with that assessment. There wasn't a shred of organization left between the soldiers and the city guards. Their numbers were halved, and they had no clue as to how many more dragon-sired might remain farther into Low Dock. Owls dove through their ranks, the avenria continued their hit-and-run tactics, and only the Goddesses knew how many lapinkin lurked in the sky, ready to spear another hapless soldier.

"There," Lyssa said, tapping his shoulder. Three city guards armed with spears had cordoned off an avenria in a corridor. They kept calm, a heroic effort in and of itself, and did not fall for her attempts to bait them out of formation. Together Devin and Lyssa rushed to join the guards. The avenria, seeing them coming, turned and fled, leading the five of them on a chase.

"Wait," Devin shouted at them. "Too far! We can't get…"

They emerged the next street over, and the avenria was not alone. Six men and women garbed in black stood ready with their hands raised and a prayer on their lips. The three guards tried to interrupt them, but the avenria held firm, her long blade shoving aside their spears and forcing a retreat.

"Anwyn of the Moon, hear me!" the six chanted in unison. "Before me stands one who would take my life. Before me stands pride and vengeance. Strike them down. Teach them, through your holy lash, humility."

Horror washed over Devin's mind as he watched the three guards cry out. Enormous gashes burst open across their chests, two to a man, as if invisible swords cleaved their flesh down to the bone. They dropped, their bodies immediately going into shock.

"Ravencallers," Devin said, the word foul on his tongue.

"Only one shot left," Lyssa said, her tone grim. She lifted her pistol and aimed it at the avenria.

"Then make it count."

Devin dashed at the six Ravencallers. He couldn't let them release another wave of prayers. The avenria knew the same, and she kept close to the Ravencallers, her sword ready to defend them. Devin ran, instinctively trusting Lyssa to hold her shot until the last possible moment. Right before reaching the avenria, he skidded to his knees, freeing up Lyssa's line of sight. The eruption of her flamestone echoed through the night. Its aim was true, but their foe was no ordinary target.

The avenria's wings folded over her, predicting the shot the moment Devin dropped. The feathers vanished into shadow, the lead shot passed straight through to connect instead with one of the Ravencallers. The woman dropped, but five remained.

Panic pushed Devin back to his feet, and he crashed into the avenria with all his might. Their swords crossed, once, twice, the chant of the five Ravencallers behind her a ticking clock toward his death. Lyssa couldn't reload her pistols in time. It had to be him. He parried, slid closer, and caught the woman in the chest with his elbow. She was frailer than he'd expected, and the moment her upper body doubled over in pain, he cleaved through her neck, dropping her.

Devin spun to face the remaining five Ravencallers. Their prayer was almost finished, and even if he could close the distance in time, they were not alone. A second avenria dropped from the rooftops.

Except Devin recognized this new avenria was no friend of the Ravencallers. Evelyn spun as her heels touched down, her two sickles flashing red as they cut through the gathered men and women. Three died instantly, while two more turned and fled. Evelyn's wings flapped once to launch her after them. She buried both sickles in the first, landed atop his collapsing corpse, and swung her arm left, decapitating the final Ravencaller.

"Your leaders underestimated us dragon-sired," Evelyn said, her back to them. "Then again, your race always have."

"Devin, get back," Lyssa shouted. She'd finished reloading, and she pointed both pistols at Evelyn.

"Lower your aim," Devin said. "She's a . . . friend."

Evelyn glanced over her shoulder. He could see little of her face due to her long hood and dark beak, but he swore he saw hints of a smile in those blue eyes.

"Yes," the avenria said. "Quite an unusual friendship, wouldn't you say?"

Lyssa's pistol never wavered.

"A friend," she said flatly. "With those who took Low Dock from us?"

"Do I look like I'm helping the Forgotten Children?" Evelyn asked. The old woman sounded exasperated. "Or do you doubt your own eyes?"

Lyssa's gaze bounced between the two of them, and after a long second, she lowered both barrels. Devin sighed with relief.

"Do you know where more are?" he asked Evelyn.

"I do. They're making their way toward the church. I suspect those inside will be next once the battle finishes."

"Then I'm going with you."

Lyssa took a step backward.

"I won't have any part of this," she said. "We need to rejoin the others."

"I'm not abandoning my sister," Devin said. "You heard Forrest's retreat order. They're going to leave her to die."

"And I'm not abandoning our Vikar, not on the word of . . ." She didn't finish the sentence. She didn't need to. "I'm sorry, Devin. Orders are orders."

Lyssa dashed back through the alley. Devin quietly watched her go.

"Logarius will gather his forces once the humans have fled," Evelyn said. "I will help you kill more human Ravencallers, but I will not fight my own kind. You face Logarius alone should he try to breach the church's walls."

"Not alone," Devin said. He took advantage of the pause to

load flamestone and shot into his pistol. "Adria's still there, and that's all that matters."

"Such love for family," Evelyn said, and this time he was certain she smiled darkly at him. "I would commend it, but I am not blind to the truth. It likely leads you to your death, Soulkeeper, but while you fight on, consider me your dark-winged guide."

# CHAPTER 19

The only thing keeping Tesmarie from breaking down in tears was the need to keep Tommy alive. If she could at least manage that, then perhaps this abysmal night would have a silver lining.

"Hurry, hurry, this way!" she shouted at him and his friend, Malik. A trio of lapinkin gave chase. One of them soared high into the air, her spear at the ready. The faery's eyes widened.

"No, no no no," she shouted, her wings buzzing in her ears. Her hands traced runes in the air as she flew, encasing an invisible bubble around the two men. When the lapinkin descended, her spear aimed to impale Tommy through the chest, she hit the bubble and then slowed as if her entire body swam through molasses. The rip of the wind through her clothes rolled in slow motion. Tommy glanced over his shoulder, saw the lapinkin there, and blanched.

"*Aethos glaeis surmu*," he quickly shouted, and with a wave of his hand formed a wall of ice that spread from one side of the street to the other. The lapinkin emerged on the other side of the time-slowing bubble and crashed unseen into it. Tesmarie winced, fearing the damage and broken bones the poor lapinkin most certainly suffered. If only there were a nonhurtful way to stop their fighting!

The two men ran, while the two trailing lapinkin easily hopped over the ice wall. Tesmarie bit her lip. She'd already slowed the time about her considerably. Going further would put a significant strain on her physically, but she was starting to believe she had no choice. How else might she scare off their pursuers? Tesmarie summoned her moonlight blade. If she had to draw blood, then so be it…

Blood. That was it! She quickly carved a symbol into the palm of her left hand, her teeth gritted against the pain. Once the rune was complete, she clenched her hand into a fist, words of magic flowing off her tongue.

"*Chyron aro ocpectu.*"

Chyron's magic filled the rune, and then the blood.

"Please work," she whispered. Her wings carried her on a straight shot toward the lapinkin. They readied their spears, but they were clumsy, ineffective weapons against someone so small. Tesmarie danced around the bladed tips. When their spears failed them, gales of air blasted from their palms, buffeting her about like a leaf in a storm. The world spun, the sky and the street rotating above her head. Her back slammed against a wall, and she sobbed as her head whip-cracked into the building's hard stone. Blood leaked from her clenched fist, and she refused to open it lest the magic be wasted.

"It's…going to…take more than…that," she said as she hovered in a daze.

"Stay back, faery," one of the lapinkin said. A second gust of air flattened her against the wall. "You are misguided, but that alone does not deserve death."

The wind relented. Tesmarie slumped forward and dropped several feet before her wings caught her. One of the lapinkin resumed chasing Tommy and Malik. The other stood over Tesmarie, waiting for her surrender.

"I might be misguided," Tesmarie said. "But I won't let you kill anyone."

She closed the distance between them and flung her hand in a wide arc, spraying her blood across the lapinkin's furry face. Blue drops struck his eyes, enacting the long-pent-up magic. He stumbled back a step and lifted his spear. His eyes, normally a deep brown color, shimmered pink as he gaped around him.

"What...where?"

He stabbed at the air, striking nothing. The magic had taken his sight and transported it back almost an hour. Whatever he saw, it certainly wasn't the current street, nor the two fleeing Wise. Tesmarie abandoned him to his confusion and chased after the final three lapinkin. Catching up would be no difficulty, but before she could, she saw Tommy with his hand outstretched, speaking the syllables of a spell.

"Wait-wait-wait!" she cried. The lapinkin had his spear pulled back to throw, but Tommy finished quicker. Electricity sparked about his fingertips. Tesmarie pulsed her wings, and she clenched her hand to fill it with another spray of blood. The lapinkin was so close now, and still he'd not thrown his spear.

"I'll get there, I'll get there, I'll stop him, I'll..."

Even to one who moved so slowly through time, the strike of lightning that shot from Tommy's palm to the lapinkin's chest was an instantaneous blur. She squinted and turned. She felt the heat of the blast. She smelled the scorching flesh. The lapinkin's death cry came out stilted and weak, his heart burst by the energy and his lungs likely charred. His body slumped. Tesmarie hovered above him, little diamond flecks dropping across his limp form.

"Tes!" Tommy screamed the moment the spell ended. "Oh shit, I didn't hit you with that, did I?"

To his eyes her arrival beside the dead lapinkin had been no more than a blur. She shook her head and forced her attention back to the two humans.

"I'm not hurt," she said.

*At least not on the outside.*

She flew over to him, only now realizing how uneven her trajectory was despite her efforts to fly straight. The blow to her head must have been worse than she thought. Her feet lightly touched down on Tommy's shoulder, and she grabbed his hair to steady herself.

"We need to hide," she said.

"Here seems as good a place as any," Malik said. He gestured to the boarded-up home at his right. At some point the wood planks over one of its windows had been smashed inward. Tommy climbed in first, followed by Malik. The older man stepped in gingerly, and he winced when Tommy helped him in.

"Are you all right?" Tommy asked.

"I'm fine."

Tesmarie flew in a circle, making a cursory scan of the home's sole room. Like much of Low Dock, it looked hastily abandoned, with its bed in the corner stripped of sheets and the drawers of the solitary dresser pulled out and dumped on the floor. There was a small fireplace with a flue barely large enough for her to fly through. Tesmarie hovered to the dresser and sat down on the edge.

"Why does there have to be fighting?" she sulked. "Low Dock is big enough to share, isn't it?"

"Forgive me for saying so, but that was a naïve hope," Malik said. He sat upon the bed and wiped sweat from his pale face and neck. "I appreciate your attempts to spare lives, but when both parties are void-bent on killing one another, there is only so much one can do."

Tesmarie slumped her head onto her hands.

"Doesn't mean I still can't try."

"I tried, too," Tommy added. "I—I didn't mean to kill that last lapinkin, I swear, only stun him. People can be hit by lightning and survive, you know? Sure, it'd hurt, but I thought he'd live, just a burn, he'd live…"

Tesmarie smiled at Tommy. She might not be able to comfort herself, but damn it, Tommy was a cuddly stuffed animal, and it hurt her to see him so upset.

"It's not your fault," she said. "He—he could have left you two alone. You weren't fighting. You were running. He had to know that."

Tommy nodded but said nothing. She hoped it'd at least be something.

"So how do we get out of here?" Tommy asked. "When do you think it'll be safe?"

Malik lay down onto his back and let out a groan. His hands clutched at his side.

"I don't think we do," he said.

"Nonsense," Tommy argued. "If we...Malik, is that blood?"

Between the robe's dark brown color and the dim light, it was hard to tell, but Malik shifted his head up and down.

"Took a cut when the fight started," he said. "It's nothing, I promise."

Tommy would hear none of it. He hurried to the bedside and pulled Malik's hand away. A thick smear of blood coated the thick fabric.

"*Aethos creare lumna*," Tommy hurriedly whispered. A little ball of light appeared above the bed. In the sudden brightness it was clear Malik suffered far worse than he let on. His skin, normally a soft tan, was significantly paler. A hole had been punctured in his robe's cloth, which Tommy ripped wider so he might see the wound. Blood soaked Malik's entire side, which made it that much harder to judge the scale of the damage.

"It's just a cut," Malik said, but his speech was starting to slur. "Let me sleep. I'll feel better if I sleep."

"No, you stay awake, you," Tommy said. Panic crept at the edges of every word. "Stay awake, damn it."

Tesmarie flew closer, her arms crossed over her chest. She felt so helpless. Tommy ripped the cloth further, then used a clean stretch of his own robe to mop up the blood. At long last he found the wound. It didn't appear to be much, just a cut about the length of Tommy's thumb.

"It's not deep," Tommy said. "At least, I don't think it's deep. He's just losing so much blood!"

He tried tearing the bottom of his robe, but the tough fabric refused.

"Here, I'll help," she said. Her moonlight sword carved through it with ease, allowing him to rip a large chunk free and then press it against the wound. Malik gasped against the sudden pressure.

"We—we can handle this," Tommy said. "Just some pressure, yeah? Stop the bleeding, then cauterize it with a little fire magic. That's all."

Tears were starting to build in his eyes, and he sniffled. After a moment he pulled the cloth back and placed his fingers along the wound. He whispered the words of a spell, keeping the intonations as calm and quiet as possible to lessen its power. Fire plumed out from his touch. It burned the skin, cauterizing the wound. Malik cried out at the pain, but his strength was clearly sapped.

"All right, you can sleep now," Tommy said. "We'll keep you safe, right, Tesmarie? Nice and safe."

"That we will," Tesmarie said. She smiled, determined to keep Tommy hopeful no matter how unsure she was herself. Her heart felt scraped raw from all the death and hurt.

"All right," Malik said. He chuckled despite his awful circumstances. "If you insist..."

Tesmarie lowered herself to the bed and then sat. Tommy paced at bedside, his eyes never leaving Malik. The minutes wore on. Sometimes they heard distant screams and shouts, other times silence. Tesmarie shuddered at the thought of the battle raging all across Low Dock. The ambush had been expertly planned, but the Forgotten Children were still significantly outnumbered. Who would win? Her gut said the humans were outmatched. They had but swords and spears against the magical gifts of the dragon-sired. Malik and Tommy perhaps could have swung the outcome, but they were here in hiding, not out there fighting. Not out there killing.

"Does it look like he's getting paler?" Tommy asked. He gestured at Malik's face. "Like, more pale than a few minutes ago?"

"I don't know," she said.

"His breathing's quieter, too."

"He's asleep. Isn't that normal?"

Her friend shook his head, not convinced. He put a hand on Malik's shoulder.

"Hey, buddy, wake up and convince me you're all right, would you?" Malik remained asleep. Tommy shook him harder. Whatever traces of calm he'd shown vanished. "Malik? Malik! Wake up, you stubborn prick, wake up!"

Malik's eyes fluttered open, and he muttered something garbled and indistinct before slumping. Tesmarie flew up a few feet, a frown locked on her face. What was wrong with Malik? The wound was sealed. He shouldn't be bleeding anymore, and she told Tommy as such.

"He—he must be bleeding inside," he said. "Oh shit, oh shit, what do I do, Tes? What do I do? Do I reopen it and look? There's—there's intestines and stuff where he was stabbed. If one's cut, if he's bleeding out in his own body...shit. Shit. Shit!"

He spun, his eyes wild.

"Wait. You helped Jacaranda once, right? Tommy said you cast a spell, and her whole body went backward before being hurt. Hurry, cast the same on Malik."

"Only a few minutes," Tesmarie said. "It's been longer than that since you sealed the cut, let alone when he first took the wound."

Tommy was stricken with panic. His skin looked as pale as Malik's, and he stuttered and fumbled for solutions.

"Adria!" he nearly screamed. "She can heal him! We need to get to her church. She'll make everything right."

Tesmarie thought of Tomas trying to carry Malik in such a condition and frowned. Goddesses and dragons help them, there was no way that Malik would live through such a journey. Unless...

"I have an idea," she said. She clenched her fist, summoning her moonlight blade. "Be quiet, all right? This won't be easy."

Tesmarie cut Malik's robe down the middle starting at the neckline, granting her access to his chest. She took the tip of the blade and carefully began carving into his skin. Unlike a lot of other magics, manipulating time was incredibly nuanced and risky. A little bit of extra fire was not a problem for those using Aethos magic. The world would not end if you read the thoughts of the wrong person with Gloam magic. But manipulating the essence of time? Dangerous, and fraught with unforeseen consequences.

That was why she needed the runes. From what her mother had told her, they were based on the different scales that grew upon Chyron's magnificent emerald body. They directed the magic, gave it strict order and meaning that mere words and thoughts could not. The rune she chose would encapsulate Malik's entire body, locking it in a flow separate from the flow of the universe.

Assuming she didn't mess it up. If she did, the magic might not enact properly, or at all.

"This should do it," she said, once the intricate carving was finished. She dismissed her sword and placed both hands atop the angry red skin. Her dark hair fell across her face as she closed her eyes and spoke the words of the spell.

*"Chyron aliu gargos."*

Strength pulled out of Tesmarie, draining an interior reservoir of power she didn't fully understand. A rainbow of colors flashed in seemingly chaotic order across Malik's body. His breathing halted. His body went rigid, almost as if he were a statue. Not a hair on his head shifted. Not a single pulse of blood moved within his body.

"What did you do?" Tommy asked.

"I've stopped his time completely," she said. "It's like what the gargoyles do during the day. The duration isn't long, exactly twenty minutes, but I think that's enough to get us to Adria's church."

"That's perfect," Tommy said. He sniffed and rubbed at his face. "We got this, you and me."

"That's right!" Tesmarie chirped. "You and I, the best of teams, we can take on anything the Cradle throws at us."

Tommy awkwardly stood beside the time-frozen body, turning and positioning his arms multiple times before finally picking Malik up. The older man's body slumped over Tommy's right shoulder, and for a brief, horrible moment, it seemed Tommy would lose his grip and send Malik tumbling face-first to the floor. Tommy caught himself at the last second, and he wrapped his arms in a vise grip about Malik's legs.

"Oof," Tommy said. "He's heavier than he looks. Maybe he needs to jog a few miles every morning."

"Or you could do a few push-ups yourself so your arms aren't as skinny as grass blades," Tesmarie said. They shared a nervous laugh. A quick word from Tommy dismissed the glowing orb of light he'd summoned, and then in darkness they returned to the broken window.

"Oh Goddesses damn it," he muttered. "I forgot about the window."

Tommy effectively dropped his friend to the street in the gentlest manner that he could. Tesmarie hovered outside, keeping watch for anyone who'd want to do the two Wise harm. With time's flow slowed about her, she'd notice any human or dragon-sired coming long before they reached Tommy. At least, that's what she thought.

The flash of shadow darker than the night racing in at her right said otherwise.

Tesmarie spun in place, dropped an inch while her wings halted, and then shot back upward with her moonlight blade out and blocking. A matching blade struck hers, and she flew back a full foot as her attacker tried to drive his weapon home. The shimmering weapon cut across her arm, and she bit her tongue to bury her cry of pain. She easily parried the next two attacks, her wings matching his, neither of them willing to give an inch. At last her attacker retreated a few feet, and when she did not chase, he hovered before her and glared.

"This treachery is shocking, even for you, Tesmarie," the faery said. He was onyx like her, but instead of a leaf-made dress, his clothes were stitched with thread and dyed black using the bark from the oaks surrounding their home. Only his face was uncovered, revealing a thin-lipped frown, green eyes, and dreadlocked hair tied behind his head.

"What are you doing here, Gan?" she asked. "You're making everything worse."

"The Matriarch sent me here as ambassador to the Forgotten Children," Gan said. "Finding you is just an unwelcome surprise."

He made a quick burst toward Tommy. Tesmarie had the better angle, and she cut him off so he'd retreat. Twice more he tried, testing her, judging her reflexes. No doubt to Tommy they were a confusing blur. After a third attempt she turned and shouted at the young man at the top of her lungs.

"Go! Get him to safety, before you run out of time!"

"It doesn't matter how fast he runs," Gan said. His moonlight blade shimmered between his fingers. "I'll catch up to him when I'm finished with you."

"Stop it," she said. "You're a bully, always have been, always will be."

"A bully?" Gan glared at her. "A bully? I am the Matriarch's

Chosen Blade. I fight for the honor of our village. What are you doing here, Tes? Befriending humans? Protecting them? How dim must you be to think yourself on the correct side. The battle's still raging. Join the righteous before it's too late."

"There's nothing righteous about any of this! Everyone's killing everyone and I hate all of it. I just want to keep my friends safe."

Gan tensed his upper body like a tightening coil.

"I see you learned nothing from your exile."

He exploded toward her, his moonlight blade gripped in both hands. Tesmarie shot to her left, saw him curl to match, and then spun about to block just before he cut her through. Their blades connected with a shower of sparks. His momentum carried him past her, and as he shifted and buzzed his wings to slow down, she took the offensive. Her sword slammed into his in a series of cuts, beating him back.

"Just leave me alone," she cried. Her fourth hit missed entirely as Gan halted his wings and dropped low. A rotation of his waist curled his legs upward. His heel caught her waist. Tesmarie groaned out her pain as she flew sideways, needing space while she recovered.

"You're strong, Tes," he said. "No doubt about that. You might not be living in a stinking, crowded city of humans if you'd stop thinking with your heart for two seconds."

Gan was trying to sting her with words, not just his blade. The worst part was that it was working. Little diamond tears collected at the corners of her eyes.

"Better here than with you," she said, and wondered if she believed it.

Gan's shimmering blade lifted in challenge.

"Then prove it."

This time Tesmarie held firm when he charged, her wings countering the force of his arrival to keep her steady in the air. She blocked his overhead chop, batted aside a follow-up, and then parried his thrust for her chest. The two had dueled only a handful of times when she lived in the onyx village. There was no doubt he'd vastly improved since obtaining the title of Chosen Blade. Most faeries would have crumbled beneath the assault, but Tesmarie was not most faeries.

She was the Matriarch's daughter, and she had been trained to wield her starlight weapon the moment her wings could bear her weight.

Gan tried to keep his offensive going, but the exertion from constantly slashing and thrusting in midair cost him his balance. His next thrust lacked power, and Tesmarie took advantage of the opening. She grabbed his wrist with her left hand and pulled. His wings fought against hers, but he could not escape. Her snap-kick to the crotch stunned him, and her follow-up heel to his abdomen knocked the breath out of him. It'd have been easy to kill him, for his body was exposed and his wings outmatched, but she couldn't bring herself to do it. Instead she cracked her fist into his nose, breaking it.

"Just—just leave," she told him. "None of this is right."

"No," Gan said. Blood dripped down his face and into his mouth. He spat a blue glob of it toward her. It floated toward her at a crawl, and she realized both of them had been increasing their time to match the other's. Her heart raced within her chest. Fighting too much longer like this was dangerous. She had to end it.

"Fine," she said. "Then I'll make you."

Tesmarie angled her body into a dive, used gravity's aid to gain speed, and then curled up and around toward him. Gan's stubborn pride kept him still. He wanted to face her strength. He wanted to outmatch her skill. Such a damn fool. His pride had cost her a home and a life among her own kind. Now it would cost him a limb.

The moonlight blades were a gift from the dragons, a weapon to battle the void in a time long forgotten. They could be summoned in either hand, though most faeries learned how to wield one only in their dominant hand. Tesmarie wasn't most faeries. She feinted an attack with her right hand, then opened her palm. The weapon faded away, only to immediately reappear into the clenched fist of her left. Gan's sword was out of position, and panic locked him in place. Tesmarie's blade sliced through his wrist, severing the hand and sending it on a slow, slow drop to the ground.

Out of kindness, she left him his dominant hand. He could still be the Chosen Blade if he desired. Why she showed him mercy, when he himself would never show her any, she didn't know. That was just the faery she wanted to be.

"You're beaten," Tesmarie said as she retreated away from the screaming faery. "Leave Londheim. You—you're not needed here."

Gan clutched his bleeding stump of a wrist to his chest. Shock replaced his angry glare. A rainbow of color swam around him as he relented his grip on time, and Tesmarie did likewise. The blood that spilled from his wrist fell like a slow rain.

"You're a traitor to your people," he told her. "Shame and dishonor upon you, Tesmarie Nagovisi. You break your mother's heart yet again."

Finally he fled. Tesmarie didn't give chase. Instead she wiped away the flecks of diamonds from her eyes and did her best to smile.

"All right, Tommy," she said. "Today is just the worst, so you better be fine when I find you, or so help me, I'll make Devin botch your reaping ritual so I can yell at your ghost."

# CHAPTER 20

Y ou spoiled our ambush," the avenria said as he stalked Jacaranda upon the rooftop. "What madness would possess you to throw your life away in such a manner?"

"I'm just trying to keep my friends alive," she said. "Sorry if that offends you."

She'd watched the initial battle between dragon-sired and humans, but instead of leaping down to join them when it was apparent they needed help, she'd found herself ambushed by her current foe. If the roof's warped slats hadn't groaned from his landing, she might not have known he was there at all.

The avenria wielded a lone blade, as long as a traditional soldier's sword, but the steel was curved up and down in waves. Something about its unnatural shape was off-putting to watch, and it made blocking and parrying a tense affair, for it never behaved quite as she expected. Best to kill the avenria quickly, she knew, but the strange raven-like man was more than an equal match to her skill.

"And we seek to reclaim a world stolen from us," the avenria said. His beak barely moved when he spoke. Instead his throat constricted and tensed, resulting in a voice that was deep and gravelly. "You do not impress me with your wit."

She'd rather impress him with her blade work, but she struggled on that front as well. The avenria slashed, and when she parried, her short sword scraped along his curved blade. The avenria closed the distance, her entire vision filled with gray clothes and black wings. She kicked, he sidestepped it and cut again. It was so quick she barely registered the movements. Her only solution was to desperately fling both her swords in the way. The avenria bashed one sword out, stepped even closer, and then looped around his weapon so it hooked the other short sword. Her weapons pinned wide, the avenria slammed his head downward.

The avenria's beak struck her forehead, and she gasped at the cloudburst of white pain that filled her mind. Only finely honed instincts kept her moving. Even a momentary daze could be fatal against an opponent so skilled and savage. She danced closer to the rooftop's edge, braced a foot on a chimney, and kicked back into a lunge. Her foe, having expected her to flee, was caught with his blade in an awkward position. One of her swords cut across his shoulder, exposing dark flesh. His blood shone violet in the moonlight.

If she'd hoped the wound would slow him, she was quickly proven wrong. He retook the offensive, his curved blade looping and slicing through the air as she fought to regain her balance after her lunge. The sound of metal hitting metal rang out a steady song. In it she heard lyrics, and they spoke to her impending defeat.

Rather than keep fighting, she turned and ran. The avenria followed, a mere half step behind her. She didn't look back to confirm. She trusted his speed, and his anger to keep him chasing. Jacaranda crossed the rooftop and leapt the narrow gap between it and its neighbor's home. This one bore a tall brick chimney, and she waited until the last possible moment to shift her angle. She hopped toward the chimney, landed lightly on both feet with her knees crouched, and then somersaulted into the air, her arms extended like a dancer's.

Their bodies collided, her weight on him. One short sword pierced through his wrist and pinned it to the rooftop's thin wood

slats. The other pressed against his throat, the edge just barely
cutting. Jacaranda grit her teeth and pushed, shoving that edge
in farther, farther, seeking the trachea underneath. The avenria
repeatedly slammed his fist into her abdomen with strength born
of impending death. Her innards heaved from a punch to the gut.
One of her ribs cracked. Her breath came in ragged, uneven gasps.

Deeper and deeper went the blade. Blood pooled across her
hands. The punches slowed, then ceased altogether. Jacaranda
slumped off him and pulled her swords free. A wave of nausea
nearly caused her to vomit. *Get up*, she told herself. *Get up now,
before someone finds you.*

The chaotic ambush was a mere two streets over. If it spilled her
way, she'd be helpless. Clenching her teeth, she forced her body to
roll off the rooftop. She had to get on her feet. She had to recover
her bearings. Except instead of landing lightly on the ground, she
collided with a man directly beneath her.

"Goddess damn it!" she muttered. She disentangled herself and
staggered up. By some miracle she'd not cut the man with her
swords upon landing, but he looked fairly woozy himself.

"Get—get back!" a woman with him said. The two wore
matching black robes, and by her guess, they were husband and
wife. Both looked to be in their forties, and neither was in the fin-
est physical shape. Why in the world would they be out and about
Low Dock at this hour?

"Anwyn of the Moon, hear me!" the man she'd struck said. His
wife heard and quickly joined in. "Hold this serpent so its teeth
find no purchase."

Jacaranda's eyes widened. She crossed the distance between
them in a single lunge, and she buried her dagger down the man's
throat before he might finish another syllable.

"Turn flesh into lawful stone," the woman continued. Jacaranda
felt her muscles growing stiff, and her movements sluggish. She
glared death at the woman, fury surging through her at the thought

of becoming helpless in her own body. The woman returned that look with one of terror. "Turn willful impulse into—"

Jacaranda pulled a slender throwing dagger at her thigh and flung it. Its aim was true, the sharp point puncturing the woman's throat, ending the spell. Immediately she felt the invisible chains upon her body relent. Anger kept her moving. She pushed both her short swords into the woman's chest and twisted. The woman toppled and died, her final cry a garbled moan.

"Who are you?" she wondered aloud. Her swords had torn open her robe, revealing a pale gown that was certainly worth more than most in Londheim could afford. Large rings adorned both their hands. These two were wealthy, yet they came to Low Dock with dark magic on their lips. What could possess them so?

"Jac!" a familiar voice called from afar. She looked up to see Devin hustling toward her, a tired smile on his face.

"Hey, you," she said, but her grin did not last long. An avenria followed Devin upon the uneven and slanted rooftops. Jacaranda readied her short swords and prepared for a charge.

"Behind you!" she shouted.

The avenria leapt to the street, but instead of attacking Devin, she landed just ahead of him and peered at Jacaranda with a bemused look on her strange, long face.

"Stay calm," Devin said. "It's Evelyn. We've met her before, remember?"

Jacaranda slowly eased out of her stance.

"I do," she said. "Forgive my panic. You are not the first avenria I've seen tonight."

Evelyn looked away.

"Logarius leads them down a rotten path. Any who follow deserve their fate, even if it pains me to admit it."

Devin crossed the remaining space and wrapped his arms around Jacaranda for a quick embrace. She kissed the side of his neck and tasted sweat and blood on her tongue.

"We need to quit separating on nights like this," she said, and she smiled, because grim humor was the only emotion she felt capable of handling.

"I'll keep it in mind." He turned to Evelyn. "We've spent enough time hunting these bastards. We must make our way to the church."

"Then it is my time to leave. The Ravencallers are my prey, and none else."

Jacaranda felt relieved at the avenria's departure. It was also unnerving being in her presence. There was an aura to her, as black as the wings that stretched from her back or the shadows that pooled beneath her feet.

"Safe travels to you," Devin said, and he bowed. Evelyn crossed her left arm over her chest and extended her right arm as she bowed in return.

"I wish you both the best luck one might find on this dark night."

Her wings wrapped about her body, fully encasing her as she dashed through the nearby district wall and presumably out the other side.

"What is it that makes me attract the most unusual of companions?" Devin asked as he watched her vanish.

"There's something safe about you," Jacaranda said and then winked. "Or maybe you're just the only person foolish enough to keep us around."

Devin laughed as he adjusted his damaged coat.

"Goddesses, tonight has been the worst. Let's hope it ends better than it began. Adria's church is this way. Keep your eyes peeled and your ears open. I'd rather not die in an ambush this close to our goal."

It wasn't signs of an ambush that they heard as they crossed the last stretch of road toward the church, but of sobbing. Jacaranda took point, with Devin trailing behind her with his pistol at the ready. The noise came from just past the broken front door of a dilapidated home. She elbowed it all the way open and stepped inside with daggers drawn.

"Jac?" a stunned Tommy asked. The young man's eyes were red from crying. "Devin? You—you're here!"

"That we are," Devin said as he followed Jacaranda inside. "What's going on?"

Malik lay in Tommy's lap, and for a moment she thought he was dead, his body was so still. It was only after a shimmer of pink bloomed and faded over his skin that she realized some sort of magic was involved.

"Malik, he's—he's hurt," Tommy said. "Tesmarie cast a spell to keep him alive, but we need Adria's help, too, and I can't get to her. The church is surrounded, and I have to carry him, and—and—and I don't want to die getting him there because then what if he dies alone. I'd rather wait here so when he wakes, he can see me. I can say g-g…"

He was blubbering too much for Devin to make any more sense out of his words. He just kept stroking Malik's hair and sobbing. Devin knelt beside him and wrapped Tommy in a hug.

"We're here now," he said. "It's all right. We'll get him to Adria, I promise. But if we're to succeed, I need you to pull yourself together. Save Malik, cry later. Got that, Tommy?"

His brother-in-law swallowed down his next few breaths as he gathered himself.

"Yeah. I can. Just…ugh. I'm such a gross mess. Please give me a second."

Jacaranda scouted outside while Tommy cleaned his face using the sleeve of his robe. She didn't need to go far to spot what the young man meant. Two gargoyles perched on opposite ends of the street, just before their current road intersected with the crossroad directly before the church. Three foxkin stood near the steps of the church. More might lurk outside her line of vision, but she didn't want to risk getting closer until everyone was ready.

"The Forgotten Children are definitely watching the church," she said when she returned. "I believe we can break through if we act quickly."

"Are you ready, Tommy?" Devin asked.

"I'm ready." The young man stood, and he hoisted Malik into his arms and over his shoulder. "I can't cast spells like this, though. Can you two handle it?"

"You-mean-you-three!"

Tesmarie zipped in through a window and pirouetted in midair. Though her voice was chipper, Jacaranda noticed the joy did not reach the faery's eyes or smile.

"Tes!" Tommy exclaimed. "Are you all right? Did you fight that other faery off?"

"Of course I did," she said. "I'm the best."

She might be the best, but Jacaranda could also see that she was hurt. Blood wet her arm and the side of her dress. It didn't seem to bother her too much, and if she was determined to pretend she was fine, then Jacaranda wasn't going to push the issue.

"It's good to see you all together and well," Devin said, and he smiled at them. "Let's not screw that up now, eh? Take lead, Jac. My pistol will keep you safe."

"My hero," she said. "There's two gargoyles watching from above. Take one out before they dive and I'll handle the other."

"Are you sure?" Tesmarie asked. "I could talk with them first, maybe ask nicely if we can go past. We just want in the church. They might let us..."

"Do you believe that?" Jacaranda asked. Tesmarie's wings dipped and she pouted.

"No," she said. "Everyone wants to fight. I hate it."

"I'm no fan, either," Devin said. "But I'm not going to let them hurt my sister and those in her care. If it makes you feel any better, Tes, I'll wait to shoot until they attack. It's the best I can do."

Jacaranda took point, with the rest following several dozen feet behind her. She pretended not to be aware of the two gargoyles keeping watch, though in truth she watched them from the corners of her eyes at all times. The sounds of screams echoed from afar. A retreating group of soldiers, perhaps? Flickers of orange and red painted the sky. It looked like fires burned in the two districts bordering Low Dock. Distractions? Or were they positioned to cut off any potential reinforcements?

When she reached the end of the street, she stopped and put her back against the wall. The gargoyles were directly above her, and she fought to keep her eyes on the church. If she looked up, it'd give away the plan. The three foxkin standing at the church steps appeared to be the only other guards. So far, so good.

The roar of Devin's pistol was her only warning that the gargoyles attacked. Jacaranda pushed off the cold stone and dove. One gargoyle slammed the wall where she'd been, its thick claws tearing into the bricks like they were cloth. Another hit the ground and rolled, painting a trail of blue blood with its passage. Jacaranda came up to her feet only to find the uninjured gargoyle already upon her, its catlike face snarling and its muscular arms extended.

"No-no-that-is-enough!"

Tesmarie flashed across her vision, once, twice, perhaps more, her speed bordering on the impossible. Jacaranda processed a singular blue line that was the faery's moonlight blade before the gargoyle's body collided with hers. Its weight was tremendous despite its size, and she gasped as together they tumbled across the stones. Blood coated her chest, but it wasn't hers. The gargoyle's front claws were removed at the base, so when its paws should have ripped apart her rib cage, they only scraped already wounded and bleeding digits.

Jacaranda tucked her legs to her stomach and then kicked the gargoyle off her. It went down limping, and it whimpered like an injured mountain cat. Its wings spread wide. The gargoyle fled, a trickle of blood falling from it like a pitiful rain.

"Thanks," Jacaranda said as she rose to her feet. It seemed she would find no respite. The three foxkin, alerted to the battle by the sound of pistol fire, sprinted toward her with their long blades drawn.

"I—I won't fight them," Tesmarie said, her fingers pressing together as a rainbow of colors circled underneath her palms, coalescing into an orb. "You have to do it."

The faery pushed the orb directly into Jacaranda's forehead. She felt a sense of vertigo, followed by a sudden slowing of the world. When she turned to face the foxkin, it felt as if her body was sluggish compared to the commands given by her mind. Somehow she was seeing and thinking faster, though her physical self moved no faster than before.

Jacaranda grit her teeth and white-knuckled her grip on her daggers. Already she felt the magic starting to fade; whatever spell Tesmarie cast seemed to have little permanency. She couldn't waste it. Her legs pumped, sending her into a sprint, and she lowered her body and crossed her arms over her chest. Upon meeting the foxkins' charge, she exploded in a whirlwind of steel, her every nerve aflame and her heart pounding with the thrill of battle. Her feet danced beneath her, twisting her, allowing her to bow below a slash, stab one foxkin in the belly, and then rise up, her other hand parrying aside a thrust so she might counter. Her steel punched through the foxkin's throat. The magic enveloping her allowed her ample time to witness the blood begin to pour from the torn trachea.

Once past them, Jacaranda dug in her heels, her blades up to block an attack that never came. The final foxkin lurched aside, her jaw hanging from a single hinge as Devin's shot tore through the back of her head. The gruesome image haunted Jacaranda as she beckoned the others to follow.

She reached the church door first, and unsurprisingly found it locked. She beat on it to alert whoever might be inside. The last of the faery's magic faded from her, leaving her with a pounding headache. Just the act of hitting the door with her fist made her wince.

"It's Jacaranda," she shouted, earning an immediate, muffled response from Adria on the other side.

"Prove it."

The foxkin, she realized. They could disguise themselves. How could she prove her own identity to Adria?

"Devin is an asshole," she shouted. "But I love him anyway."

The door immediately unlocked and swung open.

"Come on in," Adria said. Jacaranda entered first, the others at her heels. The hall was dimly lit by candlelight, and the people inside eyed them warily. Jacaranda wondered what they might think of their motley little crew come to save them. Disappointed, she figured.

"I heard that," Devin said as he holstered his pistol.

"Which part?"

"The 'love him' part." He grinned despite his exhaustion. "So is that true?"

Jacaranda planted a kiss on his cheek.

"Asshole." She smiled despite the pain in her back and the hitch in her side. Tommy carried Malik to a corner, Tesmarie hovering protectively overhead. Devin turned his attention to Adria, who looked doubly exhausted from the stress of the past week.

"Sorry, sis," he said. "I'm afraid we're the grand sum of your rescue forces."

"We'll make do." She wrapped him in a warm embrace. "I'm glad you're here."

Jacaranda peeked out the door. Already more foxkin had replaced the ones they'd killed. She saw the first arrival of an aven-ria, his dark wings enveloping his body as he landed on a nearby roof. Three gargoyles joined him, their pale eyes glowing in the moonlight. Jacaranda tightened her grip on her daggers and muttered to herself as she shut the door.

"Let's hope by the night's end we can say the same."

# CHAPTER 21

Though outside was chaos and death, Adria felt pride that inside her church was calm and quiet. Candles burned low, and survivors huddled together, comforting one another and praying to the Sisters for mercy. Sena drifted among the groups, her presence invaluable in keeping hearts calm. Jacaranda and her brother kept watch at the front door, for which she was thankful. It allowed her to dedicate her attention to Tommy and his injured...actually, she wasn't sure what Malik was to her brother-in-law. Friend? Mentor? Lover?

"Can't you end the spell early?" Tommy asked the little faery. The four of them were tucked into the far corner of the church. A lone candle burned in the candelabra above, their only light. Malik lay on his back, his limbs weirdly frozen and his entire body occasionally shimmering a faint pink. Tommy sat cradling Malik's head in his lap, while Tesmarie perched atop Malik's knee, carefully eyeing the time-locked wound in the Wise's side.

"I cast the spell, and then it goes until it's done," Tesmarie said. "Sorry. It's only a few more minutes."

Adria glanced across the church to Devin and Jacaranda in the doorway. She prayed the Sisters gave them those minutes. So far the forces surrounding the church had not attacked. Janus's protection had saved her once, but she had a feeling he would not do so again.

"Are you injured?" she asked upon noticing Tesmarie held her arm in a peculiar way. Tesmarie pulled her hand away to reveal a nasty gash along her bicep.

"Just a scratch, really," the faery said.

"Then it shall be easy for me to heal," Adria said. "Please, sit upon my palms so I may pray."

Tesmarie's wings fluttered softly as she touched her bare feet into the center of Adria's palm. The words of the 36th Devotion flowed effortlessly off Adria's tongue. Soft, pleasant light washed over the wound, and then the faery's onyx skin was perfectly smooth as always. Tesmarie hovered to Adria's face, placed a kind kiss upon her cheek, and then returned to her perch atop Malik's knee.

"Hey, Tes," Tommy said. He coughed as if something awkward was stuck in his throat. "That faery who attacked you...did you know him? He seemed to know you."

Tesmarie rested her head on her hands and cast her eyes downward.

"Yes. I know him. His name is Gan, and he is...was my betrothed."

Adria cast a look Tommy's way. Such a sensitive topic didn't deserve prying, but Tommy wasn't often keen to such matters. Her brother-in-law caught her stare, and his next question died on his tongue.

"Sorry," he said instead.

"No, it's fine." Tesmarie sniffled. "I didn't care for him, not really. He's why I was banished from my home. Mostly why, I should say. My mother didn't exactly help."

Little diamond tears started to swell within the faery's eyes.

"You need not tell this story now," Adria said softly. "We are all heavy with burdens."

"I said it's fine," Tesmarie huffed. "Stupid home, stupid Gan, stupid—stupid everyone. I was betrothed to Gan but not by choice. My mother is Matriarch, and she set up the whole arrangement.

I didn't love him. I loved Elebell." She paused to wipe the tears away. "A neighbor caught us together and raised a stink. We were both brought before my mother, and she lectured about disgracing our family name and my betrothed's honor and other stuff I think is hogsnot. She gave us a choice—renounce our relationship, or be banished."

"I'm sorry," Tommy said. "Being banished by your mother had to have been awful."

Tesmarie shook her head.

"No. That part I could handle. I flew before the whole town and said I didn't love Gan, I loved Elebell, and not even exile would change my mind. But then Elebell, she—she refused. Being banished wasn't the worst, Tommy. Being banished alone was."

Adria's heart went out to the little faery. She'd been ready to stand against the world by the strength of her love, only to find that love pulled away, and her feet falling through the earth. No wonder she'd followed Devin from the Oakblack Woods to Londheim.

Tommy lowered a hand toward her, and Tesmarie cupped two of his fingers in an embrace. Flecks of diamond scattered across his pink skin.

"I know there's a lot of fighting and things we don't understand," she said. "But you and Devin and Jac, you've all shown me more kindness than I deserve. I don't care if Gan thinks I'm a traitor. I'm going to help you, no matter what!"

The occasional shade of pink that washed over Malik's skin suddenly brightened to a vibrant red. Tesmarie hopped off Malik's knee and onto Tommy's shoulder. The rigidity left Malik's limbs, and a sudden gasp of pain marked time's renewed grip upon his body.

"Hurry, Adria," the faery said. "He doesn't have long!"

"What...where...?" Malik gasped. His eyes struggled to focus, and she could hear groggy delirium overtaking his voice as he tried to sit up.

"Lie still," Adria said, forcibly pushing him onto his back. "I need only pray."

"It's all right," Tommy said, grabbing Malik's hand. "I'm here, right here. Just relax, and Adria here will fix you up."

Adria slipped her hands through the torn fabric and into his blood and ruptured flesh. She closed her eyes. Prayer floated across her tongue. Poor Tesmarie might have lost someone close to her, but under no circumstances would she allow the same to happen to Tommy. When her hands pulled away, the flesh was clean. Not even the spilled blood remained.

"Oh, thank the heavens," Tommy exclaimed. A long breath eased out of him as if he'd held it for hours. Tears crashed down his cheeks, his speech growing more and more indecipherable with his every word. "I thought I lost you, Malik. I thought you were gone, and if you did, I don't, I don't know what…"

Malik grabbed Tommy by the shoulders and pulled him close. Their lips brushed for but a moment, then longer as tears slipped down Malik's face as well. Tesmarie fluttered over to Adria's shoulder as she stood.

"Give them their moment," she whispered in agreement to the faery. Tommy knelt in Malik's embrace, releasing his every horrible imagined fear that he'd clung to over the past hour. Malik was calmly whispering something to him that she could not hear, but her spirit-blessed eyes could see the warm, soothing emotions rolling off Malik's soul.

Adria crossed the church, giving the two of them space, and she did not like the look Devin gave her as they approached. Sena had joined them, and her calm façade momentarily flickered with nervousness.

"Have matters worsened?" Adria asked, ensuring her voice wasn't loud enough for the huddled refugees to hear.

"Is it possible for things to be worse than they are now?" Sena asked.

"Don't tempt the Sisters," Devin said. The church doors were open a crack, and his eyes remained fixed on the outside. "Shit. You just had to say it, didn't you, Faithkeeper?"

"Why?" Adria asked. "What's wrong?"

Devin stepped aside so the other two might see.

"Their leader is here," he said. "Which means we've run out of time."

Adria surveyed the gathered forces, at least those that were visible. Three of the dark-winged creatures Devin had called "avenria" stood at the forefront of the varied and numerous forces. She saw foxkin wielding knives, tall lapinkin brandishing strange hooked spears, and even human Ravencallers scattered among the mix. Gargoyles hungrily perched on the nearby rooftops. Giant owls circled in the skies above.

"So many," Tesmarie whispered. The little faery shivered. "There's just so many."

Adria shut the door completely.

"Can we fight them?" she asked.

Devin checked his two ammo pouches and then shrugged.

"We might," he said. "You two have your prayers, and Tommy his magic. Me and Tesmarie can bring down a few as well, but you're talking about five of us trying to protect the church from all sides."

So it was as dire as she feared, and unlike when the creatures had first taken over Low Dock, their numbers were greater and their control over the district tightened. She thought of the weird Mayor's son, and his warnings. Those gathered monsters outside wanted to hang her from the steeple in a Ravencaller execution, with her guts ripped out and her rib cage opened. Did her church even matter to them or did they just care about her? She cast a worried look over those in her care, her eyes settling on Tommy and Malik cuddling.

"Sena, do you trust me?" she asked.

"Of course I do," the Faithkeeper replied.

"Then come with me, and do not fear." She turned to her brother. "Ready everyone inside to leave at a moment's notice. Bring only what they can carry."

"And if the dragon-sired choose to fight?" he asked.

A deep, rumbling voice released a vicious cry to the night.

"Chainbreaker! Come forth!"

Adria kissed her brother's forehead and gently brushed Tesmarie away.

"Hold faith in me," she said. "Now ready the others."

Before he might argue further, she pushed the doors open and stepped out into the night, Sena trailing a step behind.

Logarius stood at the head of his army, a black and silver monster wrapped in wings. Adria swallowed down her rage and distaste. She had to keep a clear head. Too many lives depended upon her. She descended the few steps to the mocking calls of the creatures. The ruckus threatened her resolve. Sena's hand sliding into hers strengthened it.

"I am here," Adria shouted from the bottom step. "What is it you desire of me?"

Logarius offered a mocking bow.

"To rid Belvua of this eyesore you call a church," the avenria said.

"And what of Viciss's orders? I was granted protection."

Logarius slid his long daggers out from their sheaths.

"We Forgotten Children must fight for our own future. Let the dragon crush us with his own claws if we commit a sin against him."

Drool landed on her shoulder. She looked up to see seven gargoyles leering down at her from the church's rooftop.

"Then we shall leave," she shouted. The creatures quieted with surprise. "This building is not worth the blood it will cost. I ask that you make way for us to exit Belvua, just as you offered when you first laid claim to this district."

A foxkin beside Logarius started to say something but the aven-ria cut him off.

"No," he said. "The rest of Londheim must be sent a mes-sage about the cost of human pride. The people you coddle were offered a chance to leave. They stayed. Let them die in the tomb of their own making."

Adria squeezed Sena's hand tightly.

"I feared as much," she said. She turned to the Faithkeeper. "Forgive me for this."

Adria ripped Sena's soul from her body. Its brilliant light, its luminescent white fire, shone like a beacon before the church. Adria held it aloft with her left hand, the right still clutching Sena's limp fingers. Logarius's Forgotten Children shrank back in fear.

"A message must indeed be sent," she said. "But it is not yours to send."

Sena's soul shot skyward, blasting through the gargoyles. A naked soul was incomprehensible power, whose very touch burned away flesh. The gargoyle's gray bodies shriveled and col-lapsed. The monsters about her screamed and howled, but their cries meant nothing to her. The soul crashed down among their forces, its speed so great it was but a brilliant blur in the night. Monsters collapsed with gaping holes in their chests. Others howled as their limbs were severed, or chunks of their sides sud-denly disintegrated.

Adria took their lives with but a thought, her mind mapping a path of slaughter and Sena's soul following it with perfect obedi-ence. Let these vicious monsters die for threatening the innocent. Let them run. Soldiers might fear them, but she was a Mindkeeper of the Sisters, and she was sick of these creatures blaspheming their beloved name. She directed the worst of her anger toward the Ravencallers, humans so lost to hatred they would kill their own.

Logarius, however, she let live. She needed someone to give the necessary order.

After those first vicious few seconds she pulled the soul back to a hover above her head. The warmth of its light bathed her with Sena's memories. Oh, if only she could dive deeper within and experience her friend's life in a far more intimate way. That time was not now, nor the church steps the place. Dozens of the Forgotten Children lay dead or dying. The collected monsters crowded closer, their weapons, be it metal or tooth and claw, bared and hungry.

"There are enough of you I may die," she told them. "But are you prepared to pay the cost? I only ask that we leave in peace. Save us both the bloodshed."

All there awaited Logarius's order. The avenria glared at her, his wings shuddering with his every breath. Rage burned in his eyes. For a moment she thought he'd resist. No matter how many died, he would see her dead. The Forgotten Children tensed with each passing second, anticipating another display of her power.

"You are a blight upon the Cradle," Logarius said. "But I will not sacrifice precious lives to snuff it out. Have your freedom. We will not lay a hand upon you until you leave Belvua's borders."

Adria bowed her head in understanding and then turned to the passive, dull-eyed Sena.

"Thank you," she whispered. She plunged the soul back into Sena's forehead and reattached its little tendrils throughout her body. The Faithkeeper jolted awake with a long, pained scream. Adria fought against the guilt that scream awakened. Sena's soul... she'd damaged it during its killing flight. Various memories, like wisps of white ether, had slipped free as it tore through flesh and bone. Would her friend notice? Only time would tell.

Adria called for her brother as Sena recovered. The door to the church pushed open and her brother stepped out. She wondered if he had watched the destruction she had wrought. She prayed he hadn't. "We're leaving."

"Is it safe?" Devin asked her, his voice strangely muted.

Adria cast a glare Logarius's way.

"It is."

Sena's hand clutched her shoulder as the Faithkeeper struggled to keep her balance. Her eyes were bloodshot. Fury bubbled beneath her exhaustion.

"I would have said yes," she said. "Why did you not ask my permission? I would have said yes."

A valid question, and one Adria had no good answer for. Sena would not have understood what she was accepting, not really. At least the burden of the event fell squarely on Adria's shoulders.

The various creatures parted as the several dozen men and women exited the church. Devin led the way, and it was his shoulder, not Adria's, that Sena relied upon for the walk out of Low Dock. Adria stayed back, ensuring not a soul remained behind. She felt the inhuman glares stabbing like pins, and she glared right back. They were shadowy beings, each and every one of them. There was no soul shimmering within their skulls. No light of the Sisters.

"You did it," Tommy said as he and Malik passed, the young man supporting his mentor's weight.

"That I did," she said, unable to match her brother-in-law's smile.

The final refugees of Low Dock marched through the streets, passing guards and soldiers strung up by their arms in front of doorways. At the cleared-out west entrance, a dozen guards stood frozen by barely concealed fear at the encroaching tide of magical creatures flanking the retreating humans. Adria was the last to leave, and she turned to offer one final good-bye to Low Dock, place of her church, and her beloved home.

Good-bye, for it was Belvua now, and it belonged to the Forgotten Children.

# CHAPTER 22

Dierk walked past corpse after corpse hanging in Belvua, his mind lost in pure euphoria. Every single dead human had been tied to doorways and rooftops, their stomachs and rib cages opened for a Ravencaller funeral. Vaesalaum wrapped about their unharvested souls with a noticeable bulge in its belly. The creature fed well, Dierk thought, and so did he.

*A million memories*, Vaesalaum replied. *Read. Eat. Drink.*

Dierk did not fall into them like he normally would. There were just too many. Instead experiences floated over him, a sampler buffet curated by the nisse. He felt phantom punches on his chin from fights, felt wetness on his erect penis from electric snippets of encounters, sometimes from a man's point of view, sometimes a woman's. The world before his eyes lost its firm reality. Walls and homes gave way to fields, to forests, to tight bedroom walls and cramped barracks. Excitement would flush through him as he watched their (his) hand strike a killing blow against one of the magical creatures in last night's battle. He had not participated like the other Ravencallers, but with so many collected memories filling him, he might as well have. Dierk walked, intoxicated, stumbling down an abandoned street with but one location in mind.

Adria's church was but a smoldering ruin of ash and embers.

*Finding her is pointless,* Vaesalaum insisted. *Enjoy the feast.*

"No," he said. "No, no, this time I will do it. This time I'll tell her."

But that meant finding her. Where might she have gone? There was no chance she'd died, he was certain of that. Sure, he'd listened in on the devastating reports delivered to his father in the dead of night. He knew the effort to retake the district had ended in colossal failure. Adria was too powerful, though. Too amazing and special to die like the rest of the humans. If only he could spot her brilliant soul, so bright it shined through walls and flesh like nothing...

"You said I now have nisse eyes," Dierk said, an idea popping into his head. "Can you help me then? Can you help me see her?"

The long creature floated in a figure-eight path before his face. Dierk realized just how much the nisse had grown since they first met. It'd tripled in length at the least. The eyeless childlike face finally hovered still in a weird stare.

*If it will make Dierk happy.*

The world darkened and lost much of its color. The souls of the guards hanging from the doorways of human homes brightened so that they were unmistakable. Their pearlescent glow was nothing, nothing at all, compared to the brilliant beacon blazing several miles away. Its light passed through stone walls as if they were translucent. The edges of its beams streaked to the heavens.

"There you are, my beautiful Adria," he whispered, a drunkard's smile plastered across his face.

Dierk left Belvua via the cistern tunnel, following Adria's light like a guiding star. For once he wore no disguise, and he did not care about any strange looks the haggard and nervous early-morning crowds cast his way. What did their opinions matter? He could barely see them through the shadowy haze. His every step felt like another person's, for the memories Vaesalaum had devoured still clung to his mind like a welcome stranger.

It was in the Church District that Dierk found her home. Vaesalaum stayed away, and not for the first time upon meeting Adria, he realized.

"Are you afraid of her?" he asked.

*Chainbreaker will see me*, the nisse said. *Chainbreaker will not like what she sees.*

Whatever. Let the strange nisse keep away. Dierk didn't need it. He didn't need anyone. Confidence surged through his veins in a way he had never before experienced in his life. He approached the modest home's door and knocked several times. Out stepped his beloved goddess-made-flesh.

"Dierk?" Adria asked, confused.

He didn't respond immediately. Her face was uncovered. Without her mask, he could see the gentle slope of her nose, the sharp prominence of her cheekbones, the pale pink of her lips. Adoration flooded his chest. Bravery powered his movements. His arms spread wide, and he wrapped her in a tight embrace. Her scent wafted up his nostrils and to his brain, painting his vision red. She felt rigid in his arms. Tired. Confused. That was fine. He'd come to help.

"I am so happy you lived," Dierk said upon pulling away. "I know you said you'd stay, but you left, and that was smart. You were smart."

"Perhaps," she said. Her arms crossed over her chest. She wasn't wearing her thick Mindkeeper attire but instead a thin shift covered by a long-sleeved shirt. Dierk could see the shape of her breasts, even see faint outlines of her nipples hardening from the cold. It was several seconds before he realized he was staring at them and not her.

"I, um," he stammered, heat flushing into his neck. "Are you well?"

"How did you find me?" she asked. "Did someone tell you I was staying at my brother's?"

He shook his head, the act almost costing him his balance. It felt like his brain was made entirely of air.

"That's partly why I'm here," he said. "I wanted you to know, I can see how special you are. I can see *you*. Your soul. It's so bright, and wonderful, and different from everyone in all of Londheim. Did you know that? How amazing you are?"

Surely she did, but she clearly didn't understand what he was getting at; that much was obvious by her constricted frown.

"I'm not sure what you're implying," she said.

"Your *soul*," he said, as if that explained everything. "It's special, and I know, deep down I know, that I'm the only one that understands."

Damn it all to the void, he was screwing this up. He could barely understand what he was saying, so why should she? Dierk shook his head back and forth, trying to dismiss the fog that seemed to have settled over him. Too many memories. Too many souls fed upon.

"I'm not sure what you are implying, but I am a Mindkeeper of the Sisters, as faithful and as loyal as hundreds of others in their service," she said. "Did—did your father ask you to check on me?"

"My father? No. Fuck no. He doesn't know I'm here."

He thought that'd make her feel better, but instead it just confused her further.

"Then why are you here?" she asked. She could tell something important was on his mind. Not a surprise. Would he be so infatuated with someone whose mind wasn't sharp as a blade? "The real reason. Tell me."

Cold sweat rolled down his neck. His armpits felt like swamps. He couldn't bring himself to look her in the eye, so he made his confession as he stared at the socks on her feet.

"I think that...I think that it could be something special. *We* could be something special, you know? If you'd like, you could come over to my father's mansion. You could stay there even, it's very nice, and we have more than enough rooms. It'd give us a lot of time to talk."

She wasn't answering. Was she flattered by the offer? Or was it too much commitment much too soon?

"You don't have to, of course," he quickly added. "We could just go somewhere warm. There's some great bakeries near our mansion. Would you like me to buy you something, maybe some shortbread or a slice of pie?"

Finally Adria found her tongue. Shock tinged her every word.

"I spent last night fleeing the only home I've known in years," she said. "I betrayed a close friend so I might kill with abandon. There's blood on my hands, of humans and monsters, and you want us to go on a *date?* How are you the Mayor's son and yet so clueless?"

That last sentence was a jagged rusty knife stabbing straight into his heart and then twisting.

"I—I didn't mean it like…I'm sorry. Please. I'm sorry, Adria. Don't be mad at me. Please don't be mad."

The Mindkeeper looked torn between anger and pity, and Dierk couldn't decide which hurt him worse.

"You need help," she said. "You barely know me, and I know nothing of you. Whatever you think you mean by '*we,*' it's make-believe. Do you understand that? It's hopeful imagination, and it has no bearing on the real world."

Breathing was suddenly, unbearably difficult. He tried to figure out the nicest thing to say, some clever argument or honest confession that would make Adria see how wrong she was, how cruel she was being, but the only thing that tumbled out his tongue-tied mouth was, "Oh. All right. I get it."

Her expression softened, but Dierk was in too much pain. He didn't want her sympathy. He didn't want her comfort. His feet couldn't move him fast enough as he turned and ran, not bothering to say good-bye. Snot dripped down his lip as he sprinted in the cold. Tears rolled down his cheeks, first a few, then a torrent. One word pounded in his mind like the world's largest drum.

*Stupid. Stupid. Stupid.*

Cute little homes dusted with snow passed by in a blur. He shoved past anyone remotely in his way, not giving a shit if it angered them. He ran, ran, ran until his lungs threatened to give out. Dierk spotted an empty crevice between two homes, hardly more than a rat hole, but it was enough for him. He more crawled than walked into it, and once in its private confines he curled into a ball and bawled into his arms. His heart ached, its tender flesh so badly ruptured he felt a physical pain across his chest. Whatever remnants of hope he'd felt were long gone, replaced with seething hatred. Stupid. So fucking stupid. Why did he think she would care one bit about his ugly, awkward self?

Vaesalaum appeared before him, its childlike face mere inches from his nose.

*Vaesalaum warned you*, the nisse whispered into his mind. *Vaesalaum will wait for the human to stop behaving as a child.*

Dierk wanted nothing to do with the damn creature. His protest was a wordless howl, but that was enough to make it shimmer into nothingness. He glared at where it'd been, his hatred quickly redirecting back toward himself. He thought with the nisse's help he'd become a better person. With power would come confidence. With confidence would come attractiveness, and worthiness for such a beautiful goddess. No one else matched his magical and political power combined. Son of the Mayor. Student of Vaesalaum. Ravencaller of the Forgotten Children.

So naïve. So stupid. So hopeless.

Alone in a dark alley, still surrounded by fleeting memories of the dead, Dierk sobbed and sobbed, utterly convinced he was the loneliest, unluckiest, most miserable person in all of Londheim.

# INTERLUDE

Fredrik Milles stood on the smooth shores of Oris, an easel wedged into the sand before him and a stick of black chalk in his left hand. He drew long, arcing lines across his canvas, molding the ever-moving ocean into fixed curls and waves. Fredrik had traveled throughout the Cradle in his youthful days, but now that he was in his seventies and the tastes of the wealthy clientele had shifted firmly over to inks, he no longer felt the same need to explore. His weekly sketches and scribbles of the ocean were enough to satisfy his subdued creative drive.

"The water's angry today," a fisherman named Perry said as he paused on his walk to the market, a string of fish slung over his shoulder. Every day Perry liked to stop and chat before leaving the coast with his haul. It was never about anything serious, just the ways of the weather and the shifts in the tide.

"Looks like some aren't intimidated," Fredrik said. With the approach of winter, the city's beaches had fallen quiet but for the fishermen and a small group of men and women swimming several hundred yards down shore.

"Eh, they're young," Perry said. "They still think death is for other people."

A few more minutes of idle talk and Perry was on his way. Fredrik turned his attention to his canvas, and he decided his drawing didn't quite catch the same anger the fisherman talked about. He brushed his stained thumb over lines, smoothing waves to shadows and highlights to match new, bolder lines. The ocean did seem strangely hostile today. The waves came crashing in with rare speed, and they pulled out farther than usual on the retreat.

*An omen of a bad winter?* he wondered. Nearly every town and city had similar signs they believed portended a bad harvest, a scorching summer, or a season of storms and tornados. Some bore truth, while others were nonsensical superstitions. Fredrik's personal favorite from his travels was a village where the elderly forced a frog to hop toward multiple sticks, with each stick representing a good, mediocre, or poor harvest. How a frog possessed this knowledge baffled him, but his painting of the town crowded around the small track had sold for a nice chunk of gold crowns, so he wasn't one to judge. Let simple people believe in superstitions and magic. It did no harm.

The ground rumbled beneath Fredrik's feet, strong enough that he had to grab his easel and hold it steady. He immediately looked to the swimmers. They may think their youth protected them from the cold, but a sudden quake like that meant strong waves that would make a mockery of their slick bodies. Thankfully he saw fishermen farther down shouting at them. Witnessing a drowning would be a sorry start to the day.

"Shit," Fredrik muttered when he realized the sudden shifting of the sand had caused his hand to errantly scrape across his drawing. Years ago such a mistake would have left him furious, but long gone were the days of him painstakingly detailing one image over weeks. He let out a long sigh and wondered if he could integrate the mark somehow, perhaps as part of a pier or a fishing pole...

Again the ground shifted, and this time he could hear its deep rumble. Distant voices screamed. Fredrik was torn between watching the receding shoreline or checking the buildings behind him for collapse. The strangeness of the ocean kept him still. The way the water moved, it defied his understanding. Pulling down, draining, yet at the same time rising in scattered, uneven portions unlike any waves he'd ever witnessed.

And then the dragon's head emerged from the water.

It bore six eyes, three on each side of its head. To call them eyes seemed strange, for they looked like enormous sapphire boulders. Its scales were slabs of emerald. The teeth of its gaping mouth were diamond. This gemstone monstrosity had a body like a snake, and as it continued to rise above the waters, Fredrik's mind struggled to comprehend the impossibility of its existence. Its body…it continued for miles and miles, a winding, seaweed-covered serpent taller than buildings and longer than the horizon.

All others fled, but Fredrik would not. He tossed his current picture aside to reveal the second canvas beneath. His chalk sliced across its blank surface. Fredrik had drawn many wonders in his life, but they all paled compared to the gemstone dragon. He relied on fierce dedication to overwhelm his terror. His mind may disbelieve, but drawing it made it real. He sketched its gold whiskers, each the thickness and length of a Helwoad Pine. He formed deep divots with the chalk to represent the ruby slabs that coated its underbelly, which was barely visible from the tilt of its neck as it approached. If only he had his paints! Their color would fail to capture the dragon's true wonder, but at least it would showcase it better than his black and gray scribbling.

A wave crashed up to his knees, but Fredrik clung to his easel and kept steady. The dragon was close now, so close. He feared his heart would break from how heavy it pounded within his chest. The dragon's chin scraped along the sand, carving itself a pathway. The shift of sand, the flow of water, it was deafening, yet the assault on his ears meant little compared to how its very existence scrambled Fredrik's mind. Monsters and magic did not exist. Though fantastical drawings of faeries and goblins were popular, he had never painted such flights of fancy. To stand before such a thing threatened to completely break his mind down to nothing and then wash him away like sand upon the tide.

The mouth stretched open, a yawning chasm with diamonds for teeth and a slick coating of onyx for a tongue. The chalk slipped from Fredrik's hand. There were no words to offer. His mind was as blank as his canvas at the start of his early mornings. From within that endless darkness walked a woman in a flawless silver dress. Her skin was smooth as water and black as obsidian. The perfection of her face would be the envy of every rich heiress throughout Oris. Her blue eyes held him captive. Her raven hair, so long it hung to her ankles, taunted his mind with its playful swish. Her only decoration was a thin silver crown woven through her hair and studded with sapphires.

"Can you write?" she asked him. Her voice was clearer than any instrument crafted by the hands of humanity.

"I can," he said. By comparison, his voice was harsh and rough as sand.

"Then write a message for me, human, and bring it to your queen."

Fredrik flipped his canvas over to its back. His first wedge of chalk was long gone to the waves, but he kept a spare in his vest pocket. He withdrew it with shaking fingers and gently pressed it to the canvas.

"What shall I write?" he asked.

"By order of Chyron the Beautiful, you are to release your hold upon the lands you call West and South Orismund, to allow the humans there to become countries free of the crown."

Fredrik wrote the words, baffled by the demand and unsure of how the Queen might respond. He knew her as an acquaintance, one luxury afforded him by his prestigious career. She was not one to give in to threats.

"You ask for much," he dared say. "We have fought wars to keep Orismund united. Why would she relinquish those lands now?"

Chyron stepped closer. Something of her demeanor changed. She seemed taller, her eyes darker, and her dress sparkling with unseen power.

"Tell her to do as I command, or I shall bury Oris beneath the waves."

Her crystalline lips kissed his cheek. All the world froze. Even the waves were like immutable stone. Fredrik tucked the canvas underneath his arm and ran every step of the way past the beachside shops, through the three-story homes of Seaside District, over the bricks of the Sparkling Bridge, and to the palace gates of Queen Woadthyn the Ninth. It was only then, when he touched the shoulder of a guard manning the giant ornate doors, that the world resumed its proper pace.

"A message for the Queen," Fredrik said, and thrust the drawing toward the surprised and frightened guard moments before his legs gave way and his heart shuddered its last.

# CHAPTER 23

The cell door slammed shut behind Adria with a violent clang. Tamerlane rubbed and stretched his jaw as she leaned against the bars and watched him.

"That contraption never gets comfortable," he said. "So, do you have news to share of the outside world? I can tell from the whispers of the guards that something exciting happened over the past few days, but they don't feel the need to share with their lowly prisoner."

"I can't imagine why not," she said dryly. Deakon Sevold was just a few cells over, struggling to breathe under the care of a physician and two Faithkeepers. It'd be a constant reminder to the guards why Tamerlane was imprisoned in the first place.

"So please, do fill me in," the man insisted. "The world is changing at a rapid pace, and I'm down here blind to most of it."

"Magical creatures have taken control of Low Dock and repelled any attempts to reclaim it. They've renamed it Belvua, and are petitioning the Mayor to acknowledge the territory as theirs."

"Low Dock?" he asked. "Isn't that your district?"

"It was."

Tamerlane tilted his head, and again she felt naked before his golden-eyed stare.

"What was it like?" he asked.

"What do you mean?"

"The night the creatures came for Low Dock. What was it like?"

She pulled the edges of her ridge cloak more tightly about her and suppressed a shiver. Goddesses, it was so cold down there. She almost felt pity for Tamerlane's lack of blanket or extra clothing beyond his torn Mindkeeper robes.

"They surrounded my church and demanded my death," she said. "To hang from the steeple of my church, to be specific. Ravencallers were with them. A fine bunch you have thrown your lot in with."

"It may surprise you, Adria, but I am not actually a Ravencaller, even if I have read the Book of Ravens and found it intellectually stimulating."

"And why not?"

"It was once a mystery, but with this old magical world return-ing, the Book of Ravens' purpose is now blatantly revealed. It argues that humans are not the dominant life upon the Cradle, and the Goddesses not the perfect, flawless creators we have been led to believe."

Adria's mind raced over the early pages of the book, chastising herself for not having read the entire thing. She'd been much too focused on the curses than the sophomoric religious rants.

"And what is it you disagree with?" she asked.

"We humans *are* the dominant species," he said, as if it were obvious. "And it will take far more than an old book to convince me otherwise. But I digress. These magical creatures wanted you dead, yet obviously you stand before me, alive. How did you survive?"

Adria questioned herself for the twelfth time that morning since deciding to come visit Tamerlane. Whatever Janus had done to her, there was no scripture or scroll within their archives detailing its significance. And now that Tamerlane had shaken her trust in her own Vikar, she feared to fully reveal her newfound power to anyone in the church. Having so few to discuss this change with stifled her mind and left her frustrated. But in this dark cell was a man physically bound to silence and possessing knowledge into things she was only beginning to understand.

"I survived by killing them until they let us go free," she said.

"Did you?" Tamerlane asked, his eyebrows arcing upward. "With another curse?"

Adria swallowed down her fear.

"No," she said. "With this."

Though a wall was between her and the nearby guard, the light of his soul was an easily visible star to her eyes. She wrapped her mental fingers around it and beckoned it to come. The soul detached from the guard's head with a metaphysical shudder and then passed through the stone. She set it to swirl about her body, starting from her legs and ending in a hover just above her open palm.

Tamerlane fell to his knees, and it looked like he might cry from the sight of her.

"The power to command a soul," he whispered.

A flick of her fingers and she sent the soul crashing back into the guard's body. After a few seconds of smoothing it down, the guard was back to normal. She heard him coughing and shaking his head, no doubt convinced he'd undergone a strange and violent dizzy spell.

"That is my gift," she said softly. "That is how I took the lives of the magical creatures."

Wonder lit his face with light long denied him within the dungeon cells.

"How?" he asked. "Please, tell me, I must know."

"An answer for an answer," she said. "Tell me how to un-curse the Deakon, and I shall tell you how I became what I am."

For the very first time since meeting him, she witnessed his confidence falter. His desire for knowledge rivaled even Thaddeus's. Adria waited with bated breath.

"No," he said. "I cannot."

"Because you do not know how?"

"Because my curiosity is not worth that monster living another second without pain and suffering."

Adria was shocked by his sudden rage. Tamerlane had always been so cocksure, as if even his own imprisonment was beneath his worry.

"Why did you curse the Deakon?" she asked.

The man quickly soothed his rage. A false smile returned to his face.

"Finally you ask the obvious question. Have you not wondered why this whole time?"

"I guess I thought it self-explanatory," she said. "You're a Ravencaller, or at least, something close to it. Of course you would hate the Deakon."

"Come now, that's it? You're far wiser than this. You understand the complexities of this world. Do I seem a man who would curse and harm another for no reason other than a lame belief that it's what I am 'supposed' to do?"

Heat flushed into Adria's neck. Damn it, how did Tamerlane keep making her feel so foolish? She was a learned scholar of the church. For him to twist her mind around so easily, it didn't just shake her confidence in herself. It shook her confidence in all the dogma and tradition she'd spent her life immersed within.

"No, you seem like a man with a clear purpose for everything he does."

"Very good. Then let me ask again...why do you think I cursed the Deakon?"

"Because you believed he deserved it," she said. "All else is complete conjecture."

Tamerlane clapped his hands twice, the mockery almost enough for her to rip his soul out of his body just to spite him.

"Indeed, but what fabulous conjecture it is. Was it deviancy? Hypocrisy? Did I interrupt dark plans and conspiracies, or was it in self-defense? I knew him well, Adria. I worked with him closely in the cathedral. We spent years collaborating on sermons and letters. What might break me? What would create such wrath within my heart? Perhaps the question you should be asking yourself is not '*how* do I un-curse the Deakon' but instead '*should* I un-curse the Deakon?'"

Adria stepped closer, and her voice fell to a whisper.

"What did the Deakon do?" she asked. "What great sin did he commit?"

"Not yet," Tamerlane said. "You're close, very close, but you're not ready to believe me."

"I could take the answer from you," she said. "I could tear your soul from your body and peer through its memories like pages in a book."

"And yet you haven't," Tamerlane said. "That alone is how I know you are not ready to hear the truth. You fear it. If the Deakon is a vile being, and worthy of his curse, well..." He slumped against the wall of his cell and sat. "Then you might have to do something reckless. Something that might land you in serious trouble with your beloved Keeping Church."

Adria stretched her hand out toward him. Tamerlane's body stiffened, as if he could feel her mind grabbing at the edges of his soul. It'd be so easy to pull it free, she thought. All his pride and intellect would mean nothing compared to her raw power. Every answer she sought, the counter to the mutilation curse, the supposed dark secret the Deakon harbored, all naked before her. He could not stop her. He could not resist.

But she could not bring herself to do it.

Tamerlane collapsed to the ground, and he gasped from a breath he'd held for the past minute.

"I'm leaving," she said, whether to him, the guard, or herself, she didn't know. She exited the cell and hurried down the cramped corridor.

"Slay your fear," Tamerlane shouted after her. "It is your one fatal flaw."

The guard she'd withdrawn the soul from nodded at her as she passed, the leather gag swinging in his fingers.

"Don't listen to the bastard," he said. "Trust me, he even gets in Thaddeus's head."

Once outside the dungeon, Adria walked the streets of Londheim, her hands clutching the rabbit-fur trim of her cloak and holding it tightly shut. The souls of those passing by were distant stars to her deeply sunken mind. *Slay your fear*, he'd said, as if it were a simple thing. Her wounded pride insisted she wasn't afraid. She had power. Authority. People had begun to sing praises to her name. What could possibly frighten her?

Her feet rooted in place. She shook her head in shame. No, she was certainly afraid. Despite her desperate need to understand her new condition, she'd not done the one obvious thing to seek answers. She closed her eyes, not caring she blocked the center of the street. She meditated on her fears, and on conquering them. Her knees turned to liquid, and already her heart beat faster at the thoughts overwhelming her. Of blue mist rising at her feet. Of walls coursing with starlight-filled veins.

"Damn you, Tamerlane," she seethed. "Goddesses fucking damn you."

She ran. It was the only way she knew to ensure she did not lose her nerve.

Adria had returned only once to the simple dilapidated home since her rescue from Janus. Devin had led the way, armed and eager for another fight, but the way inside the tunnel had been sealed off by a massive wall of steel that Janus no doubt formed during their absence. It refused Tesmarie's touch. Not even Tommy's magic had left a dent. But her magic? Her power? She'd not tried once.

"Be with me, Sisters," she prayed as she brushed away the illusion hiding the sealed doorway. The slab of steel shimmered into view. Adria touched its cold surface and closed her eyes. Inside would be a small chamber with a well, and from another secret door, there would be a tunnel. At the end of that tunnel...at the end of that long, dark passage...the beating heart beneath Londheim. The chamber of her rebirth.

"Slay your fear," she whispered.

There was no one to draw from but herself. Power surged throughout her body as she tapped her soul's seemingly infinite reservoir. No fire or lightning could break that door, but she wielded magic fiercer than fire, more intense than lightning. The door before her? Break it down. Rip it apart. She imagined it gone, and demanded the world reshape itself to make her vision true. Little tendrils of light lashed out from her fingertips and ripped their way through the steel like cracks in ice atop a frozen lake. She heard it groan in futile protest. The light continued to spread, as unstoppable as the tides. Unmaking it. Denying its very existence.

With a whoosh of unsealed air, the steel door disintegrated into stardust that fell like snow upon the floor.

"Welcome back," Adria told herself with a grim smile.

The chamber inside was as her brother had described to her. The walls and ceiling were a smooth dome, its surface like glass separating the interior from a vast star field upon the other side. A stone well was in its center, shaped like three stacked triangles rotated at slight angles so their sharp points poked out in all directions. Liquid starlight dripped into the heart of the well at a slow, steady pace.

Adria walked across the cold stone floor and peered into the well. Inside was a diamond orb collecting that starlight like a pail set out to catch rainwater. Its light was almost blinding to her sensitive eyes, yet she knew it was but a tiny fraction toward being full. Everything about the setup should have frightened her, yet for some reason she felt... comforted. The protection of the stars, no matter how real or illusionary they might be, was like a warm blanket across her cold skin. If only she could say the same of where she traveled to next.

Devin had said there was a door hidden by a secret trigger, but she need not search for it. A normal person's eyes would find nothing, but she could see the thin, swirling beam of starlight and souls underneath the floor leading directly toward the wall. A tiny little tendril of it snaked out to one of the stars, and when she pressed it, a segment of the wall faded away to allow her entrance.

From within that dark corridor she sensed a hidden voice beckoning her onward.

"I am blind, but Lyra gives me sight," she whispered. "I see darkness, but Lyra gives me light. The light I see dwells in me, and it is blinding."

A brilliant flare exploded from her palm. She captured it within her mind, calming it, weakening it so it might last for hours instead of one debilitating moment. The pure white glow emanating from her palms soothed her nerves and gave her strength to continue. Step by step, she returned to Janus's prison. Step by step, she returned to where her life changed forever.

"Here I am," she said to the great emptiness of the central chamber. "I'm back."

It was as she remembered. The ceiling seemed as far from her reach as the stars in the sky. Bone morphed into steel and back to support the dome's sides. She dared not touch the walls, but she felt certain they would be firm like muscles. Now that she had time to look, she realized the dome wasn't quite perfectly round. No, the way the supports came together near the top, not quite connecting, reminded her of standing within a giant, hollow rib cage. This place, it was still alive somehow. Dormant, slumbering perhaps, but still it gathered power, still it prepared to force its gift upon another.

And there in the center of this otherworldly locale was the broken heart.

Panic reared its ugly head as she looked upon the twisted remnants of her prison. Her shallow breathing escalated against her wishes. Invisible bugs bit at her fingertips. Goddesses help her, what was she doing here? What if Janus was nearby? She imagined the gargantuan machinery rumbling back to life. What if her rescue had interrupted something? What if the power she wielded was only the beginning?

What if. What if. What if.

Adria's heart pounded as if she sprinted in a race, yet her feet remained bolted to the ground. Her eyes locked on the broken metallic heart in the center. She was a fool coming here. What did she think she'd learn from the broken glass, metal, and membranes? A sob escaped her throat despite her not crying. She remembered Devin's panicked screams as he failed to break her out. She remembered urging him to run, her death a certainty, her fear hidden behind a fake smile. That sense of insurmountable dread returned to her, and no rational argument held sway against it.

The Mindkeeper collapsed to her knees. Real tears finally broke free. She'd not cried for herself, she realized. From the very moment she awoke from Janus's capture, she'd comforted her brother. She'd wiped away his tears and brought life back to his

beloved Jacaranda. There'd been no tears for her. There'd been no
time. No privacy.

But she had both time and privacy in this monstrous rib cage,
whose veins pulsed with starlight and whose heart was a shattered
construction of tubes and metal. Londheim was a world away,
and despite her fear, and her trauma, she allowed herself to finally
break. A twisted part of her almost wished Janus would arrive.
He was the lone being in all of Londheim who might understand
what she felt. He might even be the only one to truly know who
and what she was.

*We know what you are.*

Adria jerked her head up, her eyes wide. That voice, that cold,
slithering voice...where had it come from?

"Hello?" she asked, her own voice small and insignificant in the
gigantic expanse. "Who's there?"

*We are. We have always been. We will always be.*

Adria spun in place, searching for the speaker whose voice
seemed to enter her mind without touching her ears. Counting
the corridor she'd come from, there were six total pathways leading into the enormous center. She could only guess as to what she
might find down them. Would they be similar chambers as the
one she'd entered, or was there more to this machine capable of
granting godlike powers? She scanned the entrances, looking for a
person, a shadow, a hovering pair of eyes.

Instead, not far from the broken remains of the steel heart, she
spotted a long, slender wound in reality itself. It was like a long,
wriggling black scar torn through the air. No wider than a piece
of string, but she could see within, and her mind looped from vertigo. It seemed inside that scar was an entire world, infinitely long
and impossibly dark. There was no light, no stars, only emptiness.
Only void.

*The lines are breaking*, spoke the scar. *The stars fade. The walls
tremble.*

"Be silent," she said. Wisps of smoke floated from the scar and sank like water. It dissolved before touching the ground, but the mere sight of it filled her with a visceral revulsion. "Whatever you are, leave this place."

This voice, this presence, this void, cared not for her threats. A sudden surge of mist burst out from it, forming two long spider-silk strands that wrapped about her wrists.

*They call you Chainbreaker, but it is not humanity's chains you break.*

Adria screamed against the cold fire blackening her skin at its very touch.

*It is ours.*

Her mind blanked with horror. She tried to summon the strength of her soul, but she could not command it. She couldn't even see its phantom glow. The scar's tendrils tugged and pulled, dragging her closer to the jagged window of an impossibly endless void. Fury fought against her panic. This was not how she would die. Her mindless scream became words of a prayer she belted out at the top of her lungs.

"Blessed Sisters, I seek your protection. Bind the darkness so it may not touch my flesh. Show mercy so I may stand in the light."

For the first time since her healing powers awakened upon healing old Rosa's knee, her prayer went unanswered. The tendrils tightened. Her boots skidded against the floor.

"Blessed Sisters," Adria begged. "I seek your protection."

No anger this time. No commanding the power. She was desperate. Helpless.

"Bind the darkness so it may not touch my flesh."

Silver light sparked about her feet. The tendrils cut through flesh entirely, their spidery touch clinging to naked bone.

"Show mercy so I may stand in the light."

Waves of brilliance washed over her. The tendrils withered into flecks of ash. The moment they departed, she felt her world reawaken, and the presence of her own soul was the clearest, most beautiful sensation in all the world. Power flowed throughout her body, brilliant lightning streaking down her spine, through her arms, and out her fingertips. She grabbed its white fire and swirled it across her wrists, mending the ripped flesh. Once healed, she lashed the light against the sides of the tear. Six new tendrils emerged from inside, but they withered and broke against her might.

*You should have never been. Become ours. Heal the wound.*

"I am not yours," she seethed. "I belong to no man. No monster. No void. *Be gone!*"

Her hands smashed together. The rupture sealed shut with a tremendous hiss of air. Though silence followed, the scream of the void echoed like distant thunder within her mind, forever to stay.

# CHAPTER 24

Crksslff bounced and somersaulted across the waves inside a tiny pocket of steam. It wasn't one to feel fear often, but it did now. Devin and Jacaranda were long gone, having managed to resist the current far better than it could, given its now diminutive size. That size would continue to shrink, too, should it not escape the cistern's channel and seek dry ground.

Another rough bounce. The waterkin weren't near, so far as it could tell. Now was its chance. Crksslff directed all its heat directly beneath itself, creating a burst of steam to catapult it out of the cistern's flow and to the stone. There it lay for several minutes, shivering against the cold. There was so much moisture in the air, it irritated its flame and left it miserable.

Crksslff hopped up onto two legs when it heard an oncoming rush of water. Were the waterkin hunting it? It didn't know, and it feared to be caught in its current state. Crksslff was hardly larger than Devin's pinkie at this point. The well-fed waterkin could douse it into nothing with hardly any effort. The little firekin dashed to the far wall, its beady eyes searching. A tiny crack was all it needed, and it found one near the bottom. Crksslff quickly hopped in and shriveled its flame down to a faint spark.

Two waterkin passed by while leaping in and out of the channel's surface like dolphins. Crksslff listened for what felt like hours, but did not hear their return. At last it allowed itself to relax. A little bit of green moss grew in the crevice, and though it was thick with moisture, Crksslff had plenty of time to digest. It let its heat slowly dry the moss out, and once sufficiently warmed, Crksslff placed a tiny arm against its center. By this point Crksslff was barely larger than the flicker of fire atop a candlestick. Smoke rose in soft curls as the firekin ate. The fuel wasn't much, but to the starving firekin, it was a feast.

A day passed before Crksslff poked its head out from the crevice. The moss was gone, and had been for hours. The firekin was back to the size of Devin's thumb. Not the strongest, but it could wait no longer. While in a dry, barren environment Crksslff could survive for weeks, the thick moisture of the cistern would slowly wear away at it like a fatal itch.

So far Crksslff hadn't seen any sign of the waterkin after the first few initial searches, but it kept on its guard nonetheless as it hopped along the cold stone ground. It kept an eye out for any sort of ladder or stairs to the surface. Living among the humans presented its own set of challenges and risks, but at least the humans had not tried to kill it like the waterkin had. Plus among humanity's massive collection of clothes, knickknacks, and fluff, there was a seemingly infinite amount to eat.

The firekin did not find a ladder, but it did find square alcoves spaced out along the pathway. Most of them were empty, but the second one it encountered contained dozens and dozens of logs stacked up like firewood, and tied down with a thick burlap sack to protect against moisture. To find such a treasure belied belief, but starving firekin couldn't be choosers. Crksslff darted to the very back of the stack, hugged a thick chunk of pine, and happily burned the hours away.

Firekin did not dream, but they did fade away for long periods of time with the entirety of their focus upon the slow, steady consumption of their food. It was in this sleeplike haze that Crksslff heard movement from beyond the wood pile. Its beady little eyes snapped open. The tarp pulled away, and torchlight spilled across the logs. Crksslff kept low, confident it would go unnoticed with how far back it hunkered.

"The humans haven't retaken Belvua yet," a foxkin said to the lapinkin with him as the two loaded logs into their arms. "Maybe they'll decide to give us a place to live."

"Or maybe they're waiting until they have enough soldiers to burn the whole district to the ground," the lapinkin argued. "Stop giving humans the benefit of the doubt. They're scared children. Provoking them like Logarius has will only make things worse."

"Is it really so wrong for me to be hopeful?"

"It is if it gets you killed."

The two departed, their arms full, but Crksslff heard them give a parting greeting to an unseen third in their midst.

"It's all yours, Fifissll. We'll come back in an hour to replace the tarp."

Crksslff expected another foxkin, or perhaps a gargoyle. What it did not expect was a firekin to climb the wood pile like stairs and dive headfirst into the thick of it.

Firekin could suppress their fire by concentrating it more densely in a single space, turning their soft reds and yellows into small blue orbs. This was how Crksslff watched the other firekin crawl and weave through the wood pile. It didn't set the logs alight, nor settle down to burn. It was more like Fifissll was inspecting the logs, stroking them with burning arms and kissing away lingering wetness. Keeping the logs healthy to burn, Crksslff realized, until the others, whoever they may be, came for them.

Loneliness and yearning tugged at Crksslff's heart. Fifissll was the first other firekin Crksslff had seen since waking from their centuries-long sleep. Shyness kept it still. How might this other firekin react? Would it be happy to see Crksslff? A quick shake of the head pushed such doubts away. Had its time with the humans taught it to share their fears?

While Crksslff communicated with most beings via letters it spelled out, other firekin could understand the little pops, sparks, and whistles that emanated from their burning cores. It was with that manner of communication that Crksslff expanded back to its full size and addressed the other.

"Hello. I'm Crksslff. You?"

Fifissll froze in place, half its body wrapped around one end of a log. Its black eyes rotated ninety degrees about its head to stare back. They trembled.

"Another?" Fifissll asked.

Crksslff bobbed up and down.

"Another!" it said. "How are you?"

The other firekin snaked across the logs faster than a bolt of lightning. It circled the air about Crksslff as if unable to contain its excitement. One word sparked out from the firekin's core over and over in joyous chant.

"Happy! Happy! Happy! Fifissll so happy!"

They spun and danced and yammered at each other for what felt like hours. Crksslff could hardly believe its luck. To find another firekin in Londheim? Never did it think that might happen. They swapped stories of awakening from their slumbers. They spoke of lost families, of friends in the old times, of their favorite moments when but little embers. The foxkin and lapinkin returned to replace the tarp, but neither firekin noticed.

"Crksslff stay here long?" Fifissll asked. Its eyes glanced away. Nervous? Excited? Both?

"Fifissll want me to stay long?" Crksslff asked.

The other firekin bobbed up and down. A chunk of firewood charred black from its sudden surge of warmth.

"Stay," Fifissll said. Each word brought them closer. "Days. Weeks. Years!"

For the first day, it felt like they could indeed spend years together. They flitted among the giant wood pile, playfully chasing one another as they told stories of the before-times. Sometimes they burned side by side, saying little. The heat of one's company was enough. They had many stories, for Crksslff had been born an ember in the far west of the Oakblack Woods, whereas Fifissll had come from the east once it had grown strong enough to leave its parent flames. They swapped tales of creatures they'd encountered, faeries and dragons and talking stones.

Perhaps a day or two passed. Down there without the sun, it made it hard to know. Crksslff had not realized just how much it had ached for another firekin to burn alongside. Meeting Fifissll felt like a gift from the stars, and to be gone from its sight for even a moment was unbearable. But it was not to be. Fifissll grew restless, and finally it exited the wood pile and gestured for Crksslff to follow.

"Come with," Fifissll said. "More dragon-sired to meet."

The two hopped along the cistern tunnel, Crksslff suddenly reminded of why it had hidden in the first place.

"What if waterkin find us?" it asked.

"Waterkin friends," Fifissll said.

Crksslff let out a huff of smoke.

"Someone tell waterkin that."

Fifissll's eyes bobbed and narrowed with laughter.

"Crksslff grumpy. Be happy. Meet new friends!"

Not far, a tunnel was carved through the dirt, and at its entrance stood two spear-wielding lapinkin.

"Hey, Fifissll," said one with a smile. The rings in his ears rattled as he nodded toward Crksslff. "And who might you be?"

Crksslff paused and spoke its name very slowly while also punctuating it by spelling out the letters with elongated arms.

"Cr-ks-slff," it said.

"Welcome home then, Crksslff," said the other. "No burning anything inside, all right? We don't have anywhere for the smoke to escape."

Crksslff rolled its eyes and followed Fifissll inside.

While it had expected to find a small, cave-like place, Crksslff was stunned by the enormous, multiroom complex cut from the earth beneath Londheim. Each room had dozens of small, curtained-off juts to offer its occupants privacy. Crksslff was delighted by the variety of creatures beneath. Foxkin were the most numerous, with at least two dozen spread out in clusters. Some talked and laughed around a cook fire (not caring about *its* smoke, Crksslff noted), others played a game with chits and dice, while the oldest and gray-furred of them rocked in chairs in a far corner. Two alabaster faeries chased one another to the delight of three foxkin children, while an avenria slept bathed in shadow atop a stone perch.

"Two firekin!" exclaimed a gargoyle hanging upside-down from the ceiling.

"New friend!" Fifissll exclaimed back. "Spotty, meet Crksslff!"

The gargoyle's fur was all black but for white spots, two of which were centered upon each eye, which gave it an even wider-eyed appearance when it smiled. Crksslff held back a giggle. It had a feeling Spotty was not the gargoyle's actual name, but the nickname certainly fit.

"Hi hi hi!" it told the gargoyle before hurrying after Fifissll.

They passed an viridi softly singing by manipulating the way the air moved across her grassy scales. Crksslff noted how pale that grass was. The viridi needed sunlight, that much was clear, but here she lived below ground. The sight dampened its joy a teensy bit, and it was happy to bounce along after Fifissll, who moved with a clear destination in mind.

"Why all here?" Crksslff asked, still thinking of the sickly viridi.

"Those here not wanting to fight. Londheim our home, but we woke up with it full of humans. So now we hide."

This only clouded Crksslff's mood further, and made it appreciate Devin's cozy little fireplace all the more. They continued to the far end of the cave, which was sealed off by an enormous red curtain. Fifissll paused before it and hopped twice.

"Go in," it said. "Meet leader."

Crksslff dashed through the gap underneath the curtain and into a cavern much larger than expected. It was brilliantly lit by several dozen diamonds wedged into the smoothed-out ceiling. Works of art lay carelessly scattered about the place. Their differing styles bewildered Crksslff. It saw marble sculptures, tablet carvings, figurines made of bronze, gold, and wax. Reliefs were cut into the three walls, enameled glass cups and vases hung from nearly invisible wires, and effigies of straw and yarn lay in repose. Most numerous of all were the dozens upon dozens of canvas portraits practically piled atop one another in a corner. Every single piece of art depicted the same image, the same person, the same face: Devin's sister, Adria.

In the center of it all sat Janus, the avatar of change, a blob of silver shifting and molding to his touch.

"Hello, little one," he said without looking up from the silver. "Have you come to join our modest community?"

Crksslff trembled despite its best attempts to remain calm. The last time it faced this horrible monster, Janus had assaulted it with ice and left it near dead. Now here he was, sitting comfortably a few feet away.

"Y-yes," it said, wanting nothing more than to flee.

"Crksslff is new friend!" Fifissll said, happily bouncing in to join them.

"Wonderful," Janus said, and he smiled at the both of them. "I'm happy to see you're no longer alone, Fifi."

That smile suddenly faded as Janus and Crksslff met one another's gaze. The avatar of change tilted his head to one side, as if momentarily confused, and then his smile returned wider than before, his opal teeth flashing in the bright lights.

"Fifissll, would you mind giving me and Crksslff a moment to speak?"

The other firekin appeared worried but did not argue.

"See you soon," it said before vanishing back underneath the curtain. Janus waited until it was gone to turn his silver blob into a long spear and jam its hilt into the cave floor. His green eyes bore into Crksslff's.

"We meet again," he said. "Will you try to burn my face a second time?"

"Will you ice Crksslff and friends?"

A smile tugged at Janus's lips.

"No, I don't think so. Things proceed as they are meant to, little one. Your presence does not interfere with that. I merely wonder, why have you come here instead of remaining with that annoying Soulkeeper?"

Not an answer Crksslff wanted to discuss in the slightest. Revealing that they'd ventured into the cistern to destroy the chronimi felt like betraying Devin. For all it knew, Janus was the reason Trytis had made the colony of mushrooms in the first place.

"I ask same," Crksslff said carefully. "Why you here?"

"Viciss, in his infinite wisdom, has decided I need a break from killing hapless humans and ordered me to instead work on my art. Any art, so long as I did not use flesh and bones as my paint and canvas." He waved a dismissive hand at the chaotic pile surrounding him. "Unsatisfying, to say the least, but until the Chainbreaker takes her true place, I must remain patient. My time will come. Until then, I obey my creator."

He frowned at Crksslff.

"But you," he said. "You turn against your own kind. You've sided with humans, live among them, even call them friends. Why is that, little firekin? Why insult your very creator in such a way?"

Crksslff sizzled and huffed.

"Insult creator?" it asked. "Aethos is creator. What does Aethos think?"

A smirk crossed Janus's face.

"Aethos sides with Viciss in thinking humanity might still be saved from the Goddesses' influence. I guess we both honor the wishes of our masters in our own ways. You may remain here, Crksslff, so long as you tell no one of its location. This is a place of peace. If human soldiers and keepers storm this cave, I will know exactly who to blame." He cast his green eyes its way. "There are far worse ways for a firekin to die than ice and water. Keep that in mind during your stay."

Janus pulled the spear from the ground, quickly molding it back to a blob. It solidified as his hands caressed it, shaping it into something humanoid. Crksslff held no doubt as to whom it would resemble when finished. It quickly exited Janus's makeshift art studio and joined Fifissll in what appeared to be its home. It was a small shelf suspended with nails hammered into the stone. A collection of dry grass formed a bird's nest, which Fifissll softly burned. There wasn't much smoke, and with them so high up, it stayed near the ceiling. Crksslff dashed up the wall and joined Fifissll. A huff of frustration from dealing with Janus escaped from Crksslff's forehead.

"Everything good?" Fifissll asked.

"Fine. Confusing but fine."

Fifissll bobbed its head up and down.

"Put away for now. Be happy. Meet friends!"

And so they bounced about the underground village. Crksslff met many dragon-sired he'd seen before, and several races that were new. It danced and laughed for the lapinkin, gargoyles, and foxkin; did tricks for the avenria; and chased after Fifissll, to the delight of little viridi children. There were no cares down there, nothing to hide from. At least, Crksslff thought not, but it seemed Fifissll bore burdens it wasn't quite ready to share until they settled down for the night in their little nest of twigs.

"Big fight coming," Fifissll said. "Everyone worried."

"Humans and dragon-sired always fighting," Crksslff said. "It sad."

"We need not stay. We—we should go. Human city not safe."

"But..." Crksslff huffed a bit of smoke, its frustration going. "But why not? We safe so far."

Fifissll twisted and shivered, the narrow slant of its eyes giving away its displeasure long before it spoke.

"*Not safe*. Dragon-sired war. Humans war. Fifissll wants no part."

"What does Fifissll want?"

"A home. A wide field with lots of grass and steady wind. A place to...a place to raise embers."

Crksslff felt a longing strike it deep down into its core. Embers...Fifissll was proposing embers. Firekin were whirlwinds of emotions when they met, and they loved wild and reckless like their namesake element, but forming families was something firekin took much more seriously than most things. The creation of embers required a great deal of strength from both parties, and it often took weeks, if not months, to recover.

To leave all their troubles behind, to escape the coming war and raise a family instead, it was such a wonderful-sounding dream. But it'd mean abandoning those Crksslff had come to love just as deeply as it now did Fifissll. When would it see Tesmarie?

Jacaranda? And how would Devin survive without it keeping a protective eye on him?

Crksslff's mood, already soured by its meeting with Janus, paled completely.

"But Crksslff will miss Devin."

"Who is Devin?"

"Friend. Wise, and kind. A human."

Fifissll's distaste was hotter than its flame.

"Human over family? That is your choice?"

Crksslff whimpered.

"Sadness not a choice. Sadness is sadness. And why can't human be part of family?"

"Humans are never family. They never accept us. Never."

Frustration and helplessness washed over Crksslff like a cold rain. It hated arguing, and it hated not knowing the right thing to say.

"Crksslff was accepted," it said. A simple truth that it believed to its core. Fifissll, however, shook its head and turned away.

"Then you are fool, Crksslff."

They slept without another word between them. When Crksslff stirred, Fifissll was gone. It dashed about the community, but it found no sign of the firekin. It even went to the giant pile of logs outside the cave, but Fifissll was not there. Dejected, it returned. At the community entrance, the lapinkin guard waved it closer.

"Janus is looking for you, little one," he said.

Its flames burning low and heavy, Crksslff returned to Janus's private alcove. The avatar of change stood facing one of the walls, which was now a sheer sheet of jade. Janus's left hand was a chisel, the right hand a thick steel hammer. He was chipping and carving away at the jade, forming images with the indentations. No doubt those lines would form the face of a woman just like all the others.

"I'm sure you've noticed Fifissll left," Janus said.

"Crksslff knows."

Janus sighed and shook his head.

"Such a shame. I wish you two could have stayed here, and if not, you could have had a home in Londheim above like you deserved. Fifissll senses the coming war, just like we do. It hangs like a fog over the west. What will you do, firekin? Will you side against your fellow dragon-sired? Will you burn our flesh when the inevitable conflict comes?"

It was a question Crksslff had tried very hard not to think about, but its refusal had now cost it the possibility of a family.

"Crksslff will stay with friends," it said. "They are kind. They are good."

Down came Janus's hammer. A thick chunk of jade clattered across the floor.

"Things will get worse, Crksslff. Do not let one or two friendly humans convince you they represent humanity as a whole. Devin and Adria Eveson are aberrations. It is the rest who shall snuff out your flame when you least expect it."

Crksslff left the community. It dashed along the cistern until finding a ladder and then shimmied up its sides to the streets above. Directions weren't Crksslff's particular forte, and keeping unseen was difficult, given the bright daylight. Giving up, Crksslff settled down as an inconspicuous bit of flame burning atop discarded wood stinking of rot near a gutter. The day passed, thoroughly cold and miserable. Once night fell, and the people all but vanished from the streets, Crksslff ran until it recognized its surroundings and used them to guide itself to Devin's home.

The door was shut, but the chimney was not. Crksslff fell between the bricks and landed atop the fire. It hunkered down, unseen as it surveyed the interior. Devin sat in his favorite chair by the fire, steadily rocking it with his heels. Should it go to him? There was one other choice. It could exit Londheim and scour the grasslands beyond. There might still be signs of tiny footprints from Fifissll's passage. Tracking it would be a long shot, but in time, maybe Crksslff could find whatever calm field the other firekin chose to settle down in, in whatever place it decided to build its new life.

But that also meant saying good-bye to the only friend who had been there when Crksslff awakened in a cold, unknown world after the Goddesses had imprisoned them. It meant acknowledging that Janus was right, that humans were not family.

Before fear and doubt and sadness might change its mind, Crksslff let off a loud, cracking *pop* from the center of the fire, drawing Devin's eyes its way. It let its beady eyes widen, and it stood up from the center log.

"Puffy, you're back!" Devin said, beaming him a smile. Hearing that silly human word sent Crksslff's eyes to quivering and its flames to flickering. It dashed over to Devin, ran a circle about his chair, and then hopped atop the dully burning candle at his tableside. Its body quickly shifted, forming letters in the air. After two tries Devin understood the message.

DEVIN GOOD? it had asked.

"More than good, now that you're here," he said. "Isn't that right, Tes?"

Tesmarie waved from her cozy bed-shelf.

"Welcome back, you bubbly spark. It took you long enough!"

Crksslff settled lower atop the wick and exhaled a long, steady stream of black smoke. Its tensions and uncertainty went with it.

WHERE JAC? it asked.

"Jacaranda?" Devin said. "I'm not sure where she went tonight, but I can assure you, wherever she is, she's happy you're back, too."

Crksslff hoped so. It hoped for a lot of things, but right then, being content with its friends, be they human or dragon-sired, was the only thing that dulled the open wound of losing Fifissll to the world beyond Londheim's walls. The firekin softly nibbled on the candle wax as the hours passed, perking up only when the door opened. Crksslff raised its head, eager to greet Jacaranda, but immediately knew something was amiss.

"Jac?" Devin asked, quickly vaulting out of his chair.

Jacaranda took two steps in, barefoot with blood dripping down her arm and forehead, and then collapsed into Devin's arms.

# CHAPTER 25

"W ould you like the candles dimmed?" the bed warmer asked Jacaranda as she sat on the edge of the mattress inside an expensive room of the Gentle Rose Brothel.

"Light is fine," she said. Her fingers absentmindedly twiddled the lower fringe of her shirt. The bed warmer, while younger than her, was fairly old for his profession. In his late twenties would be her guess, with his blond hair and smooth skin still radiating youth. He was fit but not muscular, his hair long but neatly trimmed and styled, and his baby blue eyes simply to die for. Even in a crowd she could have picked him out as a bed warmer. The good ones had an effortless beauty about them.

It was good he was older, she decided as she slid farther onto the bed. At the reception area she'd requested their most skilled, patient man and then booked the room for a solid hour. It was expensive, but she'd robbed the home of one of Gerag's associates to cover the cost, an irony not lost on her.

"My name is Larsen," he said, flashing her a smile of his perfect teeth. His voice was soothing, comforting. "I was told you had a specific request in mind?"

Given her history, she should not have been so nervous, but to her surprise, her words stammered out unevenly as she tried to explain.

"I need help to relax," she said. "So I can...enjoy myself properly with my lover."

Larsen sat beside her on the bed. She sensed kinship in his gaze, or perhaps she only saw what she wanted to see.

"First-time fears?" he asked softly. "Or abuse?"

Jacaranda cast her eyes to the red sheets that felt so smooth underneath her fingertips. His hands were not far from hers, and she almost reached out to touch them.

"Abuse," she whispered, as if it were her ugly shame instead of a brutal crime performed against her.

The bed warmer touched two fingers to her chin and guided her vision back to his lovely face.

"The majority of my nervous clients are here for one of those two reasons," he told her. "Don't be ashamed. Just tell me what will make you comfortable, and I will do the rest. Is that a deal?" When she nodded, his smile blossomed. "Wonderful. Lie back, and I will do the rest."

He started with her belt buckle, and the mere proximity of his hands to her skin quickened her heart. Next he removed her boots and set them on the floor. He unfastened the button of her trousers, but he did not pull them down. Instead he removed his own shirt, exposing his clean-shaven chest, and then set the shirt down beside her. The scent of oils and perfume trickled into her nose.

"Are you comfortable with a kiss?" he asked. It didn't sound like he was asking for permission, but instead proposing something wonderful and wicked. She quickly nodded yes. He kept his weight off her, but his head lowered, she felt his warm breath across her neck, and then his lips traced a line of kisses from the side of her jaw to her mouth. It took her a moment to relax and return the act. When she kissed Devin, it was like touching fire yearning to explode. With Larsen, he was cool, controlled, his tongue slipping only the tiniest bit between her lips, exciting her without overwhelming her. His hands traced steady, methodical lines down her neck, exciting her skin, until they crossed over her scarf and to the top button of her shirt.

"It stays on," she said.

His fingers withdrew without a word. Jacaranda wouldn't normally have minded, but she also wore her scarf about her neck to hide her chain tattoos. If she were naked but for the scarf, it would certainly draw his attention. While he didn't remove her shirt, he did lift it up just enough to continue a new line of kisses from her sternum down to her belly button. Only then did he pull her trousers down and off.

"I'm going to start slow," he said as he folded the pants with practiced care. "Don't panic or get upset if you don't respond immediately. This isn't a race, there's no timer, and you certainly won't hurt my feelings."

Jacaranda closed her eyes and opened her legs. Goddesses damn it all, she felt so nervous over something that shouldn't be difficult. She'd had sex countless times throughout her life. It was a physical act, that was all, which was what she'd understood so well as her soulless self. So why did this make her panic now? Why did the mere thought of Larsen seeing her naked fill her with anxiety? She was safe here, with a highly skilled, highly paid bed warmer. Gerag couldn't hurt her. He couldn't touch her.

"You're lost in your head," Larsen said.

"Sorry," she mumbled, feeling embarrassed.

"I don't want you apologizing. I want you relaxed and enjoying yourself."

His hand settled upon her inner thigh, and once she did not recoil, he guided it all the way between her legs. His fingers gently brushed her folds, teasing at her opening. She could tell it was dry, and again she wanted to apologize. Instead she bit her tongue and reminded herself that Larsen had experience with many, many women. This would hardly be new to him.

"You're beautiful," he said, and this time she did blush. It worked, his words drawing her out of her mind and to his cocky smile. Up and down went his fingers, teasing, exploring, and true to his word, he showed not an ounce of impatience. Jacaranda felt her lower abdomen tensing, and she caught herself holding her breath multiple times. Each time she let it out in a long, slow exhale. To her surprise, the third time that exhale came out as a low moan. His hand was moving in circles now, and she felt herself opening to him, her imagination even pretending it wasn't a hand there but the tip of the beautiful man's fully erect cock.

When he finally did slip a finger inside her, he didn't have to force it at all. Her body welcomed it. Jacaranda tensed, almost expecting a traumatic flash of memories. That was the worst of it, she decided, that uncertainty of how her own mind would react. Even though she remained calm, and successfully kept those harmful memories at bay, the mere worry scraped at the edges of her awareness and threatened to douse the growing heat of her body with cold water.

"Keep your breathing steady," Larsen said calmly, as if his fingers weren't currently sliding in and out of her. "Don't think. Don't remember. Focus only on my hand, all right? Focus on how good it feels. Focus on how your body is responding."

Three fingers now, and they were curling just before withdrawing, his fingertips brushing her insides in a way Gerag had never done. Gerag would never...he'd never care if she was enjoying herself...never think to find this spot inside her that sparked with pleasure at every gentle touch...

"No thinking," Larsen said, his thumb suddenly pressing down against her vulva in a not-unpleasant way. The pressure quickly drew her attention to his playful grin. "If you must think, think on what you hope I do next."

"And what is it you will do next?" she asked.

Mischief sparkled in those baby-blues.

"I guess I'll show you if you're so impatient."

His mouth settled over her, his breath warm and lustful. She couldn't see his tongue, nor could she visualize it with how the rapid motions overwhelmed her with pleasure, but whatever he did was a gift from the Goddesses.

"Ho-holy shit," she gasped. His fingers could have belonged to a machine, they were so consistent in their motions and speed. She clung to the bedsheet. Her back arched instinctively. She thought he might go faster, given her receptive response, but he remained maddeningly consistent as he carried her toward a seemingly inevitable climax. Gerag had often thought himself an expert in all things sexual, but Larsen was showing her what a true master was actually like. Gerag was a selfish lover, even his giving acts performative, self-indulgent...

*Stop fucking comparing him to Gerag!* she mentally screamed, beyond frustrated with herself.

Just like that, she felt a shift inside her. The warm cloud that had engulfing her mind chilled. Anxiety robbed some of the pleasure derived from the steady movement of Larsen's fingers. Somehow the bed warmer immediately sensed her frustration and pulled his mouth away while halting the movement of his hand.

"You can't out-think this," he said. "We want good thoughts connected to what I'm doing, not bad thoughts and bad memories." He smiled at her. "Do I have a beautiful smile?"

"Of course you do," she said.

"Good. So I want you to imagine me smiling. Don't think about your memories, your frustrations, or what brought you here. Just me, smiling. Enjoying myself, just like *you* are enjoying *yourself*. Can you do that?"

"I can try."

His hand started to move again.

"Allow yourself to be happy," he said. "Trust me. We have all the time in the world."

It took a few minutes but her body once more grew receptive to his touch. Larsen, perceptive as always, increased the speed of his hand and brought his tongue back to work its magic. Again she felt herself being carried toward climax, and as her nerves lit up, she did as he asked and thought of his smiling face. He was enjoying himself. *She* was enjoying herself. The waves came faster, harder, until pleasure washed away her thoughts completely and her body clutched at Larsen's hand, not wanting to let go. Long moments later she collapsed onto the bed, having not realized she'd lifted off it a half-inch.

Larsen withdrew his hand and stretched his upper back and neck, clearly satisfied with his work.

"Is that enough?" he asked her. Jacaranda almost told him yes, and that cowardice was enough to spur her onward.

"Not quite," she said. "I need to know for certain."

Larsen shrugged his shoulders.

"Very well," he said. "I certainly won't complain about spending more time with a woman so beautiful."

"I'm sure you tell that to all the men and women who come to you," she said.

"That I do. But this time it's not a little white lie." His teeth nibbled at her ear. "Because you're fucking gorgeous."

It wasn't much, just a deeper tone, a little rougher language, but the sudden animalistic increase in his behavior set her heart to hammering and her pulse racing with anticipation. He removed his loose trousers with one hand while the other wrapped around her waist and then up her spine. She arced into his embrace, relishing the firm presence of his chest and abs against her. For once she hated keeping her shirt on, for she wished she could feel his skin pressing against her skin, to have his hands caress her breasts. Fuck, what could that magical tongue of his do to her hardening nipples?

Larsen pressed himself against her crotch, but just before entering, he hesitated.

"Are you ready?"

A little whisper of terror protested in her heart, but it was so easily drowned out by her enjoyment.

"Yes," she said, adjusting her hips. "More than ready."

His cock slid into her, and she felt no fears, no anxiety, just an immense satisfaction that dragged a groan out of her. The bed warmer enveloped her completely, and she buried her face into his neck and gasped out breath after breath as he rocked his hips back and forth. Each thrust was a little stronger than the last, until what had been gentle motions became a furious pounding that had her digging her nails into his back and moaning out her pleasure at the top of her lungs. Even amid that magnificent exertion, he had the concentration to wrap his lips about her neck and kiss with such intensity she felt tingles streak up and down her spine.

"I'm close," he breathed into her ear. "Don't worry. I'll finish outside."

This moment she had feared above all. What it meant. How she'd react. His hips drove his cock deeper and deeper into her, their two forms hardening and gasping and clutching one another as their bodies released an hour's worth of tension, sweat, and effort. At the last moment Larsen withdrew, his right hand a blur as he stroked himself. His seed spilled across his hands and wrist. None on her, she realized, and she was surprised by how grateful she felt. Gerag had done that many times to her, and she had to suppress a shudder lest those memories steal away her current euphoria. Larsen finished, and with a contented sigh, he collapsed onto the bed beside her.

The heavy silence that followed filled Jacaranda's eyes with tears. She could hardly believe her immense feelings of relief. She wasn't broken. Sex wasn't irrevocably ruined by her servitude to Gerag. Devin might not be as skilled as Larsen (she doubted many in Londheim were), but it was something they could work toward. It was something she now knew, deep down, that they could achieve together.

Larsen shifted to sit at the edge of the bed. He saw her tears and carefully wiped them away with the thumb of his left hand. His other slid underneath a pillow and withdrew a hidden washcloth to clean himself with.

"You did good," he told her. She smiled, her mind still swimming with relief. A devilish part of her even pondered how much time remained of her hour. Perhaps there might be a little bit more fun to squeeze out of...

Larsen's easy smile vanished. His shoulders sagged, and he rolled his eyes and quietly groaned.

"Fuck, I should have known," he said.

"Known what?" Jacaranda asked, confused by the sudden change. Larsen stood and walked completely naked to one of the luxurious room's dressers.

"You can drop the act," he said with his back to her. There was no hint of his former care and gentleness. Instead he sounded mad at her, and at himself.

"I don't understand," she said.

He retrieved a new pair of black trousers from the dresser and pulled them on.

"Whatever. Tell your master that you passed the test."

Ice froze her veins. Jacaranda glanced down at her half-naked self, her shirt ruffled, her legs wet with sweat...

Her scarf, pulled halfway down her neck to expose her chain tattoos.

"What test?" she asked. It chilled her how easily the hollow, emotionless voice of her soulless self came back to her.

"I said drop it," he snapped. She tensed, waiting until he pulled a white shirt over his head. The moment his vision was blocked, she lunged off the bed. Her knee smashed into his crotch, her fist into his throat. Larsen gagged from the pain and doubled over, his movements controlled solely by reflex and not any attempt at self-defense. She tucked a hand behind his neck and pulled. The bed warmer dropped to the floor, unable to properly break his fall. His head smacked against the hard wood, adding to his disorientation. Jacaranda quickly rolled him onto his back and then braced her forearm against his throat. She may have surrendered her swords to the men at the brothel's entrance, but she didn't need them to kill.

"Listen carefully," she told Larsen. "Make a noise, and I crush your windpipe. Call for help, I crush your windpipe. Struggle? Crushed windpipe. You get the idea?"

Larsen nodded with what limited motion was available to his head. He was staring at her, but his eyes didn't seem to be focusing correctly. She wondered if she'd given him a concussion, and if so, whether that was good or bad. Right now, she wanted answers.

"You said I passed a test," she said. "What test?"

"Owners sends us soulless to test their acting skills," Larsen said once she relieved a bit of pressure from his throat. "If they're poor, we're to freshen up their training."

All this was new to her. She'd thought only Gerag trained the soulless.

"Why not send them back to Gerag?" she asked.

"Who's Gerag?"

Jacaranda bashed him across the mouth, then clamped her other hand down over his face to hold in his muffled cry.

"Stop lying," she said.

"I'm not," he said through bleeding lips. "Whoever trains the soulless first doesn't want them sent back. We're the best new owners can do."

New owners. That meant Larsen might know who the potential buyers were. Under normal circumstances, Jacaranda would have been excited by the possibility of clues as to where Gerag had vanished. Right now she was naked, weaponless, and straddling a bed warmer who knew of her existence. She felt humiliated, confused, and very, very pissed.

"Who are the buyers?" she asked.

Larsen didn't answer immediately. He was staring at her chain tattoos, and with eyes that no longer looked concussed.

"You can't be a soulless," he said. "No training could accomplish this. Why the tattoo? Is it a disguise?"

Goddesses above, she wished it were.

"Answer the question," she hissed, ignoring his.

"I don't know names," Larsen said. "Do you think anyone would be so stupid? Servants bring the soulless here for training. Everything hushed. Everything hidden. Whoever sent you surely knows that."

So he thought she was an agent sent to uncover information on the soulless sex ring. Not a bad theory, honestly, and one she didn't mind playing up. The problem was, he'd seen her face. He'd seen her tattoos.

"Is there anything you've noticed?" she asked. "Anything at all?"

Larsen was starting to relax. A good sign. His tongue might loosen because of it.

"One of the buyers sends servants with a strange tattoo on their wrists," he said. "Three thick dots between their knuckles. That's all I know."

Jacaranda allowed him to stand. He got up with a limp and a wince.

"Damn, did you have to knee me there?" he asked. "Look, I don't know who you are, or who sent you. Just—just let me go, and I won't tell anyone, all right?"

"Sure," she said. Her voice sounded dead to her. "It's a deal."

He'd seen her face. He knew her secret. She tried to tell herself not to go through with it. She tried to tell herself she was better than this. Who she was. Who she wanted to be.

The moment his hand touched the doorknob, she grabbed his head in both hands and slammed it forward. His forehead made a sickening crack from the contact, but it wasn't enough. He let out a sharp cry. His legs went limp. Jacaranda slid both arms around his neck, and as he fell, she used that momentum to aid her. One tight clench. One sharp twist. The reverberation of the snap traveled up her arms and iced her lungs. Larsen immediately went limp, and she smelled shit and piss as his corpse evacuated its bowels.

Jacaranda slid to a sit with her back braced against the door. She absurdly straddled the bed warmer's head in her hands. Tears flowed as her breathing hitched with uneven sobs. He'd never harmed her. No, worse. He'd *helped* her, and yet she killed him. She was a coward. A murderer. Mere minutes ago she'd been overcome with joy. Was that how fleeting her happiness would be in this world? Was she cursed to kill and destroy, all because the Goddesses had failed to deliver her soul upon her birth?

"I'm sorry," she whispered. She brushed his beautiful face with shaking fingers. "I'm sorry, I'm so sorry."

A hard jolt from the other side of the door broke her out of her miserable reverie.

"Open up," commanded a deep voice. It was one of the Gentle Rose's guards. Jacaranda lurched to her feet and grabbed at her clothes. Damn it, how did shit go so fucking sideways so quickly?

"One moment," she said. She jammed a leg into her trousers and frantically pulled at the fabric.

"Larsen? Is everything well?"

Larsen was meant to respond with specific phrases to indicate if he was safe or not. Obviously the bed warmer wouldn't be offering any of them. The door was locked, but she knew without question that the guard possessed a key. She pulled on the other leg of her trousers, then fixed the scarf so it properly covered her tattoos. No time for her boots. She grabbed her belt, but instead of putting it on, she looped it into a circle.

Jacaranda opened the door a crack before the guard needed to use his key. The burly man hesitated. He couldn't see Larsen's body, not with how it was positioned. She was a woman, smaller than him, her face wet with tears. She relied on that uncertainty. He had a short sword strapped to his waist, but he'd not drawn it. Not yet.

She wouldn't give him that chance.

"Sorry to interrupt," the guard said. "But is—"

Jacaranda leapt through the crack, and upon their collision, she slid the belt over his head and to his throat. Her momentum continued, and she pulled on the leather with all her might as her bare feet hit the floor. The guard staggered, but he managed to keep his balance despite the crushing weight around his throat.

*Well. Shit.*

The hallway was narrow, and purposefully built so. There was no getting around the burly guard. He drew his short sword with one hand while the other grabbed at the belt around his neck. Jacaranda released the leather, allowing him a sudden, shrill gasp. She wouldn't win in a straight strength contest, and the narrowness of the hallway mitigated her superior mobility. She had only one real chance, and that was through sheer, raw savagery.

The guard stabbed at her as she closed the distance, but his face was turning red and his vision blurred by the tears in his eyes. Jacaranda sidestepped the weak attack and then leapt atop the man. Her legs wrapped about his waist, holding her in place as she rammed a thumb into each of his eyes. He less screamed and more gagged out his protest. His arms flailed wildly, and Jacaranda had to bite down a scream as the sharp edge of his sword clipped her arm. Deeper. Her thumbs had to go deeper. Her fingers clutched the sides of his face as he tried to buck her off. He slammed her against one wall, then the other, the impacts piercing her vision with stars. Blood poured down her arms, both his and hers. Deeper. Into the skull. Into the soft matter beyond.

There was no sudden kill moment, not like with Larsen. The guard's movements merely slowed, his breathing turned ragged and uneven, and then his limbs went limp. None of it seemed real. She withdrew her thumbs, saw the mess of gore coating them, and felt nothing. The man's weapon lay on the floor, and she retrieved it without any sense of urgency. At least now she was armed. She tried to remember how many guards she saw when she entered the Gentle Rose. Two? Three? Wealthy clients. Expensive bed warmers. There might be more, hidden, but she couldn't think properly.

*You're in shock*, she told herself, as if understanding that would suddenly make it better.

With all the fighting and commotion, more would come. Had to run. Had to get out. She checked her scarf, ensuring her tattoos remained covered. That was important, right? She checked her arm as well. A shallow cut, more blood than real damage. Something to worry about once she was out. Jacaranda hurried to the stairs at the end of the hall, paused to catch her breath, and then sprinted down them.

The layout to the Gentle Rose was simple, with the stairs leading up to the rooms blocked off by a heavy desk and a banister with a lone latched entrance. The greeter turned upon hearing movement, his practiced smile vanishing the moment he saw she was armed. He dove over the desk, and before she could chase, a guard emerged from a curtained side room. Jacaranda leapt off the steps and onto the desk, needing its height. The guard barreled out like an angered bull, and no matter her skill, he'd have crushed her with sheer size and weight without some sort of advantage.

"Who sent you?" the guard asked as his sword slammed down upon the desk, just missing her left leg.

"No one," she said. Her heel caught his forehead. It felt like kicking a wall. He swept at her shins with his sword, and instead of parrying, she attempted to block. A poor decision, she realized, as their weapons connected. The flat side of her sword pressed against her own leg, preventing the edge of the guard's from piercing flesh but doing little to stop the force of its swing.

Jacaranda decided not to fight it further. She released the sword and dropped to the other side of the desk. Her foe's free hand caught her knee, twisting her fall into an awkward angle. Her head clipped the desk's sharp edge, and a fresh trickle of blood rolled down across her jawline. Jacaranda groped the shelves underneath despite her momentary disorientation. She couldn't delay. Delaying meant death. Her fingers closed around the two short swords she'd handed over upon purchasing her room.

"Much better," she whispered.

Jacaranda rose from behind the desk like a whirlwind. The guard threw up a meager defense, but it meant little. Jacaranda finally felt like herself. She had her weapons, an escape plan, and control over the fight. Instead of panicking, she took the offensive, cutting the guard several times to get him raging and then sidestepping his eventual desperation slash. Both swords crisscrossed across his throat. As he died, a dark, disgusted voice whispered within her mind.

*Another innocent man dead.*

But now was not the time to dwell on her guilt and misdeeds. She dashed out the door of the Gentle Rose, praying that the false name she'd offered would be enough to disguise her presence from ever reaching Gerag's ears, wherever the fat bastard might be hiding. She rushed back to Devin's house, making no attempt at stealth. Several times a passing stranger asked if she was all right, no doubt disturbed by the blood on her face and clothing. She smiled and waved them off. Keep moving, she told herself. Keep going. Get home. Get safe. The night was young, and though Londheim had been relatively peaceful since the failed attempt to retake Low Dock, it was still not a time anyone wanted to be out for long.

At last she turned down Sermon Lane, but she was still not free of intervention.

"Miss?" asked a woman not far from Devin's home. "Are you all right?"

Jacaranda glanced at her. A Soulkeeper, she realized, one not much younger than Devin.

"I'm fine," she said, pushing past the auburn-haired woman.

"Would you at least accept an escort home?"

"I am home," Jacaranda said, and she gestured at Devin's house. Thankfully the Soulkeeper let her be. Jacaranda less opened the door and more collapsed against it so her weight forced it ajar. She stood in the doorway, overcome with relief. This was home, her home, and she knew exactly why when Devin lurched from his fireside chair.

"Jac?" he asked.

Jacaranda collapsed into his arms, her face buried against his chest. For as much as she hated Gerag for damaging her, she loved Devin that much more, and through that she would overcome. No matter how broken she felt, she'd find a way to be worthy of the arms holding her close.

"Hey, Devin," she said, laughing despite her sudden onslaught of tears. "It's been a long night."

# CHAPTER 26

Lyssa stared at the closed door, the other woman's words echoing within her troubled mind.

*I am home.*

"Whose home?" the Soulkeeper whispered aloud. Her feet rooted in place. She'd come to invite Devin to a round of drinking. Not for his sake, but for hers. The rumors had been getting to her, and so she'd come to put them to rest. Devin wouldn't lie to her face. Devin wouldn't take a soulless woman as some sort of... comfort creature, no matter how pervasive the snickers she heard when gathered with other Soulkeepers in the Church District's fancier taverns. Devin had always been a bit different, she'd argued with any brave enough to say so within earshot of her, much more of a loner, but he'd never do such a disgusting thing.

But then who was the red-haired woman with violet eyes calling Devin's house her home? And why was there blood on her clothes?

Lyssa abruptly turned and left, her fingers rapidly tapping the smoothly polished handles of her pistols. She couldn't force herself to knock on Devin's door. It'd be the easiest way to get her answers, but perhaps some answers were none of her business. Let Devin have his secrets. There were a dozen things that woman could be. A friend, a relative, a prostitute, a lover...

"You could have just told me," she muttered as her legs moved faster. They carried her toward no specific destination, just a vague direction opposite of Devin's. Hadn't she and Devin always been friends? They'd been practically attached at the hip during their training inside the Soulkeepers' Sanctuary. Void's sake, she'd been his honored guest at Devin and Brittany's wedding. Then again, things had never been the same after Brittany's death.

"Soulkeeper?"

She snapped alert. A city guard was beckoning her closer.

"Is something the matter?" she asked him.

"You might say so," the portly man said. "This is beyond my expertise. Think you could come weigh in?"

It was only then she realized that two more guards stood at the entrance to a brothel, and their glares made it clear no one was to enter. Several bed warmers in various states of dress stood not far to the side, quietly chatting with and comforting one another. Lyssa shot a glance to the brothel's name. The Gentle Rose.

"I'll help as best I can," she offered.

The guard scratched at his bushy mustache.

"I pride myself in solving killings, but all this shit's gotten weirder as of late, as I'm sure you know."

"Painfully well," Lyssa said, thinking of the broken bones she'd suffered from her first entangle with a gargoyle. "So what's the story here?"

The guard led her through the door and into the small entry room. The body of a burly man lay in a pool of his own blood upon the wood floor. A pale man stood speaking with a fourth guard near a curtained doorway leading farther into the brothel. Lyssa frowned as the smell of death hit her nostrils.

"Some man not want to pay for their fun?" she asked.

"Not a man," Mustache Guard said. "A woman."

Lyssa hoisted an eyebrow.

"A woman took down a man that size?"

"Not just him. She killed another guard upstairs in the hallway, and with her bare hands by what I can tell. And she did all that after she killed the bed warmer she paid for an hour with."

Lyssa walked past the corpse and up the stairs, the city guard following.

"So why do you think you need a Soulkeeper?" she asked.

"Some skinny lass barely above five feet tall doing all this? It's got me thinking some sort of magic or monster might be involved."

Lyssa glanced over her shoulder.

"Wait, you have a description?"

"The greeter in charge of booking rooms got a good look at her. He got a name, too, but I'd bet my hide it ain't her real one. That ain't all of it, either. The greeter swears he saw chain tattoos on her throat."

Anxiety crept its little claws along the sides of her neck and spine. She reached the upper floor to find a second body lying in the center of the cramped hallway. It didn't take much to decipher his throat had been crushed by the belt looped around his neck. The savagery of it was what really shook Lyssa. At some point, both of the guard's eyes had been gored from their sockets, and she had her suspicions it was by the assailant's thumbs. His body lay in front of an open door. When she glanced inside, she found the third victim, a lovely man with his head twisted at an unlovely angle.

"Soulless killing people," the guard said. "That ain't a thing, is it? I mean, I know they can when we teach them to be guards and soldiers, but to come here and kill like some sort of assassin? That's a bit much."

"Is it?" she wondered aloud. "I want to speak with the greeter."

The two returned to the entryway. The greeter, an olive-skinned man in his fifties who had aged as gracefully as a swan, gladly accepted her offer to describe the killer.

"She wasn't very talkative, but most people coming here aren't, at least not until they get inside their rooms," the greeter said. "As for her, she wasn't very tall, maybe a few inches above five feet. Very pretty. Had violet eyes, I remember seeing them and remarking to myself of how lovely and rare a shade they were. Oh, and her hair was as red as the setting sun. A tragedy that someone so lovely could be so brutish."

Lyssa felt her insides twist and harden into stone. Her jaw clenched so tightly she had to consciously force herself to relax.

"This woman," she said. "Did she wear a white scarf?"

"She did," the greeter said, immediately perking up. "I remember because it tangled during her fight, and that's when I saw her chain tattoos. Does the scarf mean something? Do you know who she is, or who she belongs to?"

*Home*, she thought, remembering the blood on the violet-eyed woman who had stumbled through Devin's door.

"No," Lyssa said. "But I know where she lives."

# CHAPTER 27

At last the summons Cannac had been waiting for arrived at the tower. Tommy accepted the message graciously, careful to keep his body blocking any sight farther into the tower from the messenger. To the unprepared, viewing inside the tower was... distressing.

"We'll be there as soon as possible," Tommy assured the older man before slamming the door shut. He put his back against it and wiped his forehead with relief.

"Has the summons finally come?" Cannac asked from his tree-born perch.

Yes, as much as Tommy could understand it, there was a tree growing in the center of the Wise tower. The walls had expanded outward at a fairly steady rate, with the stone floor fading into a deep shadow that appeared to have no end. A thick, stubby tree simply appeared overnight at Cannac's behest, its branches perfectly shaped to form the dyrandar a comfortable chair. The floor and rug didn't even appear damaged by its intrusion. Tommy might have questioned why it didn't die without sunlight, but then again, that main floor was now bright as day, as if the sun lurked just outside his line of sight. Plus, he still wasn't sure if the tree was actually *there* there, a common issue when dealing with the dream-weaving creature.

"It appears so," Tommy said. He gestured with the tiny scrap of paper the messenger had delivered. "We are to present ourselves before the Royal Overseer at his mansion at our soonest convenience."

Cannac pushed off from his perch.

"Then let us make haste. Too much time has already passed."

Tommy retrieved Malik from his room, and together the three prepared to leave. Once he'd put on his boots and looped a scarf around his neck, Tommy looked to Cannac and raised an eyebrow.

"Um, aren't you going to...you know...make another illusion?"

The dyrandar shook his head.

"I have reconsidered its wisdom," he said. "It is time we peaceful dragon-sired ceased our hiding. Let the shadows and disguises belong solely to those who seek chaos and bloodshed."

"I'm not sure this is a wise idea," Malik said. "It's a long walk, and people are on edge. Things might get ugly."

Cannac pushed the door open. Logically, Tommy knew that the dyrandar was much taller than the entrance, yet Cannac did not even need to duck to allow his antlers passage. Tommy's stomach did a fun loop in appreciation of the constant unsteadiness of the world. As much as he loved all things magical, Tommy did miss having reality feel solid like stone instead of squirmy like water.

"I do not fear the crowds," he said. "Nor should you."

The moment Tommy stepped outside, it felt like the tower shrank behind him to its proper size, almost as if the stone exhaled. Cannac, having been there once already, needed no guide to reach the mansion. He strode ahead, not waiting for Tommy or Malik. Given the dyrandar's massive size, it meant Tommy had to walk at an unpleasant clip to keep pace.

The reactions of those nearby were about as he'd expected. Some gasped, others pointed, and a good many suddenly found their paths veering away. Tommy didn't exactly blame them.

Cannac was enormous, and his arms and chest appeared made of solid muscle.

"It's all right," Tommy called to the onlookers. "He's nice, I swear. Very nice, not scary."

"Tommy, please stop that," Malik muttered. "It's embarrassing."

"Just trying to help."

"Tommy, please stop helping. It's embarrassing."

"Fine. Fine. You don't need to ask twice."

"I clearly did."

The fearful looks and quick retreats turned out to be preferable to what happened once they turned onto one of the main roads leading to the mansion. City guards quickly set up an escort, and they looked none too pleased about it. Once there were armed soldiers to keep them safe, the mood of the crowd turned ugly.

"Get the fuck out, monster!" a middle-aged man shouted, only the long handle of a guard's spear keeping him at bay.

"Why are you protecting it?" others asked. Many joined this chorus, jeering the guards and urging them to turn on Cannac. Tommy lowered his head and focused on walking. A couple times he felt stones pelt his back and shoulders. Just pebbles, really, but he feared that might change. About thirty people followed now, with half gawking at the sight of the dyrandar, and the other half itching for a fight.

"Pay them no mind," Cannac said, his deep voice easily discernible above the din. "They act only out of fear and ignorance."

They seemed far angrier than fearful to Tommy, but then again, other people were not exactly his forte. The numbers only grew the farther they traveled. Many more shouted questions, wondering where they were going, or accusing Cannac of all manner of things. Tommy weathered their insults as best he could, but the abuse was shocking to him. Each time a stone struck his robes, he wondered if it would be the last straw, and the crowd would surge past their escort to do Goddesses-knew-what to Cannac.

Assuming he let them, of course. Tommy glanced at the serenely calm dyrandar. It would take many people to bring him down, and that didn't count whatever magic he might use in self-defense. Given his ability to distort reality as if it were a dream, Tommy feared what might happen if Cannac were truly angered.

When they arrived at the mansion, several soldiers had to rush from the entrance to help push away the last of the crowd. Tommy and Malik darted inside, with Cannac ducking the entire upper half of his body so he might fit through the doors without his antlers striking the archway. The doors slammed shut behind them, blocking the sounds of chasing jeers and insults.

"Should have used a damn illusion," Malik muttered.

"I encountered nothing beyond my expectations," Cannac said. "You did not need to escort me if you feared for your safety."

"We're not going to abandon you if things get scary," Tommy said. "It wouldn't be right."

Malik's glare seemed to indicate he felt otherwise. Together the three followed an escort through the mansion, this time to a much larger lounge area located in what seemed to be an enormous library. The focal point of the room was a long oak table that could seat thirty people, and at its very center waited the Royal Overseer, the Mayor, and an entourage of other wealthy and important members of Londheim's civil structure.

"Let's start with the most important question first," said a red-haired woman with a scar sealing over her left eye, skipping right over any pleasantries. She was General Kaelyn, the person in charge of the soldiers stationed in Londheim by the Queen to support the Royal Overseer's rule. "Did you have any part in the attack on Low Dock?"

"Have I done anything to make you suspect my involvement?" Cannac asked. Tommy was impressed by his calm demeanor. He wasn't even the subject of the meeting, yet he felt his armpits already soaking through with sweat. The others weren't entirely certain how to answer the dyrandar's question.

"I ask only because we must," Overseer Downing said. "Please, were you involved?"

Cannac stood up straighter, and it seemed a bit of fire sparked in the center of his antlers.

"No. The actions of those in Belvua are contrary to my desires."

"How is that so?" asked Mayor Becher. "Have you not already told us you are a King to these magical creatures?"

"I rule my dyrandar, and I speak for my alliance in the west. The Forgotten Children who have infiltrated your city reject all masters, clan leaders, and kings. I am responsible for their actions as much as you are for a human criminal a thousand leagues from here."

Many there still did not appear convinced.

"You granted a vision of your armies, and one was of giant rabbits with spears," Kaelyn said. "Those same creatures were part of the attack on my troops. Would you care to explain that?"

"Is one lapinkin the same as all lapinkin? Is one human the same as all humans? You are not of one mind. Why do you presume us to be? I shall repeat myself if I must, but the Forgotten Children reject our leadership. They do not follow any orders of mine, or my fellow leaders."

"There's a simpler solution," the general insisted. "You could be lying."

"I am King of the dyrandar," Cannac bellowed. The force of his voice was like a fire sweeping through grasslands. "I come without guards and subjects into your capital, and yet you accuse me of subterfuge? I seek diplomacy, but you accuse me of aiding those who seek violence and conquest by force? You insult me, humans. Was I wrong to expect better from you?"

Cannac's ire wasn't even aimed at him and yet Tommy wanted

to wither away and hide. The air sucked out of the room, and it took several long moments before anyone was prepared to speak.

"You are right," Albert said after clearing his throat. "We should show you more respect than that. Please, accept our apologies."

"Your apologies are welcome," Cannac said. "But they are not why I came to Londheim. Have you arrived at a decision as to our requests? Every day our people travel further east into vacated lands you insist are yours. There is still time to avoid bloodshed, but it is lessening with each rise and fall of the sun."

"We've already had bloodshed," Kaelyn said. "Or have you forgotten?"

The Royal Overseer admonished her with a look, then turned his attention back to the dyrandar.

"I am still awaiting much-needed word from the capital," he said. "We do not have an answer for you, and will not while we operate under such limited information."

"Then why did you bring me here?" Cannac asked. "Was it solely to question my honor and accuse me of violence?"

"No," said Nikos Flynn, the commander of the city guard, if Tommy remembered correctly. "There's one other matter. Your stay at the Wise tower is no longer acceptable. You're here so my guards can escort you to join the rest of your kind."

"Join my kind?" Cannac asked, his tone cold.

"In Low Dock," Albert said. "Or Belvua, as some call it now. We have declared a temporary truce, but given that your kind now possess land within Londheim, we feel it best that you spend your stay there instead."

Tommy bit his tongue to prevent himself from butting in. This wasn't his fight, even if it were deeply insulting. Cannac had done nothing to associate himself with those in Low Dock, not their claims on the land, nor their fight against the people, yet he would still find himself sequestered within?

"You would house a King in the stolen lands of criminals," the dyrandar said after a long pause. "I assume any protest I offer shall fall on deaf ears?"

"Would you not be more comfortable living with your own kind?" the Mayor asked, and he sounded legitimately confused.

"Comfort was the reason you made this decision," Cannac said. "But not mine. If this is your request, then I acquiesce. I seek peace, humans of Londheim. I hope you learn I am not your enemy before your paranoia and fears lead us to war."

"Not our enemy, he says, right before threatening us with war," Kaelyn practically growled. "I think we've heard enough. Get him where he belongs."

"Overseer, if I may so humbly object," Malik began, stepping between Cannac and the rest of the table.

"You may not," Albert interrupted. "This decision is final."

"You can always go with him," Kaelyn offered. She pulled a dagger strapped to her thigh and almost lazily twirled it in her fingers. "Though I don't know how long you'd last in Low Dock before some monster decides they'd rather eat you than play nice."

The Royal Overseer beckoned to the soldiers stationed at the library entrance. One opened the doors, and the other gestured for them to follow.

"Well," Tommy said as they exited, "that went poorly."

"Humans have always been reactionary creatures obsessed with the present, ignorant of the past, and fearful of the future." Cannac shook his head. "I will endure these indignities if it prevents the casualties of war. I must admit, my hopes have fallen significantly since my arrival. Scattered remnants of our kind have reclaimed portions of a city right underneath their nose, yet the humans act as if a full-scale war will be one they might win."

The guards were awfully close and listening in on such proclamations. Tommy felt his neck flush with a mixture of embarrassment and uncertainty. It felt weird to discuss such things so candidly with them there.

"Did we ever wage war before?" he asked. "Back when we lived together in the early days of history?"

"We did," Cannac said.

"And did we humans ever win?"

Cannac pushed open the doors to the mansion.

"If you had, do you think the Goddesses would have needed to banish us to slumber beneath the earth?"

Any hope Tommy had that their return trip would be easier than their arrival died the moment he exited those doors. A crowd had formed around the mansion gates, numbering at least sixty by his estimate. The four city guards assigned to take them to Belvua shouted to the soldiers nearby, demanding a larger escort.

While they waited for it to arrive, Cannac stood before the gathered throng and raised his arms high. Shimmering mist swirled between his antlers, then dispersed throughout the crowd with such speed only a few had time to let out frightened cries. The mist faded, but the colors of the people's faces and outfits seemed weirdly vibrant. A rainbow fog shimmered into view between them, and Cannac drank it in like he would a fine wine.

"They are frightened by the creation of Belvua," he said with eyes closed. "They see my entering the mansion as a symbol of Londheim's leadership surrendering to the unknown. We are monsters to be fought, not equals to be met at a diplomatic table."

The mist faded away as Cannac lowered his arms.

"The damage the Forgotten Children have done is immeasurable," he lamented. "If only our first meetings between races had been of peace and a sharing of information so we might better understand the changes of time. Perhaps then their opinion of the dragon-sired would be improved."

"Actually most people's first encounter with the dragon-sired was with the giant owls, uh, eating us," Tommy argued. "And I believe you speak for their queen."

"True," Cannac said. "Arondel shares her own portion of blame. Perhaps I am fortunate we dyrandar did not awaken near your cities. In those first early hours, anger and fear ruled over all." His face darkened. "Or perhaps Arondel and Naiser have been hiding their relationship with the Forgotten Children since the very beginning. The amount of fowl and lapinkin among their numbers is…troubling. Hrmph. I must think on this later."

Once their escort had grown to twelve, the lead guard in charge shouted for them to start their travel. Malik grabbed Tommy by the arm right when he started to follow.

"We don't have to accompany him," his mentor said quietly.

"Yes," Tommy said as he pulled his arm free. "We do."

The three marched in the center of the twelve soldiers, an angry, noisome crowd following on all sides. Their curses and shouts were beginning to lose meaning to Tommy, instead becoming a singular wave of sound that represented the dark, awful place many found themselves in since the black water washed away their normal world. He found himself blamed for crimes he could never have committed. He heard Cannac accused of deeds only the Goddesses could have performed.

Most of all, he heard him and Malik called traitors, and Cannac a monster. It was the one consistency amid the hate.

"Make way," guards shouted as they pushed through the crowd. "Make way, or we'll make the way ourselves!"

No matter their urgency, they could not move as rapidly as the lead guard wished. There were too many people. Everywhere they went, people gawked from doorways and windows, and for every rowdy man or woman who trailed off, two more seemed to take their place. Originally Tommy viewed the banishment to Belvua a cruel and misguided punishment, but now he wondered if it was the safest decision. Not for Londheim's sake, of course, but for Cannac's.

Still, other than a few bruises from stones tossed from afar, it seemed they would reach Belvua without things escalating. It was only when they reached the final road to the district gates that reality disabused Tommy of that notion. The way to Belvua was blocked by over fifty men armed with clubs and knives.

"This is bad," Tommy said, and he spun to face the way they came. Another seventy or so were still in pursuit, their faces red from shouting. The guards surrounding them barely concealed their fear.

"Keep going," one shouted to the others. "Make them disperse."

Far easier said than done. They started to shuffle forward, but the men blocking the way raised their weapons and planted their feet. They made no demands. They didn't shout like the others in tow. They simply held firm and refused to move.

"Will anyone come help us?" Malik asked the nearest guard. The burly man didn't even bother answering. The crowd closed in. The insults grew starker, the threats more vivid, more real. Tommy felt panic clawing at his skull and pecking at his eyes.

"We...we need to...we..."

He couldn't even form a sentence. He didn't know what they should do, where they should go. If only the people would stop screaming at them so he could think!

It appeared Cannac had no such difficulty. The dyrandar lifted his hands and bowed his head as if he were in isolated prayer within a church and not a street teeming with people on the edge of rioting. A low drone exited his throat. Lights shimmered into existence between his antlers. Was this it? Tommy wondered. Was this when the powerful dyrandar would finally strike back with his magic?

"Cannac, whatever you're planning, please don't hurt them," Tommy shouted. Words of spells ran through his mind, and sparks of electricity shot from his fingertips. "I'll do it. I'll protect us! It's all right if they hate me, it's all right!"

The city guards protecting them gave up trying to keep the

crowd at bay peacefully. Several started beating at those nearby with the butts of their spears, while others punched and elbowed those too close. Screams of pain and fright joined the angry. It seemed all the world moved slowly. One man tried to swing a club at Cannac. A spearhead to the gut was his reward.

That was it, Tommy knew. The final line crossed. Blood was on the ground, human blood, and the roaring crowd would not be sated until it was mixed with the blood of monsters. Electricity grew around his hands. Of all the elements at his disposal, lightning seemed the most likely for those afflicted to survive. One big strike and they'd scatter, he prayed. His hands began to swirl, the verbal components tumbled off his lips, and he visualized where the bolt would hit amid the mob.

Cannac reached over and grabbed his wrist, halting his movements.

"No," he said. "No more violence."

The collected colors between his antlers exploded like a storm unleashed. Tommy staggered, for it hit him with physical force. His mind went blank, and he felt a sensation like falling. Everyone gathered reacted likewise, startled looks replacing their shouts or cries. Tommy's stomach pitched, the falling sensation heightened, and then the emotions hit. It was a cavalcade of anger, fear, confusion, and sorrow. They rode over him like stampeding horses, and he was not the only one. Dozens fell to their knees. Weapons dropped from limp hands.

Tommy's mind struggled to understand whatever magic gripped him. He felt angry, but there was a foreignness to it. He was angry at Cannac. He was angry at creatures he'd never seen. He felt intense fear threatening to send him fleeing, but the fear was directed everywhere, at Cannac, at the guards, at the size and anger of the crowd. But he knew he didn't fear Cannac. It was someone else's fear, he realized. Someone else's panic and uncertainty.

"We are one upon the Cradle," Cannac said. His voice was a trumpet cry on a silent eve. "So live as one. Share your emotions as one. This contention must end peaceably, for the only other fate is war."

The anger steadily cooled, unable to maintain its fiery intensity when intermixed with so many other emotions. Everyone's fear was so naked, so communally shared, that the anger could not hide it. Bluster could not tame it. Tommy scanned the crowd and wished he could comfort them. If only they could see the Cannac he had seen, if they could know the intense joy and beauty found in Tesmarie's smile, and the playful cheeriness of Puffy's puffs of smoke.

Except they could. He felt his memories leaking to the others. It was a cool balm upon red and violet waves that floated through the air. Cannac's overwhelming presence joined in, and it was a dominating sensation of calm and desire for peace. More weapons dropped to the ground. A sigh escaped his lips. This was what Cannac had always hoped for, he realized. This was the peace only a dyrandar could help achieve.

The blur of a moonlight blade flashed through the crowd, horrifyingly familiar to Tommy's widening eyes. It was the passage of a creature he thought Tesmarie had defeated. The time-breaking flight of an onyx faery. Gan never slowed. He passed right underneath Cannac's chin and then was gone, vanishing like a dream.

For one long second it seemed all was fine, and then a deep red line of blood opened across the dyrandar's throat.

"No!" Tommy screamed. "No, no, no no no no!"

All color faded from the air. The hopeful silence built by the dyrandar crumbled just like his enormous body. Men and women stirred from a dream. Tommy needed no spell to sense the return of their fear, their confusion, and their anger.

"Hurry," Malik said, his hand clasped about Tommy's wrist. He dragged him out past the circle of guards, who themselves seemed at a loss of what to do. When the crowd surged for the body, the guards gave way, for a corpse was not worth their own lives. What had been angry screams became joyful cries. People took turns kicking and spitting on Cannac's form. Others beat at his chest and face with their clubs, steadily mutilating it beyond recognition.

"Don't watch," Malik said, pulling harder at Tommy's arm. "Please don't, Tomas, please don't watch."

But he had to watch. That was his friend. That was the majestic King of the dyrandar. Tommy tried to resist Malik's pull but either the older man was too strong, or Tommy lacked any of his own to resist, for he steadily retreated from the scene. With so many gathered around the body, he couldn't make out their actions anymore.

At least, not until they lifted Cannac's severed head like a prized deer.

"Look at me," Malik said, grabbing Tommy's head with both hands and wrenching his gaze away. "Just me, do you understand? Not over there. Not at the crowd. Me. Just me."

Tommy stared into Malik's lovely brown eyes as tears streamed from his own. The image replayed itself again and again. A loud, rousing cheer. The head lifting up, positioned on the edge of a spear. The dead gaze. The ripped and loose-hanging tongue.

"Tommy! Me! Look at me!"

Tommy's gaze focused as he pulled out from his mind. Streaks of ice stuck to the walls of the alley. Frost layered his fingertips. Bits more of it clung to Malik's eyebrows and chin like snow. A spell? Had he cast a spell? He didn't know. He wanted to break down in sobs, with the whole world vanishing as if it had never existed. Malik's arms wrapped around him, and he felt his mentor kiss his forehead several times.

"I know it hurts," Malik whispered. "But I need you together.

Can you keep it together, at least until the tower? They've forgotten us for now, but if they grow bored while we're still near..."

Tommy returned the embrace, and he found his strength returning. After a few long sobs into Malik's shirt, he withdrew and nodded.

"I think so," he said.

"Good." Malik grabbed him by the hand. "Now run."

# CHAPTER 28

Evelyn knelt upon the rooftop edge, her hood hanging low over her face and her wings curled tightly about her. Four Ravencallers hurried down the street below under the cover of night. Three of them held hammers, ropes, and nails. The fourth carried a corpse slung over his shoulder, a male human child maybe ten to twelve years old. No doubt the bastards had already worked their magic upon the poor boy, and now it was time for the ritualistic mutilation and hanging of the corpse.

*Logarius has much to atone for*, she thought as she followed the group. Avenria were to be the protector of souls, but now with her son's help, the humans were performing blasphemy against the gifts granted to them by the Goddesses.

*As if you're so blameless.*

Evelyn pulled her two sickles from their hooks. The soft leather of Whisper and Song against the rough skin of her hands calmed her nerves and helped push aside her guilt. Yes, she had much to atone for, but that's why she was out there in the dead of night stalking those desperate or foolish enough to be swayed by the Book of Ravens. Avenria lived long, long lives. Hopefully by the end of hers, not a single trace of that damn book would remain upon the face of the Cradle.

"Hurry up," one of the four Ravencallers admonished the others. "We won't have enough time if you keep dawdling."

"Don't worry," Evelyn said from the rooftop. Their fearful eyes turned her way. "You're about to have all the time in the world."

She spun as she descended, her arms extended. Her blades shimmered blue just before contact, heating their edges into unrivaled killing sharpness. One Ravencaller's head flew from his shoulder. Another collapsed in two, his body rent in half from hip to hip. The one carrying the body dropped it to free his hands, and the words of a curse flowed from his lips.

"Anwyn of the Moon, hear me!" he cried.

"She's busy," Evelyn said, cutting down the third Ravencaller. "Try later."

She flung Whisper end over end, its sharp point easily punching through his forehead. Its rotation continued, burying the sickle deeper so that the point punched out the top of his mouth and stuck above his jaw like a second tongue.

Just like that, the fight was over. They'd died so quickly, her heart rate had not even accelerated. Evelyn looked over the bodies. A sad ache settled over her chest. They all looked to be in their second decade of age. Incredibly young, even for humans. What promises had they been offered? What sweet lies had her son whispered into their ears? Magic? Power? Authority over humanity once they were conquered?

"War approaches and you're killing a few misguided cultists," she muttered. "What are you doing, Evelyn?"

It wasn't the first time such doubts came to her. The old world had awakened with a flourish, and barely weeks passed before factions started forming. Whispers filled local taverns of dragon-sired armies on the move. Once word of Cannac's death reached his son, Evelyn held no doubt they'd come to Londheim eager to burn the city to the ground in response.

The only question was whether or not Viciss allowed such an

act. If the living mountain stirred, no army could stand against it. That might mean Londheim's doom, or its salvation, and honestly Evelyn wasn't sure which might be better for the Cradle. War was war, and always brutal, but her few weeks in Londheim had not exactly convinced her of their ability to have humans and dragon-sired living peaceably together. Hundreds of years had passed while they slumbered, yet humanity remained very much the same upon their waking.

Evelyn flapped her wings and vaulted back to the rooftops. Such dire thoughts should no longer be hers. She'd fought her wars against humanity. She'd watched family and friends die to the prayers of Mindkeepers and the pistols of Soulkeepers. Coexistence might be hard, but damn it, a life of war was harder. She left the bodies to be found by the city guards and paced the rooftops with no particular destination in mind. The sense of movement helped her escape her own thoughts, which were none too kind.

Killing the occasional cultist would never be enough, not while her son lived.

"You're pulling leaves because you're not strong enough to cut the branches," she said. "You really are wasting your—"

Evelyn skidded to a halt atop an elegant home and clutched one of its steep pillars for balance. A sound like glass scraping against glass pierced through her mind with such force, she clenched her beak hard enough to make her jaw ache. What in blazes was that? Her stomach heaved. Something was wrong. Their creator, Aethos, had granted avenria hypersensitivity to the presence of the void, and she could feel the light of the soul within a human's body like a warm glow. This sensation, this otherworldly noise, was like a shrieking protest against all she represented.

*Keep your head together,* she chastised herself. *Focus! Where is it coming from?*

Evelyn closed her eyes and huddled closer to the shingles. This wasn't a real noise reaching her ears. That glass-on-glass sound was her mind's interpretation of something intensely wrong. A sensation of...breaking? Piercing? It faded slightly, allowing her a better understanding of its source. This noise, this sensation, was one she had not felt in ages, and never this strong.

It was the presence of the void, and it was very, very close.

"How are you here?" she wondered aloud. "How did you break through the stars' protection?"

A shiver ran down her spine and set her feathers to ruffling. She had to find it and deal with it immediately, before it could wreak untold damage upon Londheim. Her boots pounded across the shingles as she leapt from rooftop to rooftop, occasionally using her wings to grant her a boost should the gaps be large. The wretched sensation of wrongness guided her like a lighthouse, only it was not safe shores she approached but an unknown monster.

The void could take on any shape, for it had no inherent shape of its own. Even knowing this, Evelyn was not prepared for the bizarre horror that crept down the empty street. It looked like the void-monster had chosen to emulate the body of a human, only instead of walking on two legs, it crawled on all fours, with both its arms and legs disturbingly long and double-jointed. It reminded Evelyn of a four-legged spider, only it had no fat abdomen or segmented thorax. A long-necked head sniffed the ground, while a second head grew between its shoulders facing the sky. Its mouths were open, and swirling between pure-black teeth was an unending chasm. Everything about it was the absence of light, of definition, of meaning. A ravenous anti-existence, with only nebulous hate and loathing to give it purpose.

"This is what you were made for, Whisper-Song," Evelyn said as she drew her two sickles. She jammed their lower ends together and twisted. The wood connected as if it were one long branch (which in fact it had been, centuries ago) and then extended. Evelyn twirled the twin-scythe in a circle, knowing she'd need its greater reach. "Let us pray the centuries have not dulled your blades."

Evelyn leapt over three more rooftops, closing the distance between her and the monster. With how it ignored the nearby homes, she assumed it had a destination in mind. Whatever it might be, she wouldn't let it arrive. No one, not human, not dragon-sired, deserved to die in the clutches of the void.

With one head looking forward and another staring up and behind, there'd be no sneaking up on the monster. Evelyn dashed off the tall spire of a wealthy mansion and dove for it anyway, hoping her speed might overwhelm it. The monster shuddered at her approach and released a blood-chilling howl. She spun just before contact, the blades of her scythes shimmering blue as their firekin magic enacted.

The resemblance to a spider appeared appropriate, for it moved with the speed and reflexes of one. Arms and legs scrambled out of the way so that the leading scythe struck the street, cutting a deep groove into the stone and scattering pebbles in all directions. Evelyn tried to continue her momentum but a weirdly jointed arm struck her in the abdomen, knocking out her breath. She spun Whisper-Song before her, forcing the creature back lest she hack its arm off with the two twirling blades.

"*Avenria*," spoke both heads simultaneously. "*The stars moved much since we last met.*"

"Sorry," she said as she braced her legs for an attack. Her words came out raspy and weak from her attempts to regain her breath. "Can't say I remember you."

The void-monster lunged after her, and she met it with a leap of her own. They twisted together, Evelyn relying on her finely honed reflexes to carry her through. Pure black arms and legs thrashed about her, but she shifted her hips and twisted her shoulders to avoid the blows. Whisper-Song's sharp point plunged into the dark shape just above the hip.

She failed to anticipate its sudden fury at being harmed. The monster flung her away like a ragdoll. She flared her wings and flapped to slow her descent so that the hard stone didn't crack open her skull upon landing. Whisper-Song clattered to the street beside her, the blue hue fading from its blades.

"*Arrogance*," said the monster. "*Bluster. Pointless.*"

It bounded toward her, the thud of its hands and feet upon the stone like that of a panicked horse. Her hand closed around Whisper-Song's hilt as the void-monster towered above her.

"*Light must fade*," the monster gloated. "*Hunger will be sated.*"

Evelyn's wings turned incorporeal, granting her body passage through the solid stone of the street below her. The void-monster's arms pummeled where she'd been, bashing giant cracks and indents into the street. Evelyn righted herself as she fell, then shot a hand upward. Her clawed fingers hooked the stone of the street. Her descent halted, she pulled, and then shot out of the ground like a bullet. Whisper-Song's handle rolled over her shoulder, back into her grip, and then swirled. Both scythes carved through the void-monster's body, spilling shadow. Evelyn flapped her wings to carry her above, and then she ripped Whisper and Song apart so she might bury both their blades directly into the void-monster's forehead.

Their shimmering steel tore through the pure black essence, and she carved the twin blades along its body, shredding it like she would tall grass. A flailing arm caught her chest, and she flew several feet before landing painfully on her back, but the damage to the monster was already done. It broke apart, losing all form completely. Liquid shadow flowed across the stones, hissing and evaporating beneath the distant glow of the stars. With the monster's death, Evelyn instantly felt better. The glass-on-glass scraping inside her mind faded to a distant whisper. Evelyn let out a long sigh and separated the two halves of her twin-scythe.

"I am too old for this," she grumbled. Every bone in her body ached. She pushed herself back to her feet and stared at the vacant spot where the void-monster had existed mere moments before. The Cradle was like a sealed boat adrift in a vicious ocean. Once there was a leak, that leak remained until fixed. The question was... where was the leak?

Evelyn folded her wings over her face and slowly exhaled. The presence of the void was distinctly alien to everything upon the Cradle, and that meant it left a trail. No normal eyes would perceive it, but this was what the avenria had been made for. Every step the monster took scarred the very building blocks of matter it touched. It destroyed the air that contacted its skin. It absorbed all light that fell upon its body and returned none of it. The void was hunger and fury, and once Evelyn's eyes looked upon a world made of souls and shadow, the path it had taken stood out like a black scar.

Evelyn followed the path despite dreading where it might take her. The monster had snaked through a trio of homes. In each one she found furniture tossed, doors broken, and blood splashed across the walls and floor. No bodies, though. The damn thing ate them. Based on the damage, it looked like the monster had grown in size as it feasted, with the damage to the third house significantly greater than the first.

The black scar returned to the street, its trail smaller and harder to follow. Evelyn had to drop from the rooftops and scan the cold stone for signs of its passage. She found them in small, bright grooves, as if the stone had been sanded and cleaned. The path took her across the street, through an alley, and then into another home. Evelyn paused before it. Unlike the nearby buildings, this one appeared older, and completely carved from stone, whereas newer buildings used a mixture of bricks and wood. The front door was open and unlocked, and when she hurried inside, she found similar destruction to the furniture. A trip upstairs found a bloodstained bed, and Evelyn offered a prayer for the slaughtered owners.

What she did not find, however, was where the path originally began. The black scar of passage looped and circled about the home, yet she couldn't find where it had entered the home. For ten minutes she paced the property, ensuring there were no other signs of the void-monster outside the building. Then she began anew inside, retracing the creature's steps and building a timeline of destruction in her mind. At last she had the idea to check the enormous fireplace. Perhaps it had leapt from a nearby building and then scuttled down the chimney?

Sure enough, she saw signs of the void's presence within, but not as she'd expected. Power emanated from the fireplace, and she felt it on her feathers like a cool wind. Evelyn pushed her fingers to the stone and held her palm flat. Immediately the back plate of the fireplace vanished as if it had never been, revealing a long, dark passageway.

"Well now," she whispered. "What have we here?"

Evelyn curled her wings and ducked underneath to fit. Thankfully it widened out into a tall, narrow corridor. The glass-on-glass screech in her mind returned, but it was duller, and more constant. She readied her sickles just in case. Her initial assessment had placed the corridor only a hundred feet or so long, but that was born of an optical illusion due to light coming in from behind her. In truth it continued in pitch blackness for hundreds of feet without curving. Evelyn tracked her progress mentally with each footstep, picturing where she might be if topside.

Evelyn knew without a doubt where she was when she reached the corridor's end: directly below the entrance to the humans' Cathedral of the Sacred Mother. Before her was a strange, domed room, and its wonders danced in her eyes. Despite knowing her curiosity might be her undoing, she lifted her sickles and stepped inside.

"What is this?" she wondered. Stars surrounded her in all directions. It felt like standing atop the highest mountain in all the Cradle, alone with the sky's wonder. A triangular well was built in the center, a diamond orb hovering just within. Starlight trickled down into it in a thread thin as spider's silk.

Evelyn buckled her sickles at her hips and approached one of the walls, if "wall" was what one should truly call it, for it was more like a window to heavens so far away. Once she removed a glove, she lovingly brushed her naked hand across the stars. She felt their presence on her scaled skin. Protecting them. Keeping the void at bay.

*The void was nothing,* her mother had told her when she was a small child cuddled in her wings. *Empty, without thought or want or care. Then the three Sisters came to this barren place. They brought light into the darkness. They brought with them love, and joy, and creation. But the void had spent eternity comfortable in its nothingness, and now there was a light shining upon it, giving it shape. That light was the First Soul the Sisters brought to humanity. The void has sought to destroy it ever since. It will rip apart everything so it might sleep in peace.*

Evelyn had squirmed in her mother's lap and buried her beak against her chest.

*The Faithkeeper called it a dragon,* she'd said, the reason she'd brought the matter up in the first place. She'd lurked nearby during one of the ninth-day sermons the humans held in the market near Belvua, listening as he ranted about the void-dragon, and how it would swallow them all in darkness for tolerating the dragon-sired's perversions.

*The five dragons are the Sisters' children, beloved creators of the Cradle,* her mother had said. *The void is no dragon. It is emptiness given a mouth. It is apathy given teeth. It has but one desire, to return to a time when it had no desires. That is why we were made, little one. The stars hold the void at bay, but sometimes there are long shadows in deep places. Places we must go.*

Places like this, Evelyn knew, and she readied Whisper-Song.

The scar ran four feet long vertically, though its width was barely more than a strand of hair. It wriggled and squirmed like a trapped worm. The stars to either side of it were noticeably dimmer than the rest, and she had a feeling at least a few had winked out completely. Evelyn stood before the scar and readied her sickles. This scar, it was like a tunnel of near infinite length, and through which the earlier monster had entered their world. The question was... could she seal it?

The sounds of voices broke her concentration. People, here, now? Evelyn didn't know who, but her gut screamed to hide. She cast her eyes about the domed room. There was nowhere to go. The floor was perfectly smooth, as were the walls. Based on the echo of the voices, which reverberated multiple times in the long hallway as to render the speech indecipherable, she had only a minute at most.

Evelyn flapped her wings and chose the best place she could think of. Just above the arched entryway there were stretches of shadows before the stars began, and she sank her wings into them, allowing her body passage. She sank her body into the stone, all her extremities going numb as her flesh and feathers became incorporeal. When she ceased moving, only her hooded face remained free. It'd be safer to vanish completely, but she had to see who the voice belonged to, and if they were the one responsible for the wriggling void scar.

When her son entered the mysterious room with a fellow avenria, she questioned the wisdom of her decision.

"I see no sign of it," Logarius said after a moment. "Do you?"

The other avenria shook her head.

"Nothing. Wherever that void creature went, it's gone now."

So they were tracking the same monster as her. Well, no wonder they couldn't find it. Whisper-Song had put a fitting end to that nightmarish entity.

Logarius approached the wriggling scar and lifted his right hand.

"At least we know where it came from," he said. Shadows began to coalesce around his fingers. Evelyn watched as her mind began to swim with spots. She could not breathe in her current state, and even the flow of her blood was momentarily halted. Remaining like this beyond a minute or two was a dangerous risk, but what was this place, and what was its connection to her son?

"This construction is dangerous," the other avenria said as the scar sealed shut. "We're running a very big risk by not dismantling it."

"Dismantling it poses far greater risks than leaving it be," Logarius said. He let out a deep breath, his body clearly taxed by sealing the rift. "We're almost ready, Ilia. The occasional void tear is something we can handle."

As much as Evelyn wished to know what that plan of his might be, she could endure no longer. She sank all the way into the stone and then allowed herself to fall. Cool air greeted her as she dropped free into the long corridor. Her lungs gasped in a grateful breath. The darkness mixed with her wings to keep her hidden, and after a brief respite, she sprinted down the corridor. Whatever her son planned, it was greater than she could handle alone. As much as she hated the idea, it was time for her to find help.

Thankfully for her, she knew just the Soulkeeper for the job.

# CHAPTER 29

Dierk relaxed in his chair, the heat of the nearby fireplace welcome upon his cold skin. Just an hour ago he'd joined Vaesalaum on a trip to a dark street corner and drank the memories of a murdered man in his sixties. There'd been dozens of joyful moments in his soul, time spent with families, and an adventurous trek across the Cradle from his original home in Nicus, across the South Orismund grasslands, and up the river to Londheim after a stint as a fisherman in Wardhus.

*To have a life like that,* Dierk wondered. More and more he felt a calling toward something greater, to relaxed moments with friends and family and songs around campfires without caring if one butchered the words or could not hold a tune. Dierk had lived his whole life carefully measuring his every step. To dip into the existence of another who moved through the world with carefree abandon was...exhilarating.

*Such a life is not meant for Dierk,* Vaesalaum said from his perch above the fire. The nisse looked practically obese from its recent feedings. The cheeks of its face were puffy, and its belly, while still not particularly large, looked swollen on its lanky, serpentine body. Dierk didn't bother to argue. Honestly, he knew he should be paying attention to the conversation happening on the couch nearby, where his father and the Royal Overseer were having a frustrated argument over their combined futures.

"We can't count on troops from Wardhus and Stomme," his father was saying. "If they're going through anything like us, they will keep their soldiers close to home."

"You really believe they'll commit treason?" Albert asked.

Soren shrugged and sipped from his short, wide glass.

"Overtly? No. But how many excuses might they pile atop one another to explain not coming? Disrupted trading channels, destroyed crops, monster attacks; they could tell us anything and we'd have no choice but to believe them."

Albert rubbed his eyes and groaned. Londheim's leaders had a meeting during Dierk's absence about how to deal with Belvua's seemingly permanent presence, and they'd come no closer to a solution than when they began. Albert had accompanied Soren back home, the two letting off steam as they drank in private. Dierk had quietly joined them upon returning to the mansion.

"You're probably right," Albert said. "As much as it stinks to high heavens. I sent riders to both Steeth and Trivika when this madness first started, and I'm yet to receive a response from either. Both the church and the crown appear either oblivious to our struggles, or uncaring. Neither one's good for us out here in the west."

"Then we make do with what we have," Soren said, ever the practical one. His father never acted as if things were out of his control. He presided over Londheim like he did his own home, with an iron fist that seemed much softer and gentler when in public. "The walls of Londheim are strong, and the emergent miracles of the keepers in producing food for the poor have alleviated much of the threat of riots. We'll endure. These trials will not break us."

"Easy to say, but when an army of inhuman creatures finally arrives at our gates, what in Lyra's name are we supposed to do about it?"

Dierk's ears picked up at the mention of an army. He knew plenty about the Forgotten Children and their takeover of Low Dock, but the idea of full-blown armies of dragon-sired marching across the lands ignited his imagination.

"What armies?" he asked, and thankfully his father gave him an approving nod.

"There's three that we've received confirmed reports of," Albert said. "And they match the threats that strange deer-like King showed us. There's the rabbit people to the east, more of the dyrandar crossing the Triona River to the south, and pretty much in all directions we're hearing reports of...what did Cannac call them? Viridi? Grass people. They seem capable of creating fortresses of dirt and grass in mere hours. Driving them back will be a nightmare, assuming we ever build a sizable force capable of marching out of Londheim in the first place."

"Give it time," Soren said. He drained his glass and stood to refill it from a nearby shelf that held over a dozen different bottles of wine. "And keep sending your updates to the east. Once the shock of these changes passes, neither church nor crown will allow our lands to be stolen from us by these...*monsters.*"

That earned a laugh from Albert, and he held out his glass so Soren could refill it along with his own. Both of them were visibly intoxicated. Their previous meeting must have been pretty awful for them to be so eager to drink away its frustrations.

"Yes, these fucking monsters," Albert said. "But how in the world do we wage a campaign to retake our lands when we can't even take back a single district in our own city? It doesn't exactly inspire confidence."

The atmosphere was so relaxed, and Dierk's mind still floating from his stolen memories, that he didn't even hesitate to offer his advice. After all, the solution seemed so obvious, so easy.

"Why not just give the creatures in Belvua amnesty and start living with them peacefully?" he suggested.

Both older men stiffened in their seats. Dierk realized how badly he'd misjudged the room by their bloodshot glares.

"Amnesty?" Soren asked. "Do you know how many of my guards those creatures have murdered? How many innocent people they've forced out of their homes?"

"Homes in Low Dock," Dierk added, bewildered by his sudden courage. "Innocent people you didn't give two shits about until the creatures moved in."

Albert tried to break the sudden tension with a charming laugh, but even that was beyond his charismatic capabilities.

"The people in Low Dock may be poor but they are still our people," he said, flashing that winning smile of his that had earned him his position in the first place. "Though I will admit that perhaps we should be more willing to listen to the troubles and complaints of these creatures instead of viewing them as mindless monsters trying to steal our lands. Had I done so, the tragic loss of Cannac might have been prevented."

"Indeed," Soren said, his eyes never leaving Dierk. "Albert, it's late, and we've both had a bit too much to drink. I hope you don't mind if I call it a day so I might have some time to speak with my son."

"Of course, of course," Albert said, pushing himself up from the padded couch. "I'll try to visit tomorrow. General Rose promised an update on her new recruitment drive."

"I look forward to it."

The two shook hands and then Albert retrieved his coat from a polished wood hook and exited the lounge. The door shut, swallowing Soren and Dierk in silence. Soren remained where he stood, looking nowhere. It was almost as if he were counting. The moment he reached his set number, he whirled on Dierk, grabbed him by the front of his shirt, and flung him against the wall.

"Where the fuck do you get off proposing such an idea?" his father seethed, his face inches away. Dierk's entire vision filled with those angry, bloodshot eyes. "Amnesty? You'd have me dismiss all their crimes and recognize their claim on Low Dock? How can you be my son and yet so damn stupid? Don't you realize how weak that would make me look?"

"What does it matter if—"

Soren struck him across the mouth to shut him up. Blood shot from his lip to splatter little red flecks across the bricks of the fireplace.

"Albert may seem like my friend, but he is still an elected politician with his own agendas and his own circle of friends," his father continued. "You absolutely cannot criticize my view of Low Dock's people without making me appear heartless or cruel. Appearances matter, damn it. Albert left this mansion debating mercy for monsters and convinced my son thinks he can backtalk his own father."

Soren's fist slammed into his stomach so hard Dierk thought he'd vomit.

"Fucking—"

A second fist, this to his chest.

"—un—"

A third fist, again in the stomach. Dierk's knees quivered, and he fought back sudden tears.

"—acceptable."

Dierk crumpled to the ground as Soren walked to the wine shelf. He drank straight from a bottle as Dierk gasped and struggled for breath. He sniffled despite hating himself for his tears. He let out a soft moan of agony despite hating his weakness. All the while Vaesalaum floated overhead, taunting him.

*Dierk's father reminds Dierk of his place. Crying on the floor. Pathetic.*

Soren finished his long draught and set the bottle down atop the shelf with a thud.

"You're no longer allowed in any of my meetings, official or otherwise," he said, his back to him. His voice was calm, collected, as if they were discussing the weather. As if Dierk weren't crying on his knees with his insides trembling in pain. "I'm done trying to groom you as a proper replacement. At this point I'll be lucky to have my career survive your careless intrusions."

*A shame,* Vaesalaum said. *You lose your usefulness. Should nisse seek another to instruct?*

"No," Dierk gasped through clenched teeth.

Soren slowly turned.

"Excuse me?" he asked.

Dierk hadn't meant to address him, but now that his cold fury was directed his way, he felt an eerie calm wash over him. He rose to his feet, spat blood upon the carpet, and grinned at his father.

"Never hit me again," he said. "If you do, I will make you regret it like you would not believe."

"You're right," Soren said. He picked up the bottle he'd previously drunk from and downed the last of the wine. Once it was empty, he held it like a weapon. "I don't believe you. Has something crazy dug root in your head, boy?"

He calmly approached, but Dierk sensed a change in his father. This could be it. This final outburst might be the last straw. That glass was thick, and should it break, its edges would be sharp. Dierk pulled back his shoulders and extended one of his hands. He stared in the eyes of his father, and in them he saw something far more monstrous than anything he'd seen in the presence of the Forgotten Children.

"Anwyn of the Moon, hear me," he said. Immediately he felt power gathering inside his chest. It flowed out his fingers, invisible to the physical world but visible to his nisse-blessed eyes in the form of thin strands of spider-silk. The words of the third chapter of the Book of Ravens flowed across his tongue. They wrapped about his father, holding him in place as he listened with frightened rapture. Vaesalaum circled above him, a smile on its blind face.

"Before me stands a man disgracing the light of his soul. His mind rejects peace. His heart rejects love. Break his pride. Split his stubbornness. Give to me, in my superior wisdom and faith, *control*."

Soren's body convulsed. Drool rolled down the sides of his mouth. He squirmed and raged against invisible chains that kept him rooted in place. Dierk clenched his hand into a fist, and he channeled every piece of his willpower into that spell. It didn't matter that his extremities went numb and dark spots started to clutter his vision. He was done being humiliated. Vaesalaum had given him power. The Book of Ravens had taught him how to wield it. The beatings, the insults, the cruelty: today it all came to an end.

Something cracked in Soren's mind, and at last his limbs fell still. He stared at Dierk with a perplexed expression on his face.

"What is it you want?" he asked.

"I want you to grant amnesty to the magical creatures," Dierk said. "And I want you to recognize Belvua as the new name and identity of Low Dock."

"That's insane," Soren started to say, but a convulsion cut him off. His head jolted to one side, and he flexed as if lightning were coursing through his veins.

"All right," his father gasped, suddenly out of breath. "I'll do it."

Dierk felt his heart pound in his chest. Was this it? Was it that easy? It felt like a cloud over his family mansion had lifted. The fear and care that had guided his every step no longer felt necessary. The looming, terrifying specter that was Soren Becher...had he truly defeated it?

"And I want to be at every meeting of yours," Dierk added. He felt drunk on his newfound freedom. "No, change that. I want permission to go in your place and make decisions in your name."

Again Soren rebelled against the idea, but it didn't last as long as the first time. Eventually his muscles relaxed, and the fiery spirit died in those gray eyes.

"Of course," he said. "It's only proper that my son take a larger role in politics. After all, everyone knows you'll be my successor one day."

Dierk laughed and skipped in place. His smile spread ear to ear.

"You hear that, Vaesalaum?" he asked the fat ethereal thing still hovering over Soren. "You still think I'm useless? Still think I'm pathetic?"

Vaesalaum curled into a circle that resembled a bow.

*Vaesalaum proven wrong. Vaesalaum happy Dierk finally showing true self.*

"Damn right," Dierk laughed. He rushed to the wine shelf and drank of vintages his father had expressly forbidden. The warmth spreading through his stomach could not compete with the joy in his chest. It felt like a vise had been removed from his rib cage. It felt like those moments near the end of sex in the lives he relived. It felt *so fucking good.*

"Is that all?" Soren asked, still patiently waiting in the center of the lounge.

"Oh, trust me," Dierk said as he wiped a bit of spilled wine off his chin. "We're just getting started."

# CHAPTER 30

Adria sat before Alma's Greeting, a long line before her stretching down the many steps and into the street. Midday bells chimed from one of the cathedral's towers behind her.

*Three hours,* she thought as the next in line came forward, seeking healing for her crippled leg. *I've been at this for three hours.*

There was a time when healing only a few people had driven her to exhaustion, but now at hour three she still felt capable of harnessing the power of her faith to mend flesh and banish sickness. That she was getting stronger was undeniable. What it meant, however, she was still uncertain.

"Mindkeeper?" asked the crippled woman.

"Forgive me," Adria said, snapping back to attention. "It has been a long day."

She put her hands upon the woman's leg and prayed the 22nd Devotion, and she tried not to wince at the sight of her wrist, which still bore the scars from the void's touch. Moments later the crippled woman practically skipped down the cathedral steps, a joyous smile on her face and a song on her lips. Adria used that joy to fuel herself when exhaustion tugged at the borders of her mind. The next in line started to move, but a novice blocked the way at the behest of Faithkeeper Sena.

"You need not push yourself," said Sena. She had joined Adria in healing the sick at the start of the day, but tired after only a few prayers. Still, that was more than she could do the day before, a growing in power that many were starting to experience.

"I'm all right," Adria snapped, harsher than she meant.

"No, you're not," Sena said. "And you best realize that before you injure yourself."

Adria paused before responding. Things had been tense between them ever since she'd used Sena's soul to defend the church. Outwardly, her friend had insisted she understood, and forgiven her. Adria, however, could see her hidden emotions swirling within her soul, and it hurt her to see the little flickers of fear and doubt that had begun to grow.

"I will take a break if I need one, I promise," Adria said.

Sena didn't appear convinced, but she squeezed Adria's hand and then gestured for the novice to bring up the next in line. It was a woman carrying an infant that looked just shy of a year old.

"What is your need?" Adria asked.

"It's—it's my son," the woman said.

"Is he ill?"

"No, I don't think so. His crying. It isn't normal. And he doesn't play. I think...I think he's soulless."

Adria felt a pang of sorrow in her chest.

"Soullessness isn't an illness to be healed," she said.

"I just want to know," the woman insisted. "Please, can you look at him?"

Adria closed her eyes for a moment and then reopened them. The world dimmed, but amid that world shone hundreds of twinkling stars. They were the souls of the people gathered before her, shimmering within their skulls. That little boy, though? She saw only dark. Adria blinked away the vision and sadly shook her head.

"I'm sorry," she said. "Alma did not deliver your boy's soul to his body upon his birth."

The woman clutched the child closer to her. Tears swelled in her eyes. She acted like her son had been handed a death sentence, and in a way, he had been.

"The church will take him in if you are unwilling," Adria said softly. "He will be fed, clothed, and bathed. No harm will come to him."

"Please," she whimpered. "There must be something you can do. There must! You're the Sacred Mother reborn!"

"I am not the Sacred Mother," Adria said with a sharper edge than she'd intended. The Sacred Mother was the first woman granted a soul, and whose progeny had populated the Cradle with life and light when humans had been mere soulless animals. That wasn't her. She bore no sacred blessing from the Goddesses. She was a freak granted power by Janus and his strange, frightful machine beneath the city.

"But you command souls!" the mother said, and her panic increased to match Adria's ire. "You can help him, I know you can, I know it!"

A pinprick of panic stabbed at Adria's throat. Yes, she commanded souls, but there was no soul there to command.

Wasn't there?

"Come along now," the young novice nearby said, stepping between Adria and the mother.

"Wait," Adria said. The novice glanced back at her. "Just... wait."

The mother froze and held her breath, anticipating a miracle. Adria prayed she might give her one. Her eyes shifted, returning to the world of souls. Ever since she'd awakened with this power, there was one matter she had been fearful to address. Though it hovered at the edge of her vision, she had not looked, nor probed it with her mind. To do so might mean answers, and that knowledge frightened her.

Her head tilted. Tamerlane had admonished her to stop being

fearful of her strength, and of the knowledge she might gain. So be it. Her eyes focused upon the silver thread that split the sky. Always there, a seemingly infinitely long river of light. Not a star. Something even farther away. A celestial flow of memories and emotions. The destination of every soul she sent to the heavens after their body's passing.

Adria put her left hand on the boy's forehead and lifted her right to the heavens. Her eyes narrowed on that silver river. This child, this soulless being, felt like a gaping wound. A part of him was missing, and she could almost feel what it was, like forming the shape of a man based on his shadow. Her right hand clenched into a fist, and she felt a previously untouched power within her mind rip open.

"Forgive me, precious Alma, if I overstep," she whispered. "But I must try."

From deep within that river of souls, she called for the gift the boy should have been granted upon birth. A soul. A seed of power, to be filled with memories and emotions over the course of a lifetime. From a world beyond their own, across a distance her mind could not fathom, the tiniest little speck of light shot down and plummeted straight into the boy's forehead. He quaked within his mother's arms and then let out a long, frightful wail.

The boy's mother stared in shock. Soulless children didn't cry.

"Praise be to Alma," Adria said as she felt her mind collapsing back in on itself, the world among the stars receding and the river of souls returning to a barely perceptible scar across the sky.

"It wasn't Alma," the mother said as she kissed her crying child. "Thank you, Mindkeeper. May all three Goddesses bless you!"

She sprinted down the steps and shouted Adria's praises to any who would listen. A quick look from Adria to the novice let him know she was done for now, and he blocked the top of the line while shouting for the rest to disperse. Faithkeeper Sena took Adria by the arm and pulled her close.

"Adria, what you did—"

"Is only what Alma wishes," Adria interrupted. "Or do you cling to old beliefs that the soulless are born unloved and unwanted by the Goddesses?"

"You know I don't believe that," Sena snapped. "But this goes beyond prayers and miracles. You pulled a soul down from the heavens! That is Alma's divine place, not yours."

The two retreated further, for Adria knew what she would say next should not reach any layman's ears.

"Where was Alma upon his birth?" she asked. "Why was his soul not granted to him? If I can spare him an empty, pointless life, than I shall do so, Sena. Look at his parents. *Look at them*. Look at their joy. Would you tell me that it was wrong what I did, to cause such happiness?"

"Do you not hear yourself?" Sena asked softly. "Tread carefully, Mindkeeper. The first taste of blasphemy is often the sweetest."

Blasphemy? Her dear friend would accuse her of *blasphemy*? Before she could respond, a novice came running over to Adria, her face and neck shining with sweat.

"Mindkeeper Adria," the young girl interrupted. "Vikar Thaddeus requests your immediate presence and insists it is most urgent."

"Did he say the reason for this urgency?"

"'The death we feared has come,'" the novice said. "Those were his exact words."

A fresh wave of panic washed away Adria's exhaustion. There was only one person that could be. The Deakon had finally succumbed to his curse. If that were true, then...

"I must be going," she told Sena.

"Of course."

"The Vikar awaits you in the Soft Voice," the novice offered.

But that wasn't where Adria headed. She dashed down the steps and then made her way around the western wall. She passed the

Scholars' Abode, passed the main entrance to the Sisters' Remembrance, and ducked into the unassuming door to the hidden cells below.

"They've already taken the body," the guard manning the interior door told her as he unlocked it.

"I'm not here for the body."

Once inside, she rushed past the other poor soul cursed with Malformation and stopped before Tamerlane's cell. As usual, the former Mindkeeper lay slumped against the back wall, looking as relaxed as could be. She glanced to the guard accompanying her and then pointed.

"Remove his gag."

The guard gave her a wary look.

"Are you certain?" he asked.

"Very. Now do it."

He did as told, unlocking both the cell and the gag.

"Be careful," he told her. "With the Deakon dead, he's not got much left to lose."

"I'll be fine."

The guard left them to their privacy. Tamerlane massaged his jaw and observed her with a faint smile on his face.

"What happened to your wrists?" he asked.

Adria grabbed her left wrist on reflex. Two bright white scars circled around the bone, a permanent reminder of the black tendrils that had grabbed her.

"A brush with the void," she said. "I healed the flesh and bone, but no amount of prayers seems to remove the scars."

"The void? My, my, it sounds like you have a tale to tell."

"Have you no urgency?" Adria said. "The Deakon is dead, which means Thaddeus has no more use for you. The church may send your executioner at any moment."

Tamerlane shrugged.

"Perhaps. Would it be better if I panicked? I'm not sure that's how I'd prefer to spend my final moments, if these are in fact my final moments." He laughed. "Or perhaps *you* are my executioner, Adria. I did not initially consider that a possibility, but it would have a nice stroke of irony to it."

"Irony?" Adria asked.

"My greatest hope being my eventual murderer. Maybe *irony* isn't the right word. Appropriate, perhaps, given the sad state of our world? But forget about me, Adria. I'm glad you came, because I have a request to make of you."

"And what is that?" she asked. There was one request in particular she feared he might make, for if he did, she wasn't sure how she'd react.

His easy smile faded.

"Become the next Deakon of West Orismund."

She swallowed down a sudden knot that tied itself directly in the center of her throat.

"You're insane."

"No, I'm perfectly sane," he said. "With Thaddeus finally dead, they'll need to elect a new one. In normal times one of the three Vikars would be an easy victor, but these are not normal times. You told me you were the first keeper to display powers of healing. That makes you special in everyone's eyes, deserved or not. And should you display your command over souls to the rest of the keepers, I am convinced they will vote for you. Do not let this opportunity slip away! Become our next Deakon. Usher in a new age of wisdom, starting right here in Londheim."

For a moment she dared imagine herself in that role. To have every keeper in West Orismund under her command. For the Vikars of Dawn, Day, and Dusk to serve her expressed will. The responsibility filled her with panic, but even amid that panic, she felt an inkling of excitement. She wouldn't need to hide her power anymore. There'd be no one to judge her but the Ecclesiast all the way in Trivika on the other side of the Cradle. She might even be able to help her brother reveal Jacaranda's condition, and that of potentially hundreds more awakening soulless.

Adria shook her mind free of the daydream. Tamerlane was still staring at her, and his smile had returned. He'd planted a seed, and was clearly quite proud of it. He barely knew her, yet he was always pushing her to go one step farther, and believing her capable of greater things. But still, there was that one damning act he'd committed against Deakon Sevold.

"Tell me why you cursed the Deakon," she said. "I have to know, and I will take it from your mind by force if I must."

Tamerlane sat up straighter. His fingers tapped at his pursed lips.

"So be it," he said. "I think you are finally ready to believe me. Deakon Sevold kept a small harem of soulless boys to serve as his sexual playthings. It's not even that well buried a secret within the Cathedral of the Sacred Mother. I'm sure all three Vikars know about it, at the least. When I confronted him about this, he threatened my expulsion from Londheim, and that would only be after cutting out my tongue for speaking such 'baseless' accusations."

Adria shook her head, unsure why but feeling immediately defensive of the deceased leader.

"No. That can't be true. Deakon Sevold was a good man, a great man."

"I'm sure he believed he was," Tamerlane said. "But since the reaping ritual is the only clear proof of the Keeping Church's authority upon the Cradle, its scholars and keepers have elevated the importance of a soul to the absolutely highest status possible, beyond even what I believe the Sisters intended. This means all creations *without* a soul become worth less and less. We clear forests and burn fields without a care to the damage. Animals are not shared companions upon the Cradle, but exist solely to serve our needs. As for the soulless? Well, are they not akin to the animals? And Sevold absolutely had his needs."

Adria's need to refute his logic bordered on desperation. Deakon

Sevold had personally chosen all three current Vikars during his life-long appointment. His decisions, and those of his subordinates, had shaped much of the theological discourse the last three decades. To have all of that tainted with such sickening, horrific misdeeds...

"What proof do you have of this?" she asked. "The soulless boys, where are they?"

"Shuffled out among the various churches would be my guess," Tamerlane said. "The Keeping Church is rotten to the core, Adria. If I knew my words contained real power, I'd never have so clumsily confronted the Deakon. When I spoke the curse, it was mere hours before the crawling mountain arrived at Londheim. I only wished to express my anger at the sick bastard prior to my exile, and I'd hoped that having my insults come from the Book of Ravens would only irk him further."

The worn, dirty man chuckled.

"You can imagine my surprise when the Deakon's body actually twisted and changed into that disgusting heap. Sevold's screaming brought in guards and keepers, and since it was just the two of us in the Deakon's room, there was no hiding my guilt. They brought me here, to my cozy little cell, and tried to beat, cut, and burn the cure out of me."

"And what is that cure?" she asked. "How do you undo the curse?"

"The one who gives the curse must relinquish their hatred of the cursed," he said. "And I assure you, that was never, ever going to happen, no matter how badly they tortured me."

Adria paced before Tamerlane in his cell, her fingers massaging her temples. Damn it, she was too tired to think straight. Everything he said, it could so easily be truth, and so easily be a well-sculpted falsehood.

"How do I know you're not lying?" she asked. "You have no proof. This could just be one last attempt at saving your own skin."

"You command souls," Tamerlane said. "Stop fearing the truth. Touch my memories. See for yourself. Or are you afraid to remove the shield of doubt that allows you to cling to safe inaction?"

Adria set her jaw and clenched her fists.

"Fine," she said. "Though the Sisters have mercy on your wretched soul if you are deceiving me."

Tamerlane's soul shone brightly before her eyes. She felt herself falling into it, pulling at the millions of strands containing memories, senses, and emotions. Adria kept a single thought focused in her mind, using it as a beacon to guide herself to the proper memory. After a time she found it. The sensations of her own body faded, replaced by those of Tamerlane's. She saw through his eyes. She felt the ruffle of his robes upon his skin. Proof of Thaddeus's crime, she demanded. That was where Tamerlane's very soul had brought her, and it was that instant of time she witnessed.

She stood in Thaddeus's office inside the Old Vikarage. Just inside the doorway. Time refused to move, giving the memory an otherworldly quality. As if everything were frozen in glass. Adria viewed the scene from Tamerlane's perspective. She saw Thaddeus, saw his nakedness. Saw the soulless boy.

Tamerlane had not explained how he'd obtained his proof. How he had walked in during the act. Adria tore herself from the memory and back into her own body. Wet tears slid down her face, and her entire chest hitched tightly with growing anger.

"Why did you not tell me?" she asked. Her voice shook with rage. "Why did you not *warn* me?"

At last Tamerlane stood. He crossed the distance between them slowly, cautiously, as if she were a deer and he a hunter. Once close enough, he wiped away her tears with his thumbs. His touch was rough, but his movements kind, and she wished she could melt into him and cling to his frame as the last remnants of his awful memory faded.

"Because I needed you to feel the same shock I felt," he said. "I needed you to understand why I would speak such a curse, and why I would cling to that anger no matter my fate."

Adria pulled away. Her mind was made up. She spoke quickly, with urgency that Tamerlane had stubbornly resisted.

"Go," she said. "Hurry. I will ensure the guard lets you past."

"You put yourself in danger by doing so," Tamerlane said. "Are you sure?"

"Very," she said. "They'll look for you, so do your best to hide."

"Come find me at a store on Jagged Alley," he said. "The name is Sam's and Sally's. I'll be waiting for you tomorrow night, after the reaping hour has come and gone, and not a moment sooner." He bowed, took her hand in his, and kissed her knuckles. "Thank you, precious Mindkeeper. I know not what you are, only that you are unlike any other soul upon the Cradle."

Adria held her other palm against the knuckles, the warmth of his kiss seeping into her skin. She used that sensation to pull herself free of her mind, and help focus the resolve she knew would be required. Upon exiting Tamerlane's cell, the stationed guard saw them and started to panic.

"Tamerlane goes free," she ordered.

"That ain't allowed," the guard insisted.

Adria ripped his soul out from his body. The guard immediately went still.

"Go," she told Tamerlane. The other Mindkeeper bowed once more and then hurried down the tunnel. After she gave him a good minute's head start, she returned the soul to the guard. The man blinked and swayed on unsteady feet. No doubt he was trying to process the momentary vacancy of his soul, and of how he'd allowed Tamerlane to escape without lifting a finger to stop him.

"The Vikar will hear of this," the guard said as he stumbled toward the exit.

"I know," she said. She crossed her arms and shivered against the cold. "Trust me, I know."

Adria waited inside Tamerlane's cell. She knew it wouldn't be long. Several times she heard a commotion from the inner door, some hushed arguing, and then silence. After half an hour, Vikar Thaddeus appeared from down the hall. He walked alone, a small lantern cradled in his hands, but she could sense the souls of at least a dozen city guards stationed just outside the inner door.

"Hello, Adria," he said, as pleasantly as if they'd bumped into one another in the cathedral library. "It seems you've had an eventful day."

"I have."

She almost asked him then and there if he knew about Sevold's sick desires. Tamerlane would have wanted her to do so. A cowardly part of her held her back. She'd already lost her respect for her longtime Deakon. Was she truly ready to see her beloved Vikar in a newer, much darker light?

"I've alerted the city guards to Tamerlane's escape," Thaddeus continued. "Though I am not particularly hopeful. Tamerlane has always been fiercely intelligent. He'll find a hole somewhere to crawl in until the moment is clear for him to flee Londheim."

"If he flees at all," she said. "I have the impression he is not done with the church."

"Is that why you released him? He whispered sweet lies into your ear?"

"I released him because it was the right thing to do."

Thaddeus straightened up, and he leveled his silver eyes her way. Such wizened fire would have cowed her a mere year ago, but not anymore.

"And who are you to make such a decision?"

In answer she stretched out her hand and grabbed hold of the souls of the dozen city guards Thaddeus had brought with him. They ripped free of their physical bonds and soared toward her like fireflies. Thaddeus staggered away as they swirled about her body, the souls burning like brilliant stars, and she their orbital center.

"I don't know what I am," she said. "But I know I possess power beyond any Vikar, any Deakon, beyond even the Ecclesiast herself."

"You speak heresy," Thaddeus whispered.

"The truth can never be heresy," she countered. "No other person commands souls as I do. No one but the Goddesses."

Her Vikar stared at the swirling orbs of light. His initial fear and shock shifted to wonder.

"I always knew you were special," he said softly. "Even back when you accepted your post in Low Dock, I believed you were destined for far greater things. If this is your gift, then you are indeed a unique wonder upon the Cradle. But Adria..."

He stepped closer and clasped her hands in his dry, wrinkled own. Adria shifted the path of the souls so they revolved around the two of them, keeping him safe.

"Adria, please, I beg of you, do not abandon the church's teachings. Don't abandon our wisdom. I will not deny that you possess incredible power, but power does not remove the limits of authority. It only proves all the greater their need. Please, keep faith in the Goddesses and their creations!"

Adria returned the souls to their proper owners. The world darkened without their light.

"I have not lost my faith in the Goddesses," she said. "Only my confidence in those who serve in their name."

"And perhaps you are right to do so," Thaddeus insisted. "But the world is in a very dark place right now. The people need succor. They need comfort. We can provide that, if we work together."

Her eyes narrowed.

"How?"

"Vikar Forrest wants nothing to do with being Deakon, which leaves Vikar Caria as my only other real contender. Publicly throw your support to me. With you at my side, the vast majority of keepers will vote along with you."

"And why should I do this?"

The old man smiled at her.

"Because if I am Deakon, then I must appoint a successor to take my place as Vikar of the Day. There is a woman from a humble church in Low Dock who I think would be the perfect candidate."

So Vikar Thaddeus sought the role of Deakon, just as Tamerlane had theorized. Adria headed for the exit, wanting nothing more to do with the dank, foul cells.

"Will you accept my offer?" Thaddeus asked as she passed.

"I'm not sure," she said. "It depends."

"On what?"

Adria banished her fear and panic and accepted the only future that awaited someone such as her. To run from it was cowardice. To embrace it was proper. It was divine.

"On if I decide to become Deakon myself."

# CHAPTER 31

The sun crested over the walls of Londheim, and beneath its rising light the first of the wayward ghosts faded away. Devin held Jacaranda's hand and let out a long sigh as the two watched Brittany's ghost shimmer.

"I think you'd have liked her," he said. "She shared Tommy's sense of humor, and the more absurd, the better. Never met a man or woman she couldn't win over with her smile. She also wouldn't tolerate anyone's nonsense, mine in particular."

"You don't seem too prone to nonsense," Jacaranda said. "In fact, you're the most level-headed person I know."

"Fresh-faced and newly appointed Soulkeeper Devin was a bit more opinionated and stubborn." He squeezed her hand. "By the Goddesses, you should have been there when I suggested she retire from her position so we might have children. She lifted that giant sword of hers and demanded I spread my legs. '*I'm a Soulkeeper until I die,*' she tells me. '*So we better hack off that sack of yours lest children become an issue.*' That shut my mouth pretty damn quick."

The sobs of an elderly man nearby paused their conversation. Over one hundred people crowded the graveyard. What had once been a shunned, almost cursed place was now another wondrous attraction that collected both gawkers and heartfelt family members. The gathering ruined a bit of the mystical feeling Devin

had experienced that very first time witnessing the wayward spir-
its, as well as confirmation that the ghosts saw nothing of the real
world. If Brittany called out to him, as she sometimes did, it was to a
phantom that only she might find.

"Do you still miss her?" Jacaranda asked. She seemed focused on
the old man weeping on his knees before a softly swaying ghostly
woman in her late seventies.

"I think I always will," Devin said. "She was a piece of me."

"It's strange to realize this, but I've never lost anyone," Jacaranda
said. "I've never had anyone to be attached to for most of my life.
The closest I can think of was Marigold, and I knew her for only
moments. Even that loss cut deeper than I knew was possible."

"The greater your love, the greater the hurt upon its loss. You
may not have known Marigold well, but you loved her for what
she was, and what she endured."

"Is it worth it, then? To love someone so deeply?" Jacaranda
cast her gaze to the ground. "Brittany died six years ago, yet still
you weep over her grave."

Devin took in a long breath and let it out slowly. He was in no
hurry to answer, not with how important that question was to
him. It helped that he felt more and more comfortable discussing Brittany around Jacaranda. Expressing his love toward his lost
wife did not put into question what he felt toward Jacaranda now.
Such a sentiment should have been obvious, but Devin knew he
was pretty good at missing the obvious when it came to love and
family.

"Losing Brittany was the greatest pain I have ever felt in my
life," he said as he shivered against a cold wind blowing through
the graveyard. "Yet I would rather experience it a hundred times
over than lose a single second of time I spent with her. Yes, Jac, it is
worth it. More than worth it. I think it's the sole reason the Goddesses put us upon the Cradle, to love and be loved."

The two fell silent, and they watched as Brittany's ghost shim-

mered into morning mist. Devin felt a soft ache upon her departure. Would it ever get easier? he wondered. Then again, did he
ever want it to?

"Do you...do you think you could love me as much as you
loved her?" Jacaranda asked softly. She didn't look at him, only
stared straight ahead. He could feel her grip on his hand tighten.
She was nervous, so nervous, and she shouldn't be.

"Absolutely," he said. He leaned over and kissed the top of her
head. "The most I can give is all my heart, and if you'll keep putting up with me, you're welcome to have it."

Jacaranda laughed even as a stray tear worked its way down her
cheek.

"Goddesses above, you're so lame sometimes. It's a good thing
you're not a poet. Your sentimentalism would cause vomiting."

The two joined the line of people exiting to the street. Devin
had feared that particular graveyard would be overflowing once
word spread, but every graveyard throughout Londheim had
experienced similar wandering ghosts. It seemed wherever there
were enough buried souls, their memories took on physical form
and began to wander while the moon was full and the reaping
hour near.

"I bare my heart and you return it with mockery," Devin said,
nudging her with his elbow. "Just like Brittany. Apparently I have
a type."

They broke from the rest of the crowd, making their way back
to Devin's home. They kept hand in hand, like little schoolchildren
in love despite the both of them being in their thirties. Devin didn't
mind. Physical contact was obviously complicated for Jacaranda,
and however way she chose to show her affection was good enough
for him. He only wished he'd taken his glove off first, so he could
feel her skin against his skin, the chill morning air be damned.

"Hey, Devin," she said once they were alone in the quiet street.
"There's something I think we need to discuss."

Devin wondered if this would be about her returning last night bleeding and injured. Adria had come over just before bed, weary but still happy to heal the wounds with a prayer. So far Jacaranda had not explained where she had gone or what happened, other than that it involved ties to Gerag's illicit trade.

"I'm all ears," he said, pretending not to be worried or nervous.

"I've been thinking about...what I am. And the people I'm putting at risk by keeping my condition hidden. I think it's time I present myself to the Keeping Church."

This was it, then. The moment Devin had feared since she'd awakened. His boots clacked atop the stone, and they seemed to fall all the heavier.

"You put yourself at risk doing so," he said. "I hope you understand that."

"I do. But you already know about Marigold, and I heard rumors of more soulless awaking in the east. Many more." She shuddered in his grasp. "And that those who awaken are declared mad and put to the death."

Shivers nearly caused Devin to miss a step.

"Where did you hear that?"

"In the market, when the first boats from Stomme arrived. It makes sense, doesn't it? I'm not the only one. Why would I be? But if people see the initial reactions of an awakening soulless and decide it is some sort of madness, or even worse, ignore them instead..."

Then innocent awakened were being murdered. Devin wished it weren't true, but deep in his gut he knew it the case, just as there were an underground sex trade of soulless despite the Keeping Church's insistence otherwise. When faced with two possibilities, the bend of the world almost always curved toward the darker.

"We need to be careful," Devin said as they paused before the door to his house. "I'll speak with Adria about arranging a meeting with her Vikar, though that may take time given the Deakon's death. Your connection to Gerag makes things all the trickier. We'll need to prove you were soulless, and no, some tattoos won't be enough. Your knowledge about Gerag's business will help... but they might also think you were a part of it, with the tattoos as some sort of... disguise."

His ideas clearly hurt Jacaranda, and he could tell she wanted to argue his points. Instead she nodded and thrust open the door.

"I have to try," she said. "If it saves lives, then it's worth the risks."

The two were so preoccupied with one another that they were both inside hanging up their coats before they noticed the intruder. Devin startled and dropped his hat, then immediately blushed with embarrassment.

"Hello, Evelyn," he said. "It's nice to see you again."

The dark-clad woman bobbed her head, and it seemed her lower beak shivered up and down. Laughter? He couldn't tell. She leaned against the wall beside the fireplace, her wings seemingly made entirely of shadow instead of feathers. Not a terrible decision, given the somewhat cramped conditions of the room. Tesmarie sat on her shoulder, looking as pleased as could be.

"Forgive me for startling you two," Evelyn said. "I have matters of utmost importance to discuss."

Jacaranda finished hanging her coat, but he noticed she kept her short swords belted to her waist. He had no reason to fear the strange woman, but Devin decided it was a wise decision. He hung up his pistol and ammo pouches, but he leaned his sword against his elbow as he sat down upon the couch.

"This morning's been one of important conversations," he said. "Go ahead, Evelyn. Tell us what you came to tell."

"Don't worry," Tesmarie said to Evelyn, her wings aflutter as she left the avenria's shoulder to land atop her bed-shelf. "We can talk more once you're done, all right?"

"Very well, onyx one," the avenria said. She turned her attention to Devin and Jacaranda. "I suppose I should introduce myself fully, for it will perhaps add gravitas to what I am about to request. My name is Evelyn, and not counting our centuries of sleep, I have led the avenria as their clan leader for the past seventy years, inheriting the role from my father upon his death. Much of that time I warred against humanity's relentless westward expansion, and I have spilled the blood of hundreds of your kind upon Whisper-Song's blades."

"Should I be worried?" Devin asked, and he was only half-joking.

Evelyn waved a hand at him dismissively.

"I tell you this so you understand my mind-set during the final ten years before your Goddesses sealed us away. Humanity was a wildfire. Nothing stopped your spread. You took and you took, and the dragons were given no choice but to accept this. They themselves were the Goddesses' creation, after all. But we weren't. We were the dragon's creations and felt no love for your Goddesses. We fought. We died. And all the while, your newly formed Keeping Church preached this as proper and good, for we were soulless wretches, and you humans were precious, perfect children of precious, perfect Goddesses."

"I'm not sure I understand where this is going," Devin said.

"Because you have no patience or foresight," Evelyn said. "Let me state it plainly, then. I am the author of what humanity refers to as the Book of Ravens."

That got Devin's attention. He shifted farther onto the edge of his seat. The blasphemous book of Ravencallers? The mysterious, unknown author was right here before him?

*Shouldn't you be called . . . a ravenkin?* Jacaranda had asked upon first meeting Evelyn. In that light, the name of both the book and Ravencallers seemed painfully obvious in its inspirations.

"I've not read it," Devin said. "But I know of it. It attacks the Goddesses and challenges their role over humanity."

"That is because it is the angry scribblings of a woman who lost her grandchild in an unending war." Evelyn crossed her arms and looked away. She sounded so tired, so worn down by life. "I wanted to show your race that the Goddesses were not all-knowing, all-loving, and all-forgiving. I wanted to prove the creations of the dragons were equal to humanity, but I could not do that so long as they believed us imperfect and themselves perfect."

"And so you taught humans curses?"

"Those curses are not mine," Evelyn snapped. "They belonged to your Mindkeepers and Faithkeepers, and they were wielded against us at every battle. Your kind thought of these curses as holy fire descending from the heavens and righteous fury wielded by noble warriors of the Goddesses. They didn't see the hatred and anger in them. They didn't see the torn flesh and mutilated corpses. I did. And I wanted every last human to see them, too."

Jacaranda touched Devin's shoulder to keep him from speaking. He wanted to argue against her claims, for it painted the church in such a dire, blasphemous light, he felt an instinctive need to defend it. Instead he kept silent, knowing his emotions and logic were compromised.

"I saw you fighting when we marched into Low Dock," Jacaranda said. "You were killing Ravencallers. Why would you do such a thing, when you yourself wrote the book?"

"Because I wanted the church's positions challenged," she said. "I wanted the dragon-sired to be seen in a new light. What I never wanted was to create a cult focused on harming others and mutilating souls for twisted pleasure and gain. We avenria were made to protect the Cradle from the void, which still had a strong presence upon the Cradle in the very earliest days of creation. Now I find my son has perverted his very purpose and begun harming and manipulating souls for his own benefits."

"Your son?" Devin asked.

"Yes, my son. Logarius, the leader of the Forgotten Children."

Devin could hardly believe what he was hearing. The Book of Ravens, the sudden rise in Ravencallers throughout Londheim, the takeover of Low Dock and rebranding as Belvua...it was all tied to Evelyn and her son.

"Why are you telling us this?" he asked.

"Because my son has begun to meddle in things far beyond his understanding, and I cannot stop him alone. Below the city, I have discovered certain...machinery that manipulates the stars' protection and mimics the powers of the Goddesses. I need help destroying it."

Devin stood. A change swept over him, his curiosity replaced with steadfast determination. He saw the same change go through Jacaranda. They shared the same understanding. Janus's machinery was powerful, dangerous, and should never be used again. He strapped his sword back to his belt and retrieved his pistols.

"We know of what you speak," Devin said as Evelyn watched them prepare. "We thought it was destroyed after it changed my sister. If you know how to tear it down, then lead the way."

"Should I come?" Tesmarie asked. "This sounds super-important."

"Of course," Devin said. He offered her his coat pocket, and she quickly hopped inside.

"Will you be safe traversing during the day?" Jacaranda asked as they gathered at the door.

"Not as safe as during the night," Evelyn said. "But I will be fine if I stick to the rooftops."

"All right then," said Devin. "Let's go."

He pushed the door open and stepped outside to discover a full squad of city guards waiting in the street with their swords drawn. Two Soulkeepers stood at the ready, a man named Wilt whom Devin was vaguely familiar with, and a woman Devin knew all too well.

"Make this easy for all of us," Lyssa said. Her gaze was locked

on to Jacaranda and her swords. "Surrender your weapons and…
what in Anwyn's is that?"

Devin glanced over his shoulder. They'd seen Evelyn. Holy
shit, this was bad.

"Lyssa, wait," he said, hoping to talk things down, but the
avenria would have none of it. She vaulted toward the ceiling and
then passed straight on through, her wings a wide, misty stretch
of darkness. A second later she reappeared on the rooftop, her legs
already pumping to leap over one home to the next.

"Chase after her!" Lyssa shouted, sending Wilt into a sprint
toward the rear of the building. Devin trusted Evelyn to escape,
but there was a faery who might be more stubborn.

"Go, quickly," he whispered as he patted his coat pocket. Tesmarie zipped out of it in a blur, but instead of fleeing, she paused in
the air, her hands clasped before her chest and little diamond flecks
in her eyes.

"Devin, what's going on?" she asked.

"Don't worry, now go!"

The faery obeyed, her wings carrying her into the sky and far
beyond the reach of the stunned city guards. Devin wished he could
watch her go, but Jacaranda had still not relinquished her weapons.

"Don't fight," he said. "Trust me, I'll get us out of this, all right?
Just don't fight."

He dropped his sword and pistol to the dirt. Jacaranda hesitated, still debating. There were so many, but with Evelyn leading
several after her, Jacaranda might be able to escape. Part of him
hoped she would, for at least her life would no longer be in his
own hands. Somehow, someway, he'd fucked everything up, and
now the church was at his doorstep demanding answers.

"So be it," Jacaranda said. She lowered her short swords to the
ground and pushed them away from her. Guards barked orders at
them, and at their command, he and Jac bowed their heads and

placed their hands behind their backs. Manacles slapped down across his wrists. Devin bit his tongue and swallowed his ire. He wanted to demand an explanation, but he'd only be wasting everyone's time. He knew why they were there.

"I thought you'd always have my back," Devin told Lyssa. The woman flinched as if he'd slapped her. Instead of arguing, she strode over to Jacaranda and pulled the scarf from her neck, exposing her chain tattoos.

"That's what I thought," she said. She turned to the soldiers. "Take them both to the cathedral."

They marched Devin and Jacaranda through Anwyn's Gate, through the Soulkeepers' Sanctuary, and out into the Deakon's garden that surrounded the Old Vikarage. Though the triangular building was most often used as a shared living quarters for the three Vikars and the Deakon, there was one room within that harkened back to the oldest days of the Keeping Church: the judgment room.

"On your knees," a novice ordered. In the center of the room was a recessed triangular stone, its dull gray in stark contrast to the polished hardwood of the rest of the floor. Devin kneeled into it, the odd angle and his manacled arms forcing his body to bow. Surrounding him were four raised lecterns. The three Vikars stood at their respective positions, the lecterns emblazed with gold symbols representing Dawn, Day, and Dusk. Only the center lectern remained empty, and would be until a replacement was voted in for the deceased Deakon.

"With the Deakon's absence, it is the responsibility of the Dawn to begin this judgment," Vikar Caria said. Like the other two, she wore a slick black suit, immaculate, tailored to her form. There were no windows in the judgment room; it was instead lit by a dozen hanging lanterns. The shadows danced across her angular face, adding a sharp edge to her beauty. "Soulkeeper Devin Eveson, you are accused of the illegal capture and possession of a soulless individual, of lying to your superiors, of trafficking with enemies of West Orismund, and of using a captured soulless for purposes of pleasure. Have you any words to say in defense of yourself?"

Devin looked up at the three Vikars. Thaddeus and Caria seemed disgusted by him, whereas Forrest appeared unable to meet him in the eye.

"You see these events in a dire light," he said. "You must understand, Jacaranda is not soulless. While I traveled with her to Oakenwall, Alma granted her a soul during the reaping hour. She thinks, feels, and acts as a free-willed woman. Talk with her. Spend time with her. The truth is clear as the midday sun!"

The Vikars stared at him with mixed expressions of shock and disgust.

"Awakened?" Forrest said. "Are you certain?"

"Of course I am certain," Devin insisted. "I was *there*. I saw her soul return. I've spoken with her, about her past, her servitude toward Gerag, about what it means to be awakened."

"And why did you not bring her to us?" Thaddeus asked. "We could have borne witness to such a miracle ourselves. You're a bright man. You understand the incredible ramifications of such an event."

Devin felt his neck flush.

"I left the decision to Jacaranda," he said. "Bringing her situation public put her life at risk. I would not do so against her wishes."

"And so you lied to me," Forrest said. "I asked you if the rumors of your keeping a soulless were true, and you lied right to my face."

"It was no lie, for she *wasn't* soulless. And even if you disagree, I did so to protect her."

Forrest slammed an enormous fist down upon the lectern.

"I am your superior! If you wanted her protected, then you should have told the damn truth, and *I* would have protected her."

Devin bowed his head.

"I did what I thought was right," he said. "I understand the consequences of my actions. Do what you must. All I ask is that you treat Jacaranda with kindness and compassion."

"Kindness? Compassion?" Caria lifted a small sheet of paper before her and scanned its contents. "From what testimony we have already heard, this soulless woman attacked and killed three men at the Gentle Rose brothel. Have you any justification for those murders, Devin?"

A memory of Jacaranda staggering through his doorway, her clothes stained with blood, flickered through his mind.

"I can offer none," he said. "For this is the first I have heard of such murders."

The three Vikars leaned toward one another, their height and distance allowing them to whisper without Devin clearly understanding. Whatever they discussed, they were displeased. After a moment they reached some sort of decision.

"Jacaranda's nature is crucial to understanding these events," Thaddeus said. "I believe, though, that if given time to speak with Jacaranda, I can break through any façade, no matter how well trained, to confirm whether or not she is soulless. For now, let us move on to other matters. Who was the black-garbed creature accompanying you at the time of your arrest?"

"Her name is Evelyn," Devin said. "She's an avenria who knows of a place important to the Ravencallers, and she came to me seeking help destroying it."

"I've read the description of this…Evelyn," Thaddeus said. "It matches the race of many others who attacked our soldiers and keepers in Low Dock. Why would you think she would help you against the Ravencallers?"

"Because these magical creatures are just like humans," Devin said. "They're not of one mind. They don't always agree. Other avenria might have attacked our people, but Evelyn fought the Ravencallers that night. I know, because she saved me from one of their curses."

"Is that so?" Forrest asked. "I don't remember that detail when you gave your report on the night's events. More lies, Devin, even if by omission?"

Devin winced, and he had no defense to offer. He'd kept so much of his life hidden from the church since the black water swept away Dunwerth. It was foolish to think it wouldn't one day catch up with him.

"You show emotional attachment to a murderous soulless," Caria began. "You ally with, what did you call it? An avenria? A member of a race that has killed dozens of our faithful, and Soul-keeper Lyssa also reported that a strange black faery was hidden on your person when you were arrested. Taken together, these events make me question your loyalty to humanity. Your logic, and your faith, may well be compromised."

Devin straightened his back, manacles and awkward angle be damned.

"My faith in the Goddesses has never wavered," he said. "Those I have befriended are kind, wondrous people, be they human or not. We are capable of living peacefully alongside these newly awakened races. I believe that with all my heart. Again, judge me as you wish, but I will not apologize for what I have done."

It seemed the Vikars were not prepared for how confrontational he might be. The claim that Jacaranda was no longer soulless disturbed them particularly, and he caught whispers of her name as the three took a moment to quietly discuss among themselves.

After a few minutes they returned their attention his way, and Thaddeus cleared his throat to speak.

"It is clear we cannot pass proper judgment upon you without speaking with Jacaranda to ascertain her status," he said. "Until then, given the seriousness of the charges leveled against you, you shall remain in our custody."

Devin sensed the meeting at an end, and he pushed himself to his feet.

"Please," he asked. "May I see Jacaranda so I know she's all right?"

"And let you potentially manipulate her testimony?" asked Caria. "No, Devin. There will be no contact between either of you. If she is a soulless with a newly granted soul as you claim, then we shall deal with the theological ramifications in due diligence. If not…"

She shook her head.

"Then your time as a Soulkeeper is at an end."

# CHAPTER 32

M aster Dierk?"

Dierk looked up from his desk and smiled. Ever since casting the domination curse upon his father, he'd made the servants refer to him as Master. It gave him a sense of legitimacy he never knew he needed.

"Yes?" he asked.

"The Royal Overseer is here," the well-dressed servant said.

"Very well," he said. "I'll be right there."

One of the commands he'd given his father was that anytime someone came to meet with him, Dierk would also be summoned to participate. As expected, Soren had struggled a bit against it, but not as much as that first day. So long as he cast the curse every night, Dierk found himself with another twenty-four hours of a subservient father. It was everything he had ever dreamed.

He pushed away his book and stretched. It was a dry tome detailing the rights of traders and shopkeepers during times of famine and war: just the sort of thing his father would have forced him to read. Unlike before, Dierk dove into it with a hunger. The idea of being in charge and making important decisions was no longer some distant future possibility. The time was now, and suddenly he found himself craving information to ensure he made the right decisions or wasn't taken advantage of.

Granted, he could always ask his subservient father for advice, but really, that was his least desirable course of action.

Dierk joined Albert and Soren in the same lounge as before. Unlike before, the doors were closed and locked, and Dierk had to knock to be let in. He could tell from the looks on both their faces that something serious was afoot, but he couldn't begin to guess what.

"All right," Soren said. "Now Dierk is here, we can begin. Tell me the letter in full."

Dierk sat in a chair across from Albert and listened to the report. It was short, vague, and baffling in its implications.

"The Queen has cast us aside," Albert said. "She's informed me that West Orismund is to consider itself alone in the west. We shall receive no aid, no troops, and in return she expects no taxes or tributes to be paid in return."

"I don't... what does that mean?" Dierk asked.

"It means West Orismund is effectively a free, independent country," Soren said.

Dierk glanced at his father. It was always interesting observing how he acted under the curse. So often he behaved as himself, as if he weren't even aware the curse was upon him. It was only when he tried to act against Dierk, or break one of his rules, that a change came over him. The offending behavior would be cast aside, and then Soren would smoothly follow any given commands as if nothing had happened.

"A free country," Albert said, nodding in agreement. "It's damn ridiculous. We spend weeks waiting for word from the east, and when it comes, it's to tell us we're on our own."

"But why would she relinquish authority over us?" Dierk asked, still not believing it. "She fought a war against South Orismund for attempting to secede, yet now she would let us go without a single shot fired?"

Albert rubbed his hands over his brown hair cut close to the scalp.

"You ask good questions, young man, but I have no good answers for them. If I were to hazard a guess, it's that the trials we face are ones that they themselves share. Perhaps the Queen has decided to focus her resources on the eastern coast and abandon the west. Perhaps the Queen is no longer Queen, and we'll receive word of an imposter or a coup. Until that happens, we have to act on what information is available."

"How *do* we act on this information?" Soren said. "And who all is aware of it?"

Neither man had a drink, and Dierk found himself desperately needing one, so he hopped up and poured two glasses of wine from the shelf. After a moment he caught himself and poured a third. It would look strange if he did not get one for his father, too.

"Thank you," Albert said, accepting the glass. "And so far I have told no one of this message. Considering your status as Mayor, I felt it best to inform you first so we might together plan on how we consolidate power. Without the Queen's authority, both our positions are in a precarious spot. Worse, with the bulk of West Orismund's troops in either Wardhus or Stomme, either general there could side with a wealthy landowner or Mayor in an attempt to seize control. That's even assuming we keep West Orismund together as a single nation, which right now feels like a monumental task." He shook his head and laughed darkly. "We can't even handle things here in Londheim. Why would anyone trust us now?"

Dierk's mind scrambled for a proper plan of action. He wanted to make these decisions himself, but this was far out of his league. He gestured to Soren and beckoned him to offer a solution.

"We need to act fast," his father said. "First things first, we keep this information close to our chest. The longer it takes for word to spread of the Queen's abandonment, the more time we have to consolidate power. Until then, we need to focus on fostering a sense of identity for West Orismund, one that is wholly separate from the east. Perhaps a name for these lands that was used before the crown officially took control. We also need to rename your position. If the people of West Orismund view you as their anointed king, their chosen ruler, we have a shot at preventing anarchy."

Albert stared into his cup and nodded along.

"I'm not sure I'm ready to be some sort of king," he said.

"Then step aside, and allow someone else to do it," Soren said. "But you know damn well no one else in all the west is as skilled at manipulating both lords and commoners as you are. You have to be the lynchpin in this, Albert, or we'll see our lands descend into a rabble of competing city-states that..."

Fire exploded in the air between them. Dierk cried out and sank into his seat, his arms crossed defensively before his face. He waited for the heat to hit, to char away his hair and skin, only it never came. Instead a deep roar shook the furniture. The sound of it hit Dierk's stomach like a sledge, and immediately he felt overwhelming rage streak through his veins like lightning. His hands turned to fists. His teeth clenched together so tightly he feared the enamel would crack.

"Overseer? Where...is...Overseer?"

Dierk dared open his eyes. The fire was not fire, but a burning sphere of light. Its edges were not smooth like a ball, but jagged, warped, the way the brighter portions curled through the darker resembling something like exposed veins. An image flickered in and out of focus within that steadily growing sphere, that of a robed and horned dyrandar holding a staff.

"Cannac?" Albert asked. The Royal Overseer sat dumbfounded, the light of the dreamfire casting long shadows across his face.

"You would speak his name?" the dyrandar asked. He whirled on Albert, and suddenly it felt like he were a hundred feet tall, towering beyond the ceiling, beyond the walls, all else receding away into shadows until they were gnats before an enraged bull. His head tilted, his eyes focused, and it seemed he finally saw Albert clearly.

"Overseer?" he rumbled. "Ruler of Londheim? Are you the monster before me?"

Albert sat up in his chair, and he looked as dignified as one could be when facing a furious god.

"I am Albert Downing, Royal Overseer of Londheim," he said. "And who...whom do I speak with?"

The dyrandar shook his fists. His antlers flickered with golden light.

"I am Shinnoc, son of Cannac, new King of the dyrandar and general of the united dragon-sired, and I vow upon my dreams and nightmares to destroy Londheim with such savagery, even the dust that swirls in the morning light will not dare lay upon your ruin."

The fire withered. The dyrandar folded in on itself. As quickly as it came, the vision broke, the spell cast upon the three breaking like thin glass. With its departure, light seemed to return to normal. Dierk's ears rang from the dyrandar's cry. A heavy weight left his chest and shoulders, and he sucked in air as if newly granted the ability to breathe. The three men exchanged looks, surprise and bafflement keeping a firm hold of their tongues.

"It seems word of Cannac's death reached beyond the city," Albert said dryly at last.

"No shit," Soren said. "An army marching toward our city, right as Queen Woadthyn has abandoned us to our own devices? The timing is beyond suspect. We've been isolated, starved of information, and now soon to be besieged."

"We'll be fine, won't we?" Dierk asked. "Londheim's never fallen. We have our walls, and we have the river."

"And they have a goddess-damned mountain," Soren said.

"A mountain that has not moved in weeks," Albert cautioned. "And whose motivations we cannot begin to guess, so let us not waste time in making assumptions."

He crossed the room to refill his drink, which he'd spilled at some point during Shinnoc's abrupt appearance. Outwardly he seemed calm, but Dierk caught the shake of his hands as he tipped the bottle over to pour.

"All that matters now is how do we act on this perceived threat?" Albert asked upon retaking his seat. "Is there a way to salvage all this, or do we turn our tails and run east?"

Dierk's father looked his way. Confidence filled him. This was it. This was his time to step up to the grand task. Deep down, Dierk knew his father would have called for the most practical of solutions and ordered a massive evacuation. Londheim was in no shape for a siege, not when they couldn't hold a single district from the dragon-sired insurgents. But Dierk knew things Soren did not. There was power lurking in Londheim, power they were yet to tap.

How many soldiers could Adria alone destroy with the might of her soul?

"We don't run," Dierk said. Though it likely seemed a suggestion to Albert's ears, to Soren's imprisoned mind, it was an order. "We stand firm and fight for our home."

A brief flash of pain marked his father's face. A momentary resistance, but it meant little against Dierk's spell.

"We tell the truth," Soren said, suddenly calm and focused. "In our moment of need, the Queen has turned her back to us. We'll use that rage to unite the people under your rule. We'll come up with a new title for you, a new name for our kingdom, and dozens of promises and bribes to keep the wealthiest merchants and landowners in line. We'll prepare our soldiers, and we'll hope that reinforcements arrive from Wardhus and Stomme. If there really is an army out there, it's going to take time to gather together and march east. We'll have plenty of warning before they arrive. When they do, we'll be ready."

Albert rose to his feet and offered his hand to Soren.

"Thank you," he said, and glanced to Dierk. "Both of you. It is good to know that I will have your aid in these coming tribulations."

Despite the fear and unknown of Shinnoc's threat, it felt so good seeing the Royal Overseer acknowledge him in such a way. Dierk's smile spread ear to ear. Perhaps, in a year or two, he wouldn't even need to keep his father around as a puppet. He'd be ready to step into the role in full. With Soren obeying his every command, it wouldn't be too hard to act out some sort of unfortunate accident while in the public eye.

Once Albert was gone, Soren slumped like a puppet dropped by its master.

"What should I do now?" his father asked.

"Umm..."

Dierk glanced at the nisse. Vaesalaum hovered in a rapid circle above the fireplace, and for some reason the creature looked angry. Why didn't it say something? Deciding it best to find out, he shrugged and told Soren to prepare for West Orismund's newfound independence.

"Very well," his father said. He left his glass unfinished and exited. Once finally alone, Dierk turned to the nisse with a raised eyebrow.

"Is something the matter?" he asked it.

*Vaesalaum wonders why Dierk is acting strange.*

Dierk straightened his spine and pulled back his shoulders.

"I'm finally living up to my responsibilities. Londheim needs a Mayor who understands the ways of this new world."

*Dierk is not Mayor. Father is Mayor. Did Dierk forget?*

"And I'm the one who commands my father," he said. Unlike the other way around, like it had been all his life. "Why do you care? Didn't you want me to be in charge?"

The nisse looped in a sideways figure eight, the motions steadily carrying it farther and farther away.

*Vaesalaum hungers. Dierk no longer learns. Dierk no longer brings in bodies.*

It was true. Ever since he'd cast the commanding curse on his father, he'd kept busy talking with advisors and ordering around servants just to get them acclimated to him being in charge. Some took it in stride, while others cast sideways glances and whispered when they thought he wasn't listening. With all that on his plate, Dierk had spared no time to find a dead body for him and the nisse to plunder its memories.

"Why not go yourself?" he asked. "You don't need me to feed."

*Vaesalaum does. Nisse only share. Gloam made us that way.*

"Well, I'm sorry, but I've more important things to do."

*More important? Human speaks nonsense. Human has forgotten where his loyalties lie.*

A frightful chill passed through him. Vaesalaum had rarely referred to him simply as "human" since that first day they met. There was a coldness to it, a change that hardened his stomach into a rock.

"Were you not paying attention?" he asked. "War is coming. My loyalties are to protect Londheim and the people who serve me."

*Protect?* The bloated thing stopped its swirling movements and instead hovered in place. Its childlike face scrunched into a bitter frown, and for the very first time, Dierk noticed sparkling black teeth behind those thin lips. *Dierk was to accept the new. Dierk was to eat and learn and obey. Dierk was to prepare the way for the dragon-sired conquerors.*

A list of curse titles from the Book of Ravens zipped through Dierk's mind one by one, and he wondered if any would be useful against the otherworldly creature. All his newfound confidence and self-worth threatened to tumble down like a tower of twigs. How many of his decisions had been at the nisse's guidance? He'd gone from crying in a basement to secretly ruling the city as shadow Mayor. Why had he been so stupid as to not think Vaesalaum would want something more in return?

"Sorry," Dierk said. "It seems we each didn't get what we wanted from this relationship. You—you can go now. Find another pupil."

He hadn't meant it to sound so dismissive, but his fear was growing. Vaesalaum might not have eyes, but those sunken, hollow spaces seemed to bore into him with increasing intensity.

*Vaesalaum gave much to pathetic human,* the nisse said. It hovered closer. Its incisors grew, and grew, so that they jutted well past its lower lip. *Vaesalaum found crying child pissing self in fear. Gave him power. Gave him purpose. Vaesalaum will not be cast away so easily.*

Dierk retreated to the wall. What could he do to it? For that matter, what could it do to him? The creature was ethereal. It'd never shown the ability to harm another being, only plunder the memories of its soul after death.

*Does Dierk think Vaesalaum can do no harm? Come, stupid human. Come see. Come feel. Come remember.*

It lunged forward and buried its teeth directly into his forehead. No mark, no blood, but the pain was indescribable. Dierk's mouth locked open in a silent scream as his limbs thrashed. He felt the world receding around him into pure darkness. It was akin to when Vaesalaum brought him into the memories of another, only this time they were his own. The physical world was gone to him. This was Vaesalaum's domain.

"Dierk?" his father asked. Dierk whirled around, so stunned he had no time to remove his hand from his pants. He was a child again, five, maybe six? The details of his room were blurry, encased in a strange smeary fog, but the disgusted look on his father's face was as detailed as the very first time it happened. He yanked Dierk's hand out of his pants, the motion strong enough that he fell backward. When he landed on his rear, the back of his head struck the side of his dresser. Warm blood spilled down his neck.

"That is not proper for a boy," Soren thundered at him. "Do you understand me? Boys are to behave."

"I'm sorry," he cried. Horrified anguish filled him. The world was an enormous mystery full of dangers. Only his father kept him safe. So why was he yelling? Why was he so angry? Dierk wiped at his neck, and when he saw his hand coated in blood, he shrieked. Still Soren only stared down at him. Why didn't he care? Why didn't he help him?

"You only get what you deserve," his father said, and then he left him sobbing on the floor of his room.

"Wait!" Dierk shouted, tears streaming down his face and snot trickling from his nose. "Daddy, wait!"

The door slammed shut. Dierk flung his body against it and beat on it with his tiny fists as he wailed, but he didn't dare open it. Whatever pain he felt now would not compare to the anger he'd face if he opened that door against his father's wishes. So he cried, and kicked the door with his bare foot until blood began to drip upon the carpet from his split toenails. At last he slumped to his rear, buried his face into his knees, and sobbed.

The memory dimmed, and in the spreading darkness Vaesalaum hovered back into view.

*Does Dierk want to live this again? Time moves slow within the soul. A thousand years will pass before your body will be found and woken. A million memories. Dierk will break. Dierk will crumble. Nothing will remain.*

Dierk thought of living through that embarrassment and pain a second time, and then a third, and a fourth. Despair crashed down around him, and he felt an urge to beg for mercy. Dierk refused to give in. He fought back against the despair with seething rage. He would not be made helpless again. He would not be turned into a simpering child.

"Same goes for you," he said as he jumped into the air. He wasn't a child, damn it. He was a young man, tall, proud, and goddess-damned furious. The strange rules of the dream-world changed his physical representation to match his self-identity. Vaesalaum tried to scamper away, but its movements were sluggish, for it was no longer a slender little creature of dreams but instead a bloated, obese thing grown fat on memories. Dierk caught the nisse in his hands and held it tight.

"This is your world, isn't it?" he asked. Vaesalaum squirmed but Dierk's fingers easily sank into its soft, bloated body. "This is where you are real."

*Stupid human! Let go. Let go. Let go, let go, LET GO!*

Blue blood began to spill across Dierk's fingers as he punched through flesh. The nisse turned and sank its black teeth into his wrist. Pain of a thousand cuts and broken bones rushed through him, but none of that could compare to his feeling of triumph over the damn creature. He wasn't helpless anymore. This time, he was in control.

"You're a vulture," Dierk seethed as he steadily pulled his fingers farther and farther apart. "A fucking carrion beast growing fat off the dead."

The shriek coming from Vaesalaum's childlike face no longer resembled words. It was a mindless pained cry, and it sparked memories of the cries small cats used to make when he skinned them alive. He clenched his teeth, and he channeled all the frustration and helplessness the memories had bestowed upon him into irresistible strength.

"I don't need you!" he screamed. "I'm better than you! I'm better than you all!"

The nisse let out one final howl as Dierk ripped the shimmering beast in half. Blood splashed across his shirt, his trousers, the floor...and then it vanished. The darkness around him popped like a bubble, revealing the calm, quiet lounge located in his family's mansion. He was free. The dream world was gone, as was Vaesalaum.

Dierk gulped in long lungfuls of dry air. It was over. No presence lingered in his mind. No voice waited to mock his decisions or question his wisdom. The nisse was dead. Dierk was free.

"I did it," he told the empty room. "I did it. I fucking *did* it."

There was no stopping him now. His father obeyed his commands. The power of the Book of Ravens remained at his disposal. Vaesalaum, who had tried to steer him toward its own goals, was now a husk lost in a dream somewhere. He looked back at all the times he'd cowered, and he wanted to laugh at his old self. This was easier. Life was always better as the foot than the footstool.

It was time to complete his takeover of the mansion, and for that, he'd need Three-Fingers. After a quick detour to his room, he returned to the lounge. There was a small wine shelf against one wall, along with a cabinet of glasses, and he retrieved two and set them on a tray.

"Tell Three-Fingers I'd like to speak with him here," he ordered after whistling for a servant.

A few minutes later, Three-Fingers ducked his head underneath the door frame and stepped in. He tucked his thumbs into his belt and grinned at Dierk as if he were the funniest thing alive.

"I'm sure you've noticed the changes here," Dierk said, trying to sound casual.

"That I have, you clever bastard," Three-Fingers said. His lopsided smile split his face. "Your father was always too stubborn for his own good. He'd never accept the new order shaping up here in Londheim. A little magical persuasion will go a long way in ensuring a peaceful transition."

"I was thinking the same thing," Dierk said. He lifted the two glasses and offered one to Three-Fingers. "I was also thinking of elevating your role within the Becher Estate. I need a right-hand man that I can trust."

"Already making smart decisions, too," the giant man said as he accepted the glass. "Get people loyal to you and not to Soren. It's six years until the next mayoral election. Keep him as a vegetable until then, I say, and then run in his place. People'll vote for who they know. They're sheep that way."

"To herding the sheep," Dierk said in toast.

"To herding the sheep."

They both downed their glasses. A long sigh escaped Dierk's chest. Good. Everything would be fine now.

"Damn, what vintage was that?" Three-Fingers asked as he squinted at the glass. "That tasted like whale spunk."

Dierk took the glass from him, put it on the tray beside the other, and then carried both to the other side of the room. He'd hate to have the expensive glassware damaged.

"Nothing special," he said as if his heart weren't hammering in his chest. "Just a little something for our celebration."

When he turned around, Three-Fingers had already dropped to his knees. His face was red, and long beads of sweat trickled down his neck. When he spoke, he had to force the words out through a rapidly shrinking larynx.

"But...why?" he asked.

Dierk knelt by his side, and he wondered if he should try to comfort the dying man or not. Did he even know how?

"Nothing personal," he said. He watched the veins start to pop in the man's temples. He'd witnessed dozens of memories of death, but this was the first he'd killed since that frantic time in his father's cellar when Vaesalaum first came to him. It felt different now. He was calm and collected. The situation was under his control.

"You're the only one who knows of my connection to the Ravencallers," he explained. "I can't risk anyone finding out. Londheim must be ruled by humans, and those humans ruled by me. Don't you see? I've learned so much, but in the end, it's time I think for myself."

Three-Fingers swiped at him with his mutilated hand, but his strength was already waning. His mouth opened, but no more words came out, just a pained wheeze. It'd be only moments now before his heart gave completely.

"Don't fight it," Dierk whispered. "Go peacefully. I tried to give you that much."

Three-Fingers collapsed onto his stomach. His eyes lost their focus. Convulsions rocked through him, and the smell of piss and shit filled the room as his bowels let loose. In that final moment, when the dying man's body locked into rigid form and his head tilted back as if he were trying to break his spine, Dierk felt a sliver of pleasure rock through him, a hundred times stronger than when he'd brought a knife to the bodies of cats in his father's basement.

Dierk counted to thirty before he thrust open the door and shouted at the top of his lungs.

"Someone? Anyone? Come quick, I think he's having a heart attack!"

# CHAPTER 33

Adria's cautious gaze bounced between the owls patrolling the sky and Jagged Alley, where a single Soulkeeper might notice her meeting with Tamerlane in the long, narrow street connecting two of the southern districts. So far both sky and ground were quiet, and she prayed they stayed that way. She expected to find the disgraced Mindkeeper approaching from either direction, but to her surprise, the man's head poked out of the window of Sam's and Sally's storefront.

"Come in," he said. "The door is unlocked."

His head vanished back behind the thick curtain. Adria checked her surroundings one last time and then pushed inside. From what she could tell, the store sold cheap jewelry, and she wondered how much of it was stolen. The stairs to the second floor were curtained off, and Tamerlane emerged from behind them with a smile on his face that put Adria's heart on alert. Unlike all their previous visits, he was clean-shaven and freshly bathed, with his hair smoothly combed so that his long bangs were pulled back from his face.

"It is good to see you again, Adria," he said.

"It seems you've found an interesting place to hide," she said. It was warm inside so she removed her scarf and thick outer coat. Her mask, however, stayed firmly in place. "Do the owners know you bunk here?"

"They do," he said as he scooted past her to the door. "They're a lovely couple of ladies who spent most of their lives living on the streets. I helped find them a home and a proper place of work. The Ecclesiast could arrive from Trivika and they'd still lie to her face about my whereabouts."

He locked the door, then gestured toward the heavy curtain.

"Please, we can talk more comfortably upstairs."

The second floor was fairly small, just a single room with a street-side window. Blankets were piled in the center to form a bed. A stack of books lay beside it, the collection a bizarre mishmash of penny stories, news pamphlets, and barely held-together legal texts.

"I'm sorry I don't have better accommodations for you," Tamerlane said. "I'm sure you'd be more comfortable sipping tea in the grand archives."

"I'm not here for tea or comfort," she said. "I'm here to check on you."

He smiled and gestured to his meager surroundings.

"Compared to the conditions of my last abode, this room is a palace. Plus I don't have to listen to the wheezing and hacking of Deakon Sevold or that other poor soul inflicted with the mutilation curse."

Adria walked to the window and peered past the curtain to the outside. The streets were empty. Good. It didn't appear anyone had followed her from the cathedral.

"The church has arrested my brother," she said, broaching the subject most pressing to her heart.

Tamerlane sat cross-legged on his bed and tilted his head to one side.

"Under what pretense?" he asked.

"He's a Soulkeeper for the church and for the past weeks he's housed a soulless woman who ... well, is no longer soulless. Alma delivered her a soul during the reaping hour, awakening her from her former state. Somehow the church found out, and they arrested him this morning under accusations of smuggling soulless, using one for pleasure, and a bunch of other shit I know is nonsense."

"An awakened soulless," Tamerlane said. His eyes sparkled with curiosity. "The theological implications are many. Does this mean Alma was weakened, but is now stronger? How does a soul react to a body it has not occupied for years? I'd love to speak with this woman. Why did your brother not bring her to the church?"

"Because he feared how the church might react," she said. "Surely a sentiment you can understand."

Tamerlane laughed.

"That I can. But if she is as you say, in clear possession of a soul, then surely your brother will be proven innocent of these accusations...assuming the church's motivations are pure."

"That's what I'm worried about." Adria sat opposite Tamerlane on the blanket bed and rubbed her throbbing temples. "I feel my faith in the church fading, and I hate it. It's like a slow death in my heart. Have things always been this way, and I blind to it, or has the newly blossomed world of magic and monsters changed our leaders?"

Tamerlane reached out and placed a hand on hers. She flinched but did not pull away. His fingers were surprisingly soft, and his touch lit up her skin with pleasant tingles.

"Do you know why I found the Book of Ravens so appealing?" he asked. "Our fellow colleagues see its claims as blasphemous and contradictory, but what I see is a humanization of our Goddesses. They are immensely powerful beings who love us dearly, but they are not omniscient. They are not all-powerful. They have granted us our free will, and they delivered to us their most precious gift, our souls. For that, we owe them everything. But they also suffer doubt. They question themselves. They are prone to anger, jealousy, and sorrow. The weight of this world is a heavy burden, one they willingly took upon their shoulders and gladly endure. They are not perfect, and that comforts my soul greater than any hymn or prayer ever could."

Adria remembered the secret interior of the Sisters' Tower, of how the triumphant Goddess statues were actually exhausted and weeping. She wondered if Tamerlane's understanding matched how humanity first perceived the Goddesses before centuries of dogma and study.

"I don't understand," she said. "How do you find comfort in believing our Goddesses are not perfect?"

"If they are not perfect, then how can we be perfect?" he asked. "We can't. It is impossible, and yet we strive toward perfection in the same manner as our Goddesses. I see no clearer example of how we are their children, and lovingly made in their image."

Adria drummed her fingers atop her knees as she thought.

"You never answered my question, though," she said. "Has the church changed, or was I blind?"

That earned her a laugh from the handsome man. Goddesses above, he appeared so much younger than when manacled in that dark cell beneath the Sisters' Remembrance.

"Just as I take comfort in knowing the Goddesses are not perfect, so, too, do I understand the church cannot and will never be perfect. Some see that as a failing of the Goddesses. I see it as blindingly obvious, and proof that we must remain ever vigilant against those who would use our faith as a means to power. Deakon Sevold was one, and he suffered the fate he deserved. If you're as special as I believe you to be, perhaps it will be your fate to cleanse away the rot that has festered within the cathedral walls. I can think of no one more suitable for the task."

Adria wished she could dismiss such lofty ambitions as nonsense. The events of the past week made that impossible.

"I'm a Mindkeeper without a district to call her own," she said. "Even if I wished to root out problems within the church, why would anyone listen to me, or grant me such authority?"

"Because of your tremendous gifts. Only you can hold yourself back from your true potential. Burn brighter than the stars! Don't deny your gifts to the people for fear of how others may react."

"It's not others," Adria snapped, much harsher than she intended. "It's *me*, Tamerlane. I'm afraid of what I might do, and what I might become. The more power I wield, the more paralyzed I feel. What if I choose wrong? What if the path I take is not one of wisdom but of folly? And now here I am, criticizing the church, questioning its doctrine...what if I embrace blasphemy? What if I turn my heart from the Goddesses?"

Tamerlane shifted closer to her, his look one of naked adoration. She felt herself craving his attention, but more so, she yearned for him to calmly explain away her fears. It always seemed so simple to him, so obvious. What she would give to have that confidence. Perhaps she lacked it within herself, but if she could find it in another...

"The Keeping Church has pushed and pushed the idea that this life upon the Cradle is but a stepping-stone toward the true reward of eternal life with the Goddesses," Tamerlane said. "They cannot be more wrong. Our souls represent permanence, not to our internal identities, but for our very actions. This life we live, these choices we make, become everything. Kindness shown to a stranger echoes throughout eternity. The love we feel, and the love we give to another, will linger unchanging in a cosmic memory. With this gift of the Goddesses, the fleeting becomes divine. While the church would have us trudge with eyes closed and heads bowed just hoping to make it to the heavens, I would have us walk with a song and a yearning to help and befriend others."

The small room steadily faded away until it was just him and her, their eyes locked, their voices low.

"Your time in Low Dock was a blessing," he said. "Keep the least among us in your heart, and seek to make the world a better place for those in need, and I believe you will always choose the path that will have the Goddesses smile upon you."

Adria felt tears building in her eyes. Tamerlane's passion was a beautiful flame burning with intensity she had not felt since her earliest days as a novice.

"This power I have," she said. "The ability to touch and manipulate souls...it's such a burden, Tamerlane. I don't know how to view it as a blessing. I don't know how to turn this weight into a song. I feel like I can do so much good, and I know that I have, yet all I can think of is the lives I have taken."

"Human lives?"

"The magical creatures that tried to prevent our escape from Low Dock. I tore them apart with such ease, it frightens me."

He brushed her mask with his fingers as if he were wiping away tears. The contact felt more personal, and she herself more naked, than if he had wiped her actual cheek.

"Soulless beings," he said. "Dust in the wind. Feel no sorrow for their passing, only disappointment that they would use their fleeting, impermanent time on the Cradle to spread hatred and pain."

He was so close to her without touching that his presence overwhelmed her. Not since her fumbling days as a novice had she kissed another man or woman, let alone slept with one. She felt a glimpse of that awkward, conflicting desire return, of yearning for a touch that simultaneously frightened her.

"And what should we use our time for?" she asked.

Tamerlane leaned even closer.

"We should comfort those in need," he whispered. "Share in our burdens and tribulations. Embrace one another." His fingers trailed to the back of her spine, twirled through the curls of her dark hair. "Love one another."

"Love one another?" she asked, unable to hold back her laugh. "How poetic. How naïve."

"I am nothing if not a dreamer."

Adria brought her hands to her mask. Slowly she pulled it upward, just enough to expose her mouth. She'd meant to remove it completely, but she could not bear to have it gone.

"Then kiss me," she said. "And I shall show you a dream."

He leaned closer but then hesitated, as if not fully believing her. Adria closed the rest of the distance, her lips clumsily pressing against his. The contact sent a tingle up and down her spine, though the physical act was but a prelude. She kissed again, keeping him close, as her eyes shifted to a sight granted to her by Janus's machinery.

Tamerlane's physical self steadily faded away like shadows before a torch. The light of his soul shone brighter, clearer, visible even through her porcelain mask. It swelled over her vision, its luminescence so great she felt tears building in her eyes. Her hands clutched the sides of his face, and little silver threads gathered upon her fingertips. She pressed her mask to his forehead and stared, the brilliance of his soul swirling closer. Closer. Her own soul reached out to meet it, its spiderweb strands passing through her hands and a thicker stream between their foreheads forming like a streak of lightning.

And in that meld, she sensed his every emotion for her. It wasn't love, like she anticipated. It wasn't even lust. Tamerlane worshipped her. He saw divinity within her, and it humbled and excited him in equal measure. That adoration was infectious, so powerful it burned away her doubts like a cleansing fire. She let it fill her. Her own heart may be weak, but if she could take strength from another, to let his certainty fuel her actions, then perhaps they might together shape the future of Londheim.

The little spiderwebs untangled as they pulled back their lips from a kiss that had lasted only a few seconds in the physical realm but felt like an age in the spiritual. Her heart felt ready to burst in her chest as her entire rib cage shook with each beat.

"Damn," he said. His eyes were glazed over, and he gasped in air as if from a sprint. "Just...damn."

Adria pulled her mask low over her face, and she smiled behind the porcelain.

"Don't get used to it," she said. "I'd hate to spoil you."

Tamerlane escorted her back down the stairs. Before leaving, she felt obligated to share one last worry that plagued her mind.

"Vikar Thaddeus wants me to publicly support him as the new Deakon," she said. "If I do, he has promised me the position of Vikar of the Day."

Tamerlane cast her that half-cocked grin she was beginning to love.

"I had hoped you would set your sights far, far higher than that. Was I wrong?"

"No," she said. "I don't think you were."

Adria exited the jewelry shop and closed the door behind her. The cool air hit her sweaty skin, and she closed her eyes and breathed it in deep. It felt like a fog had lifted from her mind. Goddesses help her, she could get used to this. Confidence filled her to the brim. It was time to start throwing her weight around, beginning with freeing her brother from his imprisonment. Temporarily removing Jacaranda's soul from her body and floating it before the three Vikars would prove beyond a shadow of a doubt Devin's story. And if they questioned this ability, or demanded an explanation, she would give it. To the void with them if they feared what she could do, or how she wielded her power.

Her eyes opened, but she was not greeted to the soothing light of the stars, for there were no stars to see, only a thick river of smoke flowing across the night sky.

# CHAPTER 34

The rattle of the bolt on her prison door was Jacaranda's only warning she was about to have visitors. She slid off the bed and took in a deep breath. As far as prisons went, Jacaranda figured she could do much worse. The room inside the cathedral was plainly furnished, but the bed was comfortable and the room warm. She'd paced it many times, and she trusted she could turn several items into weapons if matters called for it. She doubted any true hardened criminals spent time in there, only misbehaving keepers needing a day or two of slap-on-the-wrist punishment.

Two men in matching brown robes stepped inside, short swords strapped to their leather belts. Both were pale skinned and with shaved heads, and they were younger than Jacaranda by many years. She briefly thought of assaulting them, but so far she'd no reason to act so drastically. From the moment of her arrest, she'd been well treated.

"Turn around," one of the two said. "Hands behind your back."

She did as she was told. They tied her at the wrists, then turned her about.

"Follow me."

They led her out the door and into the long corridor that ran through the eastern wall surrounding the Cathedral of the Sacred Mother, one man behind her, one man ahead. The starlight coming in through the windows confirmed the late hour. Not too surprising that whoever wished to see her would want it done in the quiet.

"Where are we going?" she asked as they walked.

"No talking," the one behind her said flatly. She doubted she could get a rise out of that one.

"Am I to meet with someone?" she asked the man in front.

"No talking," the man behind her repeated. Jacaranda rolled her eyes and accepted she'd just have to wait.

The men led her to the southeastern corner of the enormous triangle formed by the outer wall, where there was built a great bell tower. They led her up the winding stairs, and with each floor, Jacaranda felt more certain of her destination. The bell tower was known as the Soft Voice, and it housed the many Mindkeepers of the church. At the very top would be their Vikar, Thaddeus Prymm.

A plush waiting room with embroidered couches and stacked bookshelves greeted the three upon exiting the stairs. A door with a triangular window blocked off the Vikar's office. It opened immediately, and out stepped Thaddeus.

His gray hair was neatly parted, and startling silver eyes peered at her from behind his spectacles. He braced his weight on a cane, his hands neatly folded atop its silver head.

"Remove her bindings," he said.

The two men immediately obeyed.

"Thank you," Jacaranda said as she crossed her arms before her. "Vikar Thaddeus, I presume?"

"You presume correctly," the older man said with a smile. "Please, come into my office."

Inside was even more lavishly decorated. Two padded chairs faced an ornate fireplace to her left. Opposite them was a couch with red cushions, a gilded frame, and a matching small table. A mahogany desk larger than most people's beds was directly across from her, with symbols to the Goddess Lyra carved directly into the wood. Bookshelves lined the walls, their contents older than Thaddeus and no doubt worth a small fortune. The other two men closed the door and positioned themselves on opposite sides.

"Have a seat," Thaddeus said, and he gestured to the couch. A gleaming silver tea set rested on a tray in the center of the table before it. A cup was already poured for her, with faint wafts of steam rising from its black surface.

"A drink for a soulless?" she asked as the Vikar sat opposite her and took a matching cup in hand. "Such extravagance."

"Yet I've been told you aren't soulless," he said, sipping his tea. "Perhaps I wish to see how one reacts to the offer, soulless or otherwise?"

Fair enough. Jacaranda sat and took the cup in hand. She made a show of blowing across it while testing its smell. Next she sipped a bit across her tongue, and just as she had with the giant fungal creature, she spat it back out while pretending to take an additional sip. The lingering bitterness raised a dozen alarms inside her mind.

The tea was poisoned with wolfsbane petals.

"Thank you, this is lovely," she said as she shifted to a more relaxed seated position. The movements disguised her spilling a bit of the tea upon her hip. "So why is it I am here? For you to judge whether or not I am soulless?"

"That is a large reason," Thaddeus said. "And even if you are soulless, I'd like an explanation of what you've been doing living with Devin. Perhaps you could enlighten me?"

Jacaranda didn't know what game the Vikar was playing, but for now she'd play along. She told of her time with Gerag, how he used her for his own personal pleasure as well as his bodyguard. She detailed the underground trade of soulless, how they were smuggled in by boat, and of her role in escorting them to and from the mansion. Thaddeus listened to it all intently.

"What of your awakening?" he asked. "When did you regain your soul?"

Jacaranda hesitated. Telling anything other than the truth was a huge risk. If her story didn't match Devin's, then the Vikar might doubt they spoke the truth. The bitter poison in her tea made her think the truth, however, was far from what the Vikar was interested in. She stalled by pretending to take another long sip, shifting her legs again, and then wiping her mouth with her arm. She spat the tea out upon her sleeve, then positioned that arm across her waist to hide its wetness. It was risky, allowing so much of the poison into her mouth even if not swallowing, but she had to keep the act going.

"It happened during the reaping hour on our travel back from the Oakblack Woods," she said, having skipped over everything involving the songmother and the alabaster faeries. "Nothing seemed to have caused it. I slept outside, and then my soul descended from the sky."

The tea was starting to grow cold, and the cup was half empty. Jacaranda timed it in her head, analyzing what she knew of that particular flower. Its first symptoms were weakness of muscles, a racing heart, and light-headedness. She decided enough time had passed that she should be showing signs, so she hesitated for a moment to exaggerate her breathing.

"Sorry," she said. "I...need a moment to catch my breath."

"Take your time," Thaddeus said. Though his words were kind, his tone was not. She could see his patient, fatherly façade melting away to whoever he was on the inside. The cold silver in his eyes appeared more appropriate by the minute.

"I'm not sure why I need to tell all this," she said, deciding to push the conversation toward what she was interested in. "Surely it's obvious I am not soulless?"

"Oh, it's quite obvious," Thaddeus said. "Which is why you're talking to me, alone, instead of with the other two Vikars."

Now she was getting somewhere. *Look confused*, she told herself. *Like the world is spinning and your heart won't slow down long enough for you to think.*

"I don't...what? Why?"

Thaddeus sat back on his desk, his cane resting across his lap. The more she emphasized her supposed symptoms, the more he relaxed around her.

"You know far too much, Jacaranda. You're a loose end that needs to be cleanly cut."

Thaddeus snapped his fingers, and one of the two guards came forward to grab her by the arms.

"Let me go," she said and pretended to weakly resist.

"Don't bother," Thaddeus said. "My soulless are expertly trained, as you should well know."

Jacaranda glared up at the shaved man, and sure enough, he had that calm, steady gaze that was still second nature to her. So that was why there was no baiting reactions out of them on the way to Thaddeus's office. But if they were soulless, why didn't they have the required tattoos across their throats? She pulled against her captor's grip, testing his strength, and the movement shifted his long sleeves, revealing the three dots tattooed between the soulless man's knuckles.

The sight of those tattoos set Jacaranda's heart to pounding for real. Those dots, their placement along the knuckles...it was exactly what Larsen described when she interrogated him at the Gentle Rose. But that meant Thaddeus had bought those two soulless from Gerag...

The last few scattered pieces fell neatly into place. The unknown but wealthy buyer that abducted Gerag to keep their identity a secret. The source of the rumors that reached Vikar Forrest about her and Devin living together. It was Thaddeus. The Vikar was one of Gerag's clients. No, more than that. The Vikar was almost certainly responsible for Gerag's sudden disappearance.

"You," she said, spinning back toward him. She barely caught herself in time to pretend her muscles weren't cooperating, and that her speech should be slurred. "You took Gerag. You've been a part of this all along."

The old man smiled sadly at her.

"The public is too sentimental to handle some of the world's harsher truths," he said. "And the nature of soulless is one of them."

"And what's a soulless woman's nature? To be your personal fuck toy?"

Too strong. The man holding her tightened his grasp on her arms, and she made a show of collapsing to her knees.

"Your crude language is unnecessary," Thaddeus said. He slowly rose to his feet. "The Sisters do not make mistakes, Jacaranda. That is a cornerstone of our belief, and without that, the Cradle becomes nothing but meaningless chaos. You were denied a soul at birth for a reason, and that soul residing within you now most certainly does not belong to you."

"You bastard," she said. "This is who I am. This is who I was *meant* to be."

"You were meant to be a sack of meat that followed orders," Thaddeus snapped. "No different than an ox strapped with a harness and forced to work the fields. Gerag understood that. Your resemblance to a human causes undue sentimentality, but once stripped of that, your kind offers many varied uses. If you resembled what you truly are, such as one of the soulless monsters that have recently awakened, the populace would have an easier time understanding that truth."

"You're sick," she said, having had to choke down an urge to throttle him the entire time he prattled.

"I am practical. You are the last person I should have to tell this to, aren't you? Of how soulless feel nothing, care for nothing, and want nothing. Even the animals of the forest seek out needs beyond mere food and drink. Dogs will play. Birds will sing. But you..."

He knelt beside her and gently brushed his thumb across her cheek.

"You merely exist. You're an unnecessary glimpse at a world without the Sisters, and the Cradle will be much better with your passing."

"If Devin finds out, he'll—"

"Devin will die once I'm done with you," Thaddeus interrupted. "Killed during a failed escape after he ordered you, his obedient soulless, to make an attempt on my life. No one will question it. My word against the tattoo on your throat, Jacaranda. We all know who the world will believe."

"Killing me stops nothing," she said. "Others are awaking all across the Cradle. I'm just the first."

The Vikar stood. His patronizing look of pity made her want to scream.

"Except you're not the first, Jacaranda. Five of Alma's Beloved have already awakened over the past several years. They were properly and quietly put down, just as you will be. Perhaps we've seen the last of the soulless now that the strength of the Sisters returns to our keepers. If so, no one will miss you and your kind. You'll fade away, aberrations that marred the Cradle for a few decades and then died off."

Jacaranda collapsed to the floor, feigning complete paralysis. Enough listening to this disgusting old man justify his wretchedness.

"Finally," Thaddeus said. "Cave her skull in."

The moment the soulless raised his foot, Jacaranda swept her legs in a direct collision with his knee. He toppled instantly, but it wouldn't be enough to keep him down and out. His soulless nature would have him keep trying to kill her until his own life was lost. Jacaranda stayed on her back and lifted her legs so she could bring

them down with all her might upon his exposed throat. The flesh
crunched inward upon contact with her heels.

Jacaranda was on her feet before the soulless let out his dying
gasp. Her hand closed about the hilt of his short sword. Instincts
set her to rolling. The other soulless's blade punched into the carpet and then scraped upon hitting the stone floor underneath. Jacaranda coiled her legs like a spring and then vaulted back at him.
Her shoulder struck his chest, they toppled, but his weapon was
out of position, while she'd braced for impact. The tip of her short
sword punched through his stomach and out his back. When she
landed atop him, he convulsed, the pain overriding his ability to
follow Thaddeus's orders.

She caught movement from the corner of her eye and kicked.
Her foot struck Thaddeus in the chest. The old man toppled over
his desk, slid, and landed on the other side. Jacaranda rose to her
full height and yanked her short sword free. She twirled the bloody
weapon in her hand, taking pleasure in the groan of pain she heard
from the opposite side of the desk.

Thaddeus staggered to his feet, his silver eyes wide with fear.
He was sputtering something, a meaningless protest, she thought,
but then the words finally registered inside her mind.

"Anwyn of the Moon, hear me!"

*Oh, fuck me,* she thought as she broke into a sprint. His each
and every word added an unseen chain across her body. Her steps
slowed. Her teeth clenched as she fought onward, closer, closer,
her sword seeking blood.

"Hold this serpent so its teeth find no purchase. Turn flesh into
lawful stone. Turn willful impulse into silent obedience. May the
body remain still so the heart and mind listen."

She froze with her sword three inches from his heart. Her every
muscle locked tight. Her eyes could move, and her lungs draw
breath in and out, but that was all. Helpless, completely helpless,

and to a man that much more of a monster than she had ever realized.

"It seems I won't need to fake any bruises from your escape attempt," Thaddeus said with a pained chuckle. "You're good, very good. I see why Gerag was so distraught by your betrayal. No matter. I thought to give you a quick death, Jacaranda, but instead I think I will have you join Gerag in his imprisonment. There's some poetic justice in it, don't you think?"

He limped to one of the bookcases and retrieved an old, leather-bound tome with its title embossed in gold: *The Book of Ravens*.

"The mutilation curse should suit you perfectly," Thaddeus said as he limped back to her. His eyes sparkled with sick pleasure as he flipped it open and began to read.

"Anwyn of the Moon, hear me! This flesh before me hides its rot. This smile belies its sickness."

A lancing wave of the worst pain Jacaranda had ever felt traveled from her head to her toes. It felt like her bones were at the edge of breaking. Her every inch of skin stretched as if eager to tear. Horror gripped her heart, yet her frozen frame could only offer quiet tears in protest.

"These bones deny the weakness within."

And those bones were shivering like reeds in a thunderstorm. Jacaranda could not see it, but she felt her rib cage begin to extend. She was helpless, helpless, once more a prisoner in her own body.

"Anwyn, hear me, Anwyn!"

Anwyn may or may not have heard, but Jacaranda did. She heard Thaddeus condemning her to permanent imprisonment. She heard him locking her within her body. It would be just like when she was soulless, except this time she'd be keenly aware of her circumstances. Her wants and desires would remain, only to be denied by the foul magic holding her limbs in place. A scream built inside her, born not of the agonizing pain she felt but of absolute horror and revulsion at returning to the way things had been. The scream started in her mind, but as Thaddeus shouted the word "*Tear!*" the force of it reached her lungs, and her throat.

Her limbs moved an inch, and then another. Thaddeus's eyes widened, the next word stumbled upon his tongue, and suddenly the invisible chains weakened. It wasn't much, but Jacaranda didn't need much. Just a single thrust of her sword, crossing the last few feet between her and Thaddeus. The point easily piercing Thaddeus's jaw, through the floor of the mouth, and out to spear the tongue. The curse halted, and with it the excruciating pain. The invisible chains that held her departed, and she collapsed to her knees with a long, frantic sob.

The wounded Thaddeus took hold of the sword's hilt and staggered backward. Jacaranda wiped the tears from her eyes as she fought to recover control. It felt like his curse had twisted her body to its absolute breaking point, and though the strain had faded, the exhaustion remained. The Vikar started to pull the sword out from his jaw, but by his sudden gag, it seemed like the pain was more than he could bear.

"Not yet," Jacaranda said, rising to a stand. She grabbed the hilt from him and guided him back into his chair at the desk. "I've a question for you first."

Once he was seated, she scanned his desk. The Vikar had several sheets of paper strewn about it, and she grabbed one plus a stick of charcoal and shoved both into Thaddeus's hands.

"Where is Gerag?" she asked. "Where have you imprisoned him?"

Thaddeus held both paper and charcoal, but he did not yet write anything, only glared back at her.

"Answer me," she said, and she shifted the sword the tiniest bit. Thaddeus whimpered. "If not, I'll begin twisting."

That finally set his hands to moving. Jacaranda waited until he was finished and then yanked the paper from his grasp. The handwriting was atrocious, but she could make out the location. It wasn't far. She stuffed the paper into her pocket and then grabbed the sword hilt with both hands. Until today, she'd never met the man, yet he was responsible for so much of her torment.

"You deserve worse," she seethed. "But this must do."

She ripped the blade from his jaw, looped its edge about, and then slashed it across his throat. Thaddeus gasped a torrent of blood and then collapsed upon the carpet. Jacaranda watched him die with grim satisfaction. Her hand dipped into her pocket, and she pulled out the scrap of paper.

"One down," she whispered. "One to go."

# CHAPTER 35

The corridor was long and dark, allowing Jacaranda ample time to envision how she'd kill Gerag when she found him. Would she strangle him? Would she bleed him slowly one cut after another so he could truly appreciate who was killing him? Or would she do something appropriate to his crimes, such as cutting off his testicles and making him bleed to death through his cock? This was her moment, her time to finally repay years of abuse...and yet she found her pulse quickening, her throat constricting, and her breath shallow in her lungs.

"It seems the church is full of secrets, none of them pleasant," Jacaranda whispered as she walked the dank corridor. Sneaking out of the quiet cathedral had been simple enough, and once she'd reached the Sisters' Remembrance, only a single guard posted by a door had tried to stop her. Her short swords had made quick work of him. Beyond she'd found weathered cells on either side of the stone path, all of them empty.

All but one.

There in a forgotten prison built beneath the Sisters' Remembrance, after countless nightmares and daydreams of how she'd react, she confronted her former master. She'd anticipated rage, or hatred, or contempt, none of which matched the overwhelming confusion and horror she felt looking at the mutilated, deformed mess that was now Gerag Ellington.

"What—what did they do to you?"

Hardly anything resembled the man who had once owned her body. His rib cage was extended and twisted as if the bones were attempting to escape. Most of his hair had fallen out, exposing sickly pale skin covered with sores. His arms looked like they'd been broken in multiple locations and incorrectly set. A sweat-and-pus-stained blanket lay over his naked body, which had lost a staggering amount of weight. The only part of him that resembled his former self were those brown eyes. They stared at her as he wheezed, his bloated tongue unable to form words.

"The mutilation curse," she said, hovering back at the cell door. She thought of the way the Vikar's words had pulled and twisted at her body with every syllable. "He cast it on you, didn't he?"

Gerag sucked in a raspy breath and then groaned it out. There would be no talking, not with him. He lifted his hand toward her, and she grimaced at the sight of it. Half the fingers were bent backward. The other half were curled downward with seemingly an additional knuckle, making them resemble legless centipedes.

Jacaranda drew her sword and stepped closer. She tried to summon the hate he deserved. He'd been despicable. Even when she was soulless, and could feel no emotions, he'd inflicted pain and torment on her. His need to harm, and take pleasure in that harm, was insatiable. He'd cherished her, even as he hurt her, for she'd been his most precious possession. Pins, clamps, long strips of leather: He'd harmed her with all of them, but always in a most careful way to ensure he never left a scar.

"You can hear me, can't you?" she asked him. "Lift your hand again if you do."

Another long, ragged breath. Another lift of those deformed fingers. Jacaranda felt some of her rage flicker to life.

"Good," she said, and she knelt closer. "Now you know how it feels, you bastard. Now you know what it's like to sit inside a body that won't listen to a damn word you give it. How do you like feeling powerless? Feeling worthless?"

No lifted fingers this time. Instead his breathing turned thick and wet, and it was only after a long moment she realized what he was doing.

He was laughing at her.

Jacaranda's arms shook. Her lower jaw trembled. Tears built in her eyes, and she fought a whirlwind of emotions far beyond her capabilities of understanding. Here he was, wretched and broken, and he would laugh at her? Mock her?

Even worse, despite her holding the sword, and him lying helpless before her, she felt his sway over her. With but a laugh he could send her tumbling back through a thousand memories. How many times had he praised her beauty? How many times had he used her for his pleasure? Nearly all of her thirty years of life had been under his slavery. There wasn't a moment he didn't lord over. There wasn't a memory he didn't dominate. Did he even know she was awakened now? Or had Gerag merely thought Devin had stolen her from him?

"I'm free of you now," she said. "Can you tell? I'm not soulless. I'm not helpless. And I'm not *yours*, you hear me, Gerag? I'm not fucking yours."

Those brown eyes of his twinkled. She could almost hear his mocking words.

*Who are you trying to convince, Jacaranda?*

She could leave him there. Few beyond Vikar Thaddeus likely knew the grotesque man was below the Sisters' Remembrance. She could leave him to suffer and starve, undergoing pain far beyond what she could do to him with her sword. The desire was tremendous. She could just turn around and leave, confident in his death and never to see him again.

Yes, she could flee. But would she be able to live with herself if she did?

Jacaranda sat on the cold floor and faced her broken master. Still his eyes watched her. When he could manage, he made that sick, mocking laughter. He wanted victory over her, she realized. He needed it more than anything, for it was the last comfort left to him upon the Cradle. Killing him in a rage would not deny him it, either. Perhaps the truth could cut him, for its edge was often sharper than a sword.

"Listen to me, Gerag," she said. "Are you listening?"

His fingers raised an inch, then lowered.

"Good. I want you to know I awakened when returning from Oakenwall, and from that moment my choices have been my own. And do you know what has happened since then? I've met a man I love. I've spent time with him, talking, laughing, walked through gardens holding his hand. He's comforted me when I've broken down in sorrow. He's been there for me in the dark nights I've struggled to forget everything you made me do."

She stared into those beady brown eyes, refusing to look away, and refusing to allow him to do the same.

"I've made friends, good friends who I'd die for and who would die for me. I've eaten cakes and tasted sweet cream for the first time. I've laughed, I've loved. I've found joy, the one thing you never, ever gave. The one thing you never, ever could give."

At last she looked down at her sword, and she lifted it up so it caught the light of the torch upon its sharpened edge.

"I'm going to kill you, Gerag, but it's not out of anger or hate. I—I feel tired, and drained, and nothing but disgust for this miserable wretch you've become. Who I am, and who I will be for the rest of my life, are my choices now, and I choose to end your suffering out of pity. Once you've bled out your last, and I leave this cold, dark cell...I will be free of you. Forever."

Jacaranda stood, and she met his gaze once more. His mockery was gone. No more laughter. Finally she saw rage in his brown eyes, but she had no rage to offer in return. That well was exhausted.

"Not a murder," she said. "A merciful end to a cruel chapter."

Jacaranda smoothly slid her blade across Gerag's wrist. The skin parted with ease, opening the vein. Dark blood poured across the stone as Gerag forced out a deep, garbled sigh. She steeled her jaw and stared the monster in the eye. She wouldn't look away, she promised herself. Not until the life in those eyes was gone.

Gerag gasped in his breaths. He lifted both his hands toward her. His tongue moved, but he could form no words. The blood flowed.

Her former master died.

A thousand memories burned and died within her mind. She released them all, let them bleed out of her like the blood pumping from Gerag's sliced wrist. She cried, softly at first, then great chest-wrenching sobs as the weight of a million abuses fell from her shoulders. Part of her couldn't believe the truth. The monster that had hounded the edges of her vision was gone. No matter what future awaited her, it would not be a return to slavery. This moment, this relief, was life-giving. It was pure.

It was nothing like she expected, and everything she ever needed and more.

# CHAPTER 36

Tommy had not yet worn a groove into the floor of the Wise tower's cold stone, but he was doing his best as he paced in front of the enormous fireplace.

"I just don't know if it's the right thing to do," he rambled. "I mean, it's not a question of *could* but *should*. I *could* blast open the cathedral walls with a few boulders of ice and then roast any guards with fire who try to stop me, but I don't think Devin would take too kindly to such a rescue. I mean, would he take kindly to *any* rescue? Damn it, that'd be all kinds of embarrassing to break him out only for him to refuse to leave his cell."

"Having a friend assault a prison and burn your guards to death certainly doesn't scream 'I'm innocent,'" Malik said. He sat at a small table near a window, the light of his candle reflecting off the frosted glass. For the past hour he'd listened to Tommy's various escape plans and tortured logic while hardly saying a word.

"You're right, it doesn't!" Tommy said. "Good thing you're here to help me work through this."

"I more meant that as a—sure, Tommy, happy to be here for you, too."

"Don't forget me!" Tesmarie said. She perched upon the fireplace mantel, her head resting on a pillow made of cotton fluff. "I'm here, too!"

"But you've offered no advice," Tommy said.

"Well, that's because I'm as confused and worried as you are, but we're at least confused and worried together, which is far better than alone."

"Wisdom from the littlest among us," Malik said, and he set aside the book he'd been attempting to read. "Tommy, you're going to give yourself a heart attack if you keep pacing like that. We don't even know if they're in the church's possession or the city guards'. Plotting any sort of rescue is foolhardy."

Tommy blushed and forced his legs to stand still. Jitters pulsed through him, and he clenched his hands into fists and fought an urge to run around screaming. Goddesses help him, Devin and Jacaranda were being held prisoner, awaiting a fate Tommy couldn't possibly know for certain. Every fiber of his being hollered for him to go to their aid. When he next spoke, his movements increased with his every word, until he was once more pacing the room.

"Sorry, I just, I don't—I know I'm powerful, and there's spells I've not even tried because, well—they scare me. And this scares me. What if I find out something bad happened and I just sat here with my thumbs up my ass, doing nothing? I don't want to spend the rest of my life thinking, 'If I'd just tried to help them, maybe things would be different. Maybe they wouldn't be spending their life in chains, or banished. Or worse, what if I just watch and do nothing, like I did with—did with—'"

Tommy was so lost in his own head, he never heard the scrape of Malik's chair on the floor as he pushed it back, nor saw his approach. The older man's hand settled on his shoulder. Tommy startled, and with a slight blush in his cheeks, he turned to face him. He expected a wise speech or a firm but gentle admonition to get his shit together. Instead Malik wrapped his arms around him and pulled him close.

"Cannac was not your fault," he said. "And neither is any of this.

If there is one constant in this chaotic world, Tommy, it is that you of all people will always make the right choice. Maybe not the best one, or the most practical, but it'll be the right one, because I have never met a man whose heart is as open and loving as yours."

Tommy leaned his head on Malik's shoulder and sniffled. He felt like a such a child, and the age difference between them didn't help that none, but it felt so good to have strong arms holding him close. Their bodies pressed together, and Malik did not pull away. Even better than that contact was knowing that someone trusted him so deeply.

"Thank you," he said softly. Part of him had fantasized about such an embrace for weeks, and he thought to say something romantic, if not confess his aching desire for them to be together. "I'm sorry I'm such an idiot," he said instead, to the horrified disappointment of that part of him.

Malik kissed his forehead. The warmth of his lips spread through Tommy's body like hot coals tossed into a bath.

"Never change," Malik said. A bit of his old respectability replaced his emotional vulnerability, and he pulled out of their embrace. "I hope you've calmed down now, so we can discuss this rationally."

"I think so." Tommy wiped his nose on his sleeve and caught Tesmarie watching them from her perch, a gigantic grin on her face. Upon being noticed, she fluttered between them and pressed her hands together over her heart.

"You two are so cute," she said. "Are you officially a couple now? Because I think you've been a couple for a while, but no one wanted to admit it."

Tommy's blush, which had only been a bit of red in his cheeks, now bloomed to a full-on crimson wave across his neck. He started to stammer out a response about professionalism and seniority when a flash of blue left a streak across his vision.

In one moment Tesmarie was before him, and then she was

gone. He spun, trying to follow a sudden battle that proceeded far beyond the capabilities of his eyes.

The twin blue and black streaks flashed in multiple circles seemingly at once, and then they collided together against the far wall.

"Tes!" Tommy screamed. A single blue streak rebounded, and suddenly Tesmarie was in front of him, her moonlight blade in hand and blood on her torn dress. Her left arm hung limp, and it seemed she slumped to one side as she hovered.

"I'm-sorry-Tommy-no-time-no-time-I-need-help-so-don't-move-don't-move!"

She cut her moonlight blade into his forehead. Tommy's confusion and shock kept him still through the pain. What was going on? And the symbol on his forehead, he remembered Devin describing something similar. Was she about to use her time magic on him?

"*Chyron enthal tryga!*" she cried when finished and then slammed both her palms flat into the center of her carving. Tommy felt like he staggered backward a dozen feet and out of his own skull despite his physical form remaining perfectly still. His stomach cramped as if to vomit. His own body felt weird to him. His heart thumped once in his chest, and for a sanity-breaking moment he could feel every single ounce of blood slide through the miles of arteries and veins contained within his physical structure. He was breathing in, he realized, a seemingly infinite draught of air that kept going and going, as if his lungs were a million miles wide and the air were a crawling liquid making its way down his throat.

"T..."

It took a few minutes, but finally his eyes finished their lazy crawl to focus on Tesmarie hovering in front of him. She was saying something, but what? Did it matter? It'd take like an hour for her to finish. Instead he directed his gaze past her to the far wall.

"O..."

As he'd suspected, Gan was the sudden attacker. The faery was pinned against the far wall, though Tommy couldn't seem to make out how. His wings were free, and they were frozen in mid-beat. Strange colors washed over him in gentle waves, a mixture of pinks and yellows cast as if from a multicolored sun in the sky.

"M-M…"

Even Gan's face was frozen, a look of triumphant hatred pulling his mouth into a grinning snarl. Blood, Tesmarie's blood, splashed across his dark clothes and face, like azure war paint.

"Eeee!"

Tommy's mind and body snapped together like a coil stretched to its maximum and then released. His heartbeat resumed its normal pace, as did his breathing. Upon looking around, he realized "normal" might not quite be appropriate to his situation. Devin had described the slowly moving world Jacaranda inhabited, but no story could do justice compared to witnessing the hypnotic dance of Tesmarie's two pairs of wings working in tandem. Malik recoiled in surprise just to his right, and Tommy watched his every motion play out in a hypnotically slow speed.

"What's going on?" he asked, his voice sounding strangely hollow to his ears. "And are you all right? You're hurt!"

"It's Gan!" Tesmarie said. She grimaced against a wave of pain and held her injured arm closer to her chest. "I blinked him out of time, but he'll be back soon. I can't stop him, I need your help!"

"*My* help?"

Before she could clarify further, the colors surrounding Gan faded out. The faery turned toward them both, his wings resuming their steady beats.

"You should have run," he said. A shift in his body sent him rushing toward them both.

"Not anymore," she said. "This time, I'm not alone!"

Tommy wished he shared her confidence. He had no weapon, and in the confusion he'd barely given thought to casting any spells. Gan crossed the space between them, no longer a barely perceptible flash, but as Tommy dove aside and then rolled across the stone floor, he decided the faery was still pretty fucking fast.

"What do I do?" he shouted. Gan twisted, switching targets so that he chased after Tesmarie instead. She darted about, not even attempting to match blades, given her injuries. Instead she cut at sharp angles, relying on surprise to stay just inches ahead.

"Anything!" Tesmarie screamed back at him.

Tommy cracked his knuckles and then extended his hands.

"*Aethos!*" he shouted, the spell simple enough he only needed to think the other two key words in his mind. A small ball of fire materialized at the end of his finger. Despite the life-or-death struggle, Tommy's eyes widened with joy as he witnessed in detail the way the magic manifested. The three words of the spell, *Aethos creare par-fulg*, cut into the air as if he'd written them with a burning quill. He saw them for but a flash before they shriveled and compacted into a tiny yellow ball that resembled a little sun. That ball expanded outward in layers, first orange, then red, until it was the size of his fist.

The problem with witnessing this fascinating creation was that the fire moved at far too slow of a pace to catch the speedy Gan. Whatever magic Tesmarie had granted to Tommy did not extend to magic he himself summoned. Gan almost leisurely lifted up and over the ball, which struck the wall and fizzled out harmlessly. The spell did accomplish one thing, though; it gained Tommy the faery's attention.

"I may miss out on the fun tonight," he said as he bee-lined straight for Tommy with his moonlight blade raised in his lone hand. "But killing you will make it so very worth it."

Tommy fled in the opposite direction, past a nearly frozen Malik, whose mouth was open in an O. He reached the side table, lifted Malik's book, and spun about with it wielded in both hands like a club. It might not be much against most foes, but it could still batter about a little faery if swung with enough force. Gan hovered just out of reach, and he zipped back and forth, feinting attacks. Playing with him, Tommy realized.

"You're such a…frog-kissing stone-humper!" Tommy shouted, trying to figure out what might be offensive to onyx faeries. He swung at Gan, missed, and received a stinging cut across his wrist as his reward. Gan retreated from his retaliatory swing, and he'd have cut again if not for Tesmarie zipping in and blocking. Her body recoiled a foot from the impact. There was no doubt she was suffering from her injury. Tommy cast another spell before Gan might take advantage.

"*Aethos creare empas*" slid out of his fingers in silver, faster than the words could exit his tongue, and then the writing brightened, elongated, and became a streak of lightning with a definitive, spear-like shape. This time when it flew at Gan, it crossed the distance at breakneck speed. The faery dove aside, but unknowingly he judged wrong, bringing him into contact with the final third of the lightning spear. The energy swirled into him, and it would have been beautiful if not for the scream of pain and the fury in Gan's eyes after it passed.

"You…damn…human," he said. Tommy's blood chilled in his veins. There'd be no toying with him after this. That look promised murder.

Tommy dodged aside the faery's charge as he would a missile, then scrambled up to his feet and ran. Tesmarie followed after, trying to distract Gan, but there'd be no taking his attention away. The three scrambled and flailed, a chaotic frenzy knocking chairs to the floor and books into the air, all things moving with a slow, mesmerizing pace as if the air were honey and clung to every object. Several times Gan slashed his blade across Tommy's arms and chest, stinging cuts that steadily grew in severity.

"Will you just stop!" Tommy shouted as he raced past a frozen Malik. The older man was turning, vainly trying to follow the battle in his far more rapid flow of time. His lips were pulled back and his tongue extended between his teeth. Malik was clearly saying something, but his words were coming out so slowly they were a meaningless drone to Tommy's ears. He dodged around his dear friend, dropped to one knee, and shoved his hand into the fireplace.

It was a gamble, but he prayed that in this slower time flow the fire would not be able to transfer its heat to his skin at the same, dangerous rate. He grabbed a log, and he lamented the heat and pain that prevented him from more closely observing the almost liquid-like nature of the flames as they wrapped about his intruding hand for the brief second he held the log. When he spun, Gan was there, moonlight blade ready to stab.

Tommy smacked him out of the air with the burning log, then let go before it charred his fingers. Gan let out a soft "yelp" as he flew, his wings momentarily curling around his sides instead of flapping. It would have been an opportune moment to attack, but Tommy was too busy blowing air across his fingers and holding back tears. Holy shit, that hurt! Tesmarie zipped to his shoulder, landing lightly on both feet and steadying herself with a hand against his neck. From the corner of his eye he saw the blood dripping from her wounded arm, and it hurt his heart.

"Enough of this!" Gan screamed after righting himself in midair. His good hand looped about, and Tommy saw the briefest hint of magic words float like smoke in front of the faery before a flash of red washed over Gan's body. Where there had been one faery were now three, and they moved with eerie synchronicity. When Gan flew in for the attack, the others trailed like phantoms milliseconds ahead or behind, and then there were more, four, five, a dozen similar Gans rushing toward them, as if he were seeing a dozen timelines of Gans coming in to kill him.

Tommy froze, bewildered at what to do or where to go. His instincts screamed out in danger, but his mind was muddled. He was going to die, he realized then. He was going to die, and his only final thought was how goddess-damned stupid he was, standing there instead of dodging.

A flash of light burst from Malik's hand, interrupting the faery's charge. He pulled up immediately, his eyes spread wide and his arms out at his sides.

"Wh-what?" Gan said. The after-images vanished one by one, until a single Gan hovered in confusion. "Mother? Mother, please, I promise I didn't steal it!"

Tommy didn't know who Gan was talking to, or why, but he refused to waste this brief moment. His hand stretched out, and he cast the only spell that seemed to have worked that night.

*"Aethos creare empas!"*

The lightning spear struck Gan in the center of his chest. Power swirled through him, eliciting a horrific shriek that scraped like icy fingers across Tommy's spine. The faery's wings went still, and he dropped like a fall leaf, weaving back and forth as he fell.

"You did it," Tesmarie said, sounding more tired than joyful. She quickly fluttered up to Tommy's forehead. "Thank you, thank you, now forgive me, this might feel awkward."

She touched his skin and ended the spell. Tommy's stomach heaved, and his normal flow of time hit him like a stampede of horses. He rocked back on his heels, his senses returning to him one by one. Malik stood facing the both of them, his hand still outstretched from casting his spell.

"Did it work?" he asked. Tommy answered by lifting him off the floor in a gigantic hug.

"You magnificent bastard, what did you do?" he asked.

"I wasn't sure what use I could be, but there was a Gloam spell that muddles the mind, and I thought it might be useful. I see that it was. If something had happened, if... you know what, Tommy? Fuck it."

Malik grabbed Tommy's head in his hands and shoved his mouth against his lips. Tommy practically melted in Malik's arms as the kiss dragged on and on. The inner workings of his brain ceased to function. The world faded as he closed his eyes and relished the moment, wishing it could continue on and on forever. When Malik finally pulled away, Tommy gasped, realizing he hadn't even been breathing.

"What about protocol and etiquette?" Tommy asked.

"I've nearly died twice in the past week. To the void with rules and etiquette."

Tommy laughed, because any other reaction was beyond him. His hand ached, the cuts across his arms stung like mad, and his heart pounded in his chest at a mile a minute. He wished he could spend time figuring things out, but he realized Tesmarie was crying, and that couldn't go unaddressed.

"Tes?" he asked as he pulled away from Malik. The faery stood over Gan's body. Little flecks of diamond trickled down her cheeks.

"Yes?" she asked, her smile failing to mask her sadness.

"Are you all right?"

She sniffled and brushed away some of the diamond dust at the corner of her eyes.

"I'm fine, promise," she said. "He hated me so much he hunted me down. I wish I knew for what reason. Is it for rejecting him? Or for helping you?"

"Tes..."

He extended his arms as if for a hug, and she responded by flying to his chest and burying her face into his robes. He gently closed his arms and tucked his fingers against her back, hugging her as best he knew how.

"You're the absolute best," he told her. "Don't you ever doubt that."

After a moment he felt her pull back so he released his fingers. She fluttered up to his face, planted a kiss on his cheek, and then floated toward the window. Malik, who had patiently waited beside the two, wrapped an arm around Tommy's waist and pulled him close. Together they watched as Tesmarie pressed her face to the frosted glass.

"Is something wrong?" Tommy asked.

"Something Gan said has me worried." She frowned and then fluttered to the door. She was much too small to open it, and realizing that, Tommy hurried over to help her. Cold air billowed in the moment he cracked it open. He shivered, thought to get a coat, and then halted. Terror constricted his rib cage and froze his limbs faster than any winter wind.

"Oh no. No no no."

The Cathedral of the Sacred Mother loomed high above the surrounding district, and its towering spires and steep triangular rooftops roared with flame, lighting the night sky orange and crimson, a night sky filled with the silhouettes of owls and gargoyles witnessing the destruction commence.

# CHAPTER 37

Devin sat with his back against the door of his prison and hummed a quiet hymn. His accommodations were quite pleasant as far as prisons went, for it wasn't truly a prison. There were two rooms within the Cathedral of the Sacred Mother that had been converted into a makeshift stockhouse. It was generally used for quarantining younger keepers accused of petty crimes outside the cathedral grounds. The city let the church punish their own, so long as the crimes were small enough and the public made no outcry. There was a sparse but clean bed in the corner, a chamber pot underneath it, and a small table with a chair for him to read at or eat his meals.

*Could be much worse,* Devin thought as he hummed along. *They could have sent you to the city prison.*

He had two opposing ideas as to why they had kept him and Jacaranda in the stockhouse. One was that they viewed his crimes as minor enough so he didn't belong in the city prison. The other was that they wanted to bury any and all mention of a rogue Soulkeeper and his soulless lover.

The doorlock clicked above his head. Devin let out a confused grunt. As best he could tell in his windowless room, it was well into the night. Who might be coming for a visit? He hopped to his feet and turned. A few possibilities bounced around his head. All were better than the woman who finally did step inside the door and then shut it behind her.

"Hello, Devin," Lyssa said. She removed her tricorn hat, and he noticed she picked at its five raven feathers as she held it at her waist. "Trouble sleeping?"

It seemed as if she was the one with trouble sleeping. Dark circles spread underneath her eyes. Her arms were crossed tightly over her chest, and she hunched as if she could vanish entirely into her heavy leather coat.

"Sleeping is all there is to do in here, sleep and pray, and I think the Sisters are tired of listening to me."

Not the faintest hint of a smile touched her face. Devin could feel the tension and awkwardness in the air as thick as the fog rolling off the Septen River on a cold autumn morning. He glanced at the pistols buckled to her hips. Were they loaded? he wondered. She couldn't view him as that dangerous, not if she was coming in alone at night. What then?

"Why?" she finally asked.

"Why what?" he shot back. "You'll need to be specific, Lyssa. There's quite a bit that's happened since I was arrested."

Her slender face was so passive, so controlled. That wasn't like her at all. She normally wore her emotions on her sleeve at all times.

"Why her?" she asked. "Why a soulless? I told you to come to me, didn't I? I said I could be here for you, like I've always been here for you. I don't know if I should feel hurt, or insulted, or just overall very, very pissed. It'd be nice if you could help me sort this out so I know the proper way to be angry with you."

"It's not like that at all," Devin insisted.

"Then what is it like? Did you steal her from Gerag before someone killed him, is that it? A free, fancy servant that'll obey your every whim?"

"She's not a servant! She awakened, Lyssa! She was once soulless, but not anymore."

Lyssa leaned back against the door as if she'd been slapped. "Horseshit."

Devin let out an exasperated sigh.

"Go next door, spend five seconds talking with her, and you'll find out I'm telling the truth. Her soul was given to her during our trip to Oakenwall. I swear by all three Sisters I saw the moment her soul came down from the stars themselves to enter her body. She's awake, alive, and aware just like you and I are, Lyssa."

Lyssa's anger slowly melded into shock.

"That's never happened before," she said. "Not in the eighty years the soulless have appeared on the Cradle."

"And that's why I kept it a secret," he said. "Jacaranda had enough to deal with learning to control her own life. I didn't... I didn't want the church to take her into custody and study her like they would some ancient textbook or scroll passed among the scholars. Besides, I promised her, if she made herself known, it'd be her decision, not mine."

Lyssa pulled the chair out from underneath the desk and sat facing him on the bed. He could feel her gaze studying him intently, and he tried not to wither beneath it.

"Tell me about her," she said.

And so he did. He told her of how she'd been when first they met, her a soulless in Gerag's control. He told her of the moment her soul returned outside Oakenwall, of how she'd not even known how to breathe in those early confused moments. He told her of trips to the market, her first time eating sweets, of shopping and mirrors and the constant threat of Gerag discovering she was alive. He talked until her hand reached out to his and clutched his fingers to stop him.

"I've only heard you talk about one other person this way," she said softly, and they both knew exactly who she meant. The silence fell heavy between them. "Why didn't things work out between us, Devin? I thought after Brittany's death, you'd just need time, but time didn't help. It only pushed you further away."

He owed her honesty, he knew that. But what was the truth? He'd entertained thoughts of them together, especially in the long months after. Amid his depression, he'd clung to her, finding brief sparks of joy between the sheets. And yet when things seemed ready to advance, he'd fled into his work, covering thousands of miles and a dozen missions in the lands west of Londheim.

Devin could not look her in the eye. He stared at her hand upon his, gaze lost in the little whorls of her skin.

"When I think of you, when I think of *us*, I—I can't help but fall back into how it was. It reopens a wound I used you to heal. It's not fair, I know it's not fair, but moving on from her meant moving on from you." He took in a long breath to steady himself. "If I was a better man, I'd have asked for your forgiveness years ago. I knew it hurt you, and I always pretended to never see it. I'm sorry."

A rumble shook the ground. From somewhere in the distance came a scream, and many others quickly echoed it. Lyssa bolted to her feet, her pistols already drawn.

"What's going on?" Devin asked.

"I don't know," she said. "But I'm going to find out."

She hurried out the door, and Devin was keen to notice she did not lock it behind her. He almost followed after her, almost, but until he knew more, he wasn't going to risk worsening his situation with a jailbreak. He didn't need to wait long. Lyssa returned almost immediately, but instead of entering the room, she flung the door open and beckoned him to exit. Smoke floated above her head. Screams added urgency to her words.

"You're needed, Soulkeeper. The cathedral's under attack."

Devin hurried out and immediately hooked a right to the adjacent room.

"Not without Jac," he said. He slid back the bolt lock and flung open the door.

Empty.

"Where is she?" he asked as he stepped into the plain room that mirrored his own. "Where did they take her?"

"I don't know," Lyssa said, pulling on his arm. The smoke was already thickening. He could feel the first taste of it burning his throat. "But you'll have to trust she's all right."

*Please, Sisters, keep her safe*, Devin whispered in prayer. Lyssa hurried to the cabinet nailed to the wall opposite the stockhouse rooms and flung open the doors. Devin's weapons and ammo pouch were piled neatly on one of the shelves, and he quickly belted them to his waist.

"Who would dare attack the cathedral?" he asked as she impatiently waited.

"The Forgotten Children, most likely," Lyssa said. "It seems they're not happy with just Belvua under their control."

Devin drew his sword, and he steeled his emotions for the coming battle. No matter how worried he felt, he couldn't dwell on Jacaranda's safety. Distractions led to mistakes. Mistakes meant death.

"Lead the way," he told Lyssa. "And if anyone notices I'm free and objects, make it clear you helped me, yeah? I'd rather not die to friendly fire."

"You escaped on your own," she said with a wink. "What? If we survive this, I'd rather not get court-martialed and stuck in a room next to yours."

The two stockhouse rooms were built into a secluded lower section of the eastern-facing outer wall, whose only exit led farther into the cathedral grounds. The two Soulkeepers dashed up the stairs, through a cramped entryway, and into the courtyard beyond.

The courtyard of cherries was a blood-strewn battlefield, one without lines or formations. Keepers, novices, and even a few Alma's Beloved were fleeing toward Alma's Greeting in an attempt to escape the rapidly growing fire consuming the great cathedral.

Devin absorbed the shock of the sight like a body blow. The cathedral had felt timeless, eternal, its stone as old as Londheim itself. Now its stained glass windows were broken, and smoke billowed out them in giant, expanding plumes. As for the courtyard, various members of the Forgotten Children darted about, killing without mercy. Devin watched two young novices emerge from the training yard to his right, only to be cut down by a trio of foxkin blades. The monsters licked the blood off their weapons' edges and then added their howls to the sounds of chaos overwhelming the night.

"Side by side," Lyssa said. "Overrun them while they're still scattered and blood-drunk."

"Try to make it quick," he added in return. "We've work to do this night."

It was one thing to cut down unarmed children. It was another to face the wrath of Soulkeepers. Devin's pistol announced his presence, driving lead through the nearest foxkin's heart and turning the two survivors his way. His sword battered aside a panicked block with ease, he stepped in close so his shoulder could ram the foxkin off balance, and then he decapitated him with the returning swing. The last one braced her legs, anticipating a charge from Devin. Instead Lyssa buried two lead shots into her throat, firing them so close together, they sounded like a single explosion.

Devin spared a glance to the novices the foxkin had cut down. Sadness and anger warred within him in equal measure.

"Goddesses help me, what a nightmare."

The ground shook beneath him, and through the trees he could just barely see the eastern wall of the inner cathedral collapse amid ash and smoke. Devin prayed that all within had escaped beforehand. Two children fled the noise toward them, each wearing simple bed robes. He waved for them to near, and though one did, the other continued running. Upon seeing the foxkin and gargoyle chasing, he understood why.

"The gargoyle's mine," Lyssa said, taking off into a sprint. Devin holstered his pistol so he could wield his sword with both hands. There was no time for him to reload.

"To me!" he shouted, ensuring the fleeing boy turned his way. The foxkin shifted his attention to Devin, and he snarled like a rabid animal.

"Stubborn keepers," the foxkin said. "Lay down and die if you wish to avoid suffering."

"Sorry," Devin said. "But I've no plans for that tonight."

The foxkin assaulted with his twin daggers. Pain shot through Devin's arms with his every swing. He grit his teeth and endured. Lyssa could handle the other, of that, he had full faith. Once she did, they could finish off this one. He focused on parrying the foxkin's quick hits, relying on the occasional feint to force the dragon-sired back. It took all his concentration, but Devin could tell he had far more training, and the foxkin was used to his speed being enough to win a fight.

It seemed the foxkin realized his predicament. He retreated, dipped his head, and opened the third eye directly across its forehead. Colorful smoke wafted out its edges, and Devin forced his gaze away lest it alter his mind. That temporary opening was all the foxkin needed. Instead of charging Devin, it sidestepped him, grabbed the boy he'd defended, and put an arm around the boy's neck to hold him still. His other hand pressed the edge of a dagger into his back.

"Stay back or I skewer him," the foxkin said. Devin lifted his sword in a show of surrender. He dared not even a glance at Lyssa sneaking up behind the two.

"Let him go and run away," Devin said. "That's all. Just run away."

Before he could respond, Lyssa lunged, driving her short sword into his skull. It was fatal, but the foxkin had a half-second of life in him to react, jamming his dagger between the boy's shoulder blades. They both dropped, blue and red blood pooling together.

"Damn it," Lyssa seethed, seeing the wound. Devin rushed to the boy, his own curse dying on his lips. Not fatal, but it would be soon. Before he might administer aid, a torrent of wind knocked him to one knee. A black-furred lapinkin approached, his spear twirling in his grasp. The body of a dead Soulkeeper lay not far behind, the corpse slumped against a tree trunk.

"I'll keep him off you," Lyssa said, her hands a blur as she sheathed her sword and began reloading her pistols. "Help him if you can."

Devin tried not to worry as he checked the boy's back. The wound was deep, and there was so much blood. No impromptu bandage would suffice. He looked about, spotted a Faithkeeper fleeing toward Alma's Greeting wearing only her shift, and sprinted to intercept her.

"Not yet," he told her as he latched on to her wrist. She spun on him, her eyes wide with shock. "We need your help."

He practically dragged her back to the boy bleeding out upon the grass.

"I have no bandages or cloth," the Faithkeeper said upon seeing him. The helplessness in her voice stirred anger inside Devin for reasons he couldn't explain.

"I don't want bandages," he said. "I want you to pray. The 36th Devotion, it can help him. Pray, and *mean it*."

The frazzled Faithkeeper dropped to her knees above the child, and she pressed both hands upon the bleeding hole in his back. Tears fell upon her bloodstained fingers. The words of the devotion flowed off her tongue, and she was not even halfway finished when Devin knew it would take effect. Light shimmered underneath her hands, blood fading and skin knitting together before the Faithkeeper's command.

*Maybe they all can harness the Sisters' power*, Devin wondered. *They just need lives to depend upon it.*

A scream diverted his attention to an ashen gray avenria walking straight through a thick tree trunk, her slender sword cutting down an unsuspecting novice fleeing from a foxkin at his heels. She shook blood off the blade, then turned her blue eyes their way. Devin stood before the Faithkeeper and lifted his sword.

"Pray for me," he told her, an idea popping into his head. "The 5th Devotion."

She obediently prayed as the avenria calmly approached, the devotion's lines tweaked slightly so it applied to Devin and not herself.

"Lyra of the Beloved Sun, hear my prayer. His body is weak, his legs unsteady, and his burdens beyond what he may bear. Grant him strength to walk in your name. May he stride tall through fields of strife, and care not for the danger, but only for your blessed light."

The words flowed over him like a cool wind amid desert heat. His sword cut through the air like it weighed nothing. His foe tried to match his newfound speed, and her lone blade should have been faster than Devin's larger, heavier sword. It wasn't. He parried her first thrust, sidestepped her second, and lunged with his arm fully extended. The tip pierced through her inner ribs. He set his feet and pulled, ripping the sword out the side of her rib cage and dropping her instantly.

A gargoyle attempted to ambush him while he was distracted with the avenria. Devin's feet shifted, and his sword continued the arc it'd begun when tearing out the rib cage. The sharp edge caught the gargoyle in mid-leap and sliced through its neck until hitting the spinal cord. Its frighteningly heavy body continued onward, just barely missing Devin due to his side step. The gargoyle's claws cut thick grooves through the earth, and its momentum halted only upon slamming into a cherry tree. Its body seemingly hardened, a trick of time Devin recognized and refused to believe. He sprinted closer, flipped his sword downward so he might hold the hilt in both hands, and buried his sword deep into the gargoyle's chest where he believed its heart to reside.

Immediately the creature's body and time returned to normal, blood gushing from both neck and chest as it flailed its death throes.

"Share your prayers with others," he said to the Faithkeeper. "We are all in need of Lyra's strength."

The woman nodded, looking in awe of what her prayers had accomplished. Lyssa rejoined him, her short swords wet with fresh blood. Two young boys wearing simple novice robes followed a step behind her.

"We need to get these people out of here," she said.

"Alma's Greeting," Devin said. It was the closest major exit, as well as the largest. "That's where most should be fleeing."

"Then let's go."

A wide, bricked path led between Alma's Greeting and the cathedral proper, and once Devin's group had exited the rows of trees, he had his first good look at the enormous gate. Its thick wooden doors were splintered and off-center. The stone supports were heavily cracked and collapsed inward, effectively sealing the doors both shut and immobile. A large gathering of keepers held firm before it. Four Soulkeepers formed the outer perimeter, holding dragon-sired at bay with their pistols and swords. In the deep center of the group hid the youngest among them, some barely older than six or seven.

Destroying the cathedral wasn't enough, Devin thought as he glared at the collapsed gate. The dragon-sired wanted every last soul to perish. Several times he saw shimmering golden light wash over the humans, a shield reminiscent of what Sena and Adria had cast about their church. So it seemed the rest of the keepers were realizing the extent of their powers. A group of five dragon-sired guarded the stone pathway from their direction, two gargoyles, two lapinkin, and an avenria. They darted in and out toward Alma's Greeting, never pressing too hard. Instead it looked like they were merely trying to contain the keepers. Waiting until the cathedral was ash and their forces could regather.

Devin dipped his hand into his bag of spellstones.

"Wait to fire until my shot hits first," he said as he slid a white and yellow spellstone into his pistol. "If it works, it'll stun the whole lot of them."

"And if it doesn't?"

He pulled the hammer all the way back.

"Then your aim will need to be a lot better than mine."

Lyssa lifted her brace of pistols and waited. Devin aimed his pistol at a spot on the ground in the rough center of the dragon-sired and pulled the trigger.

The roar of the stone echoed in his ears, but that noise was a pittance compared to the dome of sound that encapsulated the five dragon-sired. Both gargoyles dropped from the sky, and the rest collapsed to their knees with their hands clutched over their ears. The dome broke within a heartbeat, and in the ensuing silence Lyssa's pistols thundered, their aim true.

Devin didn't bother reloading his pistol, for he couldn't compete with Lyssa in that regard. Instead he rushed with his sword in hand, all while counting in his head.

*One, two, three, four . . .*

At five, Lyssa's pistols sounded again, one shot tearing straight through a gargoyle's eye, the other blasting off the jaw of an avenria. Devin tore through the remainder of the group with a vicious spray of blood, ending their lives without resistance.

"Go, hurry," Devin shouted back to his group, which had grown in number during their short trip to the center walkway. The men and women sprinted to the safety of the keepers. Devin loaded his pistol and watched the skies. Sure enough, a lapinkin dove after them, and he put a shot straight through his chest. The impact shifted the windleaper's path enough so that it crashed a few feet to the side of his intended prey, one of his legs snapping as he rolled.

The rest safely arrived. Devin joined Lyssa in sprinting the final distance to more of his fellow keepers. Vikar Caria of all people greeted him, and Devin bowed his head in deference to his superior.

"Your pistol," Caria said. "Somehow it uses magic."

"That it does," he said, not bothering to explain how or why. He turned his attention to the collapsed Alma's Greeting while rummaging through the pouch with Tommy's spellstones, seeking one appropriate for the situation.

"Stand back," he shouted, settling on a pure white stone Tommy had described as an earthquake on demand. Hoping that meant what he thought, Devin loaded it into his pistol, cocked the hammer, and drew aim upon the left side of the gate. After a pause to whisper a prayer to the Sisters, he pulled the trigger.

The pistol jerked hard enough backward, he feared it'd sprain his wrist. Stone crumpled inward as if the wall were struck by an invisible boulder, and then the entire gateway began to shake. More cracks spiraled outward, growing in size and depth until the mangled wood and stone of the gate shifted and crumpled to reveal a slender opening.

"Praise the Sisters," Vikar Caria said.

"Make sure you keep on praising them," Devin said as he shook his stinging arm. "We'll need your prayers to get these people to safety. Keep defensive and the bastards should start seeking easier prey."

"And what will you do?" she asked.

"Distract them," he said with a grin.

He ran for one of the ladders leading to the top of the surrounding wall, Lyssa at his heels. Once atop the wall, he better surveyed the battle. It seemed a similar situation had formed at the western-facing Lyra's Door, with attempts to escape halted by the dragon-sired. Soulkeepers gathered just inside the gateway, holding formation with a handful of Faithkeepers and Mindkeepers blessing them with prayers. Smoke clouded the air from the constant discharge of their pistols.

The gateway meant little to most of the dragon-sired, but it still held back the foxkin and the Ravencallers steadily gathering in opposition. Fires burned all across the cathedral, and owls dove for vulnerable novices or keepers who had not yet reached the safety of the groups. So far the Soulkeepers could only watch, for they faced opposition on all three sides. Avenria flanked them while leaping through the wall, striking down a few men and women, and then retreating back through the stone to the outside. Lapinkin dove straight into their numbers, relying on the shock of their impact to avoid lethal counterfire from the pistols.

It was a losing fight unless something swayed the flow of battle. Devin chose one of the swirling blue stones inside his pouch and slid it into the chamber of his pistol, hoping to do just that.

"Surprise is our best weapon," he told Lyssa. "Keep them off me so I can focus on the gate."

"As if I need to be told," she said with a wink.

Devin cocked the hammer all the way back and aimed.

"Just making sure. We're about to be very, very popular."

The hammer fell, piercing the spellstone. Blue smoke flashed out of the barrel, marking the exit of a shimmering sapphire orb. It crossed the distance within the blink of an eye and struck the ground at the bottom of the steps before Lyra's Door, instantly detonating. Shards of ice with jagged points grew in all directions as if they were upon the back of a frozen porcupine. Foxkin and avenria screamed as they were impaled upon the shards, macabre decorations upon a crystalline creation glowing in the moonlight.

"Incoming," Lyssa said as he slid the next spellstone into his pistol, this one a mixture of gray and black.

"Handle it."

A powerful shock wave rocked Devin's pistol in his hand. He saw no projectile, but a group of Ravencallers that clustered behind the front lines crumpled as if struck by an invisible hand, legs shattering and arms twisting in strange directions without apparent cause.

"Handle it?" Lyssa mocked him as a gargoyle crashed down toward her from the sky. She deftly avoided its landing, and her pistols boomed out their deadly protest. Devin brought his attention back to the larger battle. The next spellstone he grabbed from his pouch was an ugly mixture of pink and brown. He racked his mind trying to remember what Tommy had described it as. Something about time.

"Fuck it," he said, pulling the hammer back halfway to expose the hole into the chamber. "Let's hope you know what you're doing, Tommy."

With Lyra's Door so viciously defended, the Forgotten Children again attempted a flank, this time with a trio of avenria that simply walked through the wall using their shadowy wings. Devin aimed at the nearest of the three and held his breath. A collection of novices had tried to slow their advance before a Soulkeeper could come to back them up, and the avenria were butchering the young men and women. There was no time to wait for an opening. He pulled the trigger.

Unlike most spellstones, this offered no kick. The effect, however, was immediate. Time slowed to a crawl in a spherical radius around where he'd aimed, catching all three avenria as well as five novices. To the two Soulkeepers who had rushed over to join in, the avenria were suddenly easy prey for their pistols.

"Devin!" Lyssa screamed, stealing his attention. The gargoyle lay dead at her feet, but her focus was on the sky as she rapidly reloaded both pistols simultaneously. "A little help here!"

He had a half-second to follow her gaze before dodging for his life from a lapinkin slamming down upon the wall. The thick spear shattered through the stone with ease and then caught. The lapinkin clung to the spear's shaft and rotated forward with it, using her momentum to slam both her heels into Devin's gut. His feet left the ground, and as he sailed backward, the lapinkin extended her hand. Wind buffeted his body, carrying him several more feet toward the edge of the wall.

*Shiiiiiit*, his panicked mind wailed as he frantically reached out for anything to hold. His fingers closed about the top rung of the ladder. When the wind stopped, his body swung downward. Devin had no choice but to absorb the blow of the ladder against his chest and legs. He sucked in air through clenched teeth as his shins hit one of the rungs. He holstered his pistol, grabbed the top rung in both hands, and vaulted himself back up to the wall.

The lapinkin had pulled her spear free and positioned it toward the ladder, but it seemed he'd recovered quicker than she'd anticipated. Devin batted the heavy point aside with his wrist just before she could thrust it in for the kill, slid sideways along the shaft to close the distance, and slammed a fist directly into the bridge of her flat nose. She staggered, dazed, and Devin used that moment to finally draw his sword and bury its blade into her gut, its sharp point easily puncturing her leather armor.

Devin quickly ripped the sword free, kicked the lapinkin's corpse off the side of the wall, and turned. Lyssa faced off a second lapinkin, her short sword eager to kill but the spear's long reach proving formidable. One slipup and she could dance in and destroy him, Devin knew, but with the lapinkin able to harness the wind, it made any sort of attack a tremendous risk. The wall wasn't wide enough for him and Lyssa to fight side by side, either.

He drew his pistol. Lyssa was so close. She only needed a distraction.

"Duck!" he shouted, his pistol extended and the hammer cocked all the way back. Lyssa dropped immediately, anticipating a shot that never came. More importantly, the lapinkin heard and reacted with blistering speed. His spear pulled back and his hand extended, slamming Devin with a wall of air that was shockingly solid. Blood spilled from his nose, and if his pistol weren't empty of flamestone and shot, his aim still would have been ruined.

Lyssa was back on her feet in a flash, rebounding with the grace of a dancer. The lapinkin had overextended himself, and with how large and heavy a spear he wielded, he had no chance to compete with her speed. Her short sword cut across his face and neck, bathing his fur in a sudden shower of blood.

"Annoying bastards," Lyssa said. She kicked at one of the spears that now lay atop the wall. It barely budged.

"Imagine a full army of them working together," Devin said, shuddering. His attention returned to Lyra's Door. For a moment he feared he'd suffered a blow to the head when grabbing the ladder, for a large black splotch blurred his vision. It was only when he saw it move that he realized what he looked upon. A cloud of black mist floated above the cathedral steps toward Lyra's Door. Devin feared nothing good would come of that cloud when it settled over the keepers holding the line against the Forgotten Children. He half cocked his pistol to open up the inner chamber and then scanned for the source.

There, atop the Sisters' Remembrance. Three Ravencallers stood in a triangle beside the great statue of Anwyn, their arms raised heavenward as they recited their prayers. Such a blasphemous sight atop the mausoleum sickened Devin's stomach. He had only two spellstones left, and he pulled out a black and yellow one Tommy had called "bouncy lightning." He hoped it meant what he thought as he sighted the nearest of the three Ravencallers and pulled the trigger.

A thick blast of lightning shot across the gap between them, striking the Ravencaller in the chest before leaping to the woman beside him. It leapt into the third, then circled back around one more time, crackling through the bodies of all three. They dropped, their bodies charred and smoking.

Still, the damage from the three Ravencallers was already done. The black mist had settled over the many keepers, and they hacked and coughed as if breathing in thick smoke. A trio of owls dove in unison toward the back line of praying Mindkeepers and Faithkeepers, seeking to take advantage of their suffering. Devin reached for a spellstone but already knew he'd be too late.

The ball of flame that exploded in a ring above the mist, killing one owl and scattering the other two, was very much on time.

"Close one," Lyssa said as she pulled her other short sword free from the gargoyle's body.

"That wasn't me."

Lyssa frowned with confusion for only a moment before she pointed toward the street between the Sisters' Remembrance and the nearby Scholars' Abode. A small squad of city guards had arrived to join the fight. In the middle of their formation, looking small and insignificant compared to the burly men and women around them, stood Tommy and Malik. The two men had their hands raised, and a new barrage of magic leapt from their fingertips. Lightning lit up the sky, unerringly striking through a magnificent owl preparing for a dive. Devin grinned and pumped his fist until he realized how the dragon-sired would react to their arrival.

"We need to be down there," he told Lyssa. "If the forces in Lyra's Door don't charge, the dragon-sired can turn on Tommy and overwhelm him."

Lyssa hopped off the side of the wall and landed lightly upon the soft grass.

"Then what are we waiting for?" she asked.

Devin half slid, half fell to the ground while using one side of the ladder as a guide pole. Once his feet touched ground, he sprinted after Lyssa, catching up only because she momentarily slowed. Up ahead the battle continued in earnest. Vikar Forrest helmed the defense, the giant man bellowing orders as often as he swung his enormous axe. Devin knew he couldn't override any orders by his Vikar. His only hope was that his urgency swayed the man's opinion. Thankfully the black mist had faded by the time he arrived, sparing him that particular unpleasantness.

"Those are our spellcasters!" Devin shouted over the din, and he grabbed at the sleeve of Forrest's coat. He pointed to the road that split the Sisters' Remembrance and the Scholars' Abode. "They won't last alone. We have to help them!"

"Shouldn't you be in jail?" the Vikar asked, nonplussed.

"I can go back if you'd like."

"Piss on that." Forrest slammed his axe down so he could lean on its handle and grab a quick breather. "You want us to charge out to the streets, then we'll charge, so long as you fucking lead it."

Devin drew his sword and saluted, a mad grin spreading across his lips.

"Then may Anwyn have mercy on our souls."

# CHAPTER 38

When Evelyn was forty years old, she'd led a group of nine avenria into the port town of Wardhus with fire and murder on their mind. They ignored the rows of homes, cluttered and dirty in a way only humans could make. They easily sneaked past the guards stationed on watch, for the avenria were at home in the shadows, whereas human eyes could see only when the stars were kind to bless them with light. Once spread out, they set fire to the many boats, ten at a time, a little splash of oil and a kiss with a torch all that was necessary. They'd set fire to thirty boats and then fled beyond the city's walls to watch them burn from afar. It didn't matter that there were people asleep on those boats, nor how vital the supplies were to the life and safety of the people living there.

All that mattered was watching something the humans cherished burn.

"We are more alike than you may ever know," Evelyn said as she watched the grand cathedral catch fire from her perch atop a nearby chimney. "And that is why I must save you."

She spread her wings as she jumped, using them to guide her fall. The entire grand cathedral was consumed with fire, and the smaller, adjacent buildings that housed the various keepers were now starting to crumble as well. The surviving human remnants were gathered into two groups, barely holding off the combined forces of the Forgotten Children at the southern and western entrances. No doubt Logarius thought himself achieving a great victory, but he was blinded by rage. He was consumed by hate.

Her son did not see his dead brothers and sisters scattered across the stairs leading up to the three main gates, but she did. He did not see the future cost. Humanity had a way of absorbing defeats and letting them fuel their retaliation. He might think a glorious victory would greet him at the dawn. Instead, he would face a mob armed to the teeth and seeking vengeance. Belvua would not be safe. The Cradle itself would never be safe.

In response to the Wardhus fires, an entire human army had secretly dispatched by boat from the east and sailed into port. While the avenria slept, the army surrounded the nearby forest that they'd made into their home. At the time, Logarius had been leading a guerrilla campaign in the northwest against encroaching settlements. He'd entrusted his daughter to Evelyn's care. The forests were supposed to be safe. They were too dense and easily defended, and their lumber and game were vital to Wardhus's survival during the harsh winter months.

And yet the army burned hundreds of acres of it down to ash and cinder.

There was no safety from humans, Evelyn had learned. It was their greatest strength and vilest curse. When their blood was boiling, and their hearts filled with rage, they could make mountains crumble, and to the void with whoever might die beneath the rubble. Her granddaughter's little lungs had been unable to handle the sheer amount of smoke as Evelyn carried her during their panicked escape for the forest's edge. She'd passed quietly, peacefully, just a small, still bundle in her arms when clean air finally greeted them. The same peaceful death could not be said for those the humans captured while fleeing.

Yes, she understood her son's rage. She knew why he believed himself forgotten by the dragons who'd made them. But he had not witnessed humanity's full potential for cruelty. He had not seen how freely they would sacrifice of themselves to ensure their opponents suffered worse.

"Even now they fight you," she whispered as she surveyed the emerging battlefield. She suspected the city guard had responded quicker than her son had anticipated, along with the aid of two spellcasting humans, which together forced the Forgotten Children to fight on two fronts. The bulk of the conflict was currently focused on the western-facing portion of the cathedral's triangular outer wall. Lyra's Door had a dozen Soulkeepers holding strong, and twice that many Faithkeepers and Mindkeepers backing them up. It seemed they had started to embrace the power they had once wielded in the wars of old, for she heard their hymns floating across the battle, healing wounds, protecting fallen humans, and blinding foes with searing light.

Logarius would not take such resistance lightly. She searched for her son, knowing he'd want to be close to the action and yet still far enough back that he could direct forces to each emerging threat.

"There you are."

He was opposite Alma's Greeting, leading a squad of his Forgotten Children against a large group of humans who had escaped through the rubble of Alma's Greeting. Her son's wings were spread wide and his arms lifted in a chant. Shadows crawled from his wings along the ground like vipers, growing sharp fang-like protrusions as they reached the defensive outer line. The devotions of the keepers kept back many, but not all. They tore at the legs of the Soulkeepers, bringing down two. Seeing that power used on the humans was a splinter stabbed into Evelyn's heart. Avenria were created to protect humans from the void, and yet her son wielded the void's own power as a blade against humanity.

Evelyn drew Whisper-Song into her hands and leapt with a mighty beat of her wings. They carried her across the battlefield, and she did her best not to notice the dead dragon-sired that lay scattered upon the cobbles, killed by keeper prayers or a Soulkeeper bullet. The dead humans far outnumbered the dragonsired, but Evelyn knew humanity could endure such casualties, for their kind blanketed three-fourths of the Cradle. Could the same be said for the dragon-sired?

Evelyn tucked her wings and tilted her body so she dove heel first. Though she could have struck him unnoticed, she chose to land just behind Logarius and instead bury Whisper and Song into the backs of two human Ravencallers assisting with their own curses.

"My, my, my," she said, and she yanked her sickles from the bodies. "What a troublesome little boy my son has become."

The deep shadows across Logarius's wings retreated as he turned. His throat clucked a bitter laugh.

"Just as my dear mother taught me. Have you come to witness our victory? Or would you yet again plead for me to show mercy to the undeserving?"

Whisper and Song shimmered with blue fire as her knees bent and her head dropped low.

"Can you fault a woman for trying?"

Dagger met sickle, almost casually, a playful hit to start a battle neither desired. The two danced through the heart of the sprawling chaos, a little whirlwind of shadows and feathers. She parried aside a thrust, dashed past three city guards locked in battle with a foxkin, and quickly turned to parry another. Her son was faster than her. Youth was on his side, which meant focus and experience had to be on hers. She forced him back with a curling overhead chop, then blindly leapt backward with an accompanying flap of her wings. The moment he tried to follow, she pivoted her body, dug in her heels, and met his charge.

His long daggers were positioned perfectly to block her sickles, but she'd expected as much. Her true focus was her elbow that struck the side of his beak and her knee that slammed deep into his gut, robbing him of breath. Perhaps if she pressed harder, she could break him, even kill him, but guilt robbed her of that killing instinct. Instead she backed up, her mind racing for a way to convince her son of his folly. He needed little time to recover, and his attacks renewed with a fresh surge of anger and strength. Evelyn blocked once, twice, then cut at his neck to force out a dodge.

"You damn monsters!" a charging Soulkeeper shouted as he swung an enormous axe in a wide arc as if he meant to cut through the both of them. Evelyn dropped to her knees and arched her back like a dancer, furious that she let the bulky man get near without her noticing. The heavy steel flashed overhead, and she cried out as it nicked a gash upon the bridge of her beak. Her son reacted quicker, and with much greater aggression. He somersaulted over the axe, his wings turning to shadow so the axe head passed through them without drawing blood, and then landed upon the Soulkeeper's shoulders with his heels. Logarius's weight brought the Soulkeeper down. His daggers took his life.

Evelyn flexed the muscles in her lower back to pull herself up to a stand. Blood trickled down her beak, the pain a vicious sting that watered her eyes. She jammed Whisper and Song onto their hooks at her belt and sprinted, buying herself precious seconds to recover as her son finished off the Soulkeeper. She passed through the battlefield, her mind awash with sounds that transported her centuries into the past. She'd led so many raids against human settlements that these sights, these cries, were commonplace. The constant chorus of flamestone. The way humans howled in pain when they received a blow they instinctively knew to be fatal. The solemn prayers piercing the cacophony, bringing the power of the Sisters to counter the inherent magic of the dragon-sired.

A hunting cry stole her attention to an owl diving overhead at a trio of Mindkeepers with hands lifted in synchronized prayer. A half-second before the owl grabbed them in his extended talons, his body exploded in a shower of gore against an impassable holy circle that shimmered into existence. Evelyn looked away and pretended not to feel the splash of blood upon her clothes. Pistol shots echoed, and she felt a tug on her sleeve from a bullet missing her skin by less than an inch. Behind her, a fireball exploded in the sky like a ruptured star.

*Need higher*, she thought. *Need to face Logarius alone.*

Evelyn shifted her path again, sprinted straight for the outer wall surrounding the grand cathedral. Though her wings could not grant her flight, they could boost her leaps. Evelyn soared ten feet, kicked higher off the wall, flapped her wings again to push her back toward it, and then dug the sharp metal claws of her gloves into the stone. Another flap of her wings accompanied her pull, breaking little chunks of rubble free as she vaulted herself all the way to the top of the wall.

Too close to Alma's Greeting. The wall was unsteady, much of it cracked, and the chaotic fight underneath posed too much of a threat. She ran, her son at her heels. Up ahead, the battle at Lyra's Door raged, but here, near the corner, things were quiet, almost peaceful. At last she turned and drew Whisper-Song so she might face her son.

"Don't you understand?" she asked as she wiped blood from her beak. "We haven't reawakened to take back what was ours. This isn't some glorious return for our kind. Humanity has set its roots deep over the centuries. We cannot yet fathom their numbers. You use my book to foster a war that will only lead to our destruction."

Logarius paced at the wall's edge, his daggers twirling in his fingers. She recognized the habit, one born of unease. So many times she'd scolded him, insisting he'd give away his emotions during a fight. She thought she'd broken him of it, and perhaps for a time she had. Right now, it felt like both of them had regressed to when they were younger, he her student, she his teacher, and a tranquil forest the only witness to their constant duels.

"You truly believe we can lead a peaceful coexistence?" her son asked.

"I don't know," she said. "But it is our only hope. Your way leads to extinction."

"Not if the dragons help us! Not if they rage against the Goddesses like we know they can!"

Evelyn sadly shook her head.

"I once held congress with Viciss and Gloam. Just as the dragons made us, the Goddesses made the dragons. They will not betray their maker."

"You're wrong!" Logarius seethed as he paced. "We were forced into slumber *because* they betrayed the Sisters. The dragons are not of one mind in this matter. Some would see to humanity's extinction, and it is no impossible task. Do you know why we reawakened? The real reason for our return?"

Her son settled into a low stance, his wings folding around him like a cloak. Behind him, a fresh wave of Soulkeepers pushed out Lyra's Door, backed by the glowing hands of multiple Faithkeepers deep in prayer.

"We've returned because the Goddesses can hold us back no longer. Now is our time to stand tall and claim our rightful place, no matter how great the sacrifice. I won't live my life in fear of their retribution. I won't forgive them for what they've taken from us. Centuries passed, but they are still the same stagnant, simpleminded beasts they've always been. Let us cleanse them from the world. Once they are gone, the Goddesses will have no reason to care for the Cradle. They'll leave us in peace, to live in the world that should have been before their interference."

"Your hope is beyond foolish," Evelyn said. "It's suicide."

"Sitting around hoping the humans accept us as equals is suicide. This is the only life left for us, and we must claim it in blood."

This was it. There would be no retreat, and no convincing her son to withdraw. He leapt upon her with unmatched ferocity, his daggers displaying every shred of skill she'd passed down over the countless hours of training. She blocked a cut with Whisper, failed a parry with Song that left a stinging cut along her forearm, and then kicked at his midsection in an unsuccessful attempt to gain space. Instead he absorbed the blow and drew closer, closer, his every move meant to draw her hands out wide. Too late, she realized his goal. Too late, for his hands were upon her wrists and his daggers dropped upon the stone wall.

He slammed his head against her, beak to beak. Hers, already brittle with age and now wounded from an axe, suffered far worse. Pain whited out her mind. Blows rained down upon her. A heel to her knee crumpled her to the stone like a puppet whose strings had been cut. The handles to Whisper-Song slipped from her fingers. Panic forced her to move, to ignore the pain, but she was so disorientated she didn't even know which way to dodge. By the time she stood, she was disarmed. By the time her vision cleared, there was a blade at her throat.

"Submit," Logarius said, his chest heaving with his every breath. "Swear your loyalty, before I must live with your blood on my conscience."

Evelyn pulled back her shoulders and stared her son in the eye. She would not cower, nor would she beg. Whisper's edge hovered an inch from her throat, its blue flames licking at the soft feathers there. Blood trickled from the crack near her left nostril. Her leg ached like the void, and she wondered if she'd cracked her kneecap during their tumble. She felt every one of her many years weighing upon her back like jagged stones. She could not lift her wings, so they wrapped about her shoulders like a heavy cloak.

"Stop this murder," she said. "We won't survive the long road through hatred, only through desperate hope."

"Hope?" he asked. "Why do you think I perform this butchery?

Hope is what I fight for. The hope that a world exists free of humans, so that we may live in happiness. A world of peace. A world for our children..."

Evelyn stepped closer so that the sickle's edge pressed against her neck.

"That isn't the world you're creating," she said. She gestured to the bloody carnage and fields of corpses. "This pointless death is. If this is the world you'd seek, then cut my throat, my son. There will be no place for me within."

Whisper's blade trembled. Tears slid over the midnight feathers at the corners of Logarius's eyes.

"Humans will never accept us," he said softly. "Let us at least die raging against the world that would burn us upon a pyre."

Evelyn finally saw a spark of the little avenria she'd raised in those rare peaceful months before the long war. Before she'd sold her own soul for blood and slaughter. She reached out and gently stroked the side of her son's beak.

"If we are to die, let us die whole. Let us die pure. Not as murderers of children and innocents."

She watched Logarius's chest shudder. Whisper pulled back an inch. He could not meet her eye. He was at a loss for words. So close, she knew. So close to stepping back from the abyss he had welcomed with open arms.

The western sky lit with pale light, and the realm of souls trembled. Together they turned and bore witness to a power that never should have been granted to human hands. Death followed, and it shook both avenria to their core.

"You would have me hope," Logarius said. "I see no hope. I see only our end."

Song's hilt whipped against the back of her head, crumpling her to her knees as her son cried out for his Forgotten Children to flee.

# CHAPTER 39

Devin led the charge through Alma's Gate, roaring a battle cry. A gargoyle leapt into his path, and Devin fired one of Tommy's magical shots straight down its throat. Frost covered the gargoyle's upper body. Shards of ice ruptured its belly, and its dying shriek was but one of dozens echoing constantly through the night. Two other Soulkeepers who'd accompanied him crashed into a trio of foxkin, their larger weapons beating back the smaller creatures.

"Down!" Lyssa shouted at his side, having matched him step for step. Devin dropped immediately, trusting her enough not to ask or hesitate. A lapinkin's spear cut where he'd been, and it seemed the earth shook upon the creature's landing. The spear dragged along the ground, slowing the lapinkin's momentum, and during that brief opening Lyssa descended upon him with her short swords. Her first slash severed his wrists, denying him a chance to harness the wind to his defense. The next three were all across his throat and chest, killing him.

Devin pushed back to his feet, his hands moving with practiced ease. He had a single shot left of the magical ammunition Tommy made for him, a red and black orb whose only description he'd received upon asking was "really scary fire." Devin slid it into the chamber and fully cocked the hammer. If there was a better time to discover what exactly that meant, he didn't want to find out.

"Stand back," Devin ordered the other two Soulkeepers who had accompanied their charge. Tommy had formed a curved wall of ice surrounding him and Malik as their only defense, but it wouldn't mean much to the lapinkin and owls that hovered in the air above. Malik's hands were in constant motion, and Devin watched multiple owls veer aside when diving, seemingly confused or frightened. An intriguing defense, but whatever it might be, the lapinkin weren't affected. Heart in his throat, Devin watched three dive in unison, their spears leading.

His pistol swung up on instinct. He gave no thought to his aim, instead trusting his training. His finger squeezed the trigger. The hammer fell, and the flamestone split in half, releasing the spell. Devin glimpsed a crackling orange orb no bigger than a sunflower seed streak above the battlefield. His aim was true. The orb struck the center of the three diving lapinkin and ignited.

All light from the stars vanished beneath the sudden inferno that erupted in a perfectly contained sphere dozens of feet wide. Flames rolled across its surface, which was somehow translucent, allowing a glimpse into black lightning arcing from its center. The three bodies trapped within were dark shadows, and they dissolved into ash that blistered away into nothing against the heat. All the while it emitted a roar that sent the rest of the owls veering away.

The spell blinked out of existence, its absence leaving a deafening calm in its wake.

"'Scary fire,'" Devin whispered in awe. "Holy shit, Tommy. Next time give specifics."

Despite the distance between them, he could clearly hear Tommy's excited "whoop" as his friend leapt into the air and pumped his fist.

"Do you see that?" he shouted, as if all of Londheim hadn't just witnessed the eruption.

"Dear Sisters above, that was insane," Lyssa said. She grinned beside Devin and twirled her pistols. "Got any of those for me?"

"All out," Devin said. He holstered his pistol and gripped his sword in both hands. The rest of the Forgotten Children were regrouping, their attack clearly not going as planned. The prayers of the Mindkeepers kept guards and Soulkeepers fighting through wounds that should have been fatal. Flamestones erupted in a constant chorus from those Soulkeepers, making every dive from the owls, lapinkin, and wasps a potentially fatal mistake. The Forgotten Children were all vicious fighters, but with the pouring in of city guards that had accompanied Tommy and Malik's arrival, they were now significantly outnumbered.

Sadly the damage looked already done. The great cathedral burned on all sides. The roof had collapsed in multiple locations, the stained glass charred black, the walls crumbling underneath supports no longer able to hold the weight of so much stone. It made Devin's heart ache seeing the destruction.

"We should join up with Forrest," Devin said, and he nodded toward where the Vikar was leading a squad of four Soulkeepers against the largest group of foxkin and avenria on the steps of the Sisters' Remembrance. "If we can scatter the—"

He froze. A lone combatant tore through the foxkin before Vikar Forrest could arrive, having ambushed the dragon-sired from behind. The world slowed for a brief moment, and then Devin's legs were pumping, his heart pounding, as he rushed past his Vikar, past the Soulkeepers, and wrapped his arms around a blood-soaked Jacaranda.

"You're all right," he said, holding her against him as relief swept away a thousand lingering worries. "I didn't know where you were."

"Busy," she said, returning his embrace. "I'll tell you all about it later. What in the Goddesses' names is going on out here?"

Devin stepped away to survey the battlefield. With the foxkin brought low by Jacaranda, Forrest had veered his men farther south, engaging with a growing force of Ravencallers and avenria.

Lyssa had joined them, he noticed, instead of staying with him. Had she noticed Jacaranda as well?

"The Forgotten Children are trying to burn down the cathedral," he said, turning back to her. "Sadly I think they've succeeded."

"Not that your church deserves it, but point the way, and I'll help defend it," Jacaranda said.

"We could certainly use the help," he said, and then kissed a clean spot on her forehead. "Follow me. I think there's still—"

He had no time to finish the thought, nor did his plans for the battle matter, for they quickly became irrelevant.

Adria arrived, and she announced her presence with the strength and fury of a storm.

Nine souls swirled around her in a protective orbit. She guided them with ease. Whenever a foe dared to approach, be they dragon-sired or Ravencallers, the souls would veer off and burn straight through their chests. Various prayers from Lyra's Devotions sang from her voice in volume far beyond human capabilities. Lapinkin fled, but not fast enough to avoid their bodies bursting into flames so hot it charred them down to the bone in seconds. Blinding light lit up the sky above, sending owls and gargoyles crashing into rooftops with each searing blast that leapt from her upraised palms.

A squad of Ravencallers that had lurked near the Sisters' Remembrance turned her way, curses on their tongues. An extension of Adria's hand sent all nine souls ripping through the group, the Ravencallers' mere flesh no obstacle to the power of the heavens. Light rolled out from her in waves, somehow hardening into a substance like glass that slashed through the unarmored skin of the avenria. Nothing seemed beyond her. Nothing seemed capable of stopping her. Devin knew she was his sister, but looking upon her now, he saw only a phantom resemblance to the woman he knew.

This being was a goddess incarnate. She was a terror, an unstoppable whirlwind of holy power.

"Devin! To me!"

He turned, the cry pulling him out of his awed daze. There, down one of the smaller streets west of the burning cathedral, he saw Evelyn waving for his attention. He lifted his arms, trying to gesture his confusion for what she wanted.

"Logarius!" she screamed, and then she dashed down the cobbles.

"Logarius?" Jacaranda asked. "What of him?"

"She's not led us wrong yet," Devin said. He glanced back at his sister and the destruction she unleashed. "Adria can handle the rest here."

The two sprinted after Evelyn, leaving the last chaotic remnants of battle behind. With her dark wings, she was naturally camouflaged in the night, and her speed was greater than their own. He quickly lost sight of her and had to guess as to her direction. The sounds of the cathedral battle faded, and he strained his ears listening for the beat of wings or the thud of a boot. Soon he heard the familiar cry of steel on steel, and the two made a beeline toward the source.

Devin felt a jolt hit his heart from the sight spread out before the two-story home. A pair of avenria lay dead on either side of its doorway, their dark blue blood spilling out across the cobbles. Evelyn sat with her back against the doorframe, her head bowed low over her chest and her arms relaxed at her sides. Her wings splayed out limply behind her. More blood coated her gray clothes.

"Evelyn?" Devin asked. He knelt beside her and gently touched her shoulder.

"Oh," she said, stirring as if from a dream. "It's you. I must have dozed off."

He couldn't say for sure, given the differences in biology, but he'd wager based on the look in her eyes that she'd suffered a concussion.

"Where's Logarius?" he asked, but only after she'd gathered herself.

"Inside," she said. "The fireplace. You must…" She stopped and grimaced, her left hand releasing a dagger to clutch her waist. Devin glimpsed a tear in her shirt, and plentiful blood surrounding the area. "My son is in there. He's going to release the void and let it swallow everyone and everything in Londheim."

"We'll stop him," Jacaranda said. "Don't you worry."

Evelyn grabbed his coat when he tried to enter the building.

"I'm sorry," she said. "This was my burden, and I failed. Don't let my blunder cost thousands."

"We won't," he said, gently taking her gloved hand and squeezing it. "I promise."

The two passed through the door and into the main living room. Devin knelt before the fireplace, and sure enough, the back of it had opened up to reveal a painfully familiar dark tunnel. Together they crawled within and ran in silence. Time was of the essence. The void was a hungry, vile entity. To let it slip past the stars' protection and greedily feed upon Londheim was an unfathomable fate neither could allow to pass.

Everything of the dome within was as Devin remembered. The walls were covered with a field of stars. A triangular well rested within the center of its barren stone floor, collecting a spider silk strand of starlight that dripped down into it. A lone avenria stood at its edge, his hands raised high above his head. His continuous keening cry flooded Devin with shivers. Shadows curled around the edges of the well, which was cracked and crumbling.

"Enough, Logarius," Devin said. He drew his sword and readied it in both hands. "We won't let you destroy the city."

The avenria's hands lowered to his sides, and the hilts of the sickles buckled there. Devin recognized those weapons.

Whisper-Song, the sickles of his mother. Somehow he must have taken them from her.

"Destroy the city?" Logarius asked, tilting his head. "I am saving this city. The void won't go far beyond this district. Your cathedral, your keepers and slavers, let them be taken into darkness so we may keep our home."

"Your stolen home," Jacaranda said as she slowly walked the edge of the room, searching for a flanking position. Logarius watched her from the corner of his eye but showed no apparent fear of her.

"Again with this drivel. Do you know why we were imprisoned, humans? Do you know why all of our kind were banished for centuries by your beloved Goddesses?"

"I don't," Devin said. "But the Sisters would not have done so without reason, that I am certain of."

"Oh yes, they had their reason." Logarius gestured to the well, and to the second tunnel leading to the even grander chamber that had housed Adria when she underwent her transformation. "You were made by the Goddesses, but the dragons are our creators, our fathers and mothers. Yet those dragons spent centuries creating *this*. Machinery harnessing the power of the stars to grant your people control over souls. A way for you to exist without need of the Sisters. Freedom from the chains that have held you enslaved to their whims. So when the Sisters discovered their plan, when they discovered they might no longer be needed by their precious little pets, for first time in their celestial existences they felt fear."

Anger built with Logarius's every word until he physically shook with rage.

"We were imprisoned because of *you*. Our beloved creators tried to help you, to save you, and for that we suffered. Can you even fathom our hopelessness, humans? Can you comprehend our rage? Imagine if, despite all your prayers and devotions, the Sisters turned and gave the world to us dragon-sired. Would you still serve loyally? Would you worship the beings who openly denied you a future? Or would you *rage?*"

He pointed one sickle at Devin and the other at Jacaranda.

"You say we stole Low Dock from you. I say you stole the world." He jammed the hilts of his sickles together, locking them in place and extending them into a singular double-bladed weapon. "Come bleed upon Whisper-Song. Let fate decree which of us committed the greater crime."

Logarius spun on his heels, his wings flaring out wide so that shadow enveloped his form. The momentary obfuscation allowed him to shift his attention to Jacaranda unnoticed, deeming her at his flank a greater threat. She staggered backward, surprised by the switch and immediately forced onto the defensive. Her weapons moved with precision, but the sickles were such strange weapons, far from the usual sword or dagger she might have faced.

Devin dashed in, refusing to let Jacaranda fight alone. Logarius quickly shifted, using cover of his dark wings to provide a screen to his movements. Steel clashed against steel, Devin's overhead chop an easy thing to push aside despite him throwing all his strength behind it. Jacaranda cut for his waist, missed, and received a kick to her sternum for her efforts. Logarius tried to follow up with a fatal slash with his curved sickles but Devin denied him the opportunity. He grit his teeth against the strain as the muscles in his arm bulged, seemingly sheer willpower the only thing keeping his sword in the way of that downward strike.

"So much shit about fate," Devin said upon finally shoving the avenria away. "Just admit you want to kill me and enjoy it."

Logarius's blue eyes narrowed. A smile was impossible on the avenria's beaked face, but he suspected he received the equivalent when his foe spoke.

"You are right," he said. "I will very much enjoy ripping that wagging tongue of yours from your throat with my beak."

Logarius swirled back into motion. Whisper-Song looped with

him, constantly turning so that the two sickles appeared one singular, blurry circle of burning steel. Devin parried the first cut at his chest, then a second at his throat. Despite his every instinct warning him to retreat, he knew he had to keep up the pressure. Should the avenria get the chance to engage one on one, there was little doubt among any of the three there who would come out victorious.

Devin had fought together with other Soulkeepers, with bonds forged over hard, aching months under the hot summer sun in the training field of the Cathedral of the Sacred Mother. He knew what it was like to rely on another, to anticipate their moves and try to act accordingly. Fighting with Jacaranda was wholly different. He didn't always know what she'd do when a gleaming sickle cut her way. She might parry, she might step aside, or she might even contort in ways that seemed to defy physics, ducking her head underneath strikes while twisting and shifting her feet to dance herself out of harm's way while still maintaining her speed.

What he did know was that he trusted her without hesitation. If he found his feet out of position, she was there to pull Logarius's attention aside. Should he falter, lifting his sword to block what turned out to be a feint, one of her short swords would lash out and deflect a lethal blow. When he went on the offensive, battering Whisper-Song with chop after chop, he knew she would either pause to catch her breath or join right in alongside him, overwhelming the avenria with raw energy.

That trust, that perfect synchronicity, finally garnered them the first blood of the fight. Devin chopped overhead in a mighty swing, forcing Logarius to dodge aside rather than try to block with his sickles. Jacaranda was ready for him, cutting off the easy path of retreat. He turned, trying to bat aside her short swords while he danced away from Devin's strike. She was faster, and the end of her blade cut across the avenria's arm, spilling blue blood upon the pale stone.

A keening raven-cry was Jacaranda's reward for the cut. Logarius spun faster, and he used his wings as an additional weapon. The feathers turned to shadow and passed across Jacaranda's eyes, blinding her. Whisper-Song's long handle struck her neck, Logarius planted his feet, and then he pulled. For one horrifying moment Devin thought he was about to watch Jacaranda's head be sliced off, but her instincts were up to the task. Instead of trying to get out of the way of the sickle, she moved with it, colliding her body with the avenria's.

Logarius fumbled a moment, his weapon much too long and clumsy to be useful at such range. His beak struck the side of her face, drawing blood, and then he shifted Whisper-Song so its handle was between them and shoved. A dazed Jacaranda tumbled to the ground. Devin immediately shifted his sprint so he slid to a stop just before her, his sword up to block a potential killing blow.

That attempt never came. Instead Logarius retreated back to the center of the domed room and to the opposite side of the triangular well. Whisper-Song struck the well's side with a heavy crack. The walls shook with its reverberations. The air split just above it like a scab upon reality covering pitch black darkness. Six-fingered hands reached out from within the mass. Logarius chopped them off at the wrist, then raised his open palm. Shadows wafted off his scaled fingers, lashing the tear, sealing it away.

"We were given mastery over the void," the avenria said. He turned his attention to the severed hands thrashing at his feet. "Made protectors and saviors for a humanity that loathes us. Our very existence is a sick joke."

The hands broke apart like ice beneath warm sunlight. The formless mass they became swirled about Logarius's legs, across his chest, and settled upon his hands as they gripped Whisper-Song's shaft.

"You place blame upon us for things we never demanded," Devin said. He helped Jacaranda to her feet and prayed her injuries were not too severe. "If you would rage against the dragons and the Sisters, then do so, but this is neither."

"Their time will come," Logarius said. "Even the arrogant Goddesses will be forced to show their faces once their beloved humanity is threatened with extinction. For now, we'll start small. With this little district. With you."

The avenria ripped Whisper-Song apart at the midsection with an audible clang of metal. The void essence flowed from his hands down to the sickles, bathing their blades entirely. With every swish and movement, the sickles left a trail of shadow to linger in the air. Devin braced his legs and raised his sword, unsure of what it might mean. Jacaranda spaced herself from him, preparing to flank yet again.

Logarius lunged, his body rotating to give his weapons strength. Devin raised his sword to block. Both void-cursed sickles connected simultaneously, but they did not slow. They did not ring out with the sound of metal on metal. Instead the void ate straight through the steel, severing his sword in half.

*That's not fair*, Devin thought as he staggered backward. Logarius continued turning, bringing the sickles up and around for another slash. Devin dove away, hit the ground in a roll, and reached for his pistol. A lead shot was his only hope now. Jacaranda saw his desperation and jumped between the two to defend him, but there was little she could do to battle against a foe whose very weapons could break her own. Her honed reflexes were her best bet, and she twisted and ducked beneath strike after strike while constantly seeking an opening. Twice she cut through the fabric of the avenria's shirt or trousers, but never deep enough to draw blood. The creature was too fast, and too well trained.

"Down!" Devin shouted as he rose to his feet, his thumb cocking the hammerlock to his pistol. Jacaranda reacted immediately, granting him a clean shot. Logarius didn't try to dodge. Instead he swirled his sickles before him, the void presence floating off them.

The flamestone erupted with a deafening blast in the confined room. The shot should have struck Logarius directly through his left eye. Instead it reflected off a shield of absolute darkness.

"Such meager tools," Logarius said. "Your race cannot hope to stand against our innate gifts."

Jacaranda tried to stab him while he gloated. Logarius released the shield, the void presence returning to his sickles. This time he was prepared for her attacks. His first slash cut her short sword in half, and when he followed it up with his other hand, she blocked on instinct. The short sword dropped in pieces, same as her first. She retreated immediately, cursing with every step.

"Not fucking fair," Devin said as he pulled another flamestone from his pouch. It seemed Logarius had no desire to allow another shot. He crossed the distance in a heartbeat, feinted Devin into a dodge, and flung his wing like a disrespectful slap across Devin's entire body. He hit the ground hard on his left hip, and his cry of pain was stifled by a kick to his teeth.

"Our victory is coming," Logarius said as he lorded over him. "No matter the cost, we shall pay it gladly."

Devin reached for his broken sword only to have Logarius stomp on his fingers with his boot. He screamed, fearing them broken. Jacaranda dove at the avenria despite being unarmed. A swift kick to her midsection ended her attack. She plummeted to her knees and retched. The shadows beneath Logarius deepened, as if his wings were a river of darkness that flowed unending to the stone.

"You'll kill thousands of innocents!" Devin screamed at him. "Men and women who did you no wrong!"

Logarius shook his head. His wings shimmered.

"Do you not listen?" he asked. "A future for our kind, no matter the cost."

The shadows behind him elongated, and from within them rose a hooded face, wings, and long, curling daggers.

"Some costs are too great," Evelyn said. The sharp points of her daggers thrust into the small of his back. "And we pay without joy. Only blood."

Evelyn guided him to the ground, her daggers remaining lodged into his wiry frame. Logarius gasped and twisted to look upon the face of his mother as he collapsed. That much hurt, that much betrayal, was more than Devin could bear, and he quickly turned away.

"You all right?" he asked Jacaranda. Blood dripped from her split lip, and already he could see bruises forming across her stomach through her ripped and torn shirt.

"Could be better," Jacaranda said, accepting his offered hand to stand up. She leaned on him for a moment, and Devin took the opportunity to kiss her forehead and hold her close. When they separated, he looked to Evelyn, who knelt over the body of her son. Her wings curled about her, draping both in shadow. Soft whispers floated off her tongue as she stroked her son's head.

"Evelyn," he said, wishing he knew what to say or do to ease her hurt.

"Please," she said. "Leave an old woman to her grief."

Such a simple request, but it was all either Devin or Jacaranda could offer, and so they gave her that solitude in the chamber of magic, stars, and the void.

# CHAPTER 40

Dierk's heart was in his throat as he followed the squad of city guards toward the smoldering cathedral ruins. He'd been kept abreast of the situation when the attack first started, and once it was deemed safe, he'd subtly hinted to his controlled father that he would be the one to visit. He knew to expect significant damage, but he could hardly focus on that. Adria Eveson was also at the cathedral, and he could not wait to meet her again.

Gawkers and gossipers formed a surrounding ring about the cathedral grounds, the area far too large for city guards to fully cordon off. A few gruff shouts forced the crowd to make way. Dierk arrived at the front steps leading up to Alma's Greeting and surveyed the damage. The bell tower that housed the Mindkeepers was a hollowed-out husk. The south-facing wall was charred but not too badly damaged. Worse was the cathedral proper farther inside. Its stained windows were melted and broken, its roof collapsed, and its stone sides smeared black with char. Seemingly every empty space nearby was occupied with the body of a soldier, guard, or member of the church. Blankets covered their faces, granting them some sort of dignity as they awaited their funeral pyre.

"Thank you for coming," a Faithkeeper told him, bowing low and shaking his head. Dierk didn't know his name, nor did he particularly care. The man was waiting for him, though, so he smiled and tried to be polite.

"Anything to help," Dierk said, his eyes looking everywhere for Adria.

"While the loss is devastating, we will be rebuilding immediately," the older man continued. "The church has much saved up for such emergencies, and what we lack, we believe the Ecclesiast will happily provide."

*They don't know we've been cut off by the Queen*, thought Dierk. Though perhaps the Keeping Church would still hold ties with West Orismund, even if the crown did not. It was something he needed to look into when he had a moment to himself. With the power vacuum left by the Queen's abandonment, there was a significant chance the church tried to fill it with even greater control than they already wielded.

"Just let me know what you need, and I will do my best to ensure my father provides," Dierk said. He stood up a little straighter. There, near the wall. His Adria. His beloved wonder.

"If you'd excuse me for a moment," he said. The Faithkeeper looked confused but acquiesced. Dierk hurried toward the Mindkeeper, and he cast a look at the city guards when they tried to follow. They obediently remained behind.

Adria sat against the burnt wall, her legs curled to her chest and her head bowed low. She looked a picture of weariness, and he briefly wondered if she slept. Her left arm was braced at the elbow atop her knee, palm extended, fingers curled. A soul floated just above her grasp, its soft light shining across her mask. Adria stared into the soul with unblinking eyes, and the rest of her body moved so little she might have appeared an immaculate statue.

When Dierk joined her side, she said nothing. She did not acknowledge his presence. After a long moment, Dierk coughed and struggled to find the proper words.

"Adria?" he said.

"Yes?" she asked, her voice cold.

"I, um, I know our last meeting was…awkward."

Her eyes never left the hovering soul.

"You could describe it as such."

He blushed.

"I wanted you to know, I've put a lot of thought into who I am, and who I want to be. I'm working on it, really, truly working on being a leader. It isn't right to want you to want me if I don't believe I'm worthy of it myself. Does—does that make sense?"

It was a long, agonizing moment before she spoke again. Still her gaze remained locked on that mysterious soul.

"Dierk, I know very little of you, and what you know of me cannot be much. I do not think your attraction to me is based on anything real."

"No, it's real," he said. "It's very real. I can see how special you are, and I want all of Londheim to know it! You're right, I don't know much else about you. I would like to, but for that to happen, I need to be someone you'd care to know in the first place. So I'm trying, I'm trying real hard."

At last she stood. The soul drifted behind her, casting its subtle light upon them both. Adria's hands smoothed out the folds of her dress, her trembling fingers worrying Dierk. The woman clearly needed rest.

"That is good of you," Adria said. "But don't do this for me. Improve yourself for your own sake, not mine."

She tried to leave him, but he quickly stepped in her way.

"It's not for you," he said, his words tumbling out faster and faster as if he feared he might lose her attention for good. "Not just for you, anyway. It's for me, too. Being better, smarter. Someone worthy of you. And I'll start out by helping with the cleanup. I'll help with everything, I swear, with rebuilding, the funeral rites, more workers, you name it. Whatever it takes, I will make this right."

"You can't make this right," Adria said. She gestured to the rows of bodies that lay scattered about the yard. "All this death? How could you?"

Dierk refused to let her wallow in such misery and pity. It was a bold move, but he reached out to take her by the wrist. She glared at him, her fury strong enough to wither him to dust if she wished it. He swallowed a shard of glass wedged in his throat and forced onward.

"I can see your soul," he said. "I can sense your power. You see them, too, don't you? Their languishing souls? Not just see. You wield them. Command them. I know you can heal wounded flesh. I know, I *know* that you can also soothe their souls. Do both. Bring them back to life."

Adria pulled her wrist free of him. Her mask hid so much of her emotions, but her eyes were visible, and in them he could see a full display of her fear and hesitation.

"I have done it only once," she said. "And it left me exhausted. Over a hundred dead are here. Which few should I choose to return?"

This was it. Dierk stood to his full height, thrust back his shoulders, and tried to look as strong as he felt.

"All of them," he said. "I cannot heal, nor can I resurrect, but I can give you the strength to do so. Lean on me, and together we will create miracles."

"How?"

"The prayer of Ravencallers," he said.

"Blasphemy," she whispered.

"They are prayers answered by Anwyn, and in the past they were granted to your keepers," he argued. "Can they truly be blasphemy if they are merely forgotten powers your church wielded as their own?"

Did she believe him? He couldn't tell. Dierk felt sweat gathering at his neck. The beauty of her soul, it shone so clearly through her mask it made his heart ache. He wanted to help her so badly, to provide this wondrous woman everything she needed to rise to her true potential. If only she'd listen. If only she'd see what he was capable of.

"Show me," she said, her inner debate ending.

Dierk lowered his hands to his sides, his palms open and upward. He'd gone over the prayer dozens of times in his mind on the walk over. He only needed one final ingredient.

"Grant me the soul of someone truly worthless, whose very existence is not deserving of eternity," he said. "I do not ask this lightly, Adria. For what we will do, a heavy price must be paid."

Adria gestured to the soul she had kept hovering nearby.

"This one should suffice," she said.

"Whose is it?" he asked, unable to hold back his curiosity.

"Vikar Thaddeus's," she said. "I found it among the rubble. I meant only to confirm his death, but when I looked inside…" She shook her head with disgust. "I saw his final moments. I dipped through his sickening memories. He was a vile man, and he deserved far worse than he received."

Dierk licked his lips in anticipation. The soul of a Vikar? Oh yes, that would suffice, that would suffice, indeed. Adria relinquished her hold upon the soul, and Dierk mentally grabbed it instead. It hovered over to him, a miniature star suspended mere inches from his chest. He sucked in a deep breath and steadied himself. This was it. This was his moment of truth.

"Anwyn of the Moon, hear me!" he began. "My strength wanes. My burdens bend my back and twist my neck. Before me lies one who has walked their final steps, and whose body crumbles, and whose soul is unfit to return to your bosom. Harvest their passing so I may carry on."

The power poured from the shimmering soul directly into his chest. He gasped as his senses awakened with new life. At the ritual he'd observed, that power had been scattered like raindrops across all participants, but not now. It was his, all his, and with it came an elevation of everything that it meant to be human.

He heard the sounds of conversation thousands of yards away, each individual whisper or cry clearly defined and separate from the rest. He lifted his hands slightly, and he felt each individual cord of muscle flex or relax beneath his skin. No, beyond that. He felt the acute tingle of the command that first pulsed from his brain to those muscles. When he brought his eyes to the heavens, he saw a swirling starscape akin to the vision he'd first glimpsed during the Ravencaller ritual.

Was this what it meant to be a goddess? Was this crackling excess of power the true reward of the Aether that made up the Goddesses' beings? If only it could last forever. He felt it burning out of him, his meager human flesh unable to contain it for long. If he weaned himself on it, he might last twenty or thirty minutes, but he had a far better plan than that. Dierk extended his hand toward Adria, and he gave her of his gift.

"Pray your prayers," he told her. "Give life to the dead."

Adria walked to the nearest body, which lay with a stained sheet draped over his face to give the dead novice some meager dignity. She did nothing to draw attention to herself. Her knees touched the ground, her hand gently touched his forehead, and then she whispered a prayer. Moments later she stood and moved on, not staying to witness the novice's fingers begin to twitch and his chest heave up and down.

Dierk saw the prayer dim the light of her brilliant soul, and he renewed it with his own. He was a conduit, siphoning power from the wretched dead soul and channeling it into Adria. He felt Thaddeus's memories begin to blur. The emotions of his life faded into one another. *Good*, thought Dierk. Eternity had no need of them.

Adria prayed over a second body, then a third. She mended torn flesh. She molded together broken bones and sewed together ripped limbs. Last she soothed their souls and latched them back to their physical shells. Dierk watched with tears in his eyes. She would do it, and all through his help. After every resurrection he gave her more. She would not feel exhaustion. She would not lack strength. Dierk was there for her.

It was by the fifth resurrected that the scattered crowd realized what was happening. She'd prayed over a man whose wife wept beside him, and when he sat up, his cleaved throat mended and his mouth locked in a smile, she cried to the heavens for Adria to accept her thanks.

"Now they'll see," Dierk whispered. "They'll all see what I see when I look at you."

Adria did not address the crying woman. She didn't even look her way. She continued her pace about the torched cathedral, kneeling before bodies, praying over them, and restoring life to the dead. All the while Dierk fed her, unnoticed, just the Mayor's son off in the distance watching like everyone else. The only thing someone might wonder at was the rapidly shriveling soul beside him, now no larger than a child's fist.

On and on, a parade of miracles. A crowd steadily grew around Adria, and it moved with her amid an eerie silence. Did they believe what they witnessed? Did these men and women fear to disrupt her trance? He didn't know. It wasn't his responsibility to know. Only empower Adria. Keep her going. Keep her strong to work her wonders.

After she resurrected her sixtieth victim, that of a city guard who had come to protect the cathedral in the later moments of the battle, the crowd finally stirred as if from a dream. It began as a lone woman singing, and it grew, and grew, until a hundred sang a simple hymn that children learned during their little classes between the ninth-day sermons. Only one thing was changed.

They did not sing praises "to the Sacred Mother, may she return."

They sang praises "to Blessed Adria, the Sacred returned."

"Keep going," Dierk whispered. His heart pounded in his chest, and his head ached with the worst migraine he'd had in his life. The enhanced awareness and understanding he'd felt when first praying the harvesting curse were long gone. The Vikar's soul was larger now, but only because it had unraveled like a ball of yarn. Its light floated before him, steadily feeding into his constricted chest. If Adria could remain strong, then so would he. Every single person who had died would live. He swore it upon his name, his father's name, and upon the brittle pages of the Book of Ravens.

After eighty-four lives, nothing remained of Thaddeus's soul. Dierk gave of himself. The invisible thread connecting him to Adria tightened. He gasped in agony. Two lives. Three. Four. He told himself to take joy in their awakening. They were so close. Adria was beginning to draw on her own soul as well, complementing his waning power. The crowd thronged, now well over two hundred. They'd ceased that first song and begun a second, equally simple.

"Joy to the Goddesses on high," they sang. "May we sing ever to your wonder."

The words may say otherwise, but Dierk knew it wasn't the Goddesses they praised. It was Adria, his beloved Adria. This was everything Dierk could have ever hoped for. He felt like an adult. He felt like a hero. At the one hundredth dead, Adria stood and declared herself finished. The crowd unleashed their love, the final spell holding them back broken. They wept. They begged. They reached to touch her, just touch her, as if her clothing were magic and her skin an anathema to the ills of the Cradle.

Dierk watched the crowd swarm her and wept. No one knew his pivotal role, no one but the lone person who mattered. His relief was overwhelming. His painful childhood and strangled emotions were a shadow in the distance. No longer did he feel like a disgusting mess of vices, outsider emotions, and constant fear. Instead he felt important. He felt needed. He felt like, at long last, he stood a chance to be at Adria's side, for her to finally see his love, and for her to show her love in return.

"We fulfill each other," he said, smiling as the crowd sang her name. "Two parts come together to perform miracles. Do you see now, Adria? Do you see?"

Tears trickled down his cheeks. His joy knew no bounds.

"We were meant for one another," he laughed. His words rose in volume until he was bellowing to the sky, his voice lost amid the joyous din.

"Meant for each other! We were meant to be, Adria! We were meant to be!"

# CHAPTER 41

Adria lay across Devin's couch, her hand draped over her eyes to block the light from Puffy's fire. Her head pounded with a migraine stronger than any she'd experienced in her life. It felt like she'd undergone an entire lifetime of struggles in the span of twenty-four hours. She desperately needed sleep but it would not come. In a cruel twist of fate, she lacked the herbs she normally gave others to help them rest when anxiety or pain kept them awake. She'd given away the last of them in what felt like a different age, when the chronimi mushroom had deprived many of their needed sleep.

The fire popped twice, and then the heat coming off increased. A smile crossed her lips. She'd shivered just a little, yet the firekin noticed. Such a lovely creature. If only the rest of the magical beings could be so kind. Memories of the battle came unbidden to her mind. A deep sense of trouble accompanied them. It wasn't disgust or horror from tearing apart their bodies or charring them to ash. No, her reaction worried her far more. She felt exhilaration at the power she'd wielded. She'd waded through a chaotic fight, and all the while she'd felt...invincible. Untouchable. Unbreakable.

Everything she often felt she was not.

"I think that's finally the last of them," Devin said, entering the home with a loud bang of the door. "They're more stubborn than a kicked mule."

"Don't judge them harshly," she said. "They're only scared and desperate."

A crowd of people had followed her when she retreated to Devin's house after she'd resurrected the one hundred who'd died during the attack on the Cathedral of the Sacred Mother. They didn't seem to know what they wanted from her. Being in her presence was enough for some, while others asked for nebulous blessings. Some just wanted to be touched and prayed over, as if she were one of the Goddesses and could anoint their lives with safety and abundance.

Oh, the people needing healing did come, like they always did if she stayed in one place for too long. Not even other keepers of the church developing similar healing gifts had helped her with that.

"I know they're scared, but that doesn't remove the entitlement some of them have," Devin said. She heard his rocking chair creak as he sat in it by the fire. "A few were demanding that you see them, and there was one wealthy bastard who threatened to report me to my superior. That guy's lucky I didn't pull my pistol on him. At least then he'd have something worth reporting to Forrest."

Adria mustered up a smile. It was the best she could do.

"My brother, ever the well-mannered diplomat," she said. "It's a wonder you weren't tossed back in the stockhouse after the attack."

"Having the most famous person in all of Londheim as a sister helps with that."

Adria cracked a smile. She had visited with both Vikar Forrest and Vikar Caria and confirmed to them Jacaranda's possession of a soul. That didn't clear her of the supposed killings at the Gentle Rose brothel, but Adria had insisted Jacaranda be allowed to stay at Devin's house while that matter was investigated. With a million and one things needing attention with the cathedral's destruction,

Vikar Thaddeus's apparent death in the fire, and the still unfilled Deakon seat, neither Vikar appeared eager to argue with her on the matter. Perhaps it was an abuse of her growing influence, but she didn't personally believe so. Devin was a good person at heart. Having him, or someone he loved, be put under arrest was nonsense she would not abide.

A fluttering sound opened her eyes. Tesmarie had flown to Devin's shoulder, and she reclined back and spread her wings.

"I'm just glad you two are both safe," the faery said. "It's been a long, long night and day."

"That it has, little one," said Devin. "I'm sorry you had to endure it with us. Tommy told me about what happened at their tower. I can think of no one less deserving of such cruelty."

Adria was not privy to that story, but from the corner of her eye she saw the faery slump down a little and bat away flecks of diamond tears.

"I'm good," she said. "Everything's good. I got you, right? And Tommy, and, and...Puffy. Family, right here in Londheim! Such a crazy, crazy world."

Devin kissed the air in her direction, and she batted it away like he'd lobbed a diseased rat. Adria allowed herself to laugh. No matter how awful times were, there'd still be the good. For now, she needed to rest. Tomorrow would bring new challenges, especially within the church's power structure. Goddesses help her, what a mess. Both a Deakon and a Vikar needed to be replaced, and she would be eyed for one of those positions.

Adria closed her eyes and told herself to relax. She could worry about her powers, the implications of mass resurrection, and her new church position tomorrow. For now, she only needed to...

She awoke to a loud knocking on the door. Devin swore as he rushed toward it, futilely trying to make it cease before it woke her.

"What?" he asked as he flung the door open.

"Em-emergency, Mister Soulkeeper," a young voice said.

"Ravencallers, they—they hung twelve children in the Tradeway Square. My Faithkeeper sent me to fetch Mindkeeper Adria. He was hoping she could help."

A novice, then, come for her aid. Adria sat up on the couch and swung her feet off.

"How long ago?" she asked as she rubbed sleep from her eyes.

"You don't need to do this," Devin said.

"How long?"

The novice, a young boy maybe ten or eleven years old, turned his attention her way.

"Not but an hour ago, miss."

Adria pushed herself up onto unsteady feet. Anger stirred in the pit of her stomach. She'd crushed them at the cathedral, so in petty vengeance the monsters would slaughter children? Despicable. She couldn't allow it. She wouldn't.

"Hand me my coat," she told Devin.

"Are you sure you don't need to rest longer?"

Adria shushed him with a glare.

"I'm going," she said. "Are you coming with?"

"Let me tell Jacaranda first," he said.

Once her coat was on, she stepped outside the house. The novice bowed low and glanced about nervously.

"I'll go tell them you're coming," he said before dashing off. Adria nodded absently. The pounding in her head had faded slightly, thank the Goddesses. She felt like she could think again. After a moment her brother exited with Tesmarie atop his shoulder.

"Where's Jacaranda?" she asked.

"It's been a rough day for her," he said. "She doesn't need to see this."

The square was about ten minutes by foot, so they began in earnest. Adria walked with her hands shoved into her pockets and her head bowed. The cold air bit at her skin. It was as if her insides had turned to ice, and been like that for hours. It didn't take long before her every muscle ached. She was pushing herself too hard, but what choice did she have? If she could bring life back to murdered children, then she would do it, the toll be damned.

"Sisters have mercy," Devin whispered upon their arrival of the Tradeway Square.

Adria calmly walked into the center of the hanging corpses. Everything about it was a blasphemy intended to hurt her very soul. Three lines of bodies hung from ropes tied to the nearby buildings. They were suspended by the wrists and throat, four in each line, to form an upside-down triangle. Their chests were flayed. Their innards were spilled out in skinny wet ropes that dangled mere inches above the bloodstained cobbles. They were children, just children, yet they'd suffered.

Their souls called out to her, and she touched them one by one almost on reflex. The memories of their tortuous deaths overwhelmed her. She felt their pain, their fear, their trauma. What monsters would do such a thing?

She need not ask, for as she stood within that triangle, she saw them emerge all across the surrounding rooftops.

"Hello, Adria," said a foxkin garbed in brown clothes and a long cloak. His red and orange fur swirled together in waves. "We've been waiting for you."

Adria mentally kicked herself. The novice who'd summoned them. She'd been so groggy she hadn't noticed, but now the memory shone clearly in her mind. There'd been no soul shining within that novice's skull. A dragon-sired creature, likely one of the shapeshifting foxkin. Adria clenched her hands into fists and cursed her carelessness.

"And here I am," she said, telling herself to remain calm. "Are you the one who sent the invite?"

"Indeed. I am Gerroth, second in command of the Forgotten Children, and we have brought you here to answer for your crimes."

"Crimes?" she asked as she lifted her arms. "Here I stand amid the corpses of slaughtered children and you would talk to me of *my* crimes?"

There were at least two dozen of the creatures, foxkin and avenria mostly. They wielded crossbows, each and every one of them, and they were all pointed her way. Her brother lifted his pistol, but she ordered him to stand down.

"Don't get yourself killed," she told him. Her eyes remained focused on the foxkin in charge. "So here I am. What judgment would you hand down upon me?"

She didn't listen for his answer. The moment he spoke, she reached out in her mind for the most worthless of souls, of a being whose loss no man or woman would weep for and whose location she had gleaned from her awful foray into Vikar Thaddeus's memories. With a call, the soul streaked through stone and sky faster than the blink of an eye to hover before her.

"I have shed enough blood to last a hundred lifetimes," Adria told the gathered monsters as Gerag Ellington's soul hovered just above her palm. "But I will shed more if I must."

"We have seen your power," Gerroth said. "It is mighty, but you cannot stop us all. Accept your death with grace. You are a power that should never have been unleashed upon the Cradle."

Adria had broken her connection with the children's souls, but still the gruesome memories pricked at her like needles. Her raw mind surmounted its exhaustion with rage.

"Have you?" she asked. Her own voice surprised her. It was calm. Deathly. "Have you truly seen my power?"

Crossbows bristled. Fingers tightened on triggers. She could sense Devin preparing to defend her, but she would not allow him to risk his life. These monsters, these vicious beings, had no idea whom they threatened.

"Not yet," she whispered.

Adria clutched Gerag's soul in her curled fingers, and before a single bolt might fly, she ripped the shining beacon of light and memories in half.

The explosion rocked through the square. It struck as a physical wave first, knocking the air from Adria's lungs and sending the few bolts that did fire veering off course. That initial hit was but the prelude. A second wave followed as Gerag's memories exploded outward in a rainbow fog. Adria felt it wash over her like fire. His memories, his emotions, they leaked and swirled without reason or order. It was pure chaos, and it warped the very physical blocks of reality.

The stone cobbles became sandy beaches, wood floors, and stretches of grass to fit the essence that floated over it. Devin laughed as something terribly humorous assaulted him. Other creatures sobbed, screamed, or staggered about in dazed confusion. The sky above filled half with stars, the other half with daylight, and it constantly switched between the two as the soul essence rolled outward.

Adria stood within this center, and she felt the unharnessed power begging to be used. All that had been Gerag—a wretched, lustful man prone to abuse and torture—was now scattered dust and starlight. There would be no permanence to him beyond the memories of others who knew him.

*Good*, she thought. *May your wretched existence be forgotten.*

The shimmering vortex extended hundreds of feet in all directions. Adria could sense the lives of every single creature within its power, be they human or dragon-sired. They were shadows cast across a field of light to her changed eyes. One by one she found those dragon-sired, those horrible monsters who had tortured and maimed innocent children, and she crushed them. She tore them. She ripped apart their hearts within their chests and shattered bones without a single bruise left upon their skin. They died, helpless, confused, and lost amid a sea of memories that were not theirs.

No mercy. No forgiveness. Every last dragon-sired would die. Adria's exhausted mind raged against the hollowness of their lives, of the deaths they had caused, of the field of corpses she had prayed over one by one at the cathedral. If only the Cradle could return to how it was. If only Londheim could be the sleepy city of shadows and corridors, and she a simple Mindkeeper of a small church tucked into the corner of humble Low Dock. As the essence of the broken soul collected inside her, she felt the very powers of creation at her fingertips, but she did not create, only destroy.

The colors passed, the emotions faded, and a shocked calm fell upon the now silent square.

"Adria?"

She turned to face her brother, and saw the crestfallen horror that had overtaken him. Her heart seized in her chest.

The dragon-sired. She'd killed them.

All of them.

Every last one.

"I'm sorry," she whispered.

Tesmarie's body lay perfectly still in Devin's hands. No breath. No flutter of wings. Tears trickled down Devin's face, but his voice remained completely flat.

"Such power," he said. "Yet we seem to only destroy."

"Please, Devin," she said. "I didn't know. I just...I was protecting us. All of us. And now that they're gone, these children, I can save them, too..."

Goddesses help her, his eyes, she could not look into his eyes. She recognized that pain. That brokenness.

"And what of her?" he asked. "What of Tes?"

Adria looked upon that tiny little body, but her eyes saw only vacant gray emptiness where there should have been a soul. These creatures, they weren't like humans. Even if she mended her broken bones and reknit her shredded organs, she didn't know how to reignite the spark of life. Still, she had to try. She outstretched her hand, and without need of praying the 36th Devotion, she harnessed the starlight power inside her to undo the damage to the little faery's body. The physical form molded at her touch, but it was as she feared. Death had settled over her being. Her sparkling life was gone.

"I'm so sorry, Devin. I can't bring her back."

Let a hundred blades fall upon her neck. Let a million birds peck at her flesh. Adria would prefer anything, anything, to the look of hurt and betrayal her dear brother gave her then.

"I understand," he said, but did he really?

He left her there, amid the triangle of hanging bodies, warped ground, and mutilated walls. Only the stars above did not judge her, and she flung the children's souls to them, unable to summon the strength to restore life to their bodies.

Unable, or unwilling. She didn't know. She was too tired and broken to care.

# CHAPTER 42

Devin carried Tesmarie's body as he would a child's, if a child could ever be so small. If people spoke, he did not hear their voices. He barely tracked where he walked, but he trusted himself to arrive there eventually. Londheim was his home. His feet would know the way.

*I'm sorry, Devin. I can't bring her back.*

Tesmarie had once told him that their kind buried the dead instead of burning, but where was appropriate for one such as her? No human graveyard was worthy of her. Besides, those grounds were still viewed as places of shame. Tesmarie deserved better. He thought to bring her to Belvua so the dragon-sired creatures could bury her with the proper rituals and respect, but would they even accept her? She had not been one of them. She had fought to protect those she considered friends.

And yet, it had been one of those friends that killed her.

"You should have stayed in your forest," Devin said, and he wiped tears from his face with his shoulder. "Damn it, you should have stayed."

At last he met his destination. The crossroad oak was a creature of magic and wonder in the center of a human city. It had been a place of joy and beauty, where he'd climbed its limbs as a child and laughed as Tommy announced his appointment as a

Wise while bouncing up and down atop a blanket he'd brought for their impromptu picnic.

*Tommy.* He should be here, Devin thought, but that would mean carrying Tesmarie to find him. That journey felt a million miles too far. No, he would have to tell Tommy of where he marked her grave, and together they could mourn again for the loss. For now, the burial was at hand. Devin closed the distance between him and the crossroad oak, only for a new wave of sadness to pass over him.

The ancient tree lay on its side, its trunk clearly hacked at by a multitude of axes. A strange blue sap covered the grass and stump, its appearance disturbingly similar to blood. Whatever leaf-creatures had lived upon its branches were long gone. Toppled and naked, the tree seemed so much smaller than before, and so much less wondrous.

"I'm sorry, Tes," Devin whispered. "You deserved to have its beauty bloom above you every morning."

He gently placed her atop the grass and began to dig with his bare hands. The earth was soft around the many roots, and he needed only a small grave to bury her. Once finished, he laid her into it. Her body was stiff, and while her skin had resembled onyx while alive, it seemed she had fully transformed upon her death. So beautiful. So still.

"Who am I to pray to?" Devin asked upon his knees to the empty night. "What fate awaits a soulless creature born of dragons? Will you abandon her, Sisters? Will you reject her memory as if she were unworthy of you?"

Devin pushed the dirt over the grave, and he shed tears upon its surface.

"What of you, dragons?" he seethed. "Will you keep her memory for the millennia to come? What solace is there in your crawling mountains and black water? Take her, you bastards. Come take her, hold her, pray over her, because I can't. I can't. Goddesses help me, I can't."

He longed for Jacaranda to hold him. He wished for a light-hearted quip from Tommy to ensure him brighter days were ahead. Devin didn't see them. All he saw was an unmarked grave, a fallen oak, and a city huddled in fear. What rituals were appropriate for an onyx faery? What prayers might her family and friends have given if she'd not been exiled? Devin could only offer his memories. Of the lives she'd saved. Of the joy she'd found playing with children in the market. Of the glimpse into a wondrous world where time flowed like honey and the flap of a butterfly wing took longer than a heartbeat.

"What are we doing?" Devin asked. He leaned back and stared into nowhere with blurry vision. "What is even happening to us? I don't want this world anymore, Sisters. Please help us. I'm scared. I don't know what fate awaits Jacaranda. I don't know what my sister is becoming. Please, save us from this violence. I don't...I don't know what path to walk. I don't know if I have faith left to pray, for my only prayers are apologies for my broken faith."

His eyes closed, and he felt so empty, so cold.

"Alma of the Beloved Dawn," he whispered. It was desperation that guided him. He didn't need miracles. He didn't need the power to shake the world. He merely wanted to feel like somewhere out there, in a perfect place so opposite to their own, that a being of love and wisdom felt sympathy for his pain. "Do you hear me? Lyra of the Beloved Sun, do you hear me? Anwyn of the Beloved Moon, please, hear me. We need you, now, more than ever. *I* need you. Do you weep alongside me? Or am I alone?"

"Does it matter if they hear if they do not act?" asked a voice from his nightmares. Devin slowly rose to his feet and blinked away his lingering tears. His hand shifted to the pistol holstered at his hip, not that he would have a chance to use it. Janus sat atop the crumpled trunk of the crossroad oak, his elbows on his knees and his chin resting atop his fists. His face was passive as stone, and his green eyes betrayed nothing of the thoughts swirling behind them.

"Why are you here?" Devin asked. "Am I not miserable enough?"

Still nothing, not the slightest hint of emotion on that cold face.

"Truly? I came to kill you, Soulkeeper. Not out of malice toward you, I must admit. It's your sister. I'm forbidden from harming her, but you, well..." He hopped down from the trunk. "Your death would at least cause her some distress."

Devin took a step back and drew his sword. He tried to muster the energy to fight, to get his blood pounding and his muscles loose, but he felt so drained, so empty. Did he have any real chance of defeating Janus one on one?

"Get on with it then," he said. "It's been a long night, and I'd rather not spend more of it listening to your prattle."

But it seemed Janus had no heart for fighting, either. Instead he knelt over Tesmarie's freshly dug grave, and he softly brushed his fingertips across the dark earth.

"You wept for her," he said, his eyes downcast. "You prayed for her. I never thought humanity capable of such things. We would always be monsters, or at best, curious pets." He let out a long sigh. "I warned her, you know. I told her that living among humans would lead to her death, and so it came to pass. Your sister is an abomination, Soulkeeper. Perhaps now your eyes have opened to that truth."

"Yet you made her this way," Devin said.

"I followed orders. That's something I think you could understand."

His hand sank into the earth. The soil warped and bent by his magic. Gently he lifted Tesmarie's corpse from the grave, the dirt and grass shifting so it became an ornate oak coffin lined with silver and decorated with jade. He tucked it underneath his arm and turned with a flourish of his long black coat.

"Where are you taking her?" Devin asked.

A half smile pulled at Janus's lips as he glanced over his shoulder. Finally his passive mask faltered, and when he spoke, his voice shook with rage.

"You asked if the dragons would take her and cherish her memory for a millennia," he said. "I go to do the same."

# CHAPTER 43

Janus stood before the enormous mouth of the living mountain and waited with his fingers drumming the top of Tesmarie's coffin. Each time, the material of his fingers shifted between various stones and metals. He kept his jaw locked shut. If he weren't careful, he might say something he'd deeply regret when Viciss emerged.

"The sun has barely set," the dragon demigod said when he finally stepped out from a crack between the enormous obsidian teeth. For a brief moment Janus saw him in a vaguely human form before his eyes adjusted, and he saw his true swirling nature of stars and shadow. "Why do you come to me?"

"You know why," Janus said. "Can we talk here, or would you rather I come inside?"

In answer, Viciss turned and passed between the teeth. Janus followed.

The roof of the mouth was dozens of feet above his head, and though it was rimmed similarly to the mouth of a lizard, it was built of gray stone instead of flesh. Steel beams poked through near the jawline like manufactured bones. Janus paused at one of the teeth, admiring its obsidian structure. A normal human or dragon-sired would just see a tooth, but Janus detected its makeup at a cellular level. The tooth was built of countless sheets of obsidian layered one atop the other, so equally sized that they differed by only a few cells in length. This made the sides of the tooth almost mesmerizing in their smoothness, with not a single flaw to be found.

It'd take him years to craft one tooth with similar perfection. To build a crawling, living entity like the mountain, along with its many chambers of creation? Even with his seemingly infinite lifespan, it'd feel like ages for Janus to finish, yet it was believed that Viciss had created the physical shell for his demigod body in the span of a single day. That the dragons could be so powerful, and yet still subservient to the Goddesses, was both humbling and maddening.

The tongue they walked on was made of a flesh-like substance, but it was not truly alive for no blood flowed within it. Instead it moved powered by gears, wires, and an oily black liquid filled with strong enough magic Janus could see its glow through the tubes. Viciss halted in the very center of this three-hundred-foot-long tongue and gestured toward his avatar.

"How goes your art?" the dragon asked.

"Uninspired," Janus said. "Creating without passion leads to mundane objects and forced canvases. You robbed me of a nobler path. Why would you expect my hands to mold anything of use?"

"I wished for you to discover a purpose beyond killing and hatred. What could be more noble?"

"Actually changing the world. Creating art out of desire instead of obligation. You clamped chains on my wrists and then demanded I learn to be free. The only thing I have learned is my hatred toward such limitations."

The black-water starscape that was Viciss shook his head.

"You find pleasure in killing humanity, but there will come a day when your hatred burns for nothing. When our races live together in peace, you will have no purpose for your existence. Your inspiration is a foul well running dry. Many times I have regretted making you, Janus. Yet again I wonder at your failings, and how much fault in them I bear."

Janus ground his teeth together, changing them from opal to bronze, bronze to silver, and then back to opal. The scraping sound of metal helped calm his boiling insides.

"When our races live together in peace," he said. He pulled Tesmarie's coffin out from underneath his arm and offered it to the demigod. "Here is your peace, dragon. Take her. She is one of your children, yet she was slain and buried at the foot of the felled hive-tree. That's what awaits those who coexist with humanity."

When Viciss did not accept the coffin, Janus threw it to the floor. It shattered, spilling Tesmarie's broken body upon the tongue.

"We die, and you do nothing," he seethed. "You wanted me to let Adria accept her newfound role on her own, but that role will never be what you desire. The blood of your children bathes her hands."

"The blood of those who refuse my wisdom," Viciss said. He knelt before the faery's corpse and scooped her into his hands. "They call themselves forgotten, but those children are merely disobedient. I will not mourn their loss, only their foolish despair in thinking I have abandoned them because I did not grant their every request."

"Yes, such a bold request they have," Janus said. "A place to call home. The audacity! But what of Tesmarie? She lived alongside the humans, just as you have always dreamed. She paid for it with her life, at the cruelty of the savior you created. Unmake me if you wish, but I speak the truth. Adria is a horrifying threat we cannot face, a weapon we cannot defeat, and one you freely put into human hands. Not only that, but you would create *more* like her! You're not saving humanity, Viciss. You're engineering our own extinction."

The teeth rumbled together, just the tiniest clack, but it was louder than a thunderclap.

"Adria's failings do not change the need for Chainbreakers," Viciss said. "Until humanity can call down souls from the Aether, they will remain forever chained to the Goddesses' whims."

"Then let them stay chained," Janus said. "Why coddle them? Why try to save them? These humans have never shown you love. They're flawed failures elevated far beyond their worthiness, the runt of a litter kept strong solely by the mother's intervention. Our backs are to a wall, Viciss. At least let us die fighting a war instead of handing over the keys to our own annihilation."

Again the teeth clacked together. Janus winced against the noise, fearing he'd gone too far. A long moment passed before Viciss spoke, for his attention was solely on the dead faery he held.

"The Sisters view the Cradle as little more than a garden," he said. "They draw seeds from the great Aether river beyond the stars and plunge them into tiny, frail sacks of meat and fluid. They nurture them with crops and beasts of slaughter, bid them to bloom through love and life, and then upon their deathbeds they come for the harvest. The soul is the entire reason for existence, and it is the Sisters' granting of that gift why they believe themselves worthy of worship from their confused, pitiful humans."

"And how are we any better?" Janus asked. "You hold a corpse, not a life. The humans, their memories and their emotions, will live on. What of us? What reason do we exist? We are destined to rot and be forgotten. You built humanity a Chainbreaker. Why not deliver one to us instead?"

"Because *I* remember you," Viciss said. The entire mountain shook with his sudden rage. "You wretched avatar of mine, you would curse me for the deaths of my children but then mock their very existence? There is no reason for a Chainbreaker for the dragon-sired. They bear no need for a soul, Janus. *I am their soul.*"

Tesmarie's physical body disintegrated in Viciss's left hand.

With his right he grabbed Janus's face and flooded him with his power. Janus felt his eyes shifting, changing, all amid searing pain. When the dragon withdrew, the world shimmered in ways Janus had never before seen. He saw the distant twinkle of human souls, like stars crashed down upon the Cradle. He saw the gleaming sun that was Adria. Amid it he saw dark shadows, such as the cloud hovering before him where Tesmarie once existed. It sparkled like shattered glass, yet pulsed deeper than the night. Within that diamond darkness were the essence and memories of the dead faery.

"Upon the breaking of eternity I will voyage beyond the stars," Viciss said. "I will pierce the void, and I will float among the Aether. My children are not forgotten. They are not abandoned. They are eternal, and it was that eternal power that cast off the Sisters' hold upon us. We will not be denied."

Tesmarie's essence floated upward, to the grand peaks of the crawling mountain. Janus watched its ascension, and he crumpled to his knees upon sight of those peaks. They weren't rock, nor were they hollow. The physical manifestation of the Dragon of Change was more than an intimidating presence from within which the demigod built his creations. Within those peaks swirled deep pillars of darkness so deep and yawning, his mind threatened to break trying to comprehend the distance. In them shimmered power capable of shaping worlds. What was once Tesmarie merged within it, a drop of water poured back into a great lake from which it had once flowed. With each moment Janus looked upon it, he felt ancient memories stir within him, as if his very mind wished to fall deep inside and never leave.

"No more," Janus said. He tore his eyes away. "Why give me such a curse?"

"The Chainbreaker bears the same curse," Viciss said. "She, too, sees the realm of souls for what it is. Perhaps now you will better understand her burdens."

"I don't want understanding," Janus said. "I want to be

unleashed. Humanity is a lost cause. Surely I cannot be the only one who sees that."

Viciss extended his hand, revoking his gift of soul-sight. Janus bowed his head in thanks. Better the darkness than to go blind before the overwhelming truth.

"You hold no hope for humanity, nor believe in their ability to change," the dragon said. "But what say you, Nihil? Do you agree with my misguided avatar?"

A shimmering distortion of light and reality approached from deep inside the throat of the mountain. Light refracted at its presence.

"I have doubted this plan from the very start," Nihil said. The dragon's voice changed with every syllable, from child to adult and man to woman. Sometimes it sounded like the words were made from stones breaking together or leaves rustling through a field of grass. "We are the ones who built this world, and we are the ones who should rule it, lest we return to the glass world the Sisters first created."

Janus bent at the waist and pressed his face to the enormous tongue to show respect to another of the five dragons of creation. He'd met Nihil rarely, and every encounter had left him deeply unsettled.

"But how would you establish such a rule?" Janus asked.

"Through madness," Viciss said.

"My plan is not madness," Nihil argued. "It is necessity. If the Cradle is to survive, then we must kill the Sisters."

Janus couldn't believe what he heard, but he liked the sound of it. His pulse quickened, and he dared believe in a miracle.

"Slay the Sisters?" he asked. "Is that possible?"

"They hold forms similar to ours," Viciss said, displeasure dripping off his every syllable. "Though considerably more powerful."

"Except they are weakened," Nihil said. Its tone shifted wildly, and now it sounded like a hundred voices spoke at once, creatures of all races but of one mind. "They exhausted themselves keeping us imprisoned. In such a state they may die. First we must find them, and for that, your Chainbreaker still proves useful. She has upset the balance the Sisters so haphazardly created. It is only a matter of time before they make their presence known. And once they do..."

Nihil smiled. Janus saw galaxies breathe and die inside the demigod's eyes.

"Then we end the threat of imprisonment once and for all."

The mountain rumbled. The Cradle trembled as its legs lifted the bulk back above the enormous cavern it'd carved.

"I am not yet ready to abandon all hope," Viciss said. "But it seems others have lost their faith in a future without strife. So be it. I shall remind them I am here, I bear witness, and I have not abandoned them to their suffering."

One moment Janus was standing inside the crawling mountain's mouth, the next he was thousands of feet outside it, his hands now pressing into soft green grass instead of a weirdly not-flesh tongue. The dragon's jaw dropped as its head lifted. A roar bellowed forth from the mountain's cavernous being, more deafening than thunder and traveling for miles in all directions. Black water swelled within the back of its throat. Janus prayed the demigod would finally exterminate the human city like he should have when he'd first crawled to its doorstep.

A torrent of black water surged into the air, and for a brief moment Janus dared believe. The water arced and then split on its descent, showing masterful control befitting the demigod who wielded it. The streams struck ground, though where, Janus could not tell. He curled into himself, hollowing his bones and growing feathers from his arms. He must witness Viciss's wrath for himself, not be stuck outside the walls. A few beats of his newly formed wings and he soared over Londheim, his eyes enlarging into those more befitting a hawk.

The water ceased as Janus crossed over the tall, pointed spires of the city. Viciss's aim was squarely on Belvua and the walls surrounding it. Janus might have wished for destruction, but as he flew closer, he allowed himself to appreciate this newfound beauty.

Hive-trees grew by the hundreds, supplanting the smooth, featureless stone walls with their arcing trunks to form the new barrier surrounding Belvua. Their living leaves swirled into the air in confusion despite it being after dark and when they should be hibernating until dawn. They lit themselves with color during their panic, so that the skies above Belvua burst with red and orange lights, so numerous the street shone as if beneath a daytime sun. Janus flew through their wonder, a smile upon his face. This was the world he yearned for, one where the few and extinct flourished. Where magical creatures stood firm against humanity, unafraid of their axes and gunfire, and met their cold stone with life and wonder. This was the world he would paint, if there were no more humans to use as his brush and palette.

As if in response to the red and orange cloudburst, blue pillars of light shimmered into being to the northwest; they reached from ground all the way to the stars themselves. Janus slowed to a hover, his momentary pleasure replaced with unease, as long after the reaping hour hundreds of human souls streaked heavenward in a reverse rain that seemed unending.

"Adria?" Janus asked the silence in the sky. "What have you done?"

# CHAPTER 44

When Devin returned home, he found Jacaranda sitting in his chair by the fire. With but a single look, she knew something was amiss and hurried to him.

"It was a trap," he said, his voice sounding dull to his own ears. Her arms wrapped about his waist, and he pulled her close so he could feel her comforting presence against him. He kissed the top of her head and breathed in the scent of her hair so it could ground his mind in the present. Anything to escape the horrors of the night.

"Is everyone all right?" Jacaranda asked. The tentative way she asked, it was obvious she already knew the answer, and that it wasn't positive.

"Tesmarie," he said. His mouth opened, but he couldn't say the words. *Adria killed her.* It was too painful a confession. It was a barbed truth beyond what his currently exhausted mind could bear.

"Oh, Devin," Jacaranda whispered. "I'm sorry. I'm so sorry."

They held one another, and he fought off another wave of fresh tears.

"Let's get you something stiff to drink," she said. "Then we'll cuddle and talk until neither of us can keep our eyes open. How does that sound?"

"Like better than I deserve."

She kissed him on the mouth, then slowly removed herself from his grasp so she could head to the kitchen. Devin turned to hang up his sword and pistol, glad to be free of them for a while.

"Devin?" he heard Jacaranda say in shock. He carefully turned, his muscles tightening in case he needed to act.

A woman knelt by the kitchen fireplace. Her hair was deeper than the night sky, and it lay in spools at her feet. Her dress was starlight. Her skin was the rich, comforting color of the black oaks. She lovingly placed a hand into the fire and brushed Puffy as if petting a cat. His flame made not a mark upon her fingers. When finished, she looked their way. Her eyes were solid black, and instead of irises, he saw galaxies turning.

"Do not be alarmed," said Lyra, Goddess of the Day. "I come only to speak."

Devin dropped to one knee and bowed his head. After a moment Jacaranda did likewise. His mind reeled, a thousand questions birthing and dying without a one passing his lips. He thought of the prayer he'd uttered at the felled crossroad oak, of his rage and uncertainty, and felt smothered with shame.

"You honor us, Lyra," he said. His tongue was so dry he barely forced out the words. "But why grace our household? What may we do in your service?"

Lyra rose to her feet. Her starlight dress rippled from the movement, and it was like watching a starry sky in the reflection of a turbulent pond.

"The threat of your sister must be addressed," the Goddess said. "The dragons have disregarded sacred laws and their recklessness has broken the barrier of stars and ripped a hole in the cosmos. From this wound, the void threatens to pour forth and swallow the Cradle."

Devin stammered. How did one address a Goddess? How did one speak to the beloved being that had listened to his every prayer since he was a small child?

"Adria, she—she'll listen to you," he said. "Whatever danger she represents, she can help fix it. Let us go to her, speak with her…"

Lyra shook her head. The light of Puffy's fire shimmered through her hair in mesmerizing waves.

"I know where your sister is," she said. The look she gave him churned his insides with fear. "Do not go to her."

"But—but why?" he dared ask.

She gave him a look of love. She gave him a look of pity.

"Because what you find will break you."

Adria led the procession through the graveyard, armed novices rushing ahead to order any lingering bystanders out from its grounds. There would be other nights for them to whisper loving words to ghosts that would not hear. Tonight, Adria had much to do.

*Such power, and yet we seem to only destroy.*

Adria wished she could dismiss those haunting words as easily as she dismissed the men and women of the graveyard. Many times in the past she had seen her brother broken spiritually, but this felt the worst. They had cried at their parents' passing as children. They had wept together over Brittany's grave upon her untimely death. But this time…this time the fault was her own. To have that guilt on her shoulders made her sympathy for his pain that much more unbearable.

"The graveyard is clear," said Mindkeeper Fiona. She'd been by her side as she resurrected the dead at the grand cathedral and had not left since. Adoration clung to her every word. "Do you know where we go?"

Adria closed her eyes and let her consciousness softly spread as she touched the many lingering souls.

"Yes," she said. "I do."

Of her group, there were five novices, two Mindkeepers, Faith-keeper Sena, and a soulless woman who was a member of Alma's Beloved. She had not asked for them, for they had pledged loyalty the moment she ceased her prayers that morning. Whispers of her deeds had spread throughout Londheim faster than the wind. The Sacred Mother, they called her. Lyra's Chosen, said others. The one they all agreed on was Deakon, for who else deserved the title when the vote came next month? Even Vikar Forrest and Vikar Caria acknowledged as much when they spoke with her after the chaos at the cathedral.

"The people trust in you deeply," Forrest had said after pulling her aside in the Scholars' Abode, which, along with the Sisters' Remembrance, was rapidly being converted to house the many left homeless after the grand cathedral's fire. "Do not break their hearts. Nothing is more dangerous than wounded love."

*Please, Devin. I didn't know.*

She had brought over a hundred men and women from death's cold embrace, but it was the one she failed that broke her heart. Adria walked across the little triangle symbols that marked the graves. In each one she saw the lost souls abandoned by Anwyn in their final time of need. Why had the Goddess not taken them into her bosom?

The ground shook, and a roar like thunder followed. Adria tensed her legs as two of the women with her cried out in fear. Her head swiveled to the west, and terror lodged itself in her throat as she watched a river of black water flowing into the air. Was this it? Had the crawling mountain reawakened to destroy them all with corruption and rot like Devin had described to Dunwerth?

If its aim was to destroy, it was only a small portion of the city. She watched the water turn and crash down upon a single district of Londheim. Belvua, she realized. But why would the dragon destroy the magical creatures there?

Her answer came in a great burst of red and orange light. No, not destroy. Create. The distance was too great for her to see clearly, but it seemed like the colors moved and shifted through the air like some of the great flocks of birds that migrated south ahead of winter. There was nothing ominous about their light, only awesome wonder.

"What do you think it is?" Sena asked beside her.

"I don't know," Adria said. "But it is a concern for the morning. Come, we have our purpose here."

Adria walked to the very center of the graveyard. Her hands lifted to either side of her, and she tilted her gaze heavenward. She could feel the lost souls squirming in their graves, waiting for the time of Eschaton to ascend to the stars as promised.

"Stand still," she told those with her. "No matter what you see, do not reach out. Souls may seem like brilliant light, but they burn hotter than any fire."

Knowing right from wrong was proving a heavy task, and already she felt she'd made terrible decisions. She'd given in to her anger. She'd killed recklessly. As she solidified her position in the church, she'd need someone she trusted to guide her. Adria smiled. Tamerlane Swift, Vikar of the Day. It had a nice ring to it. At least that was one decision she felt confident in.

This was another.

Adria clutched the abandoned souls in her mind and hurtled them starward in great silver beams. They need not wait until the time of Eschaton to ascend. Let them find peace. They need not be ghosts any longer. More and more floated, a backward rain, shooting stars racing upward instead of crashing down to the Cradle. The men and women with her gasped in awe, and despite her insistence to remain still, two of them fell to their knees in prayer.

Adria knew not how much time passed, but it must have been several minutes. The novices were crying. The two Mindkeepers sang a low hymn, the verses listing the joys awaiting them in the hereafter, of meeting friends by blue rivers and embracing loved ones amid rolling hills of flowers. Adria breathed in deep, and she exhaled a growing tension between her shoulders.

"The Cradle is blessed by your actions this night," Sena said. Her friend put a hand on her shoulder. "Let it remain at this, and go home. I know what you're planning. It's too much. You would meddle where only the Goddesses should dwell."

Adria trusted Sena with her life, and she knew she should listen to her advice. It would be the smart thing to do. The safe option.

*I'm so sorry, Devin. I can't bring her back.*

Despite his sorrow and pain, Devin had shown her the way. He'd lighted her path. Yes, she could destroy, but it was life that she should embrace with her gift. There was a reason the triangle of the Sisters connected forever, one Sister to the next in equal measure, for neither birth, nor death, nor the span between, should be elevated above the rest. For so long she'd focused on her abilities to kill and command.

Tonight, she would re-create life.

"Do not be afraid," she told Sena. "All I do, I do in the Goddesses' beloved names."

"I disagree, and I won't partake in this."

"Then go. My course is set."

Sena hesitated, and then before leaving, she flung her arms around Adria and held her close. Adria kept still, and she did not return the embrace.

"This isn't the Sisters' doing," the Faithkeeper whispered. "It's yours, and I fear the guilt that guides it."

Adria watched Sena go. She knew she should be bothered, but her heart was too heavy to add yet another weight. People would always fear her power, she knew. Even those who loved her.

"Bring me the soulless," she told the others with her.

The novice in charge of the soulless woman whispered something in her ear, and she came forward to kneel before Adria. Her hair was long and blond, which was good, though her eyes were green, not blue, and her face and skin were paler than what Adria remembered. It would have to do. Adria closed her eyes, for she did not need her physical sight to see the world of the spiritual. This was it. No turning back. Her heart in her throat, she took hold of the lone soul she'd left behind in the graveyard. A mere thought sent it rising, but not to the stars.

The soul plunged into the soulless woman's body. Adria grabbed pieces of it like bundled string and stretched them through the various limbs. The soul squirmed like a trapped squirrel. Adria massaged it, coaxed the memories to reawaken, told it that those arms were hers, those legs were hers, the flesh, the blood, it was all part of her body to experience. Let its memories and emotions flow into her, to be forever cherished when the Cradle sank into the sea and the world were remade perfect and free of the void-dragon's influence.

A scream opened Adria's eyes. The woman, once soulless but no longer, shrieked at the top of her lungs. A novice held each of her arms, preventing her from clawing at her face. The woman's chest heaved as she struggled, her gaze unfocused and her legs thrashing. Adria did not shy away. Trusting her novices, she put her hands on the woman's shoulders and met her bewildered gaze.

"Welcome back, Brittany," Adria told the screaming woman. "Do you remember me?"

# A NOTE FROM
# THE AUTHOR

When I plot out a series, I tend to focus much more on the immediate events of the current book and not think too much on where I'm going beyond a vague outline. I do this so I can allow myself to be spontaneous. In other series, this has meant characters dying that I meant to have live, or other times characters living that I meant to kill off. But in each series, there will be key moments that I know are coming and will have already visualized and replayed in my mind countless times. These "big" moments are what keep me excited about a story, and keep the story moving along. Adria undergoing the transformation at the end of *Soulkeeper* was one such moment.

Brittany's return was another, and damn, was it fun to finally write that final line of greeting. I can't wait for you all to meet her. She's going to be a blast. Then again, I love most of my characters, even the disturbing, twisted ones.

Speaking of disturbing and twisted, I'm sure some of you are probably a little disappointed Janus didn't get the same spotlight like he did in *Soulkeeper*. This was a necessity to give some of the newer factions some time to shine, plus his own innate desire to "burn it all down" doesn't quite fit with the goals of the Forgotten Children. Now, though? When it comes to the next book, *Void-breaker*, we've got everything set up for him to go wild...and just like the sick little fucker, Dierk, he's got a bit of an obsession with a newly forming goddess.

It's taken some work, and I thank you for being patient, but I've set up so many pieces to play with, I cannot wait to dive into *Voidbreaker*. Adria's starting to become something the church might fear. Armies of dragon-sired are marching toward Londheim. West Orismund's cut off, alone, and its power structure is rapidly evolving. The keepers are all realizing how much power their prayers wield, and even Tommy's bullets are going to be a hot commodity after Devin's little light show. And I've still got some creatures to introduce you to, and others to bring back from *Soulkeeper*. Oh, and then there's the whole slaying a Goddess thing, and Lyra popping in to say hello.

Fun times. Such fun times.

I do need to find a way to introduce Puffy to more of the action. Hopefully you all enjoyed his POV chapter. The little thing deserves its own happy spin-off. Maybe a Keepers children's picture book? *Puffy and the Really-Bad No-Good Black Water* might not be age appropriate, though.

What was decidedly *not* fun was writing the initial moment of and then subsequent chapters following Tesmarie's death. I used to sadistically enjoy writing character deaths, knowing I'd be shocking my audience and really get their emotions going. That much younger me is long since gone and done. I dreaded writing this chapter. I hated writing it when I did. I felt horrible and sad along with Devin, Janus, Adria, and the rest. My editor can attest to this, but I debated having Viciss resurrect her, as well as other potential time-altering shenanigans to save her. Tesmarie was a source of joy for the characters, and for me. I'm going to miss her, and if it wasn't obvious enough, her passing is going to leave a very deep scar on a certain pair of siblings.

Ugh. Enough of that. Thank you to all the team at Orbit for the great work on the book, the series' sexy covers, marketing, and all that other stuff I'm terrible at but you all make look easy. Special thanks to my editor, Brit, for sticking with me and not losing her mind every time I asked for extra time or called needing to work through a particularly troublesome note.

And most of all, thank you, dear reader, for coming along with me on this journey. There's a million and one things out there vying for your attention, but you gave me your precious hours instead. I hope I repaid that with a hell of a good story. As always, I'll see you at the end of *Voidbreaker*.

DAVID DALGLISH
MARCH 18, 2019

The story continues in...

**VOIDBREAKER**

Keep reading for a sneak peek!

# extras

orbit

# meet the author

DAVID DALGLISH currently lives in Myrtle Beach with his wife, Samantha, and daughters Morgan, Katherine, and Alyssa. He graduated from Missouri Southern State University in 2006 with a degree in mathematics and currently spends his free time dying for the umpteenth time in *Dark Souls*.

Find out more about David Dalglish and other Orbit authors by registering for the free monthly newsletter at www.orbitbooks.net.

## CHAPTER ONE

Sweat rolled down Brittany's neck and forehead, little rivulets stinging her eyes while on their way to the tip of her nose. With her every push-up, the growing drops would shake until finally falling to join the puddle beneath her.

Fifty-eight. Fifty-nine. Sixty.

Her arms burned like fire. Her heart hammered inside her chest. Both spurned her on, and kept her body rising and lowering above the stone floor of her room. More drops fell, growing the puddle.

She'd have wiped her face with her shirt, but it'd be pointless. The cloth was already soaked through with sweat.

Sixty-five. Sixty-six.

On sixty-seven, her shaking arms collapsed. A soft groan thudded out of her as she landed chest first upon the floor. She closed her eyes and pressed her cheek to the cold stone. Just a little break, she told herself. Just a moment to catch her breath.

A knock on the door opened her eyes. Had she slept? She honestly didn't know. Time seemed to flow weirdly in this room of hers.

"One moment," she said.

Vertigo washed over her the moment she spoke. Brittany clenched her hands into fists and rode it out. It'd gotten better over the past week, but it still unnerved her when she spoke and heard a distinctly foreign voice come from her throat.

*You'll get used to it in time*, Adria had told her during one of their many private sessions. Maybe so, but never completely. One didn't forget the sound of their own voice.

It took longer than she'd anticipated to get to her feet. Her arms didn't want to cooperate. Sixty-seven push-ups and already her body was ready to call it quits. What a joke.

"Come in," Brittany said when she finally opened the door. Adria stood on the other side with her hands crossed behind her back. Even with her face hidden behind her black-and-white mask, there was no mistaking her. An elaborate jewel-encrusted silver pendant hung from her neck, a triangle with a bright daytime sun in the top-right corner. That pendant marked her as Vikar of the Day, a rank she was temporarily filling while Londheim awaited the election of a new Deakon to appoint an official replacement.

"Shouldn't you be wearing a white suit?" Brittany asked. She turned from the door and pulled her soaked shirt off. The novices had put a small basket in the corner for her dirty clothes, and she tossed her shirt into it while opening her lone clothes drawer. Her options weren't many, just a few various shades of gray. Adria kept offering to take her on a trip to some clothing shops, which

Brittany flatly refused. She'd not left this small, square room since her very first day back from—from whatever it was she'd undergone while dead.

"I only recently had my measurements taken with a church-approved tailor," Adria said. "It will take some time, and truthfully, I'm not sure how happy I am to leave my dress behind."

Brittany grabbed a shirt at random and turned. Adria's eyes quickly looked to the floor, which earned her a derisive snort as Brittany pulled it over her head.

"They're just tits, Adria. For Sisters' sake, they're not even mine."

Those brown eyes snapped back up to hers.

"It's not good for you to refer to your physical body as belonging to another. I believe it will slow your integration."

"Acknowledging this isn't my body is the only thing keeping me sane," Brittany argued. "My body was capable of one hundred push-ups and sit-ups without rest. This one is skinny, weak, and better suited to wielding a dagger than my greatsword. Speaking of, have you made any progress in bringing me a replacement? It'd help with my practice."

Adria gestured to the cramped room. It was four walls, a bed, a lidded chamber pot, and a clothes drawer. Nothing fancy, but given the purported destruction of the Cathedral of the Sacred Mother, everyone was making do with significantly less finery these days.

"And how would you swing it without carving grooves into the walls?"

Brittany shrugged.

"Fine. Get me a sword, and maybe I'll leave this room more often. That's what you want, isn't it?"

"What I want is for you to start living your life."

Brittany's mind flicked through a few ideas of what that might even mean. Patrolling as a Soulkeeper again? Moving back in with Devin in the home they'd shared? Or perhaps joining Bailey and Hanna on their trip to the Winding Gardens, obediently carrying her younger siblings things while...

*No, wrong, wrong,* she thought, her insides churning hard enough she had to grab the dresser to steady herself. *Tommy is your brother. Tommy, not Bailey, not Hanna.*

Her spell did not go unnoticed. Adria reached for her hand, only to have it brushed away.

"Are the memories still confusing you?" she asked, showing no sign of being upset by the rejection.

"It's getting better," Brittany said. Her fingers rubbed at her eyes, as if she could scrub away her frustrations. "Not at night, though. When I dream, I dream of this body's past. She might have been soulless, but she had a name, a family. I can almost feel myself going numb and falling into that past persona. It's... disconcerting."

"The physical body creates and stores memories and emotions," Adria said. "The soul does likewise, but for a permanent remembrance, and therefore it is much stronger. The life your soul lived will slowly burn out the old existence, I assure you."

"You make it sound like I'm murdering the previous owner. Don't talk like that again. It's creepy." She glared at the mask. "And take that thing off. I'm family, not one of your subjects needing prayers."

Adria put a hand to the bottom of her mask but then hesitated. Brittany crossed her arms, and her expression made it clear there'd be no more conversation until the mask was gone.

"If it will make you feel better," her sister-in-law said at last. She pulled the mask off, revealing her pale face and shadowed eyes. Errant strands of sweaty hair clung to her cheek and neck. Brittany fought to suppress a reflexive wince.

"You're not sleeping well, are you?"

"Is it your turn to aid me?" she asked, a small smile curling the sides of her mouth.

"If not me, I hope someone else is. You look worse than I do, and I'm recently back from the grave."

"It's merely stress. Others suffer far worse than I."

"Others suffering doesn't mean you should also suffer."

"You're right. It means I should work that much harder to stop those others from suffering."

Brittany laughed.

"I was thinking it meant you should take a nap every now and then, but you've always been the hardest worker among us. No wonder you're acting Vikar. Well, that, and the whole ability to resurrect people probably played a hand in it."

Adria visibly cringed at the remark. For whatever reason, she didn't like it when Brittany commented on her newfound abilities. There was surely a reason for that, but Adria was more elusive than a barn mouse about how or why. On the third day of Brittany's renewed life, Adria had spent several hours detailing some of the changes that had happened upon the Cradle. The stories sounded insane, of gargoyles and lapinkin, crawling mountains and time-controlling faeries living in forest villages. Wildest of all, her younger brother supposedly could wield magical spells. Imagining her doughy, kindhearted Tommy roasting enemies with fire was an image so ridiculous, she couldn't help but laugh when Adria told her.

"It's true," Adria had insisted.

"Oh, I know," Brittany had told her. "Any other time, I might have doubted you, but I'm sitting here in a stranger's body. There's not much room in me to doubt."

Adria had spent the fourth day discussing the more recent events in Londheim, of the madman named Janus, a magical renegade group known as the Forgotten Children conquering the district of Low Dock, and of the grand cathedral's burning. In all these stories, Adria remained vague about her own capabilities, insisting only that her prayers to the Goddesses were more powerful than the other keepers.

Her self-imposed break over, Brittany returned to the floor. She bent her knees, put her hands behind her head, and began her sit-ups. It hurt like the void, and it might take multiple sessions, by damn it, she was going to hit her one hundred before the day's end. Adria watched quietly for a minute, and Brittany was content to let the silence last. It was only in the silence that her sister-in-law seemed to finally relax.

That, and sometimes Adria would extend her fingers, often by little amounts and only when she thought Brittany not looking. Little prayers would whisper through her lips, so softly Brittany could not hear them. Whenever her sister-in-law did so, a soothing sensation flowed through Brittany's mind and body. Anxiety she didn't even know she had would ease, and it'd seem like her memories would clear from the fog surrounding them. It never lasted more than an hour or two, but it was a welcome reprieve.

"Is there anything else you need?" Adria asked once her hidden prayer was finished.

"Some books might be nice. Are the Tomms Brothers still printing their weekly news leaflets?"

"They are."

Brittany's body shook for a moment and then she collapsed onto her side, having not yet reached fifty. She gasped in air as she wished for the millionth time that whoever had previously commanded the soulless had ordered her to run the occasional mile to keep in shape.

"I wouldn't mind a collection of those. It'd be nice to catch up on what's been happening while I lingered in a grave for...how long was I dead, actually?"

"I'll look into acquiring some," Adria said. "As for your sword, I suppose I could ask Devin if he kept your old one after...well..."

"My what? My first death? My temporary funeral? What should we call it, Adria? It'd help if we settled on some terms so you stop dancing around everything like I'm some fragile child. I was dead. Now I'm not. It won't hurt my feelings to acknowledge that fact."

A hard smirk crossed Adria's face.

"Fine. I could ask Devin if he kept your sword after he buried you, or if he returned it to the sacred division because he couldn't bear the sight of it. Is that better?"

"Much."

Brittany shifted so she was sideways. Too much time focusing on her arms and abdominal muscles lately. Had to work the rest of her as well. She balanced on one foot and hand, then lifted and lowered her hips. Within seconds her sides were burning.

"You haven't told Devin, have you?" she asked. Her gaze lingered on the dirty space beneath her bed, as if she weren't that interested in the answer. She didn't know who she was fooling, though. The only thing keeping her going over the past week of nonstop drills and exercises was the thought of seeing him again...and yet an overwhelming fear of seeing him was also why she had not once left her room.

"It doesn't feel like it's my place to do so," Adria said. She slipped her mask back over her face and tightened the strings behind her head. "Take all the time you need, and don't rush yourself."

Brittany switched to her other side. Lift and lower. Steady, rhythmic movements. The only part of life still under her control.

"You're yet to give me an answer," she said. "How long was I dead?"

Adria crossed her arms, and no doubt she frowned behind that black-and-white porcelain mask.

"I think you should be in a better mind-set before learning this."

"I've seen your face, Adria. I know it's been years. I just want to know how many."

The woman sighed.

"Six. Six years."

Even braced for the knowledge, it still stabbed her in the gut. Six long years for everyone she'd known, and yet only the blink of an eye for her. Precious Goddesses above, Tommy was almost as old as her, in a sense. And if that much time had passed...

"Has he moved on?" she asked, halting her exercises. She struggled to force out the words in the foreign voice created by the stranger's tongue inside her mouth. "Has he found someone else?"

The soft fall of Adria's shoulders gave the answer long before her words confirmed it.

"Yes," she said. "I believe he has."

Brittany swallowed down a sudden lump in her throat.

"Good," she said. "Good for him." Damn it, these stupid tears. She didn't want them. She didn't want any of this. "Does...does he know how I died?"

Adria's head tilted the slightest amount.

"We were told you died of heart failure."

Still secret then. Adria couldn't decide if that was a blessing or a curse. Perhaps both.

"I'd like to be alone for a while," she said, pointedly dropping the subject.

"Of course." Adria dipped her head as if bowing to a superior and then turned for the door. Helpless frustration pushed one last question out of Brittany before her sister-in-law might leave.

"Why did you bring me back?" she asked. "Why give me this body, this life, if he doesn't even need me anymore? My time was done, Adria. My life, my pain, my loving and living and dying, it was done."

Even with her mask to hide her face, Adria could not bring herself to turn and face her.

"I thought it was the right thing to do," she said.

"Do you still believe that?"

Adria said the only answer Brittany would have accepted.

She said nothing.

# if you enjoyed
## RAVENCALLER

### look out for

# THE RANGER OF MARZANNA

## The Goddess War: Book One

### by

# Jon Skovron

*Sonya is training to be a Ranger of Marzanna, an ancient sect of warriors who have protected the land for generations. But the old ways are dying, and the rangers have all been forced into hiding or killed off by the invading empire.*

*When her father is murdered by imperial soldiers, Sonya decides to finally take action. Using her skills as a ranger, she will travel across the bitter cold tundra and gain the allegiance of the only other force strong enough to take down the invaders.*

*But nothing about her quest will be easy. Because not everyone is on her side. Her brother, Sebastian, is the most powerful sorcerer the world has ever seen. And he's fighting for the empire.*

# 1

Istoki was not the smallest, poorest, or most remote village in Izmoroz, but it was close. The land was owned by the noble Ovstrovsky family, and the peasants who lived and worked there paid an annual tithe in crops every year at harvest time. The Ovstrovskys were not known for their diligence, and the older folk in Istoki remembered a time when they would even forget to request their tithe. That was before the war. Before the empire.

But now imperial soldiers arrived each year to collect their own tithe, as well as the Ovstrovsky family's. And they never forgot.

Little Vadim, age eight and a half, sat on a snow-covered log at the eastern edge of the village and played with his rag doll, which was fashioned into the likeness of a rabbit. He saw the imperial soldiers coming on horseback along the dirt road. Their steel helmets and breastplates gleamed in the winter sun as their horses rode in two neat, orderly lines. Behind them trundled a wagon already half-full with the tithes of other villages in the area.

They came to a halt before Vadim with a great deal of clanking, their faces grim. Each one seemed to bristle with sharp metal and quiet animosity. Their leader, a man dressed not in armor but in a bright green wool uniform with a funny cylindrical hat, looked down at Vadim.

"You there. Boy." The man in green had black hair, olive skin, and a disdainful expression.

Vadim hugged his doll tightly and said nothing. His mother had told him it was best not to talk to imperial soldiers because you never knew when you might say the wrong thing to them.

"Run along and tell your elder we're here to collect the annual tithe. And tell him to bring it all here. I'd rather not go slogging through this frozen mudhole just to get it."

He knew he should obey the soldier, but when he looked at the men and horses looming above him, his whole body stiffened. He had never seen real swords before. They were buckled to the soldiers' waists with blades laid bare so he could see their keen edges. He stared at them, clutched the doll to his chest, and did not move.

The man in green sighed heavily. "Dear God in Heaven, they're all inbred imbeciles out here. Boy! I'm speaking to you! Are you deaf?"

Slowly, with great effort, Vadim shook his head.

"Wonderful," said the man. "Now run along and do as I say."

He tried to move. He really did. But his legs wouldn't work. They were frozen, fixed in place as if already pierced by the glittering swords.

The man muttered to himself as he leaned over and reached into one of his saddlebags. "This is why I'm counting the days until my transfer back to Aureum. If I have to see one more—"

An arrow pierced one side of the man's throat and exited the other side. Blood sprayed from the severed artery, spattering Vadim's face and hair. He gaped as the man clutched his gushing throat. The man's eyes were wide with surprise and he made faint gargling noises as he slowly slid from his saddle.

"We're under attack!" shouted one of the other soldiers.

"Which direction?" shouted another.

A third one lifted his hand and pointed out into one of the snowy fields. "There! It's—"

Then an arrow embedded itself in his eye and he toppled over.

Vadim turned his head in the direction the soldier had been pointing and saw a lone rider galloping across the field, the horse kicking up a cloud of white. The rider wore a thick leather coat with a hood lined in white fur. Vadim had never seen a Ranger of Marzanna before because they were supposed to all be dead now. But he had been raised on stories of the *Strannik*, told by his mother in hushed tones late at night, so Vadim knew that was what he saw.

"Get into formation!" shouted a soldier. "Archers, return fire!"

But the Ranger was closing fast. Vadim had never seen a horse run so swiftly. It seemed little more than a blur of gray and black across the white landscape. Vadim's mother had said that a Ranger of Marzanna did not need to guide their horse. That the two were so perfectly connected, they knew each other's thoughts and desires.

The Ranger loosed arrow after arrow, each one finding a vulnerable spot in a soldier's armor. The soldiers cursed as they fumbled for their own bows and let fly with arrows that overshot their rapidly approaching target. Their faces were no longer proud or grim, but tense with fear.

As the Ranger drew near, Vadim saw that it was a woman. Her blue eyes were bright and eager, and there was a strange, almost feral grin on her lips. She shouldered her bow and stood on her saddle even as her horse continued to sprint toward the now panicking soldiers. Then she drew a long knife from her belt and leapt toward the soldiers. Her horse veered to the side as she crashed headlong into the mass of armed men. The Ranger's blade flickered here and there, drawing arcs of red as she hopped from one mounted soldier to the next. She stabbed some and slit the throats of others. Some were only wounded and fell from their horses to be trampled under the hooves of the frightened animals. The air was thick with blood and the screams of men in pain. Vadim squeezed his doll as hard as he could and kept his eyes shut tight, but he could not block out the piteous sounds of terrified agony.

And then everything went silent.

"Hey, mal'chik," came a cheerful female voice. "You okay?"

Vadim cautiously opened his eyes to see the Ranger grinning down at him.

"You hurt?" asked the Ranger.

Vadim shook his head with an uneven twitch.

"Great." The Ranger crouched down beside him and reached out her hand.

Vadim flinched back. His mother had said that Strannik were fearsome beings who had been granted astonishing abilities by the dread Lady Marzanna, Goddess of Winter.

"I'm not going to hurt you." She gently wiped the blood off his face with her gloved hand. "Looks like I got you a little messy. Sorry about that."

Vadim stared at her. In all the stories he had ever heard, none of them had described a Ranger as nice. Was this a trick of some kind? An attempt to set Vadim at ease before doing something cruel? But the Ranger only stood back up and looked at the wagon, which was still attached to a pair of frightened, wild-eyed horses. The other horses had all scattered.

The Ranger gestured to the wagon filled with the tithes of other villages. "Anyway, I better get this stuff back where it came from."

She looked down at the pile of bloody, uniformed bodies in the snow for a moment. "Tell your elder I'm sorry about the mess. But at least you get to keep all your food this year, right?"

She patted Vadim on the head, then sauntered over to her beautiful gray-and-black stallion, who waited patiently nearby. She tied her horse to the wagon, then climbed onto the seat and started back the way the soldiers had come.

Vadim watched until he could no longer see the Ranger's wagon. Then he looked at all the dead men who lay at his feet. Now he knew there were worse things than imperial soldiers. Though he didn't understand the reason, his whole body trembled, and he began to cry.

When he finally returned home, his eyes raw from tears, he told his mother what had happened. She said he had been blessed, but he did not feel blessed. Instead he felt as though he had been given a brief glimpse into the true nature of the world, and it was more frightening than he had ever imagined.

For the rest of his short life, Vadim would have nightmares of that Ranger of Marzanna.

orbit

Follow us:

 /orbitbooksUS

 /orbitbooks

 /orbitbooks

Join our mailing list
to receive alerts on our
latest releases and deals.

**orbitbooks.net**

Enter our monthly
giveaway for the chance
to win some epic prizes.

**orbitloot.com**